CW01640615

INFERNO!

VOLUME 5

CRUSADE & OTHER STORIES
A Getting Started collection
by various authors

• DARK IMPERIUM •

Guy Haley
BOOK ONE: *Dark Imperium*
BOOK TWO: *Plague War*

• THE HORUSIAN WARS •
John French

BOOK ONE: *Resurrection*
BOOK TWO: *Incarnation*
BOOK THREE: *Divination*

• VAULTS OF TERRA •
Chris Wraight

BOOK ONE: *The Carrion Throne*
BOOK TWO: *The Hollow Mountain*

HONOURBOUND
Rachel Harrison

BLACKSTONE FORTRESS
Darius Hinks

BELISARIUS CAWL:
THE GREAT WORK
Guy Haley

THE LAST CHANCERS:
ARMAGEDDON SAINT
Gav Thorpe

RITES OF PASSAGE
Mike Brooks

KNIGHTS OF MACRAGGE
Nick Kyme

SACROSANCT & OTHER STORIES
A Getting Started collection
by various authors

RULERS OF THE DEAD
Josh Reynolds & David Annandale

• HALLOWED KNIGHTS •
BOOK ONE: *Plague Garden*
BOOK TWO: *Black Pyramid*
Josh Reynolds

EIGHT LAMENTATIONS:
SPEAR OF SHADOWS
Josh Reynolds

OVERLORDS OF THE
IRON DRAGON
C L Werner

SOUL WARS
Josh Reynolds

CALLIS & TOLL:
THE SILVER SHARD
Nick Horth

THIEVES' PARADISE
Nick Horth

CODE OF THE SKIES
Graeme Lyon

GLOOMSPITE
Andy Clark

WARCRY
An anthology containing stories
by various authors

OATHS & CONQUESTS
An anthology containing stories
by various authors

GHOULSLAYER
Darius Hinks

BEASTGRAVE
C L Werner

NEFERATA:
THE DOMINION OF BONES
David Annandale

NECROMUNDA®

KAL JERICO: SINNER'S BOUNTY
Josh Reynolds

UNDERHIVE
Various authors
An anthology featuring the novella *Wanted: Dead* by Mike Brooks

TERMINAL OVERKILL
Justin D Hill

ROAD TO REDEMPTION
Mike Brooks

LOW LIVES
Denny Flowers

KAL JERICO: THE OMNIBUS
Will McDermott and Gordon Rennie

Contains the novels *Blood Royal, Cardinal Crimson* and *Lasgun Wedding*

INFERNO!

Also available

INFERNO! VOLUME 1

INFERNO! VOLUME 2

INFERNO! VOLUME 3

INFERNO! VOLUME 4

by various authors

INFERNO!

TALES FROM THE WORLDS OF WARHAMMER VOLUME 5

INCLUDES STORIES BY BEN COUNTER, ROB J HAYES, BEN GALLEY, GAVIN G SMITH, ANNA STEPHENS, MARC COLLINS, MICHAEL R FLETCHER, GARY KLOSTER, SEAN GRIGSBY, GRAEME LYON, GARETH HANRAHAN AND GUY HALEY

BLACK LIBRARY

A BLACK LIBRARY PUBLICATION

This edition published in Great Britain in 2020 by
Black Library,
Games Workshop Ltd.,
Willow Road,
Nottingham, NG7 2WS, UK.

10 9 8 7 6 5 4 3 2 1

Produced by Games Workshop in Nottingham.
Cover illustration by Alexander Mokhov.

A CIP record for this book is available from the British Library.

ISBN 13: 978-1-78999-073-7

Printed and bound by CPI Group (UK) Ltd, Croydon, CR0 4YY

CONTENTS

INTRODUCTION

Welcome, brave traveller! You have come where many fear to tread; the perilous realm of *Inferno!*

Within these pages you will uncover occult knowledge, forgotten sagas of battle and glory, and the keys to lost lands and invaluable relics. But step carefully, for this is unexplored territory where doom lurks around every corner. Mighty foes and ferocious beasts lie in wait to challenge your martial skill. Only the strong will survive, and even they will be forever changed by their ordeal…

The fifth volume of *Inferno!* is upon us already, offering up thrilling tales from the worlds of Warhammer by a cavalcade of authors both old and new. This edition features twelve such stories, taking place in the war-torn galaxy of the 41st Millennium, the untamed wilds of the Mortal Realms and the treacherous underhive of Necromunda. And for the first time ever, we venture to the savage hellscape of the Eightpoints, the setting for Warcry, where Chaos-worshipping warbands engage in constant battle in the hope of joining Archaon's all-conquering legions.

Many of the authors featured in this volume are making their *Inferno!* debuts, while others are long-standing Black Library favourites. Ben Counter, veteran author of the Soul Drinkers series, leads the charge with our cover story 'Watchers of Battle'. Focusing on the Spire Tyrants, a warband that has left behind the fighting pits of Carngrad in favour of the far greater arena of the Bloodwind Spoil, this is a tale of bloodshed, glory and all-encompassing ambition, which provides an excellent introduction to the Warcry setting.

Guy Haley provides the climactic final instalment of the *At the Sign of the Brazen Claw* series, bringing Prince Maesa and company's stories to a chilling end. Trapped in the inn, the travellers are forced to abandon storytelling and band together for survival as their world crumbles around them...

Graeme Lyon makes his second *Inferno!* appearance with a superb story that explores the volatile magic that infuses all of the Mortal Realms in the aftermath of the Shyish Necroquake.

Appearing in these pages for the first time are such formidable talents as Gareth Hanrahan, Ben Galley and Anna Stephens, established fantasy and science fiction authors who we are thrilled to welcome to the Warhammer universe. These are not the only luminaries making their first forays into *Inferno!*. In fact, no fewer than *nine* fantastic new authors – Marc Collins, Sean Grigsby, Rob J. Hayes, Michael R. Fletcher, Gavin G. Smith and Gary Kloster among them – bring their varied and distinctive writing styles to this edition. As always, it has been a joy to welcome these fresh faces into the halls of Black Library and experience new perspectives on familiar settings and factions. It is our intention to keep bringing you a host of excellent new authors with each edition of this anthology.

Ready yourself, for the time of reckoning is almost upon you. Tales of perilous quests, shadowy cults and endless war await. Don your battleplate, let the drums of war rattle your bones and know no fear as you face the darkness ahead. Raise your axe and charge headlong into the ravening hordes that gather on the horizon. Gods willing, you will emerge victorious.

Richard Garton
Submissions Editor, August 2019

WATCHERS OF BATTLE

Ben Counter

Black Library author Ben Counter's Inferno! *debut is also the first ever* Inferno! *story from the Warcry setting. It is a typically gory, visceral tale that explores the lengths one must go to in order to achieve true greatness in the eternal warzone of the Eightpoints.*

As the warbands of four tribes converge on Bonebreak Pass, Voleska of the Spire Tyrants dreams of glory beyond battle and slaughter on the Bloodwind Spoil. As luck would have it, several of the Everchosen's elite warriors have come to preside over the coming bloodshed and observe. This is Voleska's chance to show her fighting prowess by crushing the savage Corvus Cabal, but how far must she go to prove herself worthy of joining the ranks of Archaon's armies?

'We're a long way from Carngrad,' said Kyryll as he trudged up the sludge and shale of the mountain slope.

Voleska looked up towards the sky and the peaks of the Fangs that surrounded them. 'Not so far,' she said.

'Camp's up ahead.' Kyryll peered towards the scattering of bonfires and torches on the shoulder of the mountain above them. 'Looks like the Blackblades and the Mercy Slayers made it.'

'More to watch us,' said Voleska. 'More to weep.'

It had rained blood that night. Bonebreak Pass was clotted with coagulating gore. It formed a slow, black river along the pass, draining into the foothills of the Fangs, a sluggish bloodletting that formed a portent for what was to come. The pass was one of the few relatively stable ways past the Fangs and into the regions of the Bloodwind Spoil closer to the citadel of the Varanspire. Control of it had passed from one bloody hand to the next hundreds of times over the generations. Bones and shattered skulls mixed with the loose shale and formed natural cairns, pulled apart by the coagulating flow.

A lot of people had died there. A lot more were about to.

Voleska and Kyryll made their way through the encampment towards the hide tents and bivouacs of the Red Sand Raiders. Warbands from across the Bloodwind Spoil had gathered for the coming battle over Bonebreak Pass, and the banners of several Spire Tyrants bands hung from the spindly trees clinging to the upper slopes. On another day, they would be butchering one another for the right to be called the best among the Children of the Arenas. Tonight, they were allies against a common enemy.

Voleska pulled back the flap of the largest tent. Inside, Ferenk Sunder-Spine was scratching battle plans into the loose dirt. The Head-Taker of the Red Sand Raiders was a huge man with hundreds of finger bones piercing the skin of his arms and shoulders, each taken from a kill in the arena. He looked up at Voleska's intrusion.

'What do you want?' he demanded.

'Scouted, like you said,' replied Voleska.

Ferenk grunted and poked at the battle lines he had scratched. 'What have you got?'

'The Crows have the high ground at the northern end,' replied Voleska. 'They reckon they'll swoop down on us and peck out our eyes.'

'How many?'

Voleska shrugged. 'Six, seven warbands. Couple of thousand ears hanging from the trees. Flocks of birds everywhere.'

'Were you seen?'

Voleska smirked. 'Look at me. Course I was seen.'

Ferenk looked at Voleska as if seeing her for the first time.

She was huge. Most of the time the really big competitors failed to make their mark in the fighting pits of Carngrad – they were too slow and cumbersome, and a leg tendon got cut or a gut was punctured before they could bring their bulk around to face a faster enemy. The crowds whooped when they emerged onto the sands, and they cheered when they fell. But Voleska had climbed the ladder of victories to challenge the very best, all while carrying more heft than anyone in the Red Sand Raiders. She carried a stone-headed hammer over her shoulder – a less than ideal weapon for a pit fighter, but one she wielded as if she had been born with it in her hand. What skin showed beneath her heavy garb of layered animal hides and splint mail was tanned and battered, and her lank black hair was tied severely back to show off the scar taking up the right side of her scalp.

'Not like they don't know we're here,' mused Ferenk. 'What about the Unmade? The Scions?'

'The faceless mob are on the west side of the pass,' replied Voleska. 'Opposite the Splintered Fang. Doesn't look like the Scions made it.'

'Too busy annoying the gods,' said Ferenk. 'Here. Come.'

Voleska walked up to the battle plans Ferenk had scratched out. The torchlight in the tent cast flickering shadows across a crude diagram of Bonebreak Pass and the positions of the warbands. 'What's the plan?' she asked.

'Spire Tyrants don't do subtle,' said Ferenk. 'No feints. No secret paths. No false retreats. We're going straight down the middle. Storm the heights, hit the Cabal, kill them.'

Voleska nodded. 'They think they own the mountains. They're arrogant. They'll try something. But we won't fall for it. Straight down the middle.'

'I saw you,' said Ferenk. It was unexpected. He rarely said

anything that wasn't strictly necessary. 'At the Gutripper Pits. Slavemaster Barakhor's games. You killed four men.'

Voleska shrugged. 'They were only small.'

'The last one, you knocked his head clean off.'

'Yes, that I did. Went right into the crowd. They called me the Gift-Giver after that.'

'You fought well for us, Voleska. It was obvious enough, never had to say it. But a lot of us are going to die this dawn. Maybe someone important. Maybe me. The Red Sand Raiders will accept you if you want to step in. Do you want that, Gift-Giver?'

Ferenk looked at her now, piercing and intense, in a way he never had before. Voleska felt herself tense up, as if aware of an assailant trying to flank her. 'I want... I want more,' she said.

'More than what?'

Voleska was rarely lost for words – like Ferenk, she didn't use them when she didn't have to. Now she had to fight to turn her thoughts into speech. 'More than being... one among many. That's what I fought for in the arenas, to be on my own at the top. That's what it means to be a Spire Tyrant – we got to the top in the arenas and now we're doing it in the Spoil. I'm not going to live and die as just another Red Sand Raider. That's what I want. Something more.'

Ferenk nodded. 'Maybe they'll follow you, if it comes to that,' he said. 'But whether they will or not depends on tomorrow. Take some heads, give some gifts, I can make you my right hand. You want that?'

'I'll take what the Spoil gives me,' replied Voleska.

'Good,' said Ferenk with finality. 'Of course, first of all, you'll have to survive.'

'Not planning to do anything else,' said Voleska.

'With the dawn,' concluded Ferenk, and turned back to his map of Bonebreak Pass.

'With the dawn,' agreed Voleska.

Outside, the night was turning chill. The moons were sinking as the night kept a jealous grip on the Fangs against the daybreak. The Spire Tyrants of their various warbands were resting, but few were asleep. They sparred and gambled, because the habits of the fighting pits never really left them.

'What did you mean earlier?' said Kyryll as Voleska emerged from the tent.

'When?'

'You said we weren't so far from Carngrad.'

'Because we aren't,' replied Voleska. 'Back in Carngrad, we fought for the eyes of the audience. For the lords who might hire us. The crowds. Even each other, so we knew who to respect. You think it's any different now?'

'Not many arenas round these mountains,' said Kyryll.

Voleska clipped him around the back of the head with her meaty palm. Kyryll wasn't small, but he was smaller than her, and he cringed at the impact. 'You're an idiot,' she said.

'So who are you fighting for?' retorted Kyryll. 'For Ferenk?'

'Him, among others,' she said. 'These other warbands will know not to stand in the Raiders' way when they see us tear apart the Cabal. The Cabal will remember us, too, if we let any live. They'll talk about the Ones Who Make The Sand Red, and the Gift-Giver. The Bloodwind Spoil will know we're coming. They'll beg to be the first to kneel to us. And then…'

Voleska gripped Kyryll's shoulder and turned him to face one of the nearby peaks. Bloody snow clung to the highest point, well above the line where the spindly thorn trees thinned out to nothing. On one of the peaks, against the deep dark of the night, a sharp black outline was just visible.

It was a human of immense size, bulked out by plates of spiked armour and a massive tower shield. One hand held a halberd with a bundle of skulls strung around its point.

'One of Archaon's Chosen,' said Voleska. 'Saw them while we scouted. You were too dim to notice. They're watching. Not just us, the Cabal, the Unmade, the Splintered Fang. Why do you think we're here, Kyryll? To be the biggest dogs in the Bloodwind Spoil? Maybe that's enough for you, but not me. They're watching for warriors to take to the Varanspire. For Archaon's army.'

The lone warrior didn't move. The face was hidden behind a solid steel visor broken only by a black eyeslit.

'You think they're watching us now?' asked Kyryll.

'Me, maybe. You? Not so sure.'

Down the pass, in the direction of the distant Varanspire, the Corvus Cabal's warbands held the upper slopes. They hadn't set up bonfires and torches as the Spire Tyrants had. Their presence was betrayed by the trophies they strung up among the trees. Their Great Gatherer demanded trophies be taken from their dead. The Corvus Cabal cut a memento off every corpse they left in their wake, and hung up those orphaned ears and fingers everywhere they settled. The Cabal thought Bonebreak Pass and the Fangs were theirs, and they had been labouring under that misapprehension for far too long. With the dawn they would learn the truth.

And the watchers of battle would see them fail.

They swept down from the heights in a storm of bloody feathers, shrieking as they ran. Beneath the clouds of an impending storm, at the breaking of the lightning-touched dawn, the warbands of the Corvus Cabal made their charge.

Across the pass, the Splintered Fang and the Unmade had

their own battle to fight, and perhaps the victor of that slaughter would survive in sufficient numbers to challenge for command of the pass. The winners' blood could be shed another time. For now, the Spire Tyrants had the enemy ahead of them to fight.

Ferenk held his spear high. He had used it to kill his way to fame and glory in Carngrad, and then killed his owner with it when he led the breakout of pit fighters who had become the core of the Red Sand Raiders. 'Life kept the prize from us,' he yelled. 'Now we take it!'

The Red Sand Raiders gathered in front of him cheered. They were men and women of every kind, small and fast, strong and brutal, cold-blooded killers and frenzied murderers. They were united by the old marks of combat on them, and the ugly functionality of their wargear. They carried the weapons with which they had learned to fight in the blood pits and amphitheatres. Hooked blades, nets and tridents, scythes, twinned daggers. They were united by the same fury that had seen them earn or steal their freedom from the pits.

'I heard a rumour that we're here to take the pass,' continued Ferenk, which was met by a muttering of dark laughter. 'I say we're here to take some heads! Let the rest squabble about who owns what. We are Spire Tyrants! We turned the sands of the arenas red, and we do the same to the Bloodwind Spoil! We kill and break and tear, and when there's no one else left, we take what we want!'

The other Spire Tyrants warbands had their own leaders, and they were stoking the fires in their warriors just as Ferenk was. Some of them had started their careers doing the same thing in the arenas, in Carngrad and elsewhere in the Bloodwind Spoil, whipping the crowd and their fellow fighters into a fury that could only be sated by blood.

Their words mingled with the howl of the coming storm's winds and the shrieking of the Corvus Cabal. The crow-warriors were a dark tide descending from their high ground onto the treacherous slopes above the blood-clotted pass. They had been expected to hold the heights and wait for the Spire Tyrants to come to them. They had instead chosen to force the battle and, by advancing, join it on their terms.

It did not matter. The battle plan still held. Straight down the middle, and kill them all.

The leaders of the Spire Tyrants couldn't have held them back any longer if they had wanted to.

Voleska felt the ripple of fury running up and down the Spire Tyrants' lines. The ex-gladiators broke into a charge down the slope towards the advancing Corvus Cabal. She was a part of it, carried along on their tide, and she felt her heart hammering with anticipation. It was the same sensation she had once had when the doors of the arenas were hauled open and she saw the enemy for the first time. A hot, tingling spark of anticipation that ran from her core down her arms and legs, a cousin of fear but something rooted far more deeply in her mind.

'They're fast,' gasped Kyryll as he ran beside her, his twin jagged swords in his hands. 'They'll go for the tendons.'

'Not my first tumble, little Kyryll,' replied Voleska.

The distance closed. Voleska could hear the birdlike shrieks and caws of the Cabal, a battle-tongue other warbands could not understand. They wore black feathers and avian skulls. Their faces were smeared with black warpaint. She hauled her hammer up onto her shoulder and felt its familiar, comforting weight on her.

The two forces slammed into one another. The Cabal were fast and cunning. The Spire Tyrants fought with a straightforward brutality. Blood sprayed across the shale and a dozen people died in the first seconds. A gladiator's head was sheared clean off by a razor-sharp blade. A feather-clad Cabalist was rammed through the gut by a jagged two-handed sword. A Spire Tyrant a few strides from Voleska fell back, screaming, his face torn wide open by the finger talons of the Cabalist who had dived under his guard.

With a howl, one of the Cabal leapt off an outcropping of rock. He dived down at Voleska feet first, and the murky sun glinted off the talons built into his boots.

Voleska was faster than he thought.

She swung the hammer to meet him in mid-air. The weapon's head slammed into the Cabalist's midriff. It was a blow the crowd had always adored. They loved the crunch of the spine and pelvis, the elongated grunt as the air was forced out of her opponent's lungs. They loved to see the body, lifeless as a rag doll, thrown down to the bloody sands. She flung the Cabalist's body off the head of her hammer, and she could almost hear the cheering.

Kyryll was alive, wrestling with a Cabalist who had rushed him. The two rolled on the gory slope, in danger of tumbling down into the pass. Their weapons were pinned at their sides as neither was willing to let go of the other. Voleska grabbed the Cabalist's feathered cloak and hauled him up into the air. The Cabalist dropped Kyryll and slashed at Voleska, but her reach was such that the dagger's points skimmed past her throat.

Voleska slammed the enemy back into the ground. He rolled to a kneeling position from which he could stab and slash at her abdomen. But Voleska was wise to it. She was already in mid-swing by the time the Cabalist's head was up, and there was no time for him to even throw out a hand in defence.

The hammer smashed into his face. Voleska angled the blow upwards, into the chin, a trick she had learned in the arenas when the gladiators had been given the maimed or condemned to fight for the crudest entertainments of the crowd. The Cabalist's head snapped back, the neck gave way, and his head was smacked clean off his shoulders.

If there had been an audience, thought Voleska, they would have screamed with joy and bloodlust at the decapitating blow. They would have chanted the name of the Gift-Giver.

She corrected herself. There was an audience. They were watching from the peaks overlooking Bonebreak Pass.

'Get up, little Kyryll,' she scolded. She turned to the rest of the battling Spire Tyrants. 'Onwards! Straight down the middle! Don't give these vermin the time to draw breath!'

The Spire Tyrants surged. Bodies tumbled down the slope into the coagulating gore flowing down the pass. The Corvus Cabal fell back and counter-charged, some finding soft flesh for their blades, others finding only a swinging sword or a shield boss to the face. Voleska swung her hammer in a huge arc and the Cabalists scurried away from her. The Red Sand Raiders ran into the gap she opened up, and they set about the fleeing Cabal with an efficiency born of a lifetime of killing.

Ferenk was among them. The jagged steel head of his spear found a Cabalist in the back and he pinned her to the ground, rushing up to her and slamming his foot down on the back of her head.

Voleska had a split second to gather her thoughts. She risked a glance away from the carnage, up the slope towards the peaks surrounding Bonebreak Pass like the spires of a crown.

The watchers of battle were there, unmoving. In the flashes

of lightning she could see how their black armour was banded with steel. Their shields were inscribed with glowing runes and hung with strings of skulls and severed hands. Every peak in the Fangs seemed to have one of Archaon's warriors atop it, watching the various fronts of the battle unfolding in Bonebreak Pass. Some were observing the bloodshed on the other side of the pass, where Voleska knew that the Unmade and the Splintered Fang were butchering one another. Others were watching the Corvus Cabal and the Spire Tyrants.

They were watching Voleska. They had seen her pair of kills.

'Killing is not enough,' said Voleska to Kyryll, who was scrambling to his feet to join Ferenk's advance.

'What?' Kyryll struggled to understand her above the din of clashing steel and screams.

'They're watching. Killing isn't enough. We have to show them. Like in the arenas! We are the spectacle!'

She shot her friend a grin. His face showed only confusion, which passed as he refocused on the battle unfolding around them.

She knew now what she had to do. She understood why she had fought in the arenas, and why she had broken out in a night of anarchy and bloodshed on the streets of Carngrad. Why she had joined Ferenk and the Red Sand Raiders, welding a coherent force out of so many disparate killers. It was because one day, in the chill and storm-lashed Bonebreak Pass, the eyes of Archaon would be on her at last.

'They're falling back!' gasped Kyryll. The Corvus Cabal were scurrying back towards the heights, leaving dozens of dead and maimed in their wake. The slain tumbled down the slope into the thick gore, which was swelling and foaming with the rain.

'It's a feint!' shouted back Ferenk as he finished off a

Cabalist on the ground with spear thrust to the throat. 'They want to draw us in.'

'Then let them!' answered Voleska. 'Tyrants! They are watching! Finish these vermin! Fill up this valley with the dead!'

She held her enormous hammer high over her head. The whole Spire Tyrants force could see her – she was a head taller than most of them and her gore-clotted weapon was like a standard of war brandished as a rallying point.

Some recognised the Gift-Giver from their days in the Carngrad fighting pits. Others just roared in appreciation of the bloody hammer and the toll it had reaped. They surged forward again in Voleska's wake as she ran after the retreating Cabal.

Some of the Cabalists were too slow. They were trampled underfoot or killed with blades when they stumbled. Voleska slammed her hammer down on the crown of one Cabalist's head and drove his shattered skull into his chest. Kyryll kept up with her and slashed at the hamstrings of another runner, sending him face first into the bloody scree to be despatched by the Spire Tyrants behind him.

The Corvus Cabal scrambled up the slope to the heights. They had banked on the Spire Tyrants waiting to exult in their victory, licking their wounds and regrouping, not pursuing them heedless of the trap the Cabalists were trying to spring. They never made it to the eyries strung with battlefield trophies, where thousands of crows roosted among the thorny trees of the Fangs. The front ranks of the Corvus Cabal were forced to turn and face the Spire Tyrants before they were overrun, well short of the ridge where they had hoped to mass for their counter-charge

The warriors on the peaks were still watching. They had not moved, save to turn their heads and keep the thickest of the fighting in view. They showed no reaction to the bloodshed.

Voleska had to get their notice. She had to go further.

A leader of the Cabal stood proud of the enemy lines. He stood on long steel legs, like stilts strapped to his shins. They ended in talons that he wielded as skilfully as a bird of prey, clotted with torn flesh and hair. He carried a pair of hooked blades and he shrieked in anger beneath his bird-skull helm. his arms were pierced with hundreds of feathers so that he seemed to have a pair of bloodstained wings.

Voleska had seen other Spire Tyrants killing with a flourish – a skilful decapitation, a flamboyant disembowelment – and she knew her spectacular hammer kills had competition. There was only one target for her in the unfolding bloodshed.

Voleska ran right at the Cabalist leader. He loped towards her, towering over even her prodigious height. He leaped with improbable agility, stabbing his talons down at her. She pivoted to one side and felt the claws raking down her shoulder. She roared in pain and let it fuel her, as she had learned in her first few hours as a killer in the arenas. She would always be hurt. She would always be wounded. It was her choice to use it, and not let it defeat her.

Voleska had the strength and the enemy had the speed. As fast as he was, he could not fly up out of the reach of her hammer. She held the weapon near the butt-end and swung it in a wide, circular arc, ignoring the Spire Tyrants who scattered out of the way. With a clatter the hammer knocked one of the Cabalist's stilts out from under him.

He hopped onto his remaining stilt and let out a series of staccato, shrieking syllables, a war cry in the battle-tongue of the Cabal. Voleska shifted her grip on her hammer and lunged at her enemy, driving the head of the weapon towards his midriff.

The Cabalist easily jerked sideways out of the way of the blow. His twin blades ripped into Voleska's unwounded shoulder and down her upper arm. He spun on his stilt and lashed out again, slicing a deep gash into her cheek and another into her other arm.

She had known she would be hurt. There was no way, with her relative slowness, to get into position. She had made a career in the arenas taking blows and refusing to let them debilitate her. She would feel the agony later. For now, she was right next to the Cabalist leader, his bloody wings unfolded over her, his wicked beak grimacing down.

Voleska swung the hammer down and up again, feeling her torn muscles fighting to power it out of its lowest point.

The hammer arced up and slammed into the Cabalist's groin.

Bones crunched. The Cabalist's pelvis shattered. The roar of an imaginary crowd filled Voleska's mind. Severed heads and heart thrusts got boring eventually, but every crowd loved to see a kill-shot to the groin.

Voleska couldn't leave it to chance. She had to confirm the kill before she could play to the stands and exult in her victory. The Cabalist toppled off his stilt and landed on his knees. Voleska hefted the weight of the hammer over her head and swung it down like a labourer driving a post into the ground. The hammer came down on the back of her foe's neck.

The blow compressed the enemy's body, folding it in half. The ribcage collapsed into the abdomen. The spine was turned to pulp. Blood and gore spurted out through the Cabalist's torn torso, spraying to either side in crimson wings to complement the false pinions of black feathers.

Every kill needed a final flourish, an exclamation mark.

Voleska swung an underhand blow into the shattered mess that remained of the Cabalist leader. She caught him under his ruptured chest and flung him high over the battlefield. He trailed blood like the tail of a comet and thumped into the middle of the Corvus Cabal.

Voleska could feel the tide of despair that rippled out from the corpse's impact. The dismay of the opposition was as sweet as the appreciation of the crowd. Whether they loved or hated her, it was the reaction, the emotion she sparked in the hearts of the onlookers, that drove her on.

The Spire Tyrants roared at the death. They rushed in around her and dived into the Corvus Cabal. The enemy were shattered, their feathered bodies beaten down to the scree or held aloft impaled on spears and blades. They fought back till the end, and there were Spire Tyrants whose throats were cut or whose hearts were pierced even in the moments of victory, but for every fallen gladiator, five or six of the Crows were left butchered in bleeding heaps.

Drops of blood pattered down onto Voleska's shoulders as she paused. The thunderclouds overhead swelled deep crimson, and the storm broke. With a hiss and a roar, the blood rain fell again.

It trickled down the scree in hundreds of tiny streams, mingling with the river that now flowed through the pass, foaming pink around rapids formed by piles of bodies. It streamed down the faces of the Spire Tyrants and spattered against the armour of the warriors on the mountain peaks. It sluiced down the mountainsides. The sky was rent and bleeding, as if the fury of the battle below had dealt a mortal wound to the sky itself.

Voleska panted with exertion and leaned on her hammer. The pain of her wounds was starting to hit her now. Both arms were streaming with blood, and not only from the crimson downpour. She looked up through the red rain at the watchers on the peaks.

Would that be enough? Did they care? Had they even seen her butchery of the enemy amid the swirling bloodshed? Plenty of Spire Tyrants had made spectacular kills in the last few moments alone. What made her stand out compared to them?

And then she knew.

A Spire Tyrant fought alone. They might form alliances in the arenas, and then join greater alliances outside it, banding together under leaders like Ferenk for mutual protection. But they were not born to such allegiances. Even her friendly rivalry with Kyryll had its roots in a genuine desire to outdo, to defeat, to step over on the way to something greater.

There was nothing for her on that bloodstained slope, nor in the camp where the Spire Tyrants would drink and boast past nightfall. A true gladiator did not make herself a part of that. She stood alone.

She knew what she had to do. She had never been more certain of anything in her life.

She turned to Kyryll. He looked similarly exhausted. His flesh was covered in nicks and cuts, and his arms were slathered in gore to the elbow. He grinned up at her, smearing the blood rain out of his eyes with the back of his hand. 'You were right,' he said. 'Not so different from Carngrad after all. Never gave them a show quite like this, though.'

Voleska felt the weight of her hammer as if she was lifting it for the first time. No one else in the arenas had the strength to wield it. No one had thought she could either. She had proven them wrong.

Kyryll never had the time to let the smile fall off his

features. Voleska's hammer blow caught him square in the face.

It was good that she started with him. He was the hardest to kill. Once he was down, his face staved in and ruined, the rest were easy.

It took the other Spire Tyrants several fatal moments to realise what she was doing. They were drunk on victory and their bodies were sluggish with the fatigue suddenly catching up with them. Voleska crushed the skull of one who had his back to her, then knocked the legs out from under another and finished him off with a stamp to the back of the neck.

The first Spire Tyrant to react turned to her and wrestled his blade back out of its scabbard. 'What are you...?' he gasped before Voleska rammed the head of the hammer into his chest, driving the air out of him. She swung the hammer up under his chin, shattering his jaw and snapping his head fatally back with the crack of snapping spine.

They tried to swarm her. When they came into her guard, they were mown down by the swinging arc of her hammer. They leapt at her and she swatted them out of the air where they could be killed down in the scree.

Surviving Cabalists took advantage of the sudden confusion among the Spire Tyrants to leap into the fray. More died in one-on-one struggles with the Spire Tyrants. Others were caught within the whirlwind of blood that surrounded Voleska. Crowded around by enemies, stronger than any of them and with a greater reach, she could not help but catch an enemy or three with every swing of her hammer.

The pain was gone. Her strength flowed back. The hollow inside her, that had been temporarily filled with the adulation of the crowd and the rush of victory, was brimming over with a certainty of purpose.

Ferenk faced her through the carnage. He loped over the broken bones and pulped torsos towards her. His face was a furious mass of scars twisted with anger. He led with his spear, blinded by his anger at Voleska's betrayal.

'Witch!' he snarled. 'You betray! You break us!'

'Give them a show, Sunder-Spine,' said Voleska with a blood-flecked grin.

Ferenk led with a spear thrust. Voleska shifted out of the way but he knew her too well to be wrong-footed. He snapped an elbow up into her face and caught her square on the jaw. Sparks flared in front of her eyes as her head snapped back, and she felt herself drop. She threw out a hand to break her fall, dropping her hammer, and felt Ferenk's spear grazing her cheek as he just missed a fatal stab to her face.

Voleska grabbed the haft of the spear and pulled. Ferenk came down on top of her. She wrapped a meaty hand around the back of his head to keep him from getting back up and the two rolled, wrestling, slick with blood and fighting for a grip.

Ferenk rolled on top. He tore an arm free and punched it down at her. She twisted her head and the blow slammed into her collarbone. The flash of pain told her it was probably broken. Ferenk's teeth were gritted and every ropelike muscle stood out on his lean, battle-carved body. He drew his fist back again and slammed it into the side of her head.

Ferenk's eagerness to punish her had let Voleska free one of her arms. She grabbed a handful of his lank black hair and pulled his head back. He was forced backwards and Voleska had the room to force herself up into a seated position. She wrapped both her arms around Ferenk and held him in a bear hug.

She could feel his ribs creaking against her biceps. He

hissed through his teeth as he fought to draw a proper lungful of breath. He pounded against her back but she cinched him in tighter, locking her fingers and grinding his torso. He thrashed and struggled, and his fingers found the haft of the stone dagger in his belt.

Voleska had killed men with this death grip before, but not often. Any competent fighter had a backup blade to slide between her ribs in such a clinch. Even as Ferenk pulled out his knife, Voleska powered up to her feet and threw the leader of the Red Sand Raiders away from her.

Ferenk landed heavily on one shoulder. He rolled to standing, panting down a breath, knife in hand.

'Who paid you to betray us?' snarled Ferenk. 'What did they offer you?'

'No one offers anything,' said Voleska. 'Not on the Spoil. You have to take it.'

'When I leave this pass, I will be wearing your skin.'

Voleska spat out a gobbet of bloody phlegm. 'You'll never leave.'

Ferenk ran at her, but his fury made him sloppy.

Voleska took the dagger thrust on her forearm. It sliced down to the bone, but it was just one more wound among many. Ferenk rushed into her, and she rammed a knee up into his stomach.

He folded and wheezed, almost pitching face first into the scree. Voleska drove her elbow down into the back of his head and felt the skull crack.

Ferenk was on his hands and knees now. Voleska picked up her hammer and shifted her grip to hold it just below the head, with the gore-encrusted lump of stone facing groundwards. She looked up at the closest watcher of battle, whose armoured visor was facing down at her.

'The Gift-Giver has a gift for Lord Archaon!' she yelled, and slammed the hammer down.

The blow crushed Ferenk's skull flat against the scree slope. The Sunder-Spine's brains sprayed out of his sundered cranium. His legs twitched with some primeval instinct of death, and then he was still.

No Spire Tyrants rushed in to avenge their fallen. No spat curses came her way. Voleska turned to look behind her, but through the falling rain she could see only bodies littering the slope.

They were all dead, or fled. She had done it.

She was the last one standing.

They descended the slopes as the last embers of the battle died down. Most of them turned away from the carnage and walked off into the labyrinthine peaks of the Fangs, uninterested in what the warbands had to offer them. But two of Archaon's warriors descended to the place where the Corvus Cabal and the Spire Tyrants had fought, and where only the dead and wounded remained. Save one warrior who waited for them, leaning on her giant hammer. They looked her up and down, sizing up her wounds. Up close they were huge, taller and broader even than Voleska. If they had found her wanting or too badly hurt to be used, they would have despatched her then and there. But they did not.

They turned away and headed for the northern end of the pass, in the direction of the Varanspire. Voleska gave silent thanks to the Dark Gods, and followed them.

Outside the Varanspire was a complex of dozens of forges, each one a structure of black stone and iron belching smoke. The region was bathed in infernal heat and the air was almost unbreathable with smoke and ash. Pale, skinny slave-things scurried about carrying ingots or hauling sleds loaded with swords and armour. The warriors led Voleska through the forges to one where the black iron doors hung open, revealing the glowing throats of the fires inside.

Segments of armour hung on the walls. Hundreds of swords were lined up in racks, with others in the process of being forged by a malformed smith whose enormous, lopsided musculature drove the hammer he used to beat the blades into shape. His face was hidden behind a caul of chain and it looked like he had never left his place at the anvil. He took a blade he had finished beating and plunged it into the water trough running the length of the room. A blast of steam filled the air as the superheated metal was suddenly cooled and hardened.

Voleska let her heart fill with anticipation. She had not dared believe she would join the ranks of Archaon's armies, not truly, until she saw it happen. Now she was to be fitted with the all-enclosing armour of a Chaos Warrior, ready to join the legions marching out through the Realmgates to conquer and despoil.

One of the weapons racked up for inspection was a hammer. It was the length and heft of her own, but of infinitely grander construction. Its iron head was faced with spikes and its haft was bound with the warted skin of some leathery beast. Voleska reached out to touch the weapon, imagining its killing power in her hands.

An iron-shod foot kicked her in the back of the leg. She fell to one knee, grunting in surprise. She reached out to arrest her fall and her hand found the edge of the trough containing the water used to quench the forge's blades.

But it was not full of water.

Voleska was looking into a trough full of blood. A gauntleted hand fell on her shoulder and kept her down on her knee. She struggled, but the grip on her shoulder and the weight pinning her down did not shift. It was like being held in an iron clamp. Voleska had never encountered anyone as strong as she was, but the warrior holding her was stronger by far.

They were not like her. They were not men and women. They were something inhuman. It was no gladiator of Carngrad or brave of the Corvus Cabal beneath that armour. It was no Unmade or Splintered Fang. Perhaps it had once been, a lifetime ago, but now it was something very different.

Voleska had thought the watchers of battle were searching for a warrior who was their equal, but she was not an equal.

She was not strong enough.

Panic rose in her. She had never truly felt it before. This fear was an alien thing, like a ghost that stole into her heart and turned it to ice. She tried to reach up and grab the arm pinning her down, but another hand seized her wrist and she was held fast.

Not strong enough to be one of Archaon's warriors.

She felt the sword point touch the back of her neck. The trough of blood was used for quenching the blades of Archaon's soldiers, but no mundane blood would do. It gave its strength to their arms and armour, imbuing them with the ferocity and anguish of the warbands of the Bloodwind Spoil. These facts rushed through Voleska's mind as she desperately sought a reason why she might live.

Not strong enough to serve Archaon. But strong enough to be a sacrifice.

The Gift-Giver, the Butcher of Bonebreak Pass, was chosen not to march with the armies of Archaon, but so their newly forged swords could be quenched in her blood.

The tip of the warrior's sword pierced the skin of her neck. The first trickle of it ran down her throat and dripped into the trough. The malformed blacksmith grunted in acknowledgement as his hammer rose and fell in a deafening, unceasing rhythm.

The sword punched through Voleska's neck. Ice ran through her as it cut her spine. Blood sluiced into the trough in front of her. Blackness flickered around the edges of her vision.

The last thing she saw was her lifeblood flowing into the trough, the only thing of value the servants of Archaon had seen in the Gift-Giver. Her last thoughts, before they were cut off by the passage of the blade through her brain stem, were of emptiness.

NO QUARTER

Rob J Hayes

In this action-packed war story from science-fiction and fantasy author Rob J Hayes, Sergeant Malvian Craw of the Steel Legion leads his squad in a desperate struggle against the illusive and deadly aeldari.

It's a far cry from fighting orks on Armageddon, but in the 41st Millennium greenskins are never far away… As the orks unexpectedly join the battle, Craw is forced to rely on his hard-earned experience – and an unlikely ally – in order to survive. A classic Imperial Guard story, 'No Quarter' looks at the choices one must make in the midst of battle, and shows the Warhammer 40,000 setting at its harshest and most brutal while offering the smallest glimmer of hope.

Malvian tried the vox again, but all he received was static. It was fair to say the patrol had gone to hell. Just a few hours out from the Imperial outpost, Malvian Craw and his squad of Steel Legion Guardsmen had entered the forest. They hadn't been expecting an ambush, nor prepared for one, but then it wouldn't have been much of an ambush if they'd seen it coming, and the aeldari were sneaky like that. At least two of Malvian's squad were down and he hadn't so much as seen an enemy. Calling for reinforcements was impossible due to the vox being scrambled, and they were pinned down, trading gunfire with an enemy more elusive than ghosts.

Three shards of metal buried themselves in a tree just a breath from Malvian's face. He threw himself sideways mere moments before another burst of shuriken fire shredded the bark right where he had been hiding. His coat caught on a low-hanging branch and he heard it rip even over the sound of lasgun fire and Trooper Benson's screams of pain. Malvian rolled in the thick leaf litter, crushing mud and insects beneath him, and slid to a stop, his lasgun up and ready, but he could see no targets. He saw nothing but shadows slipping between trees, there one moment and gone the next, glimpses of green armour over lithe bodies. He had no clear shot. No idea where he should even be aiming.

Malvian slithered backwards on knees and elbows, lasgun pointed ahead of him and eyes straining as he searched for a target. He was breathing heavily, adrenaline making his heart pound. Blood rushed in his ears and the noise made the battle seem a distant thing.

'Sarge?' Private Kule's voice. He was a big man, Kule, so large his uniform barely fitted him. He grabbed hold of the back of Malvian's collar and dragged him to his knees and they knelt there for a few moments. Back to back, huddled behind a great grey mammoth of a tree, scanning the forest for any sign of the aeldari.

'I'm good, lad,' Malvian said, reaching back and patting Kule on the shoulder. 'Just glad I used the latrine this morning. That was closer than a wet shave with a chainsword.'

Kule laughed but it sounded forced, humour to cover the horror. 'What's going on, sarge?' the big man asked. 'Weren't like this before today. Last lot of pointy-headed buggers we found couldn't find the trigger on a cannon. But this lot... Benson is screaming like he's being torn apart out there, and Rorak is down and he ain't moving.' He sounded scared, and he had every right to be. Up until now their scouting of the region had been easy. Nothing but a few wild beasts, and some unarmed aeldari too stubborn to move on without a lasgun up the arse as incentive. But today was different. These aeldari were different. They were organised, armed and armoured, and shooting back. And by the Emperor's shiny Golden Throne, they wouldn't sodding stay still long enough to get themselves shot. Still, it was better than fighting orks. There was little more disheartening than putting a handful of shots into a greenskin and watching it laugh at you all the while like nothing you could do meant a damn.

Malvian shook his head to clear it and pressed the button on his vox-communicator.

'Benson. Benson, can you hear me? How bad is it?' The vox had been playing up ever since they entered the forest an hour back, and Malvian was starting to think it was all part of the aeldari's plan. The squad link was spotty at best, and they had lost contact with the outpost. Not that Malvian missed the sound of the commissar's voice.

'Sarge?' Benson wailed. *'It hurts, sarge. I don't want to die!'*

Kule groaned. 'You'd think he'd never been hit before.'

Malvian frowned at a spot of forest where he was certain he had just seen movement. Gone now. 'Weren't too long back you were just as green as Benson,' he said as he turned and slipped past Kule to see where Benson had fallen. 'I had to pull an ork tooth out of your arse and you screamed yourself raw.'

'It bit me, sarge!' Kule said, as if he needed an excuse to scream at the horrors they had been through on Armageddon.

Truth was he thought Kule was lucky. They were both veterans of the war on Armageddon and both had seen more than their share of combat. That Kule had come through years of bloody fighting with only an ork-bitten arse to show for it was beyond fortunate.

'Cover me,' Malvian said. He patted Kule on the shoulder once more, and then sprinted for where Benson was lying prone on the forest floor. Shuriken fire whistled past, striking trees and dirt. The surviving Guardsmen leaned out from their cover and returned fire as best they could, but the aeldari were as good as ghosts, nothing but flashes of armour and bursts of deadly fire.

Malvian slid to a stop next to Benson and spent a moment peering into the depths of the forest, but he could see no sign of their enemy. He didn't even know how many they were fighting. Benson was lying on his back, not moving save for the odd wracking sob and one hand clutching at his stomach. His own lasgun was lying nearby; shurikens embedded the length of it. The sparks crackling along it recommended that nobody touch it ever again.

'Hold this, lad,' Malvian said. He pulled Benson's left hand away from his bloody stomach and shoved his own lasgun into the trooper's trembling grip. 'Point it that way and shoot at anything that moves.'

'I'm hit, sarge,' Benson cried.

'Aye, you are,' Malvian agreed. 'Now shut up and let me look at your scratches.'

The aeldari used nasty weapons and no mistake. They fired thin serrated discs of metal that pierced armour just as easily as the flesh beneath. Benson was studded with the things all up his right side and had at least one embedded in his chest. Blood pooled around the discs and stained his mustard uniform a dark brown. He was in a bad way and needed a medic.

'I've had worse injuries from stubbing my toe, lad,' Malvian said.

'It hurts,' Benson cried.

'So does stubbing your toe,' Malvian said. 'Now open your eyes and keep that gun pointed somewhere. I'm going to drag you back to safety and get Maine to patch you up good as new.'

Malvian grabbed Benson under the shoulders, counted to three, then started dragging the wounded Guardsman back towards their ragged line. Shuriken fire whistled past, and lasguns replied with equal severity. Benson groaned and cried, and the leaves above rustled. Then Benson screamed. He pointed the lasgun up into the forest canopy and cracked off three rapid shots. A moment later a body clad in green and white armour dropped. It fell between a couple of large tree roots, its head cracking against one with a grim finality. It didn't move.

'Hell of a shot, lad,' Malvian said as he dragged Benson behind a great tree and looked around the three Guardsmen gathered nearby. 'Maine, get over here and convince Benson he's fine. Can't be that injured. He just bagged his first kill.'

Malvian poked his head around the tree as Maine started poking at Benson's wounds. He wasn't really a medic, but he knew how to dress a wound and that made him the closest thing they had. 'What am I supposed to do with this, sarge?' Maine asked. 'Do I pull them out?'

'You'll figure something out, Maine,' Malvian said. 'Just get the lad up and moving so we can…' He trailed off as a metallic object the size of a small rock sailed out of the forest depths, arcing towards them. Malvian watched it for a moment. 'Grenade!' He turned and leapt away even as the device hit the ground nearby. Malvian tackled Maine, dragging him to the ground and a moment later the world flashed a bright, searing white and a wave of heat washed over them.

Benson was gone. Or at least half of him was gone, consumed by the plasma grenade's detonation. The other half was a bloody, charred mess that threatened to turn Malvian's stomach. The grenade had left a pit in the forest floor, and the remnants of the grenade still glowed in the centre as the miniature sun ate its way down into the earth.

'Damn it!' Malvian said, his voice carrying a familiar bitter edge. Not the first Guardsman he'd lost under his command, nor the second, and not even the tenth. The worst thing, and he hated to admit it, was that it was getting easier. He knew it shouldn't, but every loss was just a little bit easier to take.

'Sarge?' Maine asked. 'What do we do?'

'Benson's gone to see the Emperor, lads,' Malvian shouted. 'He's left us to pick up his slack. Kule, give us some covering fire. Maine and I are going to move up and shove Benson's regards right down these eldar's throats.' He glanced at Maine. 'Assuming they have throats?'

Maine shrugged and wiped at the sweat running down his face.

The vox crackled, distorted sound without sense. A cold wind blew through the forest and a moment later a sound like thunder shook the earth beneath Malvian's feet and set all the trees rustling. A sense of dread crept up Malvian's spine, something he hadn't felt since the early days of Armageddon. He looked up just in time to see the crackling of energy as a great hulking ship translated out of the warp, so close to the planet there was no way it was going to do anything but crash.

'Emperor save us,' Malvian whispered as he watched the ship plummeting downwards. Then he drew in a deep breath and roared, 'Rebreathers on. Take cover!' He reached down and grabbed hold of Maine and dragged them both over the remains of Benson and into the pit the plasma grenade had left behind.

Two seconds passed. Three. Then the earth shook violently. A moment later the shock wave hit, whipping earth and detritus all around them, shaking the trees down to their roots. A roar of flames washed overhead and the sound was deafening. Something hard struck the back of Malvian's helmet and everything went dark.

Malvian woke to darkness and an ache that seemed to travel throughout his body. There was a pressure pushing down on him, crushing him. He tried to reach up to take his goggles off, but he couldn't move. That was when it dawned on him. He'd been buried alive. He struggled, wriggling and scrabbling, pushing up against the loose dirt and detritus piled on top of him. When he broke free of the earth, Malvian found the forest had turned as grey as his hair. Dust and ash had blown in, coating the trees and fogging the air so thickly he could barely see a dozen yards in any direction. Without his rebreather, he was certain he'd be choking on the fog. Some trees had fallen, and others were leaning precariously, their roots ripped from the earth and exposed. Most of the leaves were gone, either incinerated by the wave of fire or blown off the branches by the shock wave. The crash had turned the forest from a place full of green vitality to a graveyard of skeletal husks.

Malvian staggered back a step, breathing heavily into his rebreather and fighting a wave of nausea. Whatever had hit him on the head had hit hard, and his helmet had the dent to prove it. He was lucky to be alive. He pressed the button on his vox-communicator. 'Six hundred and thirteenth, sound off.' Silence greeted him. Nothing but the sound of a fire burning in the distance somewhere and a few echoing shouts he tried desperately not to recognise.

He found a hand half buried at his feet and began digging Maine out of the earth. He was dead. He hadn't managed to get his rebreather on in time and had suffocated as they were buried alive. One more Guardsman lost under his command. Malvian tried the vox again, but no one answered him. He found Kule underneath a fallen tree. The veteran had tried to take shelter behind its bulk, only for the trunk to splinter and collapse on top of him. He had survived the war on Armageddon with nothing but an ork-bitten arse by way of injury. He had held the line time and again, and fought tooth, nail and bayonet against the green-skinned menace, only to be killed by a tree that couldn't hold its ground.

Malvian searched for survivors a while longer, ignoring the shouts getting closer, ignoring the silence greeting him on the vox. He couldn't quite believe his whole squad was dead. Some of them had served with him at the battle for Infernus, lived through the hell of that brutal siege.

A mocking laugh drifted through the fog, brutish and full of scorn. Malvian recognised the sound, had heard its like time and again on Armageddon. He turned to see an ork lumbering towards him, thick with swollen muscle and covered in cuts dripping blood. It had a mouth full of rotting, misshapen fangs, and a snarl twisted its grotesque features. Rusted red metal, dented from weapons fire, was nailed onto its head, shoulders and chest, and it carried an axe that was little more than a wedge of jagged metal bolted to a haft of wood. It was the first of the monsters, probably fallen from the ship as it was crashing, but there would be many more behind it.

Malvian's shoulders slumped and he staggered back a step. He hated the orks. He'd been born on Armageddon not long after their first invasion, and he'd lived and fought through their second attempt. He'd seen good men and women die at their monstrous green hands, and lost more friends than he cared to count. Hives reduced to nothing but bones and ash. Humans mutilated and taken as slaves. He hated the orks, and with good reason. All the men and women of the Steel Legion hated the orks. But he'd really hoped he'd left the monsters behind for good.

The ork laughed again. 'Smells like roasted 'umie,' it said as it walked past a body covered in mud and ash and charred long past recognition. The hole where its nose should have been twitched and its beady red eyes fixed on Malvian. It was a big monster and no mistake, but Malvian had one thing going for him at least; the ork was alone. For now.

Malvian looked around for a gun but could see none. He had given his own to Benson and it had vanished along with the half of him caught in the grenade. The ork advanced on him, gaining speed and swishing its axe from side to side. Malvian gritted his teeth, drew his monoknife, and lurched forward to meet the beast head-on with a bellow of rage.

Even with bright spots dancing across his vision, Malvian managed to strike first. He ducked away from an overhead smash and opened a wound on the ork's unprotected legs. But orks never went down easily and the monster just laughed and smashed the blunt side of its axe into Malvian's ribs. He went down onto one knee, struggling to draw breath, then rolled sideways just in time to avoid being cleaved in two. The ork kicked him in the chest, knocking Malvian down onto his back, and then it was on top of him. Malvian grabbed hold of the axe haft and screamed furious defiance at the brute as it bore down on the weapon, using its massive weight to drive the blade towards Malvian's face.

A burst of shurikens buried themselves into the ork's flesh, biting through its rusted armour and digging into its face. The ork stumbled away and roared, a clawed hand pawing at its bleeding mouth and cheek. It ripped one of the shurikens from its flesh in a gush of blood, stared at it for a moment, then roared again and charged past Malvian.

Malvian rolled over and saw the aeldari that Benson had shot, propped up and wedged between two large roots, its gun in an outstretched hand. The aeldari let out another burst of fire and the ork staggered from the impacts, blood spraying off to paint the forest floor crimson. Malvian pushed up to his feet and charged after the ork even as it waded forward against another burst of shuriken fire. The greenskin was almost on the aeldari when Malvian caught up to it and buried his knife in its unarmoured back. He stabbed it again and again, screaming in fury, each thrust punctuated by the sound of the aeldari's pistol firing off bursts of shurikens. Eventually, Malvian staggered back and dropped to his knees, his knife loose in his grip. The ork swayed on its feet for a few moments longer, then toppled sideways in a puff of ash and loosely packed earth. Malvian looked up to see the aeldari pointing its pistol at him.

They stared at each other. Malvian shifted the grip on his knife a little and readied to launch himself at the aeldari. He knew the eldar would get a burst of fire off, but if he could cross the distance between them at least he could take the xenos with him. Then the aeldari's arm dropped and she sighed. Her emerald-green armour was dented and scored and smudged with ash, and there was a dark lasgun burn in the leg plate. She'd be going nowhere in that state, and other than a few scrapes and the ringing in his ears, Malvian was fine. He had to get out of there before more orks arrived, and he knew more of them would be on the way. Orks never went anywhere alone, and it was clear now the crashing ship was greenskin. A suicidal but effective way to invade a world; he'd seen it before on Armageddon. There was no defence against orks mad enough to crash themselves onto a planet. And no other race in the galaxy tough enough to survive the strategy.

Malvian thrust his knife back into its belt sheath, stood, and walked a few steps away from the dead ork. He glanced about the forest, trying to find his bearings. The orks would be coming and they would be beyond counting. He needed to be away before they arrived. He needed to get out of the forest. Back to the Imperial outpost would be ideal. It was neither large nor well manned, but they had enough people and enough guns to hold out for a while at least, maybe even until reinforcements could arrive. At the very least they'd make the greenskins pay dearly for coming here. Of course, he wasn't likely to make it that far on his own and with only a knife.

He glanced back to the aeldari. Her helmet was cracked, one of the eyepieces shattered, and she was fumbling at it, ignoring him as she struggled. She'd saved him, that much was undeniable. They'd been fighting just moments earlier, trying to kill each other, but still the eldar had saved him from the ork. She was finished, wounded, unable to move. She had nothing to gain from saving him, just trading one live enemy for another. But she *had* saved him. Honour demanded he repay that. That, and she'd make a good prisoner.

'Damn it!' Malvian cursed and turned around, stalking back towards the aeldari. She hadn't moved, but upon seeing his approach she lifted her pistol from the ground again and pointed it roughly in his direction.

'What are you doing, *mon-keigh*?' Her voice was discordant but disturbingly beautiful.

'Saving your arse,' Malvian said gruffly. 'Repaying the favour.

Taking you prisoner. Pick one, I don't care. Just point that little pistol somewhere useful and don't fight me.'

The aeldari scoffed. 'Your people don't take prisoners.'

Malvian shrugged. 'Sure we do,' he said, though he couldn't remember a time they had. Then again he'd spent his entire life fighting orks and there simply wasn't any point in taking a greenskin prisoner.

He arrived at her side and bent down, only to find the barrel of her pistol pressed against his throat.

'Why?' There was anger along with the pain in the aeldari's voice. 'Why not just run and leave me?'

Malvian shrugged. 'You saved me first. Besides, there's two rules I've always tried to live by. First is never to leave the barracks without a fresh pair of socks. Very important that one. Second is when it comes to guns, bigger is always better. Well, right now I don't even have a gun, so your little shredder there will have to do.'

The pistol dropped from his throat. The aeldari was breathing heavily and each breath seemed to bring more pain. Malvian couldn't say he knew a damned thing about their physiology, he knew little enough about his own, but he doubted the fall from the forest canopy had done her much good. She reached up and flipped the final catches on her helmet so it fell free. Then she gasped in a deep breath and coughed. She had pointed ears, fine features, and skin that seemed a little too tight and smooth; but in truth, she did not seem so different from a human. Not so different at all, now Malvian looked at her. He'd expected something more... alien.

'I don't understand,' the aeldari said, her voice clearer now.

The howls and shouts were drawing closer. More orks were on their way. 'Why did you save me?' Malvian asked.

The aeldari stared at him in a way that made him feel small and insignificant. 'I killed the more dangerous enemy,' she said eventually. 'After that, there seemed little point in killing you too.'

A sting to his pride, but there was no sense in taking offence. 'Well there's plenty more of those *more dangerous* enemies on the way, and we stand a better chance of getting out of here together, I reckon. So up you get and let's go.'

'Go where?'

'Anywhere but here,' Malvian growled. 'I've seen what happens to people taken by these monsters.' He shook his head. 'I wouldn't wish it on anyone. So right now, let's just get up and get moving.' He slid an arm behind her back and lifted the aeldari onto her feet. She hissed in pain and Malvian was certain he was carrying more of her weight than she was, but at least they were moving.

'That thing was an ork,' the aeldari said as they passed the body. The way she said it sounded almost like a question.

'Aye. Don't tell me you've never seen one before?' Malvian asked. He had no idea which way was back to the outpost, only that the trees had fallen away from the crash site and so that was the direction he was going. He needed to get them out of the forest and hope his vox started working again.

The aeldari was silent for a few moments. 'It was difficult to kill,' she said.

Malvian let out a bitter chuckle as he half-carried, half-dragged the aeldari along. 'Aye, tough buggers.' Malvian stepped over a fallen tree and grunted as he lifted the aeldari over it too. She was lighter than he had expected, her armour seeming to weigh almost nothing at all, but still an extra burden to carry. 'They can survive just about anything,' he continued. He wasn't even sure why he was talking to her, but some conversation seemed better than none, helped steady his nerves. 'However much you think is enough to put one down for good, it will take more. Always more. The trick is to shoot them first and keep shooting until they go down. Then shoot them a bit more for good measure.'

'Why would you keep shooting them once they're dead?' the aeldari said, sounding disgusted.

Malvian let out a grim smile. 'It's cathartic.'

'It's barbaric.' A scream of pain erupted from far behind them, echoing through the forest, and the aeldari turned her head towards the sound. She let out a mournful sigh and Malvian guessed the orks had found a surviving aeldari. 'You hate them,' she said.

'Aye,' Malvian said. He helped her over another fallen tree and winced as she hissed in pain. 'Been fighting the greenskins my whole life, it seems. I've seen the worst of what they're capable of. Lived through it. Hordes of the monsters beyond counting, all baying for blood and screaming for war. A green tide without end, threatening to wash away civilisation in a sea of blood.' He shook his head, trying to clear the maudlin thoughts. 'They're hateful creatures with no purpose but killing. So, I hate them right back. There's nothing I'd like more than to never see an ork ever again.'

The aeldari was silent for a moment. 'I have been fighting *your* people my whole life, mon-keigh. Do you really think yourself so different from these creatures? There are hordes of you and war is all you know. Hate and killing is all you know.'

Malvian pulled them to a stop. He considered dropping the aeldari, going on without her. After all, she'd compared him to an ork and he couldn't think of a worse insult. But like it or not, he knew they had a better chance of surviving together. He started forward again, dragging her with him so roughly she let out a little cry of pain. Besides, what better way to prove her wrong than to save her life?

They continued in silence for a while, listening to the noise of orks drawing nearer. The thick fog distorted sounds, confused direction, but Malvian knew what he was hearing all the same. Greenskins grunting to each other, shouting orders or taunts. Their machines clomping through the forest, saw blades chopping through trees. The occasional burst of their primitive shoota fire. Either the brutes were finding enemies to fight, or they were fighting amongst themselves. Malvian hoped it was the latter. He hoped they all killed each other.

The aeldari seemed to be getting stronger, or perhaps just coping with her injury better. Malvian was still half-carrying her, with one of her arms over his shoulders, but he was dragging her less now. She limped with gasps of pain and growls of determination. The orks were monsters, and no doubt about it. Green nightmares given horrible form. He had thought the aeldari no different, but she looked almost human and sounded it too.

'We're being stalked,' the aeldari said as they rounded a large tree that dwarfed any of the others Malvian had seen. This far from the crash site, the forest was less affected by the shock wave, but the fog of ash and dust was still so thick he could barely see a dozen paces in front of him.

Malvian glanced about. 'I don't see anything.'

'Not surprising,' the aeldari said, her voice mocking. 'Your technology is as rudimentary as your biology. Regardless, there are two of them to our left. They are both smaller than the last one but carry primitive firearms.'

Malvian looked left. The aeldari was right. He caught

glimpses of dark shapes moving through the fog, but he couldn't make out much else. He pulled them behind a large tree and stopped, glancing around its bulk. 'We can't outrun them. We need a plan.'

'Don't all your mon-keigh plans just involve mindlessly charging towards the enemy?' the aeldari said, grimacing in distaste.

Malvian bristled at the insult. 'Well I don't think either of us are dancing through the trees like you and yours did earlier. So I guess we're going with my mindless charge idea. I'll make some noise, draw their fire, and give you a chance to fill 'em full of metal.'

'Why would you do that?' the aeldari asked with narrowed eyes. 'Willingly risk your life to distract them.'

'Standard tactics,' Malvian said with a grimace. 'Sometimes it seems a Guardsman's primary job is to distract the enemy away from the bigger guns.' He glanced around the tree again. The orks were in view now, picking their way between the trees, searching for their prey.

'You mon-keigh have such odd tactics. Do your lives really mean so little to you?'

Malvian shrugged. He had more important things to do than explain the Guard's methods. 'Are you ready? Take the shot as soon as you can. Aim for the head or neck. Body shots are nothing but wasted ammo.'

The aeldari was silent but fixed him with a hostile stare.

'Right then,' Malvian said.

He took a couple of deep breaths, then sprinted out from behind the tree. 'Look at me, you ugly green bastards!' he shouted. The orks opened fire immediately, their shootas tearing up the nearby ground and eating chunks out of the trees. Orks tended to make up for inferior tactics with superior numbers, and they made up for inferior aim with a relentless storm of bullets. Malvian headed away from the aeldari, keeping his head down and running between trees as often as possible. The distraction worked. He knew the first ork had gone down when its companion let out a roar and the bullets stopped. Malvian turned to see the ork advancing on the aeldari's cover, ripping the tree to shreds with a hail of gunfire.

'Hey, ugly!' Malvian screamed. He started running at the ork, hurling insults, but the greenskin couldn't hear him over the deafening roar of the junk it called a gun. He was just a few paces away when the ork turned his way, mouth open and grinning, full of yellowing teeth. Malvian threw himself to the ground behind a tree stump just as bullets sprayed his way, tearing up the ground behind him.

The ork grunted and the shoota fire stopped. Malvian poked his head out of cover to see the ork's shoota riddled with shurikens. The stupid monster was pulling the trigger to a series of clicks, staring at the weapon in confusion. It grunted and smacked the weapon, then pulled the trigger again. The gun let out a shower of sparks and ruptured, sending shards of razor-sharp metal in every direction, peppering the ork and knocking it to the ground.

Malvian jumped out of cover and charged the ork, knife already in his hands. The beast was on the forest floor, bellowing in pain and studded with bloody shards of metal. Malvian leapt on top of the ork and drove his knife down to the hilt through its thick skull. It twitched twice and then went still.

Malvian rolled off the body, happy all over again for his rebreather. If there was one thing he'd learned from the siege of Infernus it was that the only thing that smelled worse than a live ork was a dead one.

'Are you alive, mon-keigh?' the aeldari asked as she lurched between the trees, using them for support and putting no weight on her injured leg.

Malvian patted his chest. No bullet holes and no blood. 'For now,' he said with a grimace as he forced himself to sit up. He put a boot on the ork's face and pulled his knife from its skull with a sickening squelch.

'That was reckless,' the aeldari said, a note of concern in her harmonious voice. 'You could have easily died.'

Malvian wiped his knife on his coat and slid it back into its sheath. 'In the Emperor's service, I don't fear death,' he said, the words instinct more than true faith.

'That is because you do not understand it,' the aeldari said. She was leaning against a nearby tree, pistol still held in her hand. 'You believe that death in service to your corpse-god Emperor is the greatest honour, but you fail to comprehend what awaits after that death. She Who Thirsts waits for us aeldari in the warp, eager to consume our souls. An eternity of torment.'

Malvian shook his head at the thought. 'That's just downright unsettling.'

'Yes, mon-keigh, it is,' said the aeldari. 'That is why each of my people carries a stone.' She closed her free hand around the faintly glowing blue gem in the centre of her chest piece. 'When we die, these stones trap our souls, in the hope that they will be returned to our people instead of consumed by the Great Enemy.'

Malvian laughed. 'You really think a stone will… suck up your soul when you die?'

'Yes.'

Malvian grunted sceptically. 'Well it's not the craziest thing I've ever heard. I guess it makes sense now.'

'What does?'

'Why you saved me. If I thought some great and powerful warp-spawned beastie was waiting to gobble up my soul… Well I reckon that'd be a pretty good incentive to make sure I didn't die, even if it meant making friends with an enemy.'

The aeldari was silent for a moment, her eyes dark and piercing. Then she turned her head to stare at the trees. 'You were never an enemy, mon-keigh. You were little more than an annoyance.'

Malvian chuckled. 'Come on,' he said, using a nearby tree to haul himself back to his feet. He bent underneath the aeldari's arm and took most of her weight once more. 'We better get moving. There's no way the rest of the greenskins didn't hear our little gunfight, and I'd rather not test which of us is right about this whole death thing.'

They laboured on, Malvian certain he was doing most of the work, while the cries and weapons fire of the greenskins drew closer. Before long, they were running, or doing their best impression of it. The fog was thinning, and the shouts of the orks were more distinct. Malvian was convinced he even made out a few words, but what passed for language amongst the greenskins was barely intelligible at the best of times. He heard war machines too, the monstrosities the orks called *kanz* lumbering through the forest on rusted metal legs.

'The edge of the forest is not far ahead,' said the aeldari between gasping breaths and hisses of pain. Malvian thought he could just about see the treeline.

Gunfire sounded, far too close, and a tree nearby splintered as bullets ripped into it. Malvian ducked on instinct and the aeldari tripped, bringing them both down, rolling and sprawling in the leaf litter. Malvian scrambled back to his feet in moments and grabbed the aeldari, wrenching her up and ignoring the cry of pain.

'No time to lie around, eldar,' he growled. 'Not when we're so close to... So close.' He lurched into a run, pulling her with him. He didn't want to admit it to himself, but he knew it was all pointless. The greenskins had found them, were all but upon them. Even if they made it out of the forest, all that waited beyond was a few grassy fields and miles of open ground before they reached the Imperial outpost. Open ground with a horde of orks at their backs. The crushing realisation that it was all for nothing almost took the fight out of Malvian and he felt his legs wobble.

'I'm impressed,' the aeldari said between gasping breaths. 'I didn't think a mon-keigh could wield such determination.'

Shoota fire roared past them, joined by more and more. Trees nearby burst apart from the barrage and the ground around them was torn apart. But Malvian kept on running, dragging the aeldari with him. They would die, he was sure of that, but he would not give up. By the Emperor's shiny Golden Throne, he would get them to safety or die trying.

The last of the trees passed by Malvian in a blur of adrenaline-fuelled running, and immediately his vox began to crackle. He reached up with a hand and pressed the transmit button. 'Command, do you read?' he said between great, heaving breaths. 'Command, this is Sergeant Malvian Craw. Do you read me?'

'Sergeant?' a voice said over the vox. It sounded a lot like Commissar Vanx and was about the only time Malvian had ever been pleased to hear the sour-faced bastard. *'There's greenskins pouring from a wreck at your last-known position.'*

'I bloody well know that,' Malvian shouted, heedless of any punishment it would earn him later. 'They're shooting at us.'

Now they were out of the forest, fewer bullets were chasing them, but Malvian knew the respite wouldn't last long. The aeldari was barely even limping any more, and only her laboured breathing convinced him she was still alive. Yet Malvian kept going, dragging her along.

'Well, what you may not know, sergeant,' the commissar said, spitting the title with all the menace of a falling sword, *'is that reinforcements are on the way.'*

Malvian couldn't help himself. He pressed the transmit button. 'Well they'd better get here soon because I've got orks up my arse.'

'Take cover and look up, Sergeant Craw.' There was a smug arrogance in the commissar's voice. *'The battle-barge* Wrath of Hope *has been chasing these greenskins for weeks and has arrived in orbit. The vanguard is already en route.'*

Shoota fire whistled past and Malvian glanced up to see half a dozen stars burning in the grey sky, falling towards them. Malvian dropped and pulled the aeldari down with him. The grass wasn't tall, but it obscured them enough that the orks struggled to aim. He lay on his back, breathing heavily, and felt hope surge within him as the first of the teardrop-shaped pods crashed into the earth nearby, shaking the ground with the force of the impact. Small detonation charges blew the pod doors open, and warriors of the Adeptus Astartes in lapis-blue armour charged out with bolters blazing. Another drop pod smashed down only moments later, and yet more Ultramarines joined the fight, wading into the torrent of shoota fire the orks threw their way.

Malvian laughed at their good fortune as he climbed to his knees and pulled the exhausted aeldari up with him. Now they were out of the choking fog, he pulled off his rebreather and unbuckled his helmet, letting the breeze stir his hair and cool his scars for the first time in what seemed like forever.

'From the clutches of one enemy and into another,' the aeldari said. There seemed a sad look on her face as she watched the Ultramarines wade into battle against the greenskin filth.

'What?' Malvian said, grinning through his patchy stubble. 'We're saved.'

The aeldari sighed. 'I am not so certain,' she said.

Suddenly Malvian realised he didn't know her name, nor had he thought to offer his. It seemed wrong after all they'd been through. 'Malvian Craw,' he said, holding out his hand to the aeldari.

She looked down at his hand for a moment, a frown on her tight face, then back up at Malvian. 'Feuran,' she said, but did not take his hand.

A third drop pod hit the ground, the doors thrown open as a Dreadnought barrelled forth, each footfall shaking the ground. Then a fourth landed just a couple of dozen yards away, and another squad of Ultramarines poured out to join the battle. The last to depart the pod was a sergeant. His armour was gleaming and decorated with gold filigree over the pauldrons and chestplate, and his helmet was painted red. He carried a bolt pistol in one hand and a chugging chainsword in the other, and he stopped and stared directly at Malvian.

Malvian shot to his feet as the Space Marine approached and snapped off a salute. 'Sir,' he said eagerly, staring up at the giant imposing figure. 'Sergeant Craw of the 613th. This is...'

The Adeptus Astartes sergeant raised his bolt pistol towards Feuran and pulled the trigger. The report of the bolt pistol was damning and in the relative silence that followed, Feuran's body toppled sideways into the grass.

The Space Marine raised a hand to his helm. 'Push back the xenos filth,' he said into his vox. 'No quarter.' The sergeant lingered for a few moments longer. 'Pick up your weapon and join the fight, Guardsman.' With that, he turned and strode away towards the forest where his brothers were pushing back the greenskins.

Malvian watched the sergeant go, then dropped to his knees beside Feuran's corpse. All relief at being saved from the greenskins had vanished. His hands were trembling, not with fear, but with anger and grief. She was a xenos, true, but not like the orks. Nothing like the orks. She hadn't deserved such an ignoble end. 'I'm sorry,' he said, the tremble in his hands reaching his voice as well. 'Thank you,' he added, realising he hadn't told her before, 'for saving my life.'

Deserving or not, Feuran was dead now and there was nothing he could do about that. He wondered which of them was truly right about death. Whether some great, warp-spawned monster was really waiting for her soul once she died. Malvian glanced down at the stone embedded in her armour and he pulled out his knife, using it to pry the shining gem from her chest piece. If what the aeldari believed was true, that stone now contained Feuran's soul. He looked at it, clutching it in one hand. It seemed a small vessel to contain something so grand as a soul.

Malvian gave the little stone a shake. 'You in there, eldar?' he said, his jaw clenching so tight it hurt. 'I'll get you back home. Somehow.' He tucked the stone into a pocket of his coat and got back to his feet. The Ultramarines had pushed the orks back into the forest and there was a pitched battle happening between the trees. Malvian gripped his knife tightly in his fist and ran towards the fight. He had orders to follow, orks to kill, and a squad to avenge.

MOURNCLAW

Ben Galley

Canadian fantasy author Ben Galley brings us his first Black Library appearance with this tale of adventure and intrigue from the Mortal Realms.

In a forgotten backwater in the Realm of Beasts, professional thief Mallon Tein finds himself in trouble with the locals. Fortunately, a mysterious knight and his rag-tag band of mercenaries are around to help him out – in exchange for his valuable services. Mallon is swept away on a quest to retrieve an ancient and priceless duardin heirloom, but as they near their prize he begins to wonder if his companions – or captors – are telling him the whole story…

The mire was ravenous, swallowing Durbrord Grimbelly's boots with every hurried stride. With great heaves, he dragged them free, only to battle the next hungry puddle of muck. Clouds of hot breath escaped his mouth, wreathing his fixed scowl. If Durbrord had learned but one thing since visiting this accursed barony, it was that duardin were not naturally built for marshes.

There it was again: the snickering. An errant splash of feet in wet mud. Durbrord snatched a glance over his shoulder, seeing nothing but the curling wisps of fog and the shadow of the dark pine forest. The duardin growled, wiped the sweat from his brow, and fixed his gaze on the blurry lamps of the town ahead. As he ran, he grasped the angular shape hanging at his neck, hiding beneath his leather plate and filthy tunic.

Foliage crackled behind him. Durbrord whirled, sweeping his notched axe from his belt. He stood, tensed and ready, listening to the creaking of the insects and the drip of marsh water.

'Come out!' he challenged the murk. No answer came. The duardin's weary mind conjured up monstrous foes out of the swirling mist.

Durbrord was on the cusp of turning when a dagger came spinning out of the night. He might have been close to exhaustion, but old instincts never sleep. He ducked, hearing a squelch as the blade buried itself in a mound of mud behind him. Quick on the dagger's heels, a shape loomed from the mist. Its clawed feet thrashed through the marsh water. Durbrord recognised it immediately, even before its rank stench had reached his nostrils.

'Skaven scum!' he roared, raising his axe over his head.

Yellow eyes bulging, the ratman screeched as it brandished a black and twisted sword. Durbrord's axe spun through the air, meeting the brute's chest with a loud crack of bone splitting. Blood sprayed, and the ratman's legs flew out from under it, the creature crashing into the mud with a squeak.

With a hiss of steel, Durbrord snatched a knife from his belt and charged to his foe's side, ready to cut its foul throat. But the ratman had no fight left in it, only spasms of its claws and tail, and desperate gasps for air. Dark blood bubbled around the axe blade protruding from its breastplate of tanned hide. With every shuddering exhalation, it tried to speak. Wary, poised to stab, Durbrord leaned in, mindful to hold his breath against the stink of rotten meat and forge smoke.

'Why are you pursuing me? What do the Clans Skryre want with me?' Durbrord demanded.

'M... Mour...' The skaven's verminous gaze was fixated on the duardin's chest.

Durbrord twisted the axe. 'Speak, you beast!'

The ratman writhed in the mud, and with the last breath that passed its fangs, it whispered one word: 'Mournclaw.'

Durbrord flinched at the caw of a raven. He stared at the fingers of pines reaching above the fog, blacker than the night behind them, but unmoving. He look around him, scowling at every shadow. With a growl, Durbrord wrenched his axe from the ratman's ribcage and scrambled through a puddle. Righting himself, he turned towards the speckled lights of the town, and continued to run.

Patience is a virtue sought by many yet achieved by few. It takes a sharper mind than most to realise the worth of waiting and watching. A thief's mind, for example.

Through the narrow gap between the rim of his tankard and the lip of his hood, Mallon Tein's inquisitive eyes shifted over the tables and their inhabitants. Locals of Kurchak, mostly. Several travellers, or roaming hunters. Mallon's gaze tracked hands as they subtly checked pockets, or darted suddenly as precious metals caught the flaxen glow of torchlight. Mallon let the cackling and bragging and arguing wash over him like a tide. He was the silent, lonely boulder amidst its flow.

Mental notes had been made. Connections drawn. A group deeply embedded in the west corner looked promising. A bearded man with a gryph-hound lounging at his feet was huddled conspiratorially with a handful of other figures, trading whispers. Though his armour was a patchwork of various metals welded together, he had the look of a knight.

A distant niece of the local baron was entertaining a gaggle of silk-clad men by the fireplace, waxing on about the few occasions she and Baron Kurch had crossed paths.

Or a lone aelf, a merchant by the silver trim about his collar and the way he kept fondling his notebook. Mallon was interested in the thick rings of silver and gold on his fingers, and the fat coin purse at his side that his constant twitching intermittently revealed. The thief narrowed his eyes as he chose his mark.

Mallon was momentarily distracted as a duardin bustled into the tavern. He was spattered with mud and his face was ruddy behind a thicket of russet beard. He charged through the crowds, caring not whom he barged out of the way, and headed over to the group in the corner. Mallon assumed a bad debt or grudge was about to be settled, but the others welcomed him, swiftly enveloping him into their huddle without a word.

Mallon sighed and went back to his waiting. He nursed his single tankard of mead while the merchant scrawled away for almost an hour. It was only when another fellow approached the merchant's table and instigated a hushed discussion that Mallon saw his chance. It was a fine distraction, and he pounced like an owl spotting a mouse between the rushes. He levered himself out of the chair and made for his mark. The aelf was too busy bantering to notice the thief coming. Slipping his trusty razor into his palm, Mallon stumbled, playing the drunkard as he made his way through the throngs of revellers. As he came close, he barged into the aelf's table, spilling the remnants of his mead across the notebook. Mallon garbled an apology as he fell against the merchant. The aelf arose with a yelp, but not before Mallon had deftly slit his coin purse from his belt and pocketed it.

'My notes are ruined, you cursed oaf!' the merchant snapped.

'A hundred pardons, sire. Deepest 'pologies!' Mallon

hiccupped for good measure. 'Allow me to buy you another mead,' he slurred, already slipping backwards, as if to the barkeep. Mallon was more concerned with the door.

'Mead? I should have you flayed, man! You've cost me weeks of arithmetic!'

'Allow me to make it up to you,' Mallon said, and flicked him a silver coin for his troubles, one from the aelf's own purse, no less.

It was a mistake, Mallon realised before the silver had even landed in the merchant's palm. All his patience had been for nought. He knew it the moment he turned, and heard the two words all larcenous souls fear the most:

'Stop, thief!' came the shriek.

All eyes turned. Conversations died. Even the baron's niece finally shut her trap. Mallon was already counting the worrying number of people standing between him and the door.

The aelf waved his accusatory finger about as if he were fencing. 'That man has stolen from me! This coin he tried to distract me with is mine. See my mark on the coin's face? Thief, I say!' He held up the coin for all to see, and the distinct rune chiselled into its silver.

Hands immediately fell upon Mallon's shoulders, holding him tightly despite his struggles. He felt their grip tighten as fingers rooted through his pockets, and quickly revealed the stolen purse. Mallon flashed a winning smile as the aelf retrieved it.

'Let me explain–'

'To the chopping block with him!' some drunkard crowed, drawing cheers from all around.

Mallon's charm withered in an instant. 'The block? Wait, no! There's been a mistake!' He received a fist in his gut for his excuses and was dragged towards the door. There was nothing quite like the prospect of swift and bloody justice to liven up an evening.

'Fetch Baron Kurch's men!' came the cries.

Mallon watched in horror as the door yawned wide ahead. Before he was carried over the threshold, a booming voice cut through the eager chatter of the mob and brought them all to a halt.

'STOP!'

Craning his neck, Mallon saw the bearded knight from the corner come wading through the crowd. A wiry woman followed in his wake, a head taller than him, and so battle-scarred and weathered she looked like old pieces of hide all stitched together.

'There you are!' announced the knight in a deep baritone, looking down at Mallon. 'He is our companion.'

Mallon nodded eagerly for anyone watching, trying to cover his sigh of relief. He had never seen the knight nor the scrawny woman in his life, but he was immensely pleased they were the charitable type.

'We will pay the damages,' the man continued, 'if there are any damages now that the property has been returned.' He threw a sharp look at the merchant, whose fist was still raised in the air.

'It is the indignity of it all,' said the aelf. 'He is a thief, after all. A criminal must be punished!'

Amongst the jeers of agreement, the knight tutted admonishingly. 'He was cursed by a hedge-witch. Made strange in the head and damned with greed. He is not a criminal, he is sick! Does he deserve to be taken to the block for that?'

'He ruined my notebook. All my work…' stammered the aelf.

With a grunt, the knight produced a fingernail-sized piece of what looked like torope gold from a pocket and tossed it to the merchant. It drew a muted gasp from the onlookers. The Black Marsh Barony was famed for its torope, farmed from the colossal turtles that roamed the vast marshes. Mallon would have been impressed if it hadn't meant he was now deeply in the man's debt. At least there would be no beheading tonight, and for that he was grateful.

'All has been forgiven?' the knight asked.

The aelf picked at the gold nugget with a sharp fingernail for a moment before nodding and retreating to his seat. Mallon shrugged his way out of the tight grip of the mob. They left him be, though they seemed far from happy about it. They had been cheated of their entertainment. Mallon couldn't help but smile.

'Come… Lothar.' The knight beckoned to him. Mallon thought of the door behind him, still open. He had run from debts before, but this man looked the type that would hunt him to the edges of Ghur. Instead, Mallon followed cautiously behind his saviours, trying to ignore the narrowed looks and hushed accusations from the dispersing mob.

While the man and woman retook their seats amidst the tight group, Mallon stayed standing, meeting each of their gazes. The woman had a young lad by her side, a dead-eyed boy with a shaven head. The beak-like noses they shared told Mallon they were mother and son. Two men sat opposite: one hooded and smiling awkwardly, the other, balding and heavy-set, looking bored and half-asleep. Between them sat the duardin with his beetroot face, and the brute of a knight who had saved him.

Mallon flashed a grin. 'Well, thank you kindly for

interjecting there. Very kind of you. It's not often you find such charity in this realm. I shan't bother you any further, I really must be going, so thank you ag–'

'Malefitz,' the knight said.

Before Mallon could make sense of the word, a pair of sharp, iridescent purple ears appeared above the table, followed by two glittering eyes and a hooked yellow beak that snapped menacingly. A low growl made the feathers at the gryph-hound's neck shake. Mallon's legs did the same.

The knight ruffled the beast's ears. He still played the friend for now, but Mallon saw the hardness in his gaze. 'Malefitz here doesn't take kindly to rudeness. We did you a favour, didn't we? Least you could do is sit down with us.'

Mallon realised there was nothing charitable about this man. As with ur-gold or realmstones, there was a currency in favours, and like anything with value, they could make or break a man.

With a sigh, Mallon sat, much to the duardin's apparent dislike.

'Should've just left him to have his head chopped off, Ulriker,' he said gruffly, his stern mouth only barely visible between his thick, rust-coloured beard. 'We don't need anybody else for this job, especially not some grubby tavern brigand from the backside of nowhere.'

'You sure about that, Durbrord?' Ulriker snapped. 'Didn't we all start out nowhere?'

The duardin fell silent.

Mallon spoke up, playing tough to hide his nerves. 'I'm no common brigand. And the grubbiness is intentional. You're one to talk, duardin. You've brought half the marsh in with you, I see.'

A tense moment passed, ended only by the bored-looking

man snorting with laughter. Durbrord crossed his arms, and Ulriker's glaring expression broke into an ivory smile.

'Sharp tongue on this one.'

'Speaking of brigands, who are you lot?'

'Sharp wit, too, I see. We're mercenaries by trade, lad, and you might be just what we need.'

'Need for what?'

Ulriker leaned over the table. His fellows did the same, heads bowed. Mallon half-expected them to begin praying. 'I'm sure a thief like you is aware that the realms are strewn with old trinkets lost throughout the Ages,' said the knight. 'Some are treasures that only dreams are made of.'

'Or nightmares. Others treasures are dangerous. Objects of Chaos,' Durbrord added.

'Valuable in either case, especially when delivered into the right hands.' Ulriker narrowed his eyes. 'The Stormcast Eternals, for example.'

Durbrord and the others nodded emphatically.

'And you've found one of these treasures, I take it?' Mallon asked.

'Not quite,' said the hooded man with the ever-present yet nervous smile.

'But I might know somebody who has,' growled the duardin. 'Some*thing* who has.'

'If Durbrord's information is correct–' Ulriker began, but Durbrord's spluttering cut him off.

'Why would I lie, old friend? I've still got rat-blood on me!'

Ulriker waved his gauntleted hand dismissively. '*If* Durbrord's right, then we intend to kidnap him and make him tell us where it is. Then we can go and retrieve it,' said the knight.

Mallon shrugged. 'And then what?'

Ulriker snorted. 'We deliver it to the nearest Stormkeep and claim the reward.'

'You sound more like rogues and burglars than mercenaries,' said Mallon, wary.

Ulriker smirked. 'Not our usual kind of work, true, but if we pull it off, work will be a distant memory. I, for one, am tired of scratching a living on the fringes of the Realm of Beasts. Aren't you?'

The woman spat on the floorboards, as if the notion disgusted her. 'I still say we should just kill the bastard,' she said.

Ulriker clenched a fist. 'Perhaps we will, Elfrun, but after he has given us what we need. How many times have we been over this?' His gaze moved around his circle. 'Each of us has grudges to make peace with.' His grey eyes found Mallon. 'Or debts to settle. Unfortunately, none of us are thieves, and that's why we need one.'

'He's clearly not a very good thief, is he? Just got caught red-handed,' grumbled Durbrord.

Ulriker's stare was intense, still locked on Mallon.

Mallon raised his chin. 'First time I ever got caught, I swear.'

'Then come south with us. If you live through the next few days, your debt will be paid and many times over. You won't have to worry about robbing aelves in backwater baronies any longer.'

Ulriker had stumbled upon Mallon's desires. Whether unknowingly or incisively, Mallon didn't know. *Escape*. That was all he had ever dreamed of: of making it to the cities. Here was his chance, though not in the form he had expected.

The thief drummed his nimble fingers on the mead-soaked table. He couldn't abide their stares for long. 'I don't really have a choice, do I?' he asked.

'No,' said the knight, wearing his broad smile. 'You don't. Not unless you can pay your debt in coin or gold or torope tonight? Then we can call our business concluded. Or you can take your chances with the charming citizens of Kurchak.'

Mallon thought of his hoard, stashed in the wall of his hovel, deeper within town. It barely paid for a quarter of what Ulriker had donated to save his life.

'I cannot,' he admitted.

With that, Ulriker clapped his gauntlets on the wood and arose. The rest of the table moved with him. Even Malefitz got to his feet, tongue lolling from his sharp beak. Mallon was left sitting, quite confused as to how the whirlwind of the evening had brought him here. He looked up, feeling miniature.

'What's your name, lad?' the knight asked him.

'Mallon. Mallon Tein.'

'Well, Mallon Tein, what's your answer? Will you come with us or will you visit the block after all?' Noticing Ulriker was patting the sword at his belt, Mallon hoisted up his hood and got to his feet. There was precious little alternative, after all. This way he could watch, and wait. Patience was Mallon's virtue. Perhaps he could make it his saviour, too.

'The word treasure does have a certain appeal,' he said.

Ulriker chuckled, and as the others moved off, he clapped Mallon so hard on the back he almost pitched the thief onto his face.

'Then welcome to the Rusted Blades, Mallon Tein. Welcome indeed.'

It took half the night to traverse the bogs of Black Marsh, and Mallon spent it swatting vicious insects from his face and staring at the vast yet faint shadows of the immense turtles in the distance, and the trails of lights that clung to them.

By the time dawn rose upon the barony, the small band had reached solid ground amongst the dark clutches of the pine forests of Askan. Though the trees swayed above them, whispering unknown secrets, they felt no breeze, just the thick, cloying air between the endless tree trunks and knee-high shrubs. Their path wandered, but Durbrord led them true, following some map drawn only in his head. Ulriker seemed content to trust him, and so did the others.

By the time the sunlight rose above the trees, they had broken free of the pines and stood upon the edge of the Vilefang Wastes. There Ulriker called for a halt, and the Rusted Blades broke their fast and slaked their thirst.

Mallon sat upon a rock, digging through the meagre supplies he had snatched from his hovel before they had left town.

The bald man who had been half-asleep at the tavern noticed how empty Mallon's haversack was, and sighed. 'Not much of a traveller, hmm?'

Mallon shook his head. 'I'd always planned on leaving Black Marsh one day, when I had enough of a hoard. Always wanted to seek or steal my fortune in Excelsis. Not so abruptly as this, mind.'

'Not a fighter either, eh?'

'What do you mean? I can look after myself.'

'You ain't got no weapon.'

Mallon held up a hand, revealing the thin blade of a razor cradled in his palm.

'Ha! That little slicer?' The man laughed with abandon, drawing the others' attention momentarily.

'It does the job. I'm a thief, not a knight.'

Still chuckling to himself, the man rummaged in his pack until he found a spare knife, and handed it to Mallon.

'Here. Name's Lundrich Twice-Killed, by the way.'

Mallon took the knife and poked it through his belt between his pouches. 'And why do they call you that?'

'Because I've come back from the grave more than once,' Lundrich said with a wink. Before they could say any more, Ulriker called for them to move on.

In single file, the Rusted Blades left the carpet of pine needles and dead leaves, and put their boots to grit and sand instead. The rolling hills of the Vilefang Wastes were featureless save for the scattered, bleached monoliths that poked from the scarlet sands like the fangs of some gigantic, buried creature. The sun beat down, scorching any bare flesh, and Mallon was glad he had brought a cloak, even though he was sweating tankards beneath it.

'Where are we headed?' he asked of Lundrich, who was marching ahead of him.

'South.'

'I know that. How far south?'

'A day's journey, maybe less. To the Fiend Crags.'

Mallon had heard of that place. Evenings upon evenings spent watching marks in the taverns of Kurchak tended to lead to a lot of eavesdropping. Nothing he had heard of the Fiend Crags was good.

'But that's skaven territory...'

Lundrich yawned. 'Aye, so it is.'

'Clans Skryre territory,' growled Elfrun, walking behind them. 'And they have no idea we're coming.'

Mallon's mind might have been young, but it had been honed by tough experience. He put the pieces together. 'We're kidnapping a skaven? I expected this to be a simple job, not a suicide mission. You don't just steal idly from the ratmen.' Any thieves Mallon knew that had tried had disappeared without a trace.

'We're meaner than we look, thie–'

'Shut it, back there!' Ulriker barked, interrupting Lundrich's gloating. 'By Sigmar! You should be keeping an eye out for grots or great worms, not yammering on!'

'Aye!' Lundrich shouted half-heartedly, before yawning. By the vacant look in his eyes, Mallon couldn't help but wonder if some of the man had been left in the grave.

Afternoon saw the Fiend Crags appear on the horizon: dark and ominous. At first, Mallon thought them distant monoliths, given how jagged they were. As the leagues passed by underfoot, they proved themselves to be dominating towers of rock, surrounded by volcanic black foothills. Before the Crags lay the humongous skeletons of creatures Mallon had never seen or heard the like of. Their sun-bleached ribs would have dwarfed any tower in the Black Marsh Barony, perhaps even rivalled the spires of Izalend, if the rumours Mallon had heard were true. Their skulls still held teeth the length of pine trees, each eye socket the size of a courtyard. He shivered to think of a time when such monsters roamed the Realm of Ghur.

Ulriker called the Blades to a stop on a ridge pockmarked with great craters and pulverised boulders. There they slumped in the sand, staring across the plains of bones. Closer to the Crags, fat streaks of black smoke rose from unseen pits amongst the foothills.

'The ratmen come to hunt the beasts that roam the plains. For meat, fur and hides, for warbeasts, or just to test their foul weaponry on living creatures,' Durbrord told the Blades in his gruff tone, looking thankful for a chance to rest his legs.

'Filthy bastards,' Elfrun spat. She had a habit of doing that.

Mallon could smell the soot and char of forges on the breeze. With the evening starting to fall, an unholy green glow could be seen amongst the darker crags, sparking amidst the amber light of fires.

'You lot wait here,' Ulriker ordered, tightening the straps on his mismatched armour. 'Durbrord and I will go to the next ridge and scout ahead.'

'We will?' asked the duardin.

'Aye, friend,' Ulriker replied, standing over him. 'We'll see if your suspicions of the Clans Skryre are correct. Come, Malefitz.' The gryph-hound yowled before it bounded over the ridge.

'Hmph.' Durbrord unsheathed a battered axe and held it firmly with two hands. Its blade glowed copper in the light of sunset.

Without another word, they departed, leaving Mallon alone with the others. They worked silently, producing victuals and kindling for a quick fire. A cold was creeping across the wastes, chasing the shadow of night.

'Adalbero,' said Elfrun, already cross-legged by the small pile of wood she had built.

The hooded man, who had remained silent since the tavern, knelt by her side. Clenching a fist over the fire, he muttered to himself, sounding curiously irate. With a babbling burst of foreign words, fire sparked in his palm. He pressed it to the kindling and let it burn.

'You're a wizard,' Mallon stated, stepping into the firelight.

Adalbero took a seat on the sand. 'I am,' he said, looking proud now his smile had returned. 'I was in training, once. I hope to be again.'

'What happened?' asked Mallon, ever inquisitive. More

than that, he knew information to be both a tool and a weapon, depending on the situation. It was always wise to have one to hand.

The wizard cleared his throat. 'Clerical error. A mistake.'

'He was kicked out. Ejected in disgrace,' Lundrich chuckled. The Twice-Killed chose to lounge on the sand, eyes already half-closed, catlike. Only Elfrun's son chose the cold, keeping watch on the skaven fires.

'Shut it, Lundrich,' Adalbero snapped.

Elfrun spoke around a mouthful of cracker. 'He's right though. The Collegiate Arcane booted him out for peeking at a forbidden grimoire. We found him in a tavern last year, all covered in ash and blood, half his clothes burnt off. The place was gutted by fire. Ulriker thought the Rusted Blades could use some magic, and here he is.'

Adalbero huffed and occupied himself with the fire. His fingers moving in intricate, twitching patterns, he pulled and pushed on the flames, bending them absently to his whim.

'And how did the rest of you come to be in the Blades?' asked Mallon, chewing an apple. 'Do you all owe debts to Ulriker?'

Lundrich snorted. Elfrun spat in the sand again. 'Life debt for me,' she said. 'Two years ago, he and Durbrord saved me and Oddone from a gang of ratmen.' The young boy turned at the sound of his name, but said nothing. 'Now I get paid to exact my revenge upon them.'

Twice-Killed spoke up as he stretched. 'I clashed with Ulriker and Durbrord over a job a while back. The old bastard almost killed me a third time, so I decided to join him. I'm just here for the coins and gold, lad. And for the excitement. Once you've seen the face of death twice, you get bored quite easily.'

The wizard paused playing with the fire. 'Ulriker saved me

like he did you. Bought off the guards and murderous barkeep with torope. I'll be paid up after we find and sell the Mournclaw.'

'Mournclaw?'

'The Mournclaw Mace. What we're stealing, lad. Some grand old weapon that Durbrord knows of,' said Lundrich.

'That's the treasure? A weapon?'

'By Sigmar, you ask a lot of questions.'

Mallon threw up his hands. 'Probably because nobody has told me anything since leaving Kurchak. Only that we're on some mad mission to kidnap a skaven.'

Elfrun shrugged. 'That's because we ain't been told much ourselves. Ulriker only tells us what we need to know. The rats know of a treasure, and we're going to beat them to it.'

'What's Ulriker's story, then?'

Lundrich yawned. 'None of us know much. Only that he's a beast with a blade and a damn stubborn mercenary. He was a knight once, but found himself disgraced somehow. There's a darkness in his past drives him, but I'll be damned if I know what. Durbrord's known him the longest besides Elfrun and Oddone, and though they've never seen eye to eye – pardon the pun – they seem to trust each other. At least enough for mutual gain.'

Mallon's naturally curious mind was already bursting with questions. He had trouble holding his tongue.

Elfrun nodded. 'All I know is that Durbrord hates the skaven almost as much as I do. And that this Mournclaw job was his idea even though Ulriker acts like it was his. Ulriker's intent on delivering this Mournclaw to the Eternals. He thinks they'll restore his honour.'

'I tell you, this is personal for Durbrord, too. I can see the fire in him...' Adalbero muttered.

'How fortunate the ratmen are content in their burrows this evening, Blades,' a gruff voice admonished them. Those around the fire flinched, grabbing weapons. It was Ulriker, emerging from behind a shattered boulder with his gryph-hound.

Durbrord was behind him, a duardin spyglass in his crossed arms. 'They would have heard your gossiping from a league away,' he said.

None of the Blades spoke. Mallon wondered how much Ulriker had heard.

The knight stood over the fire. 'Our warlock's banner stands above a small rift, set apart from the Crags and only an hour's journey, as luck would have it.'

The unease settled like a rock in Mallon's gut. 'Did you say a warlock?'

'A warlock engineer, lad,' Ulriker responded. 'Problem?'

'That's madness, surely!'

The knight grunted. 'You might be afraid of a little danger, thief, but the Rusted Blades have no such fear. We have the scars to prove it.'

Mallon shut his mouth, realising his arguments would have counted for nothing. He thanked the gods he was fast on his feet. There was nothing cowardly about escaping with one's life, and he vowed to do it as soon as this situation went awry. Hopefully Mallon's debt might die with Ulriker, and he would be free to pursue his fortune once more.

It seemed he wasn't the only one with a worry to be voiced. 'In fairness, Ulriker, you didn't say we were kidnapping a warlock engineer,' Adalbero grumbled. 'That is no ordinary ratman.'

The knight sighed wearily. 'Better tell 'em it all, Durbrord, before we have a mutiny on our hands.'

Durbrord stepped forward. 'Warlock Engineer Volz Flayfang of the Clans Skryre. He's the one who's been hunting the Mournclaw. He's the one who's been sending his ratmen after me. Twice in the Amber Steppes and again last night, in the marshes, like I told you. All because they want *this*.'

Taking great care, Durbrord parted his bush of a beard and dug an intricate key from around his neck. It filled his palm from fingertip to wrist, and was made of interlocking cylinders and thick duardin runes. Mallon had never seen a key like it.

'What is it?' Lundrich asked.

'The only key to a duardin tomb. My ancestors' tomb, here in the Realm of Ghur, where the Mournclaw is hidden behind stone, lock and spell. If Volz is hunting for the key, he knows where the tomb is.'

Ulriker drew his sword. Like Durbrord's axe, it was notched and rusted in places. Mallon was curious why a knight so rich in torope gold couldn't afford a better blade, or armour that wasn't cobbled together from shards of a dozen different suits.

'Once we kidnap Volz, we'll have both the tomb and its key,' Ulriker said.

Or Volz will, thought Mallon. 'Why can't we just lure him out with Durbrord, then pounce when he's out in the open?'

'You want to use me as bait, lad?' Durbrord looked furious. 'How bloody dare you.'

Ulriker drove his sword into the black dust. 'We go into the rift tonight. Who's with me?' he barked. The Blades said nothing. Elfrun and Oddone did not hesitate, moving to stand at Ulriker's side. Lundrich shrugged, cursed, but did the same. Adalbero and Mallon were left standing by the extinguished fire.

'Fine.' Mallon moved first, leaving Adalbero to scramble after him. Let Ulriker doubt the wizard, he decided, while the thief slipped away.

The mouth of the rift in the black rock glowed like a dragon's throat. Though stretching high up the jagged cliff, the doorway to the burrow was narrow. Ribcages, those of men and other creatures, littered the sand around it, between bloody, sharpened sticks and banners with the three crossed bars of the abhorrent Horned Rat. Symbols had been blasted into the sand by some ungodly fire, declaring Skryre land, and the burrow of Volz, or so Durbrord told the Blades.

A deep rumbling from within the rift caused a tremble in the earth around it. Screams and screeches intermittently escaped into the night. The stench of death, rotten meat and forge soot was already overpowering, and Mallon had yet to even see a ratman.

Gripping the knife handle hard enough to hurt his hand, he watched the rest of the Rusted Blades move slowly down the scree towards the rift. Adalbero and Oddone crept beside Mallon, one bare-handed and the other wielding two curved shortswords. The boy seemed barely old enough to pick up one sword, never mind two. In front of them, Elfrun had an arrow nocked on a bow.

As Ulriker closed the visor of his helm, the others wrapped kerchiefs around their mouths to keep from choking on the thick air. One by one, they entered the starless dark of the rift, following the glow and noise, and feeling the heat begin to grow. Mallon tried to hang back, but to his infuriation, he found Twice-Killed bringing up the rear.

'Steady, lad,' he said.

Fine advice that was, thought Mallon.

The chilling screech of a tortured beast filled the rift. Ulriker held up his sword and the Blades froze, hugging the obsidian walls. No sooner had they halted than a hulking ratman emerged from a side tunnel. Ulriker's blade fell in a blur, hacking into the thick fur at the back of the skaven's neck. Despite the rust, the sword cut true, and the ratman managed a pitiful squeak before Durbrord's axe sliced him to the floor.

After dragging the body aside, the Blades moved on, swifter now. The rift soon split into three channels. The sound of clanging and smoke poured from one, along with the stink of charcoal. Smears of blood – some fresh, some dried – criss-crossed the roughly hewn walls.

'Where are the bastards?' hissed Elfrun.

'I only care about one of them! Volz!' Ulriker snapped. He looked around before snapping his fingers at Mallon. 'Which way would you go, thief?'

Mallon wracked his brains. Skaven minds did not work with the same logic as a man's. The tunnels seem to have been built with no reasoning. He chose the one on the far right; one that led deeper into the rock, smaller and unlit. It was an instinctual guess. 'That way,' he said.

'This way!' Sword held ready, Ulriker led them into the tunnel.

'Adalbero!' came the order.

The wizard held his hand high, fingers clawed, straining to keep a candle-flame alight.

A damning squeak rang out. Mallon caught the glint of eyes in the darkness ahead. Far too many for his liking. A dagger clattered against the wall by his head and he took cover behind Adalbero. As the skaven drew closer, Elfrun tossed her bow aside and drew a longsword. Mallon snatched up the bow from the dirt. He'd spent a youth hunting deer with a bow half this size. With a thief's swiftness, he plucked an arrow from Elfrun's quiver and sent an arrow flying into the shadow. His rusty skills were rewarded with a screech.

Four clanrats, flea-bitten and twisted runts, charged them with vicious spears. Elfrun and Oddone met their advance, batting the spears aside and swinging their swords at the ratmen's limbs. Dark blood sprayed in arcs behind her strikes. The dying squeals were matched only by Elfrun's roars of fury.

'Onwards!' yelled Ulriker, eyes burning furiously through his visor. The battle had commenced. There was no stopping it now, no matter how many times Mallon snatched looks over his shoulder.

Ratmen came at them in ones and twos and threes, and the Rusted Blades left a trail of furry corpses in their wake as they burst through tunnel after rock tunnel in search of the warlock.

'More of them are coming!' Lundrich yelled from the rear. Mallon turned and saw a green light filling the tunnel behind them. A ratman bearing a smoking metal contraption on his back sprinted into view. He brandished a butcher's knife in one claw and a glowing globe in the other. Behind him ran a score of clanrats, baying for blood.

'Man-things! Sneak-find!' they squeaked.

'Stop that ratman! Kill him!' Ulriker bellowed.

Mallon scrabbled to grab another arrow, but was plunged into shadow as Adalbero extinguished his flame. Green warp light seemed to envelope them eagerly, but it was momentary. An orb of red fire sputtered into life between Adalbero's hands, roaring and spitting fiercely. With a cry of fury, the wizard released the fireball upon the skaven. It struck the acolyte in the chest, throwing him into the clanrats. As the glowing globe broke in the spell's blast, it exploded into a billowing cloud of green gas that immediately ignited into a firestorm.

'Run!' yelled Adalbero, already sprinting for the mouth of an adjoining tunnel. The Rusted Blades followed suit without complaint.

'The gate's locked!' Ulriker yelled, driving his shoulder against it to no avail and drawing a roar from his nearby gryph-hound.

'Let me!' Mallon pressed himself against the rough iron gates the skaven had thrown together, and alongside a lock pick, he dug his razor blade into the crude lock at its centre. Within moments, Mallon had broken it, and the Blades flung themselves to safety before the fire could consume them.

Ulriker didn't hesitate. 'That'll keep them busy. We keep moving!' he ordered, pressing on. With the warpfire lighting their way, they careened over scree and rock until they saw an opening into a larger tunnel. A gang of black-furred ratmen stood there, clad in hide and mail and sporting ragged banners on their shoulders. They were listening to the explosion that had rocked the burrow. At their midst, a smaller skaven squeaked order after order.

'That must be Volz,' hissed Durbrord. 'And he hasn't seen us!'

Ulriker was seasoned enough to slice an opportunity's throat when it reared its head. 'Blades, claim your destinies!' he yelled, causing the skaven guards to turn.

Lundrich sped past Mallon. The Twice-Killed made his mark on their hide armour, stabbing like a lunatic until three ratmen were slumped at his feet. Elfrun and Oddone hacked away beside him, parrying fangs and claws with their blades.

Mallon tried his best to avoid the mayhem, attacking from the flanks and stabbing frantically wherever he could. He ducked as Adalbero was tossed aside, a spiked tail lashing him across the stomach.

With Ulriker and Durbrord cleaving away like woodcutters attacking a copse, the fight was over in moments. Mallon's head spun.

As the remaining ratmen cowered before the blood-soaked Blades, Volz Flayfang was revealed. He was a crooked, piebald creature covered in scars and patches of metal bolted into his skin. One eye glowed red; the other was encased behind an oval of ruby glass, copper and wires.

Lundrich made a grab for him, but not before the warlock engineer raised a monstrous-looking pistol and squeezed its trigger. The warpstone bullet had no chance to miss. Lundrich's head jerked backwards, a bloody hole of bone and flesh where a face used to be. Tendrils of green smoke curled from the back of his skull. Lundrich Twice-Killed was dead before he toppled to the ground, and this time, it looked highly likely he would stay that way.

Ulriker used the flat of his sword to knock the warplock pistol from Volz's hand, and with his fist, struck the ratman square in its furry jaw. Malefitz seized the ratman's arm in his teeth, and after a swift kick in the goggles from Elfrun, the engineer fell unconscious. The element of surprise had somehow won the night. The Blades almost seemed surprised as they stared at each other, breathing heavily.

All except Durbrord, who hefted his axe. 'The battle isn't over yet. We still have the tomb to find.'

The rush from the rift had been a savage, blood-soaked affair, with Mallon claiming two more ratmen and receiving a gash across the cheek for his troubles. Adalbero had proved his worth once more. It appeared his anger made his pyromancy flow, and despite being injured, he conjured a wall of flame high enough that the ratmen were blocked from pursuing.

A hurried, breathless rush ensued, back across the scarlet sands, now robbed of their colour by the night and faint starlight. Ulriker slung the unconscious Volz across his back, letting the skaven's limbs and tail dangle as they scurried across the wasteland. Adalbero had kept his spell burning long after they escaped the foothills of the Fiend Crags, and only once they had stopped for breath behind a monolith did they hear the faint screeches of the Clans Skryre, pouring out into the night.

The Rusted Blades continued to move, gasping yet determined. Soon they felt alone between the monoliths and gigantic, towering skeletons. As Ulriker led them a straight and hurried path through the graveyard, Mallon's neck grew sore from constantly looking over his shoulder.

The Blades ran, jogged and finally trudged until the sun shone upon them once more. They had reached an edge of the Vilefang Wastes, and looked out over fields where scarlet flowers bloomed between the cracks in the dead earth. Rusty grasses drew patterns in the crust. Still, the skeletons remained with them, otherworldly silhouettes stark against the dawn sky.

'Where are we?' Mallon asked of Oddone as they walked, but he received no answer. His mother spoke instead.

'The Bloodbloom Fields.'

'And here we will speak to our ratman,' called Ulriker. He pointed to a shard of an immense jawbone, still cratered with empty tooth-sockets. It protruded from the earth at an angle, and they took shelter beneath it.

The knight dumped Volz on the ground, eliciting a faint groan from the creature.

'Should just knife him now, given what he did to Lundrich,' murmured Elfrun, looking particularly twitchy. Oddone hovered close to the warlock.

Ulriker pushed her away. 'Back, I say! What would be the point in Twice-Killed's death then, you fool?'

Mallon slumped to the earth a short distance away, content to watch while the burning in his legs and lungs subsided.

'Up, rat!' Durbrord shook Volz liberally, making the ratman's tongue loll. 'By Grimnir, he reeks!'

Volz pounced. His eyes snapped open as he hooked his claws around Durbrord's neck. The skaven was quick, but the duardin was quicker, jabbing the warlock with his knife. Volz squeaked, giving Ulriker the chance to pin him to the ancient bone wall, and squeeze. Malefitz strained at his heel, eager to put his sharp beak to work.

'Behave, Volz Flayfang. We don't want to kill you, but we will if you leave us no choice.'

Mallon saw the sharpness in the ratman's red, forge-scorched eyes. There was intelligence in this beast.

'Still-quiet, I be, man-thing,' Volz rasped, baring his sharp fangs.

Ulriker released him, and the warlock slumped to the ground. Durbrord bound him with rope as Adalbero stood guard. One of the wizard's hands was clamped to his bleeding stomach, the other outstretched with fingers caged, spells ready to burst from him.

Volz stared at the wizard with amusement. 'Spell-caster. Break-burn much in sneak-fight,' he said.

'And he'll break-burn much more if you don't cooperate,' Durbrord warned him.

Volz's forked tail flicking impatiently. Oddone watched it avidly, sword ready.

'Speak-piece, fool-meat,' said the warlock.

Durbrord crouched before him, resting his axe handle in the dust. 'You know what we want, Volz. The same thing you want. The reason you sent your clanrats to steal this from me.'

The duardin revealed a sliver of the key to the warlock, and Volz stiffened.

'You tell us where the tomb lies and we'll spare your life,' he pressed him.

'Lie-speak. False-tell.'

Ulriker struck him hard and Volz spat out a tooth.

'Tell us where the Mournclaw is, Volz,' he growled.

'Knight-meat, you look clever-smart. Lead-order these others?'

'I do.'

Volz grinned, dribbling blood into his piebald fur. 'Then you die-break last. You watch-see them cry-shriek first.'

'Do you want to die, ratman?'

'You seek-find me. Need me. No-kill.'

Mallon couldn't help but point it out. 'He's got you there, Ulriker.'

The knight glowered daggers at the thief. Malefitz growled.

'Think-idea,' proposed the warlock. 'Tomb deep-hidden, hard-tough to tell-speak you where it is. Take-carry Volz with you instead. He need-must show you. Seek-find tomb together. You spare-loose me after-then.'

'Ridiculous. He's playing for time until his clanrats can find him. He'll slow us down every chance he gets,' said Elfrun.

The others nodded. Even Adalbero, straining with his magic.

While Durbrord knuckled his brow, Ulriker strode back and forth.

'Fine!' he yelled.

'Ulriker...' said the duardin.

'Adalbero, keep an eye on that rat,' Ulriker ordered. He beckoned the rest of the Blades aside, out of earshot of the warlock. 'What use is claiming the Mournclaw if we die before claiming our reward, Durbrord? If we beat them to your family's tomb, we can destroy them with the Mournclaw Mace. Him and all his clan,' he argued in a low growl. 'Think how much honour that would bring us all, when we arrive at the Stormkeep.'

Elfrun growled appreciatively. Mallon's ears pricked up, along with Adalbero's. The tomb belonged to the duardin's line, it seemed. The thief could see now why Durbrord was so invested in this mace.

'It's a weapon of Chaos, Ulriker. I've told you before, you can't wield it, no matter how strong you think you are! My ancestors couldn't, and that's why they buried it.'

'Enough! We will not discuss this now!' Ulriker barked.

The Rusted Blades watched on, eyes wide. It was Mallon who spoke up. He was tired of not having a say over his skin.

'We have to take the ratman with us,' he said.

Ulriker moved closer to Mallon, reaching out a hand and grasping his shoulder. 'The thief is right. We must keep moving no matter what. We lost Twice-Killed already,' he said, taking a moment to pause. 'I refuse to lose any more of you.'

The others murmured their assent, though they sounded far from eager about it. Mallon certainly wasn't comfortable carting the rat with them, but it seemed the only way to keep them moving. And alive.

Mallon approached the rat. Durbrord was right: the creature did reek. 'Which way, Volz? How far?'

Volz regarded the thief with a curious look in his eye, and

for a moment, he did not speak. 'South-ways, edge-boundary of Blood-fields. Day's scurry-scurry.'

Ulriker dragged the ratman up by the scruff of his neck and shoved him. 'South it is, Blades. Onwards!'

'Keep still,' Ulriker ordered the ratman as he trussed him up with another length of rope. There was so much already wrapped around Volz's body he looked somewhat like a maggot.

'If anything, it might keep the smell in,' Mallon said. At least it stopped him weaving spells.

'You better hope it does. And count yourself lucky we made up the miles today, or you wouldn't get to rest at all. We'd still be running. Not so good in the hot Ghurish sun, these skaven, but they move like a gryph-hound once it goes down. That's why you're on first watch tonight. Keep your blade close, and don't listen to a word Volz says. Skaven *breathe* lies,' said the knight, laying a heavy hand on the thief's shoulder. 'You're alive, and that means you did well. Keep it up and you just might live to be a rich man.'

Ulriker left Mallon there, somewhat alone with Volz. Malefitz was nearby, one eye open and fixed on the rat. The others were gathered around Adalbero's fire, where the wizard was busy tending his wound with the help of Elfrun. Mallon inched out his razor, just in case the skaven wanted to play dirty.

An hour must have passed before the others were fast asleep, exhausted from the brisk day's journey across the Bloodbloom Fields. Mallon stretched, eyes shifting from the fields to Volz. To his surprise, he found the skaven staring at him, the creature's red eye narrowed.

'New-blood,' Volz whispered, making Mallon flinch.

'Don't speak. You'll wake the others.'

'Care-none. You not friend-clan?'

'I'm not their friend.'

'Come-stay for coin, then. Knight-meat promise-swear you riches?'

Mallon struggled to understand the rat's speech, but he got the gist. 'In a way, yes.'

'Mournclaw,' chuckled Volz, 'its poison-curse tastes sick-strange to each who seek-want it. Why knight-meat want it?'

'Gold, I suppose. Honour. Glory.'

'Sure-think? Duardin-meat speak-true about man want-think he wield-use Mournclaw. Don't trust-believe him.' Volz paused, watching Mallon's reaction. 'And duardin-meat?' he asked.

Mallon shrugged. 'To destroy it. For his family…' Realising he was somehow entertaining the warlock's questions, he added, 'Shut it, skaven. No more questions.'

'Know-know what Mournclaw is?'

Mallon tried his hardest to keep quiet, but his curiosity beat his resolve. 'No.'

'Duardin-meat build it. Many-time year back. Bash-club for rat-skulls. Clever-smart skaven steal-take it. Change-build it. Make it ours for Horned Rat. Duardin-meat steal-claim it back. Dig-bury it for long-year, until Volz find-see.'

If Volz spoke the truth, that meant this mace rightfully belonged to Durbrord, Ulriker's ideas of glory be damned. Was it stealing if a soul claimed what was owed to him? Mallon swallowed, watching the sleeping forms around the smouldering fire.

'Knight-meat worry-trouble you?' asked Volz. 'Trust him?'

'That's enough from you,' Mallon warned the skaven.

'Volz know magic. Fool-meat warriors do not. Not even spell-caster.'

'Shut it, rat!' snarled Mallon, brandishing his razor blade close to Volz's throat. 'Or you won't ever speak again.'

Volz winked a red eye at the thief as he turned around to lie on his shoulder. 'Find-catch will clanrats. Faster-foot than man-things. No-need sleep. Will gut-kill all. Think-right when time comes, thief.'

As if hearing Volz's words, Adalbero arose from his bedroll and lumbered over to Mallon. He seemed in pain.

'Has he given you any trouble?' asked the wizard hoarsely.

'Just won't shut up, is all,' said Mallon, seeking to escape the stench of the ratman. His heart was pounding.

'What did he say?'

Mallon winced. The fact the man shared the same debt to Ulriker almost loosened his tongue but he held back, knowing better. 'Just the same old threats of disembowelment,' he lied.

Adalbero wiped sweat from his forehead. 'Ulriker will keep us safe.'

'I hope you're right.'

The wizard looked to the fire and chewed his lip. A wave of pain seemed to take him then, and he doubled up.

'Are you sure you're fit to watch him?' asked Mallon.

'Me? I'm fine. Just a scratch,' Adalbero replied, with a feeble cough. His pale forehead was slick with sweat. Earlier, it had only seemed like a minor wound, yet now the skin around the cut was turning ochre. Dark veins were creeping across his stomach, like dirt roads spreading from a foul town. Mallon didn't dare to mention the word 'poison' to the wizard, but it crossed his mind all the same.

Mallon found a space on the cold earth and stretched his hands out to the warmth of the embers. Ulriker slept in his armour nearby, chest rising and falling beneath his breastplate. Mallon idly counted the different pieces he had forged and welded together, and wondered what a knight had to do to be disgraced, and yet somehow remain rich.

He gazed at the pouch at Ulriker's side and wondered how much gold hid within. He reached out, fingers hesitant, but a quick glance told him all were fast asleep. Mallon's practised hands undid the clasp and dug inside, feeling a pouch filled with something that felt like rocks. He plucked one free just as Ulriker snuffled in his sleep, and rolled to face Mallon, one eye stuck open. The thief swiftly turned away. His nose pressed to the dust, he placed the torope nugget on the cracked earth and stared at it. He picked at it as the aelf had done before taking his knife-butt to it, and bashing it as loudly as he dared. Once, twice, thrice. The nugget dented then cracked open, revealing a thin patina of gold hiding grit and iron beneath.

Mallon clenched the knife until his hand ached.

Morning saw a cold dew hugging the Rusted Blades. The bitter and irritable crew of seven stomped out across the undulating moors of crimson grasses and defiant flowers. When a frigid wind gusted and blew clouds of loose petals across the fields, it momentarily appeared to rain blood.

Dawn had broken with cries and shouts as the Blades awoke to find Elfrun throttling Volz. It had taken both Oddone and Ulriker to drag her off him. Volz had grinned through it all. Even when the ratman was forced to march, his smile would not fade.

Elfrun and Ulriker prodded the beast ahead of them with sword-points. He had been gagged to prevent him from weaving more lies.

Mallon hung back with the hollow-eyed duardin, who seemed quieter than usual.

'How much do you trust Ulriker?' Mallon asked of him, unwilling to mince his words any longer.

'Gossiping again, thief?' replied the gruff Durbrord.

Mallon grumbled. 'Merely trying to understand this mess I seem to find myself in.'

'Humph. You and me both, lad,' Durbrord admitted. Perhaps it was the tiredness, or the way Mallon caught him eyeing Ulriker, but the duardin's tongue was loose that morning. He sighed deeply. 'I wonder if I should have ever told him of the Mournclaw.'

'Why did you?'

'Because the Mournclaw deserves to be destroyed by the Eternals, and my family deserves to be left in peace, not desecrated by some filthy rat-horde!' Durbrord growled, then sighed. 'And besides. I owe him. He found me half-drowned in a bucket of mead. Dragged me up by the beard and put an axe in my hand. Since then he's always kept me in coin, and trusted me as I trusted him. He and I are the same. Disgraced, dispossessed, and damned stubborn. See his armour? Made up of the armour of enemies he's killed, usually the most savage ones. He's a fierce man with a lot to make up for.'

'Care to tell me what?'

'It's not like me to tell a man's past for him. Let us say he was a callous man in his youth. A proud knight, skilled, but death followed him like a shadow. It cost him his honour and he's been fighting to get it back since. Most of the time, it keeps him on a virtuous path. Though, when he found out about my family tomb, and what lies inside…' Durbrord lowered his head, seemingly ashamed to have been duped. 'He's changed.'

'Take it from a thief, greed is a poison,' Mallon whispered.

As if the knight had the ears of his gryph-hound, Ulriker turned to check on his Blades and locked eyes with Mallon.

'Up front, Durbrord! According to this filthy rat, we're getting closer,' he called.

'Same-like clanrats. They come quick-quick,' Volz tittered, receiving a clap around the ears before being gagged again.

Mallon matched the knight's gaze. His had been a short life, but he had yet to let anyone take advantage of it. No thief-boss, no marauder, no baron. His life was his. Ulriker was fool enough to think he owned him.

'He lied to me, you know,' muttered Mallon, before Durbrord was out of earshot. 'That torope gold in his pocket is fake. Worth less than sand. He lied to both me and Adalbero. Ulriker sounds very adept at finding people when they're at their lowest. Most desperate...'

'Durbrord!'

The duardin swatted at a crimson flower and left Mallon alone. He stared back at the wizard, who now trailed behind, looking greyer than the sky and bent like a man thrice his age. Mallon looked past him. North, to the immense crown of ribs perched on the horizon. He would have run, if he hadn't wanted to expose Ulriker for the fraud he was.

Mallon kept to trudging, loathing the burn in his calves. Like the others, he watched every ripple of wind-chased grass, every shadow between the great skeletons. They marched in this fearful way until once again the sun followed its inexorable path into the distant black spires of the Hornteeth Mountains.

Ghur was famed throughout the Mortal Realms for its beasts, both savage and terrifying, but no thought crossed the Blades' minds except the Clans Skryre hot on their heels.

As night fell, they saw the light of fires and torches shining against the skeletons, reanimating their sun-scorched bones.

'Magic not help-save you now. Clanrats scurry-hurry,' Volz chuckled, as Adalbero failed to light a fire. The wizard was as white as milk, and now shaking. It looked as though a fever ran through him.

'Ulriker... I don't feel–' Adalbero whispered.

'Get some rest, man,' said Ulriker, preoccupied with the warlock. 'Volz, you scum. How far?'

The ratman sniggered. 'Eager-keen, knight?'

Ulriker punched him without the restraint he'd displayed previously, yelling, 'Where do we go now?'

Volz reeled from the blow, and yet somehow between spitting blood, he still managed to laugh. It was deeply unsettling.

'What truly want-for Mournclaw, fool-meat? You think-believe you can carry-wield like ratmen? Ha!' Volz squeaked with glee. 'Want-see yourself a mighty hero-warrior?'

Ulriker looked around the Blades, face earnest. Durbrord was scowling. 'Lies as always! I want nothing but the reward we'll get when we deliver the Mournclaw. That is all! He's sowing doubt in your minds!' Ulriker cried.

'He's not the only one doing that,' muttered Mallon.

Before the knight could respond, a warpstone bullet struck a spur of bone mere feet from them, exploding with a trail of green light.

'Take cover! How close are we, Volz?'

Volz nodded towards a black spear-thrust of stone that matched some of the skeletons for size. 'There-place.'

As the first war squeaks reached their ears, Ulriker hoisted the warlock up, grabbed Durbrord by the shoulder and sprinted away. 'Keep moving!' he hollered over his shoulder.

The rest of the Blades followed, chasing Ulriker as he scrabbled through the night.

Behind him, Mallon saw dark shapes rushing through the blood-red fields all around them. The starlight caught the glint of steel and glowing skaven eyes. Mallon's chance to escape had crumbled like stale bread.

Adalbero had dropped to a knee. A brown-furred ratman burst from a clump of crimson grass, jaws wide and screeching. The wizard scorched him with a hurried spell, sending him squealing.

'Come on, Adalbero!' Mallon cried, but the wizard shook his head.

'It's skaven poison! No saving me now, thief. You were right,' he wheezed. 'This is all madness.'

Another clanrat fell upon Adalbero then, stabbing him through the shoulder with a wicked dagger. The wizard roared, and Mallon heard the urgency in his voice.

'Run, thief!'

As Mallon threw himself after the others, rolling and biting sand, Adalbero burst into flame. As the thief snatched a last look, Mallon saw him as a man-shaped pyre, his skin pure white flame, his face a snarling mask of ash. Mallon made it to the cover of an enormous tooth as the fire spread outwards in a whirlwind. Adalbero's scream seemed entwined in it, elongated, burning alongside the spell. Mallon felt his hair curling in the heat.

With ratmen behind him and the Blades before him, Mallon decided to run. Using the distraction of Adalbero's spell, he managed to catch the rest of the mercenaries as they hastened through the fields. By the sound of the snarls and screeches coming from the darkness, Malefitz was wreaking havoc amongst the ratmen. Ulriker had the warlock over his shoulder. Durbrord ran alongside. Elfrun and Oddone seemed singular in their desire: follow. Mallon did the same.

'Where's Adalbero?' Ulriker yelled.

'He fell behind!' replied Mallon. 'Poisoned by a blade in the Skryre tunnels!'

'Should have mind-watched your spell-caster. Not Volz,' the rat chastised them.

They traced the edges of the Bloodbloom, running through knee-high thickets of red flowers and leaving broken vegetation in their haste.

'How far, Volz?' panted the knight.

'I told-tell. South-ways. To a rock.'

'And when we find the tomb? What then, Ulriker?' asked Durbrord, making Mallon run closer.

Ulriker sighed. 'We'll set the bastard free, and take what we came for, old friend,' he said, making Elfrun growl.

'And you expect Skryre to simply leave us be?' asked the duardin.

'They will once we get our hands on the Mournclaw,' Ulriker replied. Volz squeaked to himself appreciatively.

'Nobody will touch it but me. I told you that from the beginning. It is *my* Mournclaw,' hissed Durbrord sternly. '*My* ancestors' tomb. Remember that, old friend.'

'I will,' Ulriker snapped, vaulting a hedge of scarlet flowers. 'But I don't plan on dying alongside them because you're unwilling to do what's needed. Remember *that*, old friend. I've never led you wrong before, have I?'

Mallon fought not to speak up, and let Durbrord grumble instead. The thief glanced behind him, and in the dying light of Adalbero's fire, he saw the dark shapes regrouping. He could taste the gathering stench in the air. Ratman after ratman must have filled the fields around them. All he could do now was keep running. He refused to end up like the wizard.

As the Blades weaved around boulders and bones, Mallon found himself running beside Volz. The warlock stared at Mallon with his bulging, scorched eye, whiskers twitching as the cold wind blew.

'Close-near to end now. Clanrats almost caught-snatch you.'

'Shut it.' Mallon's feet involuntarily twitched, eager to sprint away through the grass. His knew his escape from Ulriker and his Blades would be swift. He narrowed his eyes, watching the wind send waves across the dark-red fields. There, between clumps of shifting grass, he swore he caught the faint glint of eyes staring back at him. They were being toyed with.

'They want you back alive, don't they?' he whispered.

Volz nodded. 'Important-smart Volz is to clan. Smart-thinks. Tells clanrats what to do-kill. Make big-boom weapons. Many fall-die at Volz's claws.'

'If you're so important, then you can get me out of this mess alive.'

'Clans Skryre too fierce-strong?' The warlock snickered.

'Ulriker's too stubborn to know when he's beat. Durbrord and the others don't see what it'll cost them. I'm no fool. I don't want to die at the hands of your clanrats out there.'

Volz bared his fangs in a broad smile. 'You want-make a deal?'

Mallon swallowed, finding his throat dry. Skaven were famously untrustworthy, but the thief was enormously desperate. 'I keep you alive, you keep me alive. Free to walk away.'

'And the others?'

The thief clenched his jaw. 'There's no turning back for them,' he muttered.

'Think-talk like skaven, thief-meat,' Volz hissed, his gaze even more avid than before. 'Deal?'

'Deal.'

'Mallon!' called a gruff voice from behind. 'Stop talking to that filthy liar!'

Mallon kept a plain look on his face as Ulriker caught up to them. 'He was just telling me how much he couldn't wait to eat us all.'

'I'm sure he was,' Ulriker growled. 'I'm sorry it's ended up like this, lad,' he said. 'This quest wasn't ever meant to be easy, but it's becoming desperate.'

Mallon watched the cracks around Ulriker's face tense and soften as he spoke.

'You've done me well. You all have. Even Adalbero and Lundrich, Sigmar save them. I won't let any more of you down, I promise that. Trust in me, and I'll see us through to the end. Alive, and richer than you ever dreamed. Agreed?'

Ulriker stuck out a callused hand, and offered an easy smile amid the thicket of beard.

Doubt flared once more, and then Mallon remembered how the torope gold had crumbled in his fingers. He shook the hand firmly mid-stride.

'Agreed,' Mallon lied.

A distant screech made them both flinch.

'Faster, Blades!' Ulriker roared, breaking into a sprint.

'Keep that warlock close,' Durbrord ordered. Elfrun grabbed Volz eagerly as she tore past. 'We don't stop until we reach the tomb!'

Mallon chased them, hoping to Sigmar he had chosen the right devil to put his trust in.

* * *

In the shard-like foothills of the Hornteeth Mountains, the Rusted Blades huddled up against a wall of black rock, breathless, and blades trembling. Their lungs burned as bullets zipped over their heads. Clans Skryre had parried and feinted with them the whole day, chasing them deeper into the canyons.

'Where now, Volz?' Ulriker barked, over the screeching filling the evening air.

'There-place.' The warlock stayed calm and aloof despite the madness of the chase. He nodded down a channel of rock, where the skaven's ungodly machines had chewed at the mountain. Part of the rock face lay curiously untouched.

'Hold them off! Durbrord, see to the door!' The panic in Ulriker's voice was audible. Mallon drew his knife to stand between Elfrun and Oddone while the duardin pressed his hands to the black granite.

'Duardin doors,' Mallon heard him muttering.

A yellow-furred ratman broke into view, wielding a vicious pike. Oddone ducked its blade and sliced the thigh of the skaven, pitching it into the earth. Malefitz ripped into its throat, finishing it off.

'Now-time, duardin-meat. Waste-tarry or die!' snarled Volz, slumped at the foot of the rock.

'Quiet, rat!' Durbrord was hesitating, stuck between decisions. 'Give me time!'

'We have no choice!' Mallon cried, knowing the doubt he was experiencing. Scores would have to be settled within the mountain.

Durbrord dragged the cylinder key from about his neck and pressed it against the doors in different places. It took far too long for Mallon's liking, but with a grunt, Durbrord slid the key deep into a hidden space in the rock, and turned.

With a mechanical rhythm, the rock face split at its centre, revealing a doorway and a dark passage beyond.

Ulriker was already inside, dragging Volz with him. Malefitz was close at heel. No sooner had the doorway yawned than it started to shut, and Mallon sprinted towards it. Elfrun and Oddone were too busy carving red ribbons from several hide-clad clanrats.

'Come on!' Mallon yelled after them.

Elfrun turned and ran, trying to pull the bloodthirsty Oddone with her. It was at that moment that a hulking skaven scooped up the boy from the earth and dragged him away between the rocks. Elfrun howled as Durbrord dragged her inwards, roaring with the animalistic note of a mother losing a child.

The rocks were now alive with ratmen. Pikes poised to skewer him, Mallon hurled himself inside the shrinking doorway before it ground to a close.

Sprawled on the rock, the thief looked up to see a dozen skaven spears wedged in the thin gap of light. They twitched as their owners struggled.

Durbrord found his tinderbox and filled the darkness with a sulphurous glow. Volz's eyes glowed in the light. 'What happened to setting the warlock loose?' the duardin asked.

Ulriker's chest was heaving. There was a sour look in his eyes as he regarded his remaining Blades. 'Changed my mind. We might still need him. Or we can bargain with him, if it comes to it,' he replied, meeting Durbrord's glare.

The duardin snorted. 'Glad to hear you've come to your senses,' he said. 'Come! They'll break through soon!' He strode forward as if he knew the way, ignoring Elfrun's visceral grunts of frustration. She still clawed at the rock face and spearheads.

'Elfrun, we have to keep moving!' Mallon warned her.

'Not while there is rat-blood left to spill,' she growled.

'Ulriker!' Mallon shouted after the knight, but he did not seem to care.

'Leave her! Or stay and die!' came the echo of his shout, his form already lost behind a corner.

Mallon winced, watching Elfrun's heaving chest, listening to her savage, guttural grunts. The knight knew her heart. She had chosen her fate, and Mallon still had to reclaim his. With a bellow of frustration, he left her behind, chasing the orange light of the others.

What remained of the Blades ran silently, listening to the echoing crash of rock and the roars of Elfrun behind them. The reverberations hung in the musty air long after the four survivors delved deep into the tomb.

Between his frantic footfalls, Mallon glimpsed angular duardin architecture and runes between the shadows. The air became frigid, and as the stairs flew past beneath them, Mallon began to feel the weight of the earth above him. Why duardin had such a penchant for living below ground escaped him.

As hewn tunnels turned to smooth-stone corridors lined with tiles and mortar, Mallon began to glimpse treasures between gateways and offshoots. Golden cups and silver shields, dotted between untouched suits of fine mail and plate. The thief in Mallon longed to dart left or right, but he stuck true, clinging to retribution and survival.

'Where now, Durbrord?' Ulriker snapped as they came to a fork in the corridor, both blocked by doors of thick stone.

'You ask me as if I've been here before!' Durbrord snapped. 'Not a single member of my family has entered this place for many centuries.'

'Then think like your ancestors, old friend, and fast!'

'The time for giving me orders has passed, Ulriker. You walk on my ground now. Remember that,' snapped Durbrord, his patience clearly worn away, and his suspicions worn to a sharp point.

Ulriker said no more, though he gripped his blade tighter. As did Mallon.

'Be clever-smart, thief. Time-time comes for choice-make,' whispered Volz.

'I should silence you right here, warlock,' Ulriker hissed.

'Then kill-end, as you promise-say. Won't save-free you. Clans Skryre come.'

'Durbrord!'

Brandishing his key alongside his axe, the duardin moved forward and chose the left door: deeper into the mountain. Though the oppressive rock made Mallon's heart pound, with ratmen swarming behind him, the only way was forward. He stuck close to Volz, listening to the growing shrieking behind them.

With every bend in the route, with every chamber of sarcophagi and glinting treasures they passed, the more frustrated Durbrord seemed to become. He was seething by the time they reached a door of obsidian, marked with skulls in silver, as if it belonged to a Chaos cult. It looked promising, but only a bare corridor was revealed.

'This is hopeless, Ulriker!' he yelled.

But the knight pressed on, undeterred. 'We're close. I can feel it.'

'Your stubbornness will get us killed.'

'No, it won't,' said Ulriker. 'I can save us.' A fiendish grin had appeared on his bearded face. It disturbed Mallon greatly.

'You can't wield it, Ulriker!' Durbrord accused him, abruptly snapping. 'That stinking ratman was right. You are a fool!'

Ulriker didn't reply. His smile was fixed and his feet determined. All that could be heard was Volz chuckling.

They climbed a steep upward ramp to a domed hall and found a silver door blocking their path. Across its polished surface, geometric patterns were interwoven with stout bars and rivets. There was no handle or keyhole to be seen, merely a small hollow emblazoned with a duardin rune.

Ulriker dragged his blade across the door, making sparks but not so much as a scratch. He slammed his fist against it, then the pommel of his sword, but it seemed firmer than a mountain.

'What is this?' Ulriker hissed, fists clenching and unclenching. 'Unlock it, Durbrord.'

Durbrord brandished his axe but said nothing. He seemed to be staring at the rune as if he recognised it.

'Door is blood-bound,' chatted Volz casually, as Ulriker threw him aside. 'Answers to family-kin only.'

Ulriker cursed. Mallon could see the sweat beginning to run down his cheeks.

'He's right, Ulriker.' Durbrord stepped closer to the door. His hand hovered over the hollow. 'You go no further, old friend.'

Ulriker look incredulous. 'You seek to betray me?'

'As you seek to betray us? I told you time and time again, this isn't your family's tomb. It is mine, not some trunk for the plundering. The warlock is right, curse it! You want the Mournclaw for yourself, do you not?' Durbrord yelled.

Ulriker might have puffed and snorted, turning red in the face, but he made no argument.

'You think it can restore your honour? Your disgrace? I

told you – it would change you, Ulriker, more than your greed already has. The Mournclaw would kill you. You are not strong enough. None of us are.'

Mallon recognised the thirst in Ulriker's eyes. He had seen it many times in other thieves; in men that didn't know when enough was enough.

'I say let him take it,' Mallon spat. 'Death is what a liar and a cheat like you deserves, after all.' Seeing the narrowing of Ulriker's eyes, the thief grinned without humour. 'I know about your fake torope gold, Ulriker. Your lucky knack for finding lost souls is nothing but a sham. Go ahead. Take the Mournclaw. Reap its rewards.'

'Curse you!' roared the knight.

Before Mallon could raise his knife, Ulriker struck. The knight's sword came swinging fast and hard. Mallon barely had a chance to dive wildly out of the way before he was sent reeling, arms windmilling as he teetered on the edge of the steep ramp.

Even as Mallon tumbled, he heard the clang of sword blade against axe head. He spread his arms wide, trying to stop his fall. His knife clattered away from him. He clawed at the stone once, twice, three times before he managed to arrest his momentum. He'd barely halted before he heard the scuffle of rat-claws in the tunnels behind him, and between the fighting above, Volz's incessant tittering and Malefitz's yowling.

Mallon heard Durbrord cry out. He began to scramble up the slope, not due to any notions of allegiance in his head, but to be anywhere that wasn't about to be littered with skaven.

As he saw the shapes of ratmen streaming through the mouth of the tunnel below him, Mallon reared above the edge of the slope with a cry. He sprawled on the stone, just long enough to see Ulriker slicing the axe from the duardin's hand. Blood flowed with Durbrord's outraged cry, spraying the stone beneath him. Before the axe could clatter to the floor, Ulriker had already seized Durbrord by the beard and was muscling him to the doorway. He slammed the duardin's remaining hand against the rune, and to the clanking of buried machinery, the door cracked open down its centre. A shaft of unearthly emerald light divided the hall. Ulriker bathed in it, grinning, before throwing Durbrord into the chamber ahead of him.

Treading as quickly as he dared, Mallon crept to the doorway, thanking Sigmar it stayed open now that Durbrord's bloody hand had touched it.

Inside the Mournclaw's chamber, the air was stifled and old. Ulriker, too obsessed with his prize to spare a glance for Mallon or Durbrord, strode towards the Mournclaw, cradled on its pedestal in the lone shaft of light.

It was an ugly thing, and yet the Mournclaw Mace somehow commanded awe. It was a formidable-looking weapon: a stout metal handle the length of Mallon's arm, with a crown of intricate blades and spikes atop it. The sable metal refused to shine with any light but the sickly green glow of the crystals at its core. Wide-mouthed skulls decorated the handle, frozen in the anguish of dying.

Durbrord was curled around his severed hand, feverishly mumbling the word 'betrayal' over and over as blood pooled beneath him. Mallon could have bound his hand. He could have stayed at his side, but there, deep beneath the earth, in the dark, loyalty had crumbled. Self-preservation was now the only truth to hold onto, and with a horde of skaven swarming at his heels, Mallon knew what he needed to do.

Braving the foetid warp-glow of the mace, Ulriker stood at

the pedestal and reached into the light to claim his treasure. So entranced was he by the Mournclaw that he failed to see or hear Mallon running up behind him. Only when the thief's knife plunged into his neck did he break from his reverie.

Ulriker roared, swinging a fist wide. Mallon was already crouched, and poised to plunge the blade into Ulriker's chest. He did so, his blade finding a weak spot between the mismatched metals of the knight's breastplate. Malefitz pounced at that moment, sinking his sickle claws into Mallon's arms, but Mallon's razor dug into the gryph-hound's temple. Malefitz's golden eyes rolled up before he slumped to the cold flagstones.

'You...? Out of all of them...' Ulriker gasped, mouth flapping, dark blood painting his teeth.

'*Now* we're even,' Mallon said as he reached into Ulriker's belt pouch, and brought forth a nugget of so-called torope. Mallon crushed it beneath his heel as the knight's life left him.

Mallon wasted not a second; the sound of myriad claws on stone was becoming deafening. Leaving the blade in Ulriker's chest, he surged forward to the pedestal and ripped Mournclaw from its rest. Clutching its handle, Mallon felt an icy power rush though his veins, felt darkness seep into the corners of his vision. For a moment, he was filled with notions of wielding it himself, but he could only tolerate its touch just long enough to turn, kneel, and drop it at the feet of the warlock.

Mallon prostrated himself before Volz, eyes fixed on the mace lying on the floor, and mouth busy mumbling through prayers to any god that was watching.

An eerie silence fell. Mallon couldn't help but glimpse over his bloody arm. He saw the edges of the domed hall crowded with skaven. They panted heavily and bared their teeth, but they took not a step towards him.

Mallon heard the scratching of claws in front of him and looked to see Volz Flayfang emerge from his bonds. The rope fell from him as if it had been cut hours ago. The ratman arose from the floor to his full height, now towering over Mallon. His forked tail swished gleefully at the edge of the thief's vision.

Every muscle in Mallon's body was clenched. He fought not to gag against the stench of so many skaven around him. Mallon felt his hands trembling as he gestured towards the Mournclaw.

'Take it,' whispered the thief. He felt Volz bend down, closer to him, and sniff. The ratman's whiskers fell across his ear and cheek, making him flinch.

'Thief-scoundrel last to live. Impressive.'

Mallon dared to look up, meeting Volz's red eye inches from his face. 'You have the Mournclaw. That's what you wanted, correct?'

Volz snickered. 'For such-long, I have hunt-looked for the Mournclaw. Dig-find, we did, until we see-spy magic spell impenetrable. Know we need duardin-meat and duardin-blood to break it. Rusted Blades work-kill for Volz. Exactly as he plan-see it.'

Mallon saw it now. It had been a trap from the moment Durbrord had come bustling into the tavern. Who knew how long Volz had been planning this?

Mallon had never been a groveller, but he knew its worth in certain situations: the kind that ended in either death or survival. 'Very clever, Volz. You outsmarted all of us. Now, I do believe we had a bargain. Seeing as I kept my end of it, I simply wish to leave and go home,' Mallon said. Silently, he swore never to leave the Black Marsh Barony again. His dreams of far-flung Excelsis had died with the rest of the Blades.

The thief watched, rapt, as the warlock picked up the Mournclaw Mace. Green light emanated from the crystals at its centre, stuck between the blades. Something about the weapon seemed to leak vapour, as if it boiled in the cold of the hall. Though it looked heavy, Volz appeared to brandish it with no effort. The weapon seemed to fuel him in some way, and he stretched even taller. The skaven around the hall's edge began to screech and holler in praise of their warlock. Several snapped their thick tails like whips.

'Our deal, remember?' Mallon shouted above the noise. He begun to shuffle backwards on his knees, when Volz's claws alighted on his shoulder. Mallon flinched away in fear. The ratman sighed in his ear and Mallon froze. What felt like a day of waiting passed before he felt able to sit straight, and slowly look up at the warlock standing over him. Volz was grinning as usual, and though that smile was full of sharp and bloody fangs, Mallon saw a kind of respect there, if one could see such a thing in the eyes of a beast.

'The thief. Last fool-meat alive. Better than all-lots of these,' Volz hissed, as he ran his claws over Ulriker and Durbrord.

Mallon smiled back. He rested back on his heels, glancing at the shaking body of Durbrord. The duardin was staring at him, judging even in death.

Volz balanced the Mournclaw on his furry shoulder and took a deep breath, sounding disappointed. 'Shame-shame the thief-meat was not born-lived a skaven. Would have done-proved Clans Skryre proud.'

Mallon took breath to speak. 'I–'

He never finished his thought.

The charcoal-black blades of the Mournclaw sliced through the thick air without a sound, colliding with Mallon's head before he could blink. His skull was pulverised in a flash of green lightning, leaving nothing but black blood, charred bone and the broken corpse of a thief behind.

As his clanrats squeaked in approval around him, Volz raised the bloody mace, feeling the Chaos magic burn his veins.

'Shame-shame.'

THE LAST KNIGHT: PART ONE

Gavin G Smith

Gavin G Smith brings his flair for military strategy to Inferno! *with this epic and unconventional story – the first half of the tale of the war for Leucosia.*

On a storm-wracked and isolated knight world, Lacutus, scion of the embattled House Honaratus, seeks to reunite the scattered populations of a planet whose technology has reverted to an almost medieval state. But he soon uncovers a deadly threat which has remained hidden for generations… Retreating to Leucosia's capital, Lacutus must rally the castle's few defenders against a far superior army. Their only weapons are longbows, trebuchets… and one very ancient but formidable Imperial Knight. Will Lacutus prove himself worthy of piloting Wargod *by exterminating the teeming hordes that infest Leucosia?*

Lacutus' dead eye hurt, and he'd been riding so long that he feared his inner thighs had turned to leather. He gently pulled the reins to bring Augustus to a halt on the crest of the ridge that looked down onto Innsport. Lacutus reached forward to scratch between Augustus' ears. To his mind the tireless, intelligent destrier was the best horseflesh ever to come out of the flatlands east of Landfall. He turned his attention back to Innsport. He was half-surprised to see it was still there, though mostly rebuilt, like many of the towns and villages on Leucosia after the destruction wrought by the warp storms that had plagued the system. Lacutus tried to avoid looking at the part of the sky where he knew he would see the Siren's Storm. It would look faint in the daylight, a scar on the bright cerulean blue, but he could still feel it, like a malevolent presence. Unconsciously he touched the patch over his left eye. The pain was a reminder of his shame.

Lacutus knew that to have withstood the storms, Innsport

must have a network of shelters dug into the steep hill that rose up from the waterside on which the town was built. The settlement overlooked a natural harbour guarded by stark grey cliffs on either side. The worked-stone waterside was home to a small fleet of fishing boats. The most singular thing about the harbour, however, was the crashed, semi-submerged, derelict spacecraft blocking well over half of the entrance to the bay.

Lacutus pulled the telescope out of his saddlebag and held it up to his remaining good eye. He was no judge of such things, but if he had to guess, he suspected that the spacecraft was of human design and had crash-landed there more than half a century ago. Perhaps the craft had been spat out of the warp by the intermittent storms that had cut Leucosia off from the rest of the Imperium, their patron forge world, Metalica, and seemingly the light of the Emperor Himself. In part he was pleased that the rumours of the crashed ship were true and that the wreckage seemed reasonably intact. It would provide Lydia with an opportunity to scavenge the ship for tech that could be used to get *Wargod*, the Honaratus family's sole remaining Knight Errant, up and running. On the other hand, the presence of the spacecraft made him feel very uneasy indeed. The bounties of the warp storms were seldom a blessing. Augustus, perhaps picking up on his rider's unease, snorted, his ears going up. Lacutus patted the destrier's flanks, though he had little in the way of comforting words for the animal.

Lacutus turned the telescope on the village itself. There were only a few people wandering the dry mud streets, mainly women and children. All of them shuffled around, busy at some task or another, even the youngest. That said, they all seemed hale and whole of limb from what Lacutus could see of them. No obvious aberrations. Lacutus rubbed his dead eye. It had been the lashing tendril of a warp-spawned horror that had taken it from him. He could still feel the sting of it, even now, more than three years later. Worse than the pain of his dead eye was the sting of shame he felt every time he thought of that fight. He had been less than useless in the final battle with the warp spawn. The battle that had so badly damaged *Wargod* and almost killed his father. He collapsed the telescope and put it back into his saddlebag. Then he loaded both bows on his double crossbow with two of the special bolts that Lydia had made him.

'Come on, boy,' he said to Augustus, urging the destrier forward with a gentle tap of his heels.

The people he saw in the narrow, hard-packed dirt streets, between the strangely uniform wattle-and-daub hovels, barely cast an eye his way as Lacutus rode into Innsport. He tried to get a look at their faces but with little success. The place stank of fish, but that was to be expected.

He made his way towards a two-storey longhall in the centre of town. He reckoned he would find someone of authority there, if they weren't out fishing.

'You!' he said to what he assumed was a hunched old woman, though it was difficult to tell as she was so heavily wrapped in skirts, shawl and headscarf, despite the heat of the day. The old woman stopped and angled her head towards Lacutus, though not enough for him to see her face. 'Who's in charge here?'

She just pointed at the longhall.

'Go and fetch them for me,' he told her, his voice all but a hoarse rasp, his throat dry from the road.

She said nothing. Instead she shuffled towards the longhall.

Lacutus felt eyes on him. He glanced around. Nearby, people had stopped what they were doing and were watching him, but when he tried to meet their eyes, they looked down again. He was sure it was something other than the simple deference the peasantry owed to someone of his station.

After what felt like a long time, a strange figure emerged from the longhall. He wore a very fine, ornate robe and leaned on a gnarled but well-polished hardwood staff. The man was tall, thin, with a sallow complexion, sunken cheeks and a somewhat bulbous head. There wasn't quite enough there to suggest he was a warp-spawned mutant of some kind, but it was enough to make Lacutus wary. His hand moved closer to the hilt of his somewhat temperamental power sword, Woundthirst.

'I'm Elderman Fisher,' the figure said. 'Welcome to Innsport.'

'Well met,' Lacutus replied, though it wasn't a sentiment he was particularly feeling. 'I am Sir Lacutus Honaratus of Landfall. I am re-establishing contact with all our outlying settlements now that the storms have passed.'

If the elderman was in any way intimidated by the tall, heavily built, armoured figure then he gave no indication of it.

'I see, a relative of our good and noble Lord Governor Ignatius Honaratus, perhaps!'

Lacutus frowned.

'Ignatius was my grandfather, he has been gone these thirty years. I never met him. I am the son of Lord Governor Forganus Honaratus the Third.'

A flicker of annoyance crossed the elderman's face. As this happened Lacutus felt a spasm of pain in his ruined eye.

'Do you not bow to the knight of an Imperial House in Innsport?' Lacutus asked, leaning forward. It wasn't something that particularly bothered him but he was wondering if the lack of respect for his rank was indicative of something else.

'Get off your horse.'

Lacutus straightened up.

'What?' he asked.

'Your pardons, my lord, I'm out of practice. *Get off your horse!*'

Too slow, Lacutus reached for the hilt of Woundthirst, but it was as though some invisible force was pummelling him, crushing his will, squeezing. Resistance was agony, but he fought as hard as he could until he half-dismounted, half-fell from Augustus' back.

The elderman's eyes were a solid mass of black. There was nothing human about them now.

'*Now you kneel!*' the elderman cried, pointing his staff at Lacutus.

The knight cried out, curling up in a ball in the dirt. Not even the warp spawn's lash had hurt like this. He heard Augustus' screaming neigh, and was thrown into shadow as the destrier reared. He heard the sound of a shod hoof meeting a skull. Suddenly Lacutus was pain-free and able to move.

The elderman was staggering backwards, a bloody dent in his bulbous skull. Lacutus wrenched Woundthirst from the sheath strapped to Augustus' saddle. Mercifully the power sword hummed into life when he activated it. Lacutus sliced downwards, a hurried two-handed blow. The blade clove Fisher from shoulder to near-waist. Purple ichor from inhuman internal organs splattered the knight. Lacutus pushed the elderman off his blade with his boot. Somehow the creature was still alive. Lacutus raised Woundthirst high, again, to deliver the killing blow just as the creatures exploded out of two nearby hovels. They were purple-skinned, with armoured carapaces and long, sharp, pointed tongues lolling out of their mouths. They charged on all six clawed limbs towards Lacutus. He had a moment to make a choice. He could kill the elderman and die himself, or escape and warn his father of the xenos threat here.

He vaulted onto Augustus' back. The horse needed little urging and immediately burst into a gallop. Lacutus sheathed the sword with some difficulty. Then he swung around in the saddle until he was facing backwards. The creatures were gaining on him through the dust that Augustus was kicking up. Lacutus unclipped the double crossbow and brought it to his shoulder. He squeezed the tickler once, shifted aim, and then again. If he hadn't practised this trick so many times Lacutus was sure that he would have missed, but his aim was true, despite firing from the back of a galloping horse. The bolts slammed into the vile xenos and, moments later, exploded, sending one of them tumbling sideways through the air, the other careening through the wall of a hovel. He suspected it wouldn't be enough to kill the powerful creatures but he prayed it would slow them down enough so that he could escape. He spun round in the saddle again, and gave thanks to the Emperor for Augustus.

Lacutus had ridden day and night across the eastern plains. He had pushed Augustus as hard as he dared, but despite the destrier's remarkable endurance, the mighty horse had started to flag. Lacutus was all but asleep in the saddle as they reached the foothills of the Grey Sentinels. Beyond the foothills lay the snow-capped, forest-clad majesty of the mountains.

Landfall Castle was nestled amongst the foothills. The castle sprawled across several hilltops. Built from the colony ship dispatched from Terra during the Dark Age of Technology, the castle had been strong enough to act as a shelter since the appearance of the Cicatrix Maledictum, when the tendrils of the Siren's Storm had reached for them. The city of Landfall had not done as well against the depredations of the warp, however. There was little left of the city other than blackened rubble. The survivors had moved into the castle, living in its tangle of corridors and multiple courtyards.

Lacutus was too busy trying not to fall out of the saddle to pay any attention to the blackened, salted earth of the plague pit where they had burned the infected, the cultists and the diseased minions of Nurgle. The constant pain in his ruined eye was reminder enough.

He was barely aware of crossing the drawbridge, of the guards hailing him but letting him pass through the curtain wall's gatehouse, of them doing the same as he passed through the inner wall's gatehouse. He was only peripherally aware of the runner racing ahead, though he was so bone weary he couldn't work out who the boy was going to fetch.

'What you do to Augustus?' The voice was an aggrieved low bass grumble. Ten feet of bestial-featured corded muscle towered over horse and rider. Lacutus tried to look up at the ogryn. He wore a thick leather apron, his exposed skin stained by soot from the forge. Then the ogryn lunged forward to catch Lacutus as he slid from the saddle.

Lacutus steadied himself against the ogryn's bulk.

'You ride Augustus too hard!' the ogryn protested. He had one hand ready to catch Lacutus again. Augustus was nuzzling against the other. Despite the ogryn smith's ferocious appearance, he had a way with animals, particularly horses, and particularly Augustus.

'Look after Augustus, Kark,' Lacutus managed, 'I need to see my father.'

Lacutus vaguely remembered staggering past the near-empty Sanctuary, the resting place of his ruined birthright. He made his way towards the great hall in the central keep. He felt the eyes of the peasants on him as he passed. He waved away castle guards who approached as though to help. It was important that he did this himself.

The guards were at least good enough to push open the doors to the great hall. It was like walking into light. The stained-glass window, depicting the Emperor's defeat of the arch-heretic, Horus, had been positioned to catch the light of the early-morning suns.

His father turned to face him.

'Lord governor.' In public the proper form had to be followed, despite exhaustion.

His father dropped the parchment he was examining and started towards his son, concern on his face.

'Genestealers,' Lacutus managed. The last thing he saw before he passed out was the look of abject horror on his father's face.

'You've been using yourself hard.' His father's voice sounded old and worn.

Lacutus opened his eye to look up at the lord governor's gaunt, lined face. His father, a once strong-limbed, tall man, full of energy, was now diminished, bent and frail. He had not been the same since the last time he had piloted *Wargod*. The strain of the fight with the diseased warp spawn three years previous had almost killed him. The fight had robbed his father of his vitality and he had seemed to age overnight. Lacutus blamed himself.

'Genestealers!' Lacutus cried, grabbing his father's robe. He was almost ashamed to notice that Fisher's robe had been finer.

His father motioned for him to calm himself.

'You said so before you collapsed,' his father reassured him. 'I'm going to ask you this once, my son. Are you sure?'

Lacutus understood the need for the question. All they knew of the terrible clawed changelings had come from stories told by the last representative of the Ecclesiarchy that Leucosia had seen, before they had been cut off from the Imperium. Again.

'Yes,' Lacutus told him. 'I was chased by at least two of the genestealers. It was as Deacon Ullas said.' He managed to sit up. His muscles ached but he felt well rested, though he was hungry again.

'Light of the Emperor,' his father sighed.

Lacutus was desperately trying to remember the stories the fat deacon, drunk on his father's mead, had told them. He could not remember the exact details but he suspected that the presence of the six-armed genestealers meant that the xenos had been on Leucosia for generations, though he had no idea how many.

'Father, you have to call the yeomanry.'

'I have done so,' his father told him.

Lacutus was gratified by this; his father had taken his word on faith. Calling the yeomanry this close to harvest wouldn't have been a decision taken lightly.

'You will march our forces to Innsport?' Lacutus asked. Even as he said this he thought of the futility of steel against the ferocity of the purestrain genestealers – against the power of Elderman Fisher.

'No, you will, my son,' his father said, standing up and pacing the ancient plasteel floor.

'Father…' Lacutus started.

'I am too old,' his father told him, 'and we both know it.'

Lacutus wanted to argue, he wanted to turn time back three years, as heretical as that thought might be, but he knew his father was right. His father had never been a particularly easy man to read; he had been too calm, too used to negotiations where it wouldn't profit him for others to know what he thought. Lacutus, however, knew him well enough to recognise that the lord governor was deeply worried.

'Is there something else, father?' Lacutus asked.

'You weren't the only rider I sent out. None who went north and east to the coast have returned. The problem may be more widespread.'

Lacutus tried to work out just how many of the foul creatures there could be. How many people had survived the storms only to fall to the xenos?

'How could this happen?' he asked himself.

'The people turned from the light of the Emperor,' his father told him. 'In the cold and the dark, as the storms raged far above, they prayed that the water would not become contaminated, that the machine-spirits in the mulch vats would not fail them. Perhaps some prayed to the wrong god.'

Talk of prayer reminded him of Lydia.

'*Wargod*?' he asked.

His father just shook his head. The Knight Errant still wasn't working, it seemed.

Lacutus nodded, then struggled out of bed and moved to the arched window. He was high enough in the central keep to see out over both walls towards the Sentinels. The river tumbled out of the mountains, the mist obscuring his view of the falls, and flowed down the steep ravine that ran along the west side of the castle. Lacutus sometimes thought of Leucosia, particularly Landfall Province, as a beautiful body riddled with disease. The view over the mountains was in contrast to the twisted, burned remains of the city just outside the castle's eastern wall. The landscape looked timeless but Lacutus knew from bitter experience it was protean when touched by the storms. Who knew what corruptions existed up in the high mountain passes. Lacutus shook himself out of his musings.

'We could search for Vervius,' he suggested. The mountains had made him think of the old astropath.

'We don't even know if the system is navigable again,' his father said.

Vervius had deserted them after their battle with the cult of disease. It had become too much for the ageing psyker. Before he had sneaked out of the castle, he had implied that one more use of his abilities and he would succumb to the voices in the warp. His desertion was a gross dereliction of duty. There had been reported sightings of the old astropath here and there, mostly from the hardy gnarlherds in their high pastures in the mountains. His father had sought to find Vervius but Lacutus did not think he had tried too hard. He suspected his father wanted to leave his old friend in peace. Vervius could call for help, however, assuming that help was even capable of reaching them.

'I will leave you to dress and break your fast,' his father said. 'Join me when you are ready and we will continue to plan.'

Lacutus nodded.

His father crossed his chambers, making for the door. Lacutus couldn't help but notice how loose and wrinkled the skin round his father's interface plugs was.

'Father,' Lacutus said. His father stopped and turned to face him. 'I do not fear these creatures...' he continued.

'I know that.'

'But I do not know how to fight them with what we have.'

His father nodded. 'Nevertheless, we must,' he said. Then he left.

Lacutus crossed to the chest pushed up against the wall. Woundthirst lay scabbarded across it. His shield, Faith, made by Lydia from scavenged adamantium taken from a long-since-destroyed Knight Errant, and his crossbow were leaning up against the wall. Lacutus drew the sword, turned towards where he knew distant Terra lay in the sky at this time of year and knelt down. He spent a moment looking at the familiar High Gothic runes inscribed on the blade, then he closed his eyes and began to pray to the light of the Emperor.

Wargod looked like an ancient warrior in the stillness of the cathedral-like Sanctuary. The narrow windows let in only a little light to the cavernous space. The Knight Errant was a silent suit of battle-scarred armour standing, huge, in one of the many alcoves. Once the Sanctuary would have been full of such war machines, but the depredations of time, the storms, and in the long past, the futility of internecine feuding and duels, had slowly whittled the Knights Errant down. *Thunderblade* and *Queen of Blood* had both been destroyed, their pilots – an aunt-once-removed and a distant cousin – killed, fighting the forces of the Plague God, and now only *Wargod* was left.

Wargod still wore the scars of his last battle. The warp spawn had certainly left its mark on the war machine. The Knight had fallen amongst the burning ruins of Landfall City. Lacutus' father had nearly died that day. It had taken all of Lydia's ingenuity and an oxen train to tow *Wargod* back to the Sanctuary and winch him upright in his alcove. It felt like their only hope if – no, *when* – the genestealers came.

Lacutus glanced upwards. Just under the domed roof above the Sanctuary lay the Chamber of Echoes. Lacutus rubbed the back of his neck. He knew he should have interface plugs in his flesh by now. He was past his eighteenth birthday, but there had been little point while his father had been vital enough to pilot the Knight Errant, and now *Wargod* might well be dead. Truth be told, Lacutus feared the Chamber of Echoes, as he feared *Wargod*'s machine-spirit and the ghosts of his ancestors within the Throne Mechanicum. In the face of the warp spawn he had been found wanting.

'Is it true?' The voice came from high above, echoing down through the stillness of the Sanctuary.

Lacutus looked up and saw Lydia lowering herself hand over hand down a knotted rope. She was short, shaven-headed and wore much-patched robes with many pouches for her inherited sacramental tools. He could make out the outline of her tattoos under the omnipresent oil, grime and sweat. Lydia had copied them from the skin of Volgad, the last sacristan that Metalica had been able to send. He had been her master before he had fallen victim to the plague.

Lydia reached the ground and came to stand before him, hands on her hips. She was never one to give deference to his rank, but for his part they were friends.

'Genestealers,' he told her. She looked mystified. 'Clawed changelings.'

'I thought those were just a tale to frighten children.'

Despite the beauty of Leucosia, Lacutus wasn't sure that the children of his world needed made-up horrors to frighten them.

'No, of course they're real,' Lydia muttered a few moments later. Lacutus nodded towards *Wargod*. He knew they needed the Knight Errant but there was still that trickling sense of fear, that pressure he felt from the Chamber of Echoes and its ghosts far above him.

'I've conducted all the rituals, made sacrifice to the Omnissiah to appease the machine-spirits and your ancestors, but I'm no sacristan.' Lydia hung her head. Lacutus reached out to grip her shoulder. She intended to travel back to Metalica and train with the fabled Adeptus Mechanicus the next time their ships were able to make it through, but none had come for a very long time now.

Lacutus looked up at *Wargod*. He was not sure what he feared most – that *Wargod* was dead, or that he lived and Lacutus would have to undergo the Ritual of Becoming. Lydia took him by the back of his neck. He was so surprised by her familiarity that he didn't even remonstrate with her.

'Your fear will kill you,' she told him and nodded up towards the Chamber of Echoes. 'I think we need to put the interface plugs into you sooner rather than later.'

'And you know how to do this?' Lacutus asked.

'Volgad dictated extensive guidance to me before he died,' she told him, letting go of the back of his neck, which now felt dirty and gritty.

He did not feel particularly reassured by the idea of amateur implant chirurgery.

'Sir Lacutus!' a voice cried from the huge open doorway. Lacutus and Lydia turned to see one of the castle guards. 'Your pardon, sir, but I think you should see this.'

'What are we looking at?' Lydia asked. They were standing on the eastern curtain wall, gazing out over the charred and twisted remains of the city to the plains. Beyond the horizon lay the coast.

Lacutus snapped open the telescope and scanned the plains beyond the ruins of Landfall City. It took a moment but he found the reason for his summons. There were thousands of them. At this distance, even through the telescope, they looked like insects. They moved with a strange hunched lope towards the castle. Lacutus handed Lydia the telescope and turned to the captain of the guard, who was standing next to him.

'Omnissiah preserve us,' Lydia whispered.

'Send riders out, get anyone out there back inside the castle. Under no circumstances are the riders to engage with the creatures. Then raise the drawbridge, close the gates and drop the portcullises – lock us up tight. Send a runner for my father, another to get my armour and weapons from my room. Have the yeomanry line the walls and send their commander to me, and I want the artillery observers up here as well. Tell them they fire only when the creatures are in killing range,' Lacutus finished. The captain nodded and moved away to put Lacutus' orders into action, but Lacutus called him back. 'And captain – make sure you have people watching in every direction, including the west wall. This may be a feint.' The captain nodded again and went about his duties.

Lydia handed the telescope back to Lacutus.

'The trebuchets, we could arrange a little surprise for them,' she told him, raising her voice to be heard over the shouted orders.

'Not yet,' Lacutus said as he watched the closing creatures through the telescope; he was appalled at the speed, how much closer they were already. The creatures had too many arms, some ending in vicious claws, but they also carried crude swords, clubs, maces, axes and even spears. These were not the pure xenos that had chased him from Innsport.

Instead these were hybrid creatures. Their heads were bulbous, distended, and favoured their alien parents, though some had more human features. They continued to move inexorably towards the castle. Lacutus lowered the telescope and turned towards Lydia. 'If there is anything else you can do to bring *Wargod* back to life...'

Lydia spent just a moment too long silent before nodding. He knew she had tried everything. She turned and headed down the steps, squeezing past the yeomanry and their longbows as they made their way up from the killing ground between the curtain and inner wall.

The yeomanry were a militia that consisted of every able-bodied person between the age of fifteen and seventy from the province. Membership was mandatory, as were the weekly longbow drills, not that many complained. Being able to defend their herds and flocks with a longbow was as useful for the farmers as it was for the alpine gnarlherds. As well as their bows most of the yeomanry were proficient with sword and spear, or at the very least staff and dagger. The yeomanry made up the bulk of their force, and though they were only a civilian militia the folk of Landfall Province came from hardy stock.

The rest of their forces were formed of the castle guard. These were professional soldiers, all trained to use sword, shield, spear and crossbow, and many of them could also fight from horseback. There were specialist artillerymen amongst the guard as well. They manned the mangonels and ballistae, and the huge trebuchets in the courtyards behind the inner walls. There were a few other household knights like Lacutus himself, but most had ridden out on similar missions to his own, and either weren't due to return yet, or were suspiciously long overdue.

'Sir.' The provincial commander of the yeomanry was an ancient, toothless plains herdsman named Gult. He might have been old, but a life of hard work had left him still strong enough to bend a bow. More importantly, he commanded the respect of his subordinate officers and his rank and file.

'I want your men ready to loose as soon as they are in killing range, and killing range only,' Lacutus told him. Gult just nodded. 'Who's your best shot?'

'One-Arrow Nokes,' Gult told him.

'Send him to me.'

Gult grinned toothlessly, as if he found something amusing, and shouted for Nokes.

Riders galloped out of the main gate, heading off in various directions to call those remaining outside the walls back into the castle. Mostly the horsemen were calling back scouts for the yeomanry and artillery, who were measuring distances and marking them on the few remaining landmarks in the ruined city.

Nokes turned up. She was a wiry, six-foot-tall woman of about fifty. Lacutus suspected she was a high-pasture gnarlherd, and she looked as though she were made of old leather. She just nodded to him.

'Stay with me,' Lacutus told her.

'Sir?' It was one of the artillery observers. 'Pitch?'

Lacutus gave the question some thought. It was tempting to send barrels of flaming pitch into the ranks of the hybrid monsters sprinting towards his home. He suspected, however, that they would need all the pitch they had stockpiled when the genestealer forces had closed with the castle, when they were at the walls. On the walls. The very thought gave him a shiver.

'Sir Lacutus!' The cry came from one of the towers that

were interspersed along the castle wall every hundred yards or so. 'Ballista?' Each of the towers had either a ballista or mangonel atop it.

'Not yet,' Lacutus called up and then turned back to the observer. 'Stone-shot,' he told the man. Stone-shot made sense to use against an enemy that was essentially infantry, and they had more of it than any other kind of ammunition for the trebuchets. Then his hand shot out between the battlements. 'Check your range, man!'

The observer, startled, turned and looked out over the ruins of Landfall City. It seemed the observer had underestimated the speed of the hybrids as well. They were close now. Lacutus' disgust at the inhuman ravening horde, this twisting of human flesh by alien monsters, was written all over his face.

'Four hundred yards!' the observer called; it was repeated by another observer on the inner wall and then again by the individual trebuchet commanders. 'Three hundred and fifty yards!' the observer cried, just a tinge of panic in his voice.

'Notch!' Gult cried, his order repeated along the battlements by his subordinate commanders. It looked like a ripple was running through the yeomanry as they drew arrows from their quivers and notched them on their bowstrings.

Lacutus could hear the thunder of thousands of sprinting feet, but other than that the rapidly approaching horde made little noise.

'Three hundred yards!'

Lacutus heard the fear in the observer's voice. He heard the range repeated and the cry of 'Launch!' from the courtyard. He glanced behind him to see the thick arm of the huge trebuchet rise up and then disappear behind the inner wall, as six tonnes of counterweight whipped the sling on the end of the arm and launched the weapon's payload into the air.

'Loose!' Gult cried, and again a ripple passed down the battlements as the order was repeated and the yeomanry drew their bows, momentarily dimming the light as they filled the sky with arrows arcing towards the hybrid horde.

There was an explosion of earth as the first barrel of stone-shot hit the ground, sending hybrids tumbling through the air. The barrel burst, scattering the stones contained inside. Lacutus saw hybrids go down, but many of them got back up again.

And then the hybrid charge simply stopped, as though they had received a silent order. The arrows studded down, for the most part, just in front of them. Had they kept going they would have run straight into the hail. A few of the arrows reached the genestealer ranks and fewer still found their mark. A couple of hybrids fell but most seemed to ignore the arrow or arrows sticking out of them.

'Two hundred and fifty yards,' the observer said quietly.

It was just beyond the killing range of the longbows. The trebuchets and the mangonels could reach it by firing lighter payloads, but it would not be an efficient way to use their ammunition.

'Louder,' Lacutus told the observer.

The man shouted the range out the second time.

The runner returned, sweating and gasping for breath but bearing Woundthirst, Faith, Lacutus' mail hauberk and his double crossbow. He started to wriggle into his hauberk.

He looked at the waiting hybrids, wracking his brain, trying to remember what the drunken deacon had told him. The creatures were swaying like corn in the breeze, but Lacutus suspected it was anticipation. What was clear was that they had some silent way to communicate, like psykers did.

His father was clambering the steps up the curtain wall. He

looked as out of breath and sweaty as the runner had been, though he was moving a lot more slowly. Kark, the ogryn smith, trailed after him. The other six members of Kark's family, who made up the small ogryn community in Landfall, followed the smith. All of them wore steel half-helms and breastplates, and carried door shields in one hand and wielded huge hammers in the other.

Members of the yeomanry made room for their lord as he moved to the battlements to look out at the thousands of hybrids just out of effective range. Lacutus continued to pull his mail on as his father studied their enemy.

Lacutus was tightening his belt, making sure his surcoat was straight, when his father lowered his telescope and offered it to his son. Lacutus shook his head and found his own, extending it. He saw the cloud of dust on the horizon first. Next he noticed the oxen trains pulling the trebuchets, easily the same size as their own, and wagons, presumably full of supplies. Huge, misshapen monstrosities, not much smaller than an ogryn but with too many limbs, pushed four siege towers towards the castle. Then he saw the thousands upon thousands of troops that marched with the enemy army. These at least moved like humans. Finally he saw the palanquin, itself the size of a large wagon. It was being carried by the same kind of monstrosities that pushed the siege towers. Lacutus had no idea what was inside the palanquin but it disquieted him somehow, even from so far away. His eye was hurting again.

'Fisher,' Lacutus practically spat. The elderman had emerged from within the palanquin and was standing on a platform at the head of the vehicle. Lacutus was less than pleased that he could see no trace of the near-fatal wound he had dealt Fisher in Innsport. The elderman turned towards the castle and Lacutus couldn't shake the feeling that Fisher was staring straight at him.

'Ballista on the tower!' his father called. Whatever else, he still had a strong voice. 'Can you reach the palanquin?'

'Sorry, my lord,' the ballista crew commander called back.

There were creatures moving around Fisher's feet but they were too small and far away for Lacutus to make out properly.

'The hill, just behind the palanquin,' his father said.

Lacutus shifted the telescope away from Fisher's hated features and focused on the hilltop. His blood ran cold. He saw purestrain genestealers moving low and predatorily; there were dozens of them. The hybrids they could fight, but he wasn't sure they had weapons that could hurt the purestrains. These were creatures that gave even the Emperor's own holy warriors pause. It felt like looking at his own death.

'Emperor preserve us,' he muttered, earning a sharp look from his father.

'Did you see the more human-looking ones? Many of them were carrying crossbows,' his father told him. 'They and the siege engines will provide cover but it will be the hybrids that come to scale our walls.'

That made sense, but Lacutus noticed his father hadn't mentioned the purestrains; if they climbed like they ran it wouldn't take more than a few of them to get into the castle, and they would tear the yeomanry and castle guard apart.

'They must have been preparing for this for a long time,' Lacutus said.

'Your discovery must have forced their hand. I dread to think what would have happened if we'd had no warning,' his father said. Then he turned and made for the steps. 'Hold the wall,' he told Lacutus. 'I'm going to speak with Lydia.'

'Father!' Lacutus called after him. The lord governor paused and turned. 'We may yet need to find Vervius.' Lacutus left it unsaid that finding Vervius would become all the more important if Lydia could not fix *Wargod*. His father made no reply but continued down the steps.

Lacutus turned back and realised that Nokes was watching him.

'What?' he asked. 'Do you know something about Vervius?'

Nokes took a few moments, as though reluctant to answer. 'Some here might,' she said finally.

'Where want us?' Kark asked Lacutus. Lacutus had all but forgotten the group of huge ogryns taking up much of the battlements.

'Spread your people out, one between each of the towers on the eastern wall. Anything comes over the wall, you kill it,' he said.

Kark concentrated for a moment, thinking through his order, and then nodded. He started grabbing members of his family and pushing them in the direction he wanted them to go. Finally he turned back to Lacutus.

'I think I stay here with you,' Kark told him.

Lacutus nodded. He couldn't shake the feeling that Kark, wielding his hammer, might be the only thing between him and death at the claws of one of the genestealers.

Lacutus ducked behind the merlon as a barrel full of stone-shot exploded against the wall. He heard screams and saw yeomanry torn off the battlements, falling into the killing ground between the two walls. He watched flame blossom over the battlements further down the wall as a barrel full of pitch exploded against it. There was more screaming, and more bodies tumbling off the battlements, these ones on fire. Bolts tore through the air all around them. He could see smoke rising from the courtyard. The trebuchet closest to them on the other side of the inner wall was burning. The genestealers' siege weapons, throwing lighter payloads further, had been surprisingly accurate.

On the other side of the crenel Nokes risked loosing an arrow, and then ducked back behind the wall as she was answered with crossbow bolts for her troubles.

Teams of neophytes sheltered behind crude pavise shields. They kept up a near-constant barrage of crossbow bolts from equally crude windlasses. As Lacutus watched, one of the pavise shields was sundered by a spear-sized bolt fired by one of the tower ballista teams. A vengeful yeoman cut down the fleeing neophytes in a hail of arrows.

The four siege towers, pushed by the huge aberrations, were inching their way towards the eastern wall.

More crossbow bolts forced Lacutus to duck back behind the merlon before he found a target. The towers were a significant worry. The castle was surrounded by a dry moat on three sides and protected by the river gorge to the west. That meant the bridge at the top of each tower would be exposed to the defenders, but as soon as one of them reached the battlements it would be only a matter of time before the curtain wall fell. The purestrains remained the biggest threat, however, though so far they had stayed by Fisher, as if protecting the palanquin. The archers were already concentrating their fire on the aberrations but to little avail.

Lacutus swung around, crossbow at the ready. An elongated, purple-skinned face appeared in the crenel gap. Its long, sharp tongue extended past rows of sharp teeth. Lacutus gave a cry of surprise and squeezed the tickler, loosing the bolt right into the hybrid's face.

'Ladders!' he cried, another face appearing in the crenel,

a clawed arm reaching over the wall. Lacutus unloaded the crossbow's second bolt into its face. 'Kark!'

Lacutus dropped the crossbow and grabbed for his shield, left leaning against the wall. Straightening up he saw one of the hybrids climbing through the crenel. Hissing, it threw itself at him. Lacutus managed to bring Faith up. The impact of the hybrid landing on the shield almost knocked him off the battlements. Lacutus went down on one knee and bent. He heard claws scrabbling on adamantium, and the creature slid off and into the killing zone between the two walls. He knew the yeomanry on the inner wall's battlements would already be loosing arrows at the creature.

Lacutus made to stand but then ducked as a hammer flew overhead and caved in the face of another hybrid standing in the crenel. Nokes loosed an arrow and a hybrid standing on the merlon next to Kark fell back.

'The pole!' Lacutus screamed at the ogryn as he tore Woundthirst from its scabbard and tried to activate it. Nothing happened. Today it appeared Woundthirst was just a sword, albeit one that never lost its edge. Lacutus thrust the point forward into another climbing hybrid's face and it fell away.

Kark grabbed one of the long forked poles, almost knocking Lacutus off the battlements as he did so. He thrust the pole forward, knocking another climbing hybrid out of the crenel, and then used the fork to hook the top of the ladder. The ogryn's enormous strength easily pushed the ladder away from the wall.

The flight of a crossbow bolt opened up a cut on the side of Lacutus' face, the head narrowly missing him. He ducked back behind the merlon. They had to do something about the siege towers or it was all over.

'Nokes!' he shouted. She ignored him momentarily as she loosed another arrow, then she moved behind a merlon as well, looking over at him. Lacutus pointed south along the wall. 'Go to the next tower with a ballista, tell them to attach a line to a broad-head bolt and put it into the tower closest to us!' Nokes nodded and set off. 'Kark, stay here!' The big ogryn grunted his affirmative.

Lacutus slung his crossbow over his shoulder and headed north along the battlements towards the closest tower. The air was full of crossbow bolts. He kept Faith up and heard the bolts bouncing off the shield. Arrows, loosed blind by the yeomanry on the inner wall, flew overhead. He reached the entrance to the tower and scrambled up the plasteel stairs, past the wounded and runners sent for more ammunition.

He came out onto the tower and paused for a moment to take in the full panorama of the battle. He watched as ladders were pushed up against the wall, the hybrids already climbing them. He watched the genestealers' trebuchets launch flaming barrels of pitch. Moments later a huge ball of fire blossomed up somewhere south of him, behind the inner wall. One of the barrels had found a supply of their own incendiaries.

The biggest problem remained, however, the siege towers inching forward.

Lacutus dropped his shield and reloaded his crossbow with two of Lydia's special bolts. He gestured for the ballista commander to join him. The man crouch-ran over to him as bolts shot overhead. Lacutus told him what he wanted.

'We have a bodkin loaded now!' he shouted over the din.

'Kill one of the large creatures pushing the tower, the closest to us!'

The man nodded and scampered back to his crew. The wood of the ballista's frame was studded with crossbow bolts.

Lacutus crossed to one of the crenels and put his foot on it. He was looking out over the battlements. He took aim at an aberration pushing the tower that was closest to him. He squeezed the tickler, then again. He heard the clang of the ballista firing behind him, felt the wind from the huge bolt passing him. The ballista bolt passed Lacutus' own in the air. The crew's aim was true. The bolt ran the huge creature through, bursting out of its back. Lacutus' bolts hit, one blasting a huge chunk of flesh out of the creature's side, the other an arm. The creature staggered but didn't go down. The tower had almost reached the top of the dry moat.

The ballista crew loaded a broad-head bolt with a line attached. Lacutus took the other end of the line and attached a grapple to it. He shouted a warning to the defenders on the inner wall and then threw the grapple over the battlements. Then he reloaded his own crossbow and took opportunistic shots whilst the ballista was cranked back. One of the crew screamed and fell back as a crossbow bolt took him in the cheek; he staggered away spitting blood and teeth but finally the ballista was ready. The ballista commander pushed the rest of the line off the tower so it wouldn't bisect anyone when it went taut.

'Loose!' the commander cried.

The huge broad-head bolt shot out of the weapon, and once again the crew's aim was sound. The bolt flew through the thick wood of the siege tower and into its interior. Lacutus hoped it had skewered a few of the hybrids that had been clambering up the inside of the siege engine. The tower had stopped on the edge of the dry moat. At the top of the wheeled structure a bridge was extending towards the curtain wall.

'Pull the line!' Lacutus screamed at the defenders on the inner wall. 'As much weight as possible!'

Down on the battlements Kark grabbed the line, braced his legs against the wall and pulled with all his might. His huge, corded, ogryn muscles were bulging like they might burst with the effort.

Moments later another line was shot from the ballista he'd sent Nokes to, two towers along. It hit the same siege tower. The tower was bottom-heavy but it was on wheels, and some of the weight would shift as the hybrid horde scrambled up it, eager to be the first over the wall. Both lines were taut. Lacutus didn't need it to move very much, just enough... The tower inched forward. There seemed to be confusion amongst the aberrations; too late they tried to halt the tower's progress. The front wheels went over the lip of the dry moat and the whole structure toppled forward, hitting the castle wall and breaking in two.

Further south, one of the surviving trebuchets flung a smoking, oddly shaped object at another of the towers. The object landed close to the tower and there was an almighty explosion that almost knocked Lacutus over. He was sure it must have blown some of their own people off the battlements. The siege tower was lifted into the air and torn apart. It took the defenders a moment or two to recover from the shock, but then a ragged cheer went up. It had been another one of Lydia's surprises: ancient unstable ordnance, probably intended originally for one of the Knights Errant, jury-rigged to explode and launched by a particularly brave trebuchet crew.

There were still two more towers moving, their bridges reaching out over the moat towards the battlements, and now the enemy's trebuchets were concentrating on the ballista towers. More and more ladders were going up against the wall. The dry moat boiled with hybrids clambering over each other in their haste to reach the battlements and get amongst the defenders.

'Move!' Lacutus screamed as a smoking barrel of pitch arced towards the tower he was on. He dived for the hatch. Fire chased him down the plasteel stairs. He heard screaming above and saw a burning body plummet past one of the arrow slits as the ballista crew died.

Coughing, almost blinded by smoke, he managed to make it down the stairs and back out onto the battlements. He heard clanking, a heavy chain being wound. Appalled, he realised that it was the outer gatehouse's portcullis being raised. He ran to the closest crenel and stuck his head out, oblivious to the crossbow bolts flying around him. He was even more horrified to see the drawbridge being lowered. In quick succession he thought that the hybrids had taken the wall, that his troops had rebelled and were foolishly trying to surrender, or even that some of the more human-looking hybrids had infiltrated the castle.

'No!' he screamed. 'Draw it back up!'

Yeomanry and castle guard alike stared at him as though he were mad, but none made a move to action his orders. He looked out again and saw hybrids surge towards the drawbridge over the dry moat, many of them leaping for it despite the murderous hail of arrows.

The drawbridge had finally lowered. A shadow fell across the hybrid horde as they came to a halt. Then they turned and started to run, and then they simply ceased to exist. Even up on the wall Lacutus felt the wall of heat hit him as the fleeing hybrids were vaporised.

The heat haze subsided and *Wargod* stepped out onto the

drawbridge. Lacutus stared. A ragged cheer went up from the defenders on the curtain wall, those that weren't busy fighting the hybrids that had made it up onto the battlements. The Knight Errant's thermal cannon projected a haze of hot, silent death. The carapace stub gun fired into the fleeing genestealer forces. There was an explosion of earth as the Knight's chainsword roared into life and struck out at the fleeing enemy creatures.

There was a moment of exultation, but just a moment. Beyond the main gate, one of the remaining siege towers had extended its bridge, and hybrids were boiling over it and onto the curtain wall battlements, despite the deadly hail of arrows.

Wargod turned and lifted his thermal cannon. It looked as though the siege tower had lifted itself into the air, burst into flames and then torn itself apart.

The war machine went after the fourth and final siege tower with his chainsword. The weapon's whirring teeth bit into the wooden structure, cutting through it with ease, spilling hybrid bodies like blood. The top half toppled over. *Wargod* kicked the heavy bottom half into kindling and proceeded to stamp on the fleeing aberrations, the heavy stubber firing all the while.

The Knight Errant turned his armoured head and looked back at the hybrids in the dry moat as they scrambled up the siege ladders. Lacutus could feel *Wargod*'s steps through the wall as the war machine picked up pace, running back towards the castle wall. He leapt up into the air and landed amongst the hybrids, pulping some underfoot. The Knight stamped his way north along the dry moat, the thermal cannon creating a constant heat haze as the hybrids were vaporised. The power of the cannon was such that flesh became steam. Siege ladders were kicked off the wall, or cut away, the teeth of the mighty chainsword scoring the plasteel wall of the castle. Those hybrids who escaped *Wargod*'s stamping feet, the heat and the sword, were torn apart by the heavy stubber as they tried to flee.

Wargod turned his attention south, feet now sticky with pulped alien flesh. Trebuchet-flung rocks bounced off the war machine and barrels of burning pitch exploded over his armour, wreathing parts of him in flames. It just added to the Knight's air of invincibility. It was to the crossbow-wielding neophytes' credit that they vainly shot bolt after bolt at the war machine. The cloud of missiles sparking uselessly of his armour was so thick it looked like a swarm of stinging insects. *Wargod* raised the thermal cannon casually and burning pavise shields fell to the ground. He used the weapon to clear the moat south of the drawbridge. Lacutus felt the weapon's heat, saw the earth itself catch fire – watched his father, as the indestructible god of war, stride through the flames. Then, as one, the genestealer forces turned and ran.

Amongst the flames, *Wargod* looked towards the palanquin on the hill behind the genestealer lines. He took a faltering step out of the burning dry moat. Lacutus thought nothing of it, but then *Wargod* hesitated. He did not pursue the fleeing hybrid hordes, wreak havoc amongst their siege engines, and take fire and blade to Fisher and whatever horror lurked within the palanquin. Instead *Wargod* made his way back towards the drawbridge. Lacutus could not understand why his father would not press home his advantage. There was just the slightest stagger as the Knight stooped under the gatehouse, and then Lacutus realised what was happening. He turned and ran for the steps.

* * *

He reached the Sanctuary just as *Wargod* came to a stop in the alcove. Lacutus raced up the stairs that ran around the wall, making for the Chamber of Echoes high above.

He had nearly reached the chamber when the door opened and his father, dressed in the armour he wore to pilot *Wargod*, to become one with the Knight Errant, staggered out of the chamber clutching his left arm. Even as Lacutus reached for him, his father collapsed, sliding down the stairs high above the Sanctuary. Lacutus threw himself to his knees, cradling his father in his arms. The lord governor reached for Lacutus' face, mouth moving as though he was trying to say something, and then died.

Lacutus knelt there for what seemed like a very long time, too numb for tears. Far below him he could see where the wounded had been laid out on the floor of the Sanctuary. He could hear people running up the stairs towards him. He was vaguely aware of Lydia standing over him, tears in her eyes.

'My lord…' she started.

Her words beat through his fugue. Lydia was talking to him. His father, his invincible, wise, ever-present father, was dead. He was now the lord governor. The fate of Leucosia was his responsibility, and though his father had routed the xenos forces, at the expense of his own life, there were still thousands of genestealers left beyond the walls of the castle. He could do no less than his father; he would give his last breath for those he was now honour-bound to protect. He just did not know if it would be enough.

RIVER OF DEATH

Anna Stephens

British fantasy author Anna Stephens expertly weaves conflict and tragedy with this tense, fast-paced story of survival in the face of hopeless odds.

Many of the Mortal Realms' greatest heroes are plucked from obscurity by tragic circumstance – Brida Devholm is one example of this. In her thrilling origin story, the young Brida scratches an existence as a rush-weaver in the great city of Demesnus in Ghyran. When an expedition on the River Quamus goes awry, Brida and her companions must fight the river's Chaos-tainted life tooth-and-nail to avoid consumption by the foul servants of the Plague God.

This story is considered a prequel to Anna's previous story 'The Siege of Greenspire', which appears in the anthology Oaths and Conquests*.*

'Won't his lordship get blisters on those soft hands of his?' Sati asked with a sneer.

Brida groaned. 'Don't be like that, Sats, please,' she begged. 'Eron Rush is a good man.'

Sati curled her lip but relented when Cahn, her brother, kicked her ankle. A faint blush stained the young woman's cheeks and, despite herself, Brida was glad. The twins were her oldest friends, but they both thought her marrying into one of Demesnus' ruling families was a mistake, a betrayal of the poor weavers and fishers she'd grown up with.

The burden of their resentment bit at her. Brida rubbed her palm over her lips, feeling those calluses that Eron didn't have snag against her skin. Calluses from wielding the rush-knife, from tying knots, from punting, from weaving. From scratching a living in a city once a centre of learning and power. The birthplace, if legend was true, of Saint Garradan – Gardus Steel Soul – himself!

But despite the care and wise governance of the Rush family, Demesnus was a shadow of its former glory. The city was famous for its weaving and basketry, yet the rushes that supplied their industry were failing, great swathes of them dying year after year, irrespective of their hardiness and ability to spread far and wide along the edges of the river. Some thought they had been harvested too heavily for too long, others that some new parasite or blight had found its way downriver.

Whatever was causing it, times had been especially lean this last year, and a small, selfish part of Brida acknowledged that marrying Eron Rush would put such concerns behind her. The thought shamed her; what about her friends? How would Sati and Cahn fare when they took over their parents' business? How would Brida's own family cope without her to cut rushes for them?

Cahn was laughing silently at her distraction, no doubt believing her daydreams had taken a different turn, and she felt a blush, hotter than Sati's had been, warm her cheeks, both at the implication and her own cowardice at not correcting his opinion.

She checked the binding that attached her rush-knife – a sickle as long as her forearm – to its pole, which was longer than she was tall, and listened to the twins' good-natured bickering as they waited for Eron to arrive. He'd do so in a flap, Brida knew with a secret smile: he hated being late, but he hated getting up early even more, and to get all the way to the eastern docks on the River Quamus for dawn was more than he could manage.

And then there he was, the mist cutting the brightness of the sun so it didn't flare in the burnished red of his hair the way she liked. Instead it was dull with moisture, but his eyes were alive – apologetic and laughing both. He faltered a little at the sight of Sati and Cahn, then came resolutely forward with an engaging grin. Sati was at the pole and Brida shot her a warning glare. She wouldn't put it past her friend to rock the punt as Eron clambered in.

She needn't have worried. Eron sprang off the quay into the middle of the boat with ease, balancing against its movement with unconscious grace. It impressed the twins. It did something far more interesting to Brida's stomach, but she swallowed against it and the resurgent blush.

'I'm so sorry I'm late,' he babbled, snaking an arm around her waist and kissing her cheek, the corner of her mouth. He let go before she could push him away and advanced on the twins, hand out. 'I'm Eron. Brida's told me so much about you.' He patted the satchel slung over his shoulder. 'I brought supplies so we can stay out all day. Pies, cheese, apples, salted pike. Even some beer.'

Cahn's mouth dropped open. 'Well,' he managed, standing to shake Eron's hand, 'that's a good start.'

Sati was more reluctant, her expression promising Eron all sorts of pain if he hurt her friend. Eron pressed his lips together and gave her a solemn nod, a silent oath. Sati's eyes narrowed a little, but then she huffed and shook his hand too. Brida released her breath.

'All right, daylight's burning,' she said briskly. 'Let's get moving. Sats, you've got the pole. Cahn and I will row until we reach the reed beds.'

'I'd like to do my share,' Eron said, and sat down at the oar before she could protest. Cahn shrugged and took the other, leaving Brida with nothing to do but navigate and hope they'd all get along. It was disconcerting. It was wonderful. Mostly, it was terrifying.

The morning brightened as they moved upriver from Demesnus, Cahn making Eron work hard to match his rhythm. Her fiancé was soon sweating and his smile had become a rictus, but he didn't complain and he didn't slow. He was the outsider here, and it seemed he was determined not to embarrass himself.

They all fell silent as they passed a huge reed bed. The tall brown stems were soft, bending over under the weight of their own heads. Brida knew from frustrating experience they would fall apart if she tried to weave with them, and anything she did make would hold a strange, bitter scent unlike anything she'd ever smelt before. Many of the oldest weavers were worried by the unknown blight, muttering prayers to the Lady of Leaves for intervention. Demesnus had enjoyed peace and prosperity for many years, and Brida worried that that time was coming to an end.

'Hey, Eron. Heard of the River-Watcher?' Sati broke the silence and they all jumped.

Eron nodded, grave. 'I have,' he said solemnly. 'The spirit of the Quamus. Some say he's a sort of god. That in return for an offering he will ensure a fruitful harvest from the river.'

Sati's eyes narrowed. 'Wrong,' she said. 'He's a spirit all right, and he demands offerings, but they're to stop him upending your boat and dragging you to the bottom of the river. He eats the unwary, they say. The unlucky. Those whose offering isn't proportionate to their status.'

Eron stopped rowing and they drifted slowly. Brida stood up, ready to intervene. 'Then I suppose I should make an offering that's appropriate, shouldn't I?' Eron asked. 'What would you suggest?'

Sati pursed her lips and Brida groaned inwardly. Her friend's impulsiveness had got them all into trouble more times than she cared to remember, and she had no idea what Sati might suggest to see how far she could push Eron, the rich man who'd stolen Brida away.

'Your dignity,' Sati said.

'Sats,' Brida warned, but Eron interrupted.

'A mighty offering indeed for one so stiff-necked and unfamiliar with the real work done by the good people of Demesnus,' he said, and before anyone could comment, he stood up and stripped off his coat. 'River-Watcher, accept my dignity as your offering,' he called, and belly-flopped into the water.

The boat rocked and Sati flailed to regain her balance, her mouth an 'O' of astonishment as she clung to the punt's pole.

Cahn began to roar with laughter as Eron surfaced and paddled for the side, his mouth tight with pain from the impact and a string of weed clinging to one ear. He hauled him on board and gave the other man an approving slap on the back. 'I'd say your dignity was well and truly offered, Eron,' he said approvingly. 'I'm glad too. If you'd offered the beer instead, well, we could never have been friends.'

Sati grunted, but couldn't help smiling as Eron shuddered in feigned horror at the weed festooning him. 'You're all right, rich man,' she said after a pause. 'But best get back on that oar if we're to get any work done today.'

'As you command, Lady Sati,' Eron said.

The twins laughed and Brida felt a knot of tension loosen in her chest. 'You're an idiot and I love you,' she murmured, planting a kiss on his wet cheek.

'And you're beautiful,' he murmured back through chattering teeth. 'Now get out of my way, woman, and let me row like the man I am.'

* * *

They were half a mile from the healthy reed beds when the flat-bottomed punt rocked so hard that Cahn's oar came up out of the water. Eron yelled in surprise, letting go of his oar to grab the bench and the punt's side. Sati clung to the pole, pushed deep into the riverbed. Brida, in the square prow, disappeared into the water with a splash.

It was shockingly cold this far out on the wide, swift river, and her disbelief at being knocked overboard – Brida prided herself on her skill as a sailor – meant she just hung in the water for a second. She opened her eyes; they must have hit a submerged branch or something, because there weren't any sandbanks on this part of the Quamus.

Nothing. Brida kicked for the surface, her troggoth-hide boots threatening to drag her down. Her head broke the surface and she gasped in a breath, looked for the punt. Three worried faces peered down at her.

'Brida!' Eron called.

She flailed a hand in acknowledgment. 'I'm fine. Steady the boat.' She had both hands on the side when something brushed past her legs – something big, muscular. A long, sinuous shape moved beneath her and the boat, grey and green. 'Get me out,' she said and the urgency in her voice had Cahn leaping to her side. He dragged her into the punt. 'There's something down there. It's big,' she stuttered, shuddering.

'Get on the oars,' Sati ordered and Eron slunk back to the bench. They weren't fishers, weren't equipped to deal with some of the river monsters inhabiting the Quamus. Rush-knives were one thing, but it was more prudent to just leave the creature to its own devices. They rowed hard, angling for the reeds and the illusion of safety. They didn't make it.

Sati shrieked as the pole was ripped from her hands and

then snapped like a twig. The brown water churned and a grey-green flank turned in the morning sun and was gone – beneath them. The four of them clung to the sides on instinct, riding the next impact, which sent the punt lurching cross-current. Eron and Cahn fought the oars to drag them back on course.

Another impact spun them the other way and they all saw it this time, the muscular body whipping through the water, longer than the punt – a freshwater eel mutated, grown to monstrous size and malevolent intent.

'Everyone quiet,' Brida whispered and they waited, oars in the water but not pulling.

'I think we're all right,' Cahn started, but the boat rocked again, the wood echoing to the dull boom of the eel's strike. A tail flicked up and around, scything towards the men in the waist. Eron grabbed Cahn and jerked him sideways, almost into his lap, and the tail flapped down, smashing the bench where he'd been sitting. It wriggled and was gone.

'Circling,' Sati called, her voice throbbing with fear. 'It's coming back. Row!'

'Ship those oars,' Brida countermanded. 'We're going to need them.' She stood, legs spread for balance, and hefted her rush-knife. The long handle gave her a six-foot reach and the blade had a wicked edge. She watched the river intently, blinking away the freezing water leaking from her hair. The twins both took up their knives and Eron hefted an oar with awkward resolution. They all stared down at the river as the punt slowly spun and began drifting downriver with the current, back towards Demesnus.

'Port!' Sati cried.

'Starboard!' Eron yelled at the same time.

'Which is it?' Cahn demanded, but then the boat shuddered,

the planks splintering as the eel drove into the side. 'We've got a leak!'

Brida glanced back. It was more than a leak; water was pumping from between two planks faster than they'd be able to bail. If the eel was prepared to let them bail. She saw its blunt head and square mouth arrowing through the water away from them, and the long, powerful body sliding after. Her heart was in her throat, beating so hard it was difficult to breathe.

'Twins, take position fore and aft the bench,' she croaked as it headed for them again. 'Eron, both oars, row for your life. There's an island ahead, I'll guide you in. Sats, port side – Cahn, take starboard. Slash don't hook. We don't want to drag it on board or we're all dead.'

The warm brown of Sati's face had curdled to sickly grey, but she balanced easily against the rocking, rush-knife poised.

'Careful, careful,' Cahn was muttering as Eron grunted at the oars, pulling fast and smooth while Brida threw handfuls of water out of the bottom of the boat. It was covering the tops of their feet already. If the eel managed to hit the same spot again, the punt would come apart.

Even at the height of summer, the sun wouldn't have been strong enough to cut through the chill she felt as the thing's back breached the river and she saw, clearly for the first time, that the green speckling wasn't a pattern on its scales, but rot. Gangrene. Plague.

'Alarielle save us,' she breathed and then Sati was swinging, blade winking golden as it disappeared below the surface and beneath the creature's body to slice upwards, rolling it and opening grey flesh and green putrescence. Blood gouted from its flank and, maddened by its wound or Nurgle's Rot – for it could be nothing else – it bashed its deformed, monstrous head against the punt over and over, coiling its massive body to flail at the underside.

Brida saw it foul the oar and began to shout a warning, but then the oar snapped in half with horrific force, the handle slamming up into Eron's face and knocking him off the bench. Cahn grabbed the remaining oar and hit the eel as it passed beneath them again. Brida splashed to Eron and dragged his head up so he didn't drown. He was unconscious and bleeding.

The Chaos-addled fish rammed them again, staving in three planks so the river poured through the gap. They were going down.

'Take him,' Brida shouted at the twins. 'I'll keep it busy on the starboard side. Slip out on the other and make for the island.'

'*That* island? They say it's haunted–' Cahn began, horrified.

'*Go!*' Brida screamed, because their own ghosts would haunt the river if they didn't. She had the rush-knife in one hand and the broken oar in the other. The eel lifted its head from the water, gills flapping obscenely. It watched her and she watched it, both poised, both waiting. It was just a fish, but there was intelligence there. Malevolence.

The deck rocked as the twins lowered Eron and themselves into the river with the punt between them and the monster and the island only a hundred yards away. They could make it. They *would* make it. They'd be safe. Brida didn't let herself think any further than that. The eel's head lowered so its gills lipped at the water, and she feinted with the oar, swept the rush-knife around instead. She caught the thing with the outside, false edge, knocking it away instead of slicing it open.

It dropped below the surface and Brida felt it pass beneath the boat, felt its intent. There was easier prey to be had. Prey that swam fast – for a human – but was encumbered with an unconscious man.

'No,' Brida breathed. She dropped the oar, ripped the knife free from the long handle and dived into the river, wrapping her arms and legs around the eel's tail as it flashed by beneath. She had time for one breath before it twisted and was on her, head slamming into her leg and teeth just missing flesh.

Brida hooked the sickle underneath the churning body and jerked upwards, felt the bitter edge bite in, and sawed it frantically back and forth. Green blood bloomed in the murky water and the eel thrashed, more concerned now with throwing her off. Brida tightened her legs and arm around it and kept cutting. It was longer than the punt, thicker around its middle than her thigh, and it was all lean, packed muscle. It gave a single, mighty contortion and threw her clear.

Brida struggled to the surface, dragged in air and looked around. The island was only a few strokes away – the eel had brought her right to it. She kicked desperately as Cahn splashed back into the shallows armed with a heavy stick. Then Sati darted past him, grabbed Brida's hand and hauled. Her knees caught on the riverbed and she kicked, pushed, knife-hand squelching down into the mud. Cahn bellowed and she heard the stick swing down and crack into something with a meaty thud. Water roiled and thrashed and then the big twin raced back, grabbed Brida under her other arm and, together, they got her to shore.

They didn't stop once they were past the tideline, though Brida had swallowed half the Quamus and could barely breathe. Instead, Cahn threw Eron over his shoulder like a bushel of reeds and they ran. Trees, dripping with moisture and bearded with moss, closed in around them and the rushing of the river, along with its cold breath, faded into silence broken only by their pounding footfalls and rasping breath.

They stopped in a small clearing and Cahn lay Eron on his side. His nose was mashed flat and the lower half of his face was coated in fresh blood, but his chest rose and fell. He lived. Brida let out a cry and dropped down next to him, her hands feverish on his face and chest even as she coughed and struggled for air. 'Eron? Eron, wake up. Please, Eron!'

Sati and Cahn were pacing the clearing, Brida's knife in Sati's hand. She could hear them muttering as they examined their surroundings, poking hesitantly into the undergrowth.

'Who are you?'

The three who were conscious screamed and spun to the source of the voice: a hunched figure in sweeping brown robes and a deep hood, gnarled hands clutching a driftwood staff. Nothing of its face could be seen.

'Who disturbs the River-Watcher's domain?'

'Alarielle save us,' Sati breathed, backing away until she almost fell over Brida and Eron. 'The stories are true.' Cahn retreated too and Brida stood up so they formed a barrier between the figure and her unconscious lover.

'Y-you're the River-Watcher?' Cahn stuttered. The hood nodded. 'Forgive us for trespassing, holy spirit. Er, god. We were…' He trailed off.

'Were what? Speak! Are you frightened?' the figure calling itself the River-Watcher asked. Brida's throat clicked as she swallowed, but none of them said anything. Then the figure laughed and swept back its hood to reveal a face thin and somewhat stern, yet not hostile. 'I am the guardian of the river and of the people who harvest its bounty,' he said. 'You will not come to harm from me, children. I am a friend.'

'We made an offering,' Sati began but Cahn elbowed her ribs. Their prank was no offering and they all knew it.

Brida took a threatening step forward as anger replaced the cold of the river upon her skin. 'Guardian? Then why have you allowed Nurgle's Rot to infect the Quamus once more? We were nearly killed!'

The River-Watcher's eyes narrowed and he swept his staff up and across his body. Brida flinched. 'Then it has returned again,' he growled. 'Go to my home, where it's safe. Along that path there, not far. I will be back once this atrocity has been dealt with.' He hurried off through the trees before they could respond.

'What in the realms is going on?' Cahn demanded when he'd vanished from view. 'That can't be the River-Watcher, can it? I mean, not really? It's just a story,' he added, almost pleading.

Eron groaned before anyone could answer him. 'You're awake,' Brida breathed, kneeling and using her sleeve to wipe some of the blood from his face. 'How do you feel?'

His eyes were already blackening from the blow to the face, swelling up until she could barely see the blue of his irises. He groaned again and flopped onto his back, then struggled to sit up. 'What happened?'

'The eel… the punt sank and we're stuck on this island and… and there's someone claiming to be the River-Watcher.'

Eron stared at her in confused dismay. 'River-Watcher? That was just a joke. It was just to make your friends like me.'

Brida shrugged, not knowing what to tell him. It was an old story, one every child learnt and believed for a few short years before growing up. Or at least, that's what she'd always thought. What all of them thought.

'Look, we're soaked, we've lost our boat and our supplies,

and we're trapped on an island with a madman claiming to be a local spirit,' Sati hissed, crouching opposite them. 'Whoever, whatever he is, he'll have a boat. We can use it to go home.'

Brida hesitated, then yawned, the terror and the cold catching up to her. 'Should we go where he said? His house?' she asked.

'I don't know if that's a good idea,' Sati said. 'I say we find his boat and get off this island before he comes back.' She didn't make a move towards the shoreline though; none of them did.

'We can't steal the River-Watcher's boat,' Cahn said slowly and slumped on Eron's other side, shivering.

'We should get warm,' Brida said dully. Eron was already asleep again. She stretched out next to him, huddling close. The twins crowded in on his other side. 'We'll have to move soon,' she mumbled. They slept.

It was almost dawn when Brida woke, passing from sleep to alert wakefulness in an instant. Her heart was pounding. She lay still, listening. The island was full of the rustles of small animals, insects, the first birdcalls. Eron was still warm beside her but there was… an absence. Slowly, carefully, she opened her eyes. The twins were gone.

Instinct told her to shout for them and shake Eron awake; with an effort she managed not to do either. They'd slept all night. They should have been too scared, too wary, to sleep at all. Brida rolled onto her back and examined the other side of the clearing through slitted eyes. There was a faint glow of firelight through the trees, the barest murmur of voices.

'Eron?' she whispered, scanning the trees. 'Wake up.' The voices abruptly fell silent, though they couldn't have heard her from so far away. She reached out without looking, shook Eron's arm. 'Wake up now.'

He tensed as he went through the same process upon waking. 'What's going on?' he breathed.

'I don't know. I think the twins are over–'

'Here,' Sati said loudly and they both jumped, rolled over. She laughed at their expressions. 'Finally awake,' she added as Cahn joined her. He held a flaming torch and the smiles they both wore made Brida uneasy. A touch too wide, a fraction too excited.

'Look at your face!' Cahn exclaimed, shoving the torch close to Eron and whistling. In its light, Brida could see the swelling and bruising around his nose and eyes was even worse. 'Not so pretty now, is he?'

'Sun's coming up,' Eron said as they both stood. 'We should look for a way to get home.'

'Not yet. The River-Watcher's making you breakfast – you've got to try some, it's delicious. Come on.' Sati was beckoning, already turning away towards the crackle of the campfire through the trees.

'We don't have time for breakfast,' Eron protested. 'Our families will be frantic.'

Cahn's easy-going smile evaporated. 'We're not all so fortunate in our families as you, councilman's son. If we want to stay here for a few days, that's what we'll do. You can swim back for all I care. Swim or drown.'

'Cahn!' Brida said, shocked.

The big man shook his head, puzzlement creasing his features. He forced a laugh and gave a half-shrug. 'Only joking, Eron, no offence intended. Come on, let's eat. We're starving.'

He turned away with the torch before either of them could respond, leaving them in the dawn's gloom beneath the trees.

Eron put his hand on Brida's arm, stilling her. 'If they've eaten already, why are they hungry? And why did we fall asleep so easily? I don't like this, Bri.'

Brida licked her lips. 'Me neither. Let's get the twins away from this so-called River-Watcher and find a way home. I don't like it, but we can steal his boat if we have to.'

Eron nodded and they followed their friends to the small clearing near the one where they'd slept. The River-Watcher's hut stood in a gap between two monstrous, twisted willows whose branches hung down to conceal most of the structure. In the centre of the clearing a small fire burnt in a ring of stones, and around the edge bigger stones were placed as seats. The River-Watcher and the twins were already resting, legs stretched towards the warmth of the fire. All three were eating from stone bowls perched in their laps.

The River-Watcher's hood was back in place, only the tip of his nose and point of his chin limned in orange firelight. They ate intently, paying no attention to the new arrivals. Two stones had been left free: one between the River-Watcher and Sati, the other between Sati and her brother. On each stone stood a bowl, steam curling gently from its contents.

Splitting us up. The thought came to rest in Brida's mind like a bird roosting, and once there, it wouldn't go away. *They're making us sit apart from each other.*

'What's for breakfast, then?' Eron asked cheerfully and she shot him a worried glance.

'Stew,' Cahn said, his mouth full. 'Fish stew. It's incredible.'

'Eat as much as you want,' the River-Watcher said, indicating the cauldron on the fire. 'There's plenty. Eat until you burst!' The twins laughed as if they'd never heard anything so funny.

Brida didn't know what to do. She approached the circle

and picked up a bowl, sat gingerly on the edge of the stone, feet gathered beneath her and ready to leap up and away. The bowl was cold despite the steam rising from inside, chilling her fingers.

Eron picked up his own bowl and sniffed the contents, then grinned at the twins and strolled around the circle to Brida's stone. 'Shove up,' he said, nudging her, and she scooted over until they could both – just about – sit down, pressed together at shoulder and hip and thigh. He leant in to kiss her cheek. 'Don't eat it.'

The words were more breath than sound, but they sent another tremor through her. She lifted the spoon to her mouth and pretended to eat in a pantomime that would fool no one. The twins were oblivious, scraping the last of the stew from their bowls and then licking their spoons.

'So good,' Sati said again. She patted her stomach. 'Could I…' She indicated the cauldron and the River-Watcher waved her on. She refilled her bowl and Cahn's and again they began to eat.

'You're not hungry?' the River-Watcher asked when the sun had risen into the river-mist, diffuse as candlelight through silk.

Eron and Brida jumped. 'Not really,' Eron said and touched his face. 'It seems that breaking one's nose robs one of appetite. It is no comment on your hospitality, which is excellent and appreciated,' he added as everyone turned to stare at him. He was using the voice he spoke in when trading – relaxed and friendly, hiding a steel mind behind a façade of benign interest. It told Brida how worried he was. And Eron didn't get worried; it's why she loved him, his quiet competence, his calm in the face of challenges. She could see the tremor in this Eron's hands, the glisten of sweat on his unshaven upper lip.

Not just worried. Scared.

'And you?' the River-Watcher asked, and though she couldn't see his eyes beneath his hood, his gaze upon her was as heavy as lead.

She swallowed. 'I... no, thank you.' It wasn't an excuse – she didn't have an excuse, had no idea what she could say, but movement from the twins broke the moment. They were at the cauldron again and this time they hauled it off the fire, fingers and palms blistering against the hot metal. Brida clearly heard the sizzle of flesh burning. She gasped.

Sati and Cahn dipped their hands into the scalding stew and pulled up gobbets of fish and vegetables, cramming them into their mouths, bickering and snarling at each other as they fought over the choicest meats. Meat...

Brida tipped her bowl into the light and squinted. Grey flesh, tinged here and there with green she'd originally taken for cress or dandelion tips. The eel...

Without thinking, she stood and hurled the bowl as far from her as she could, desperate only to be rid of the tainted stuff. Eron was up a second later, but his bowl sailed through the air and struck the River-Watcher hard in the face so he fell backwards off his stone. Eron lunged around the fire and snatched up the rush-knife from its place near Sati and then grabbed Brida and hustled her backwards.

The twins had stopped eating, poisoned flesh dripping from their mouths and fingers. Very slowly, their gazes switched from the River-Watcher's prone form to Brida and Eron. As his head came around, she saw Cahn's eyes were leaking pale green tears. They rose to their feet with an inhuman fluidity, as if their bodies contained thousands of tiny bones like a snake's.

Eron brandished the knife at them and pushed protectively

in front of Brida. There was the sound of cloth tearing. Over it a different sort of tearing – wetter, meatier. To their right, the River-Watcher rose to his – its – feet, the robe splitting and falling from its bloating flesh.

If it had ever been human, it had been aeons ago. If it had ever been beautiful, it was but a maddening, distant memory subsumed in filth. Wide mouths ripped open in its sickly flesh as it grew ever larger, gaping grey lips rimed with rotten blood out of which putrid entrails bulged. The hair on its head was stringy and a shocking blond, the final vestige of its former humanity. Fingers as thick as bulrushes clicked and flexed, ragged black talons punching through the ends and reaching for them.

Its head swelled, cheeks and nose spreading until the eyes were almost hidden. Its throat distended like a bullfrog's, but no words emerged – instead a tide of pus, acrid enough to sting their eyes, gushed from its mouth onto the grass, blackening it instantly. It beckoned to them.

Brida tore her gaze from Nurgle's disciple as Eron stiffened. Sati was smiling, a hungry feral rictus. Her fingers stretched and then hooked, the flesh opening at the knuckles and weeping black blood. 'Hungry,' she growled. 'So hungry.'

She took a shambling step towards them, her belly suddenly distended and flopping over her waistband, an empty sac begging to be filled. Next to her, Cahn grunted as one of his eyes exploded, spraying thick, viscous liquid into the fire to hiss and squeal as though it were alive. They advanced; so did the Rotbringer.

Eron flailed his hand back and found Brida's, gave it a desperate squeeze. 'Go,' he yelled as Sati lunged, hooked fingers clawing for his face and screaming her hunger on blasts of foul breath.

He swung the knife, the outside edge smacking her hands away, and then Brida was running, and he was on her heels, and they were racing headlong through the trees blanketing the island, no destination in mind, nothing but to get away, get far away and never look back.

The Rotbringer's unearthly laughter rose behind them, laughter that bubbled and gasped through a pus-filled throat, great dolloping splats of putrid mirth. Beneath his retching, the drumming of pursuing feet.

'Head for the river,' Eron panted as they raced through the trees ahead of the twins.

'The eel,' Brida gasped back, but of course it was dead – the Rotbringer had fed it to her friends. She screamed as a branch whipped into her face beneath her eye. Tears blinded her but she stumbled on, Eron's fist in her sleeve as he dragged her faster and faster through the trees and around the undergrowth. Ghyran's voracious plant life seemed as healthy as ever, but Brida didn't trust anything now. Already Nurgle's Rot could be seeping into her skin from the cut beneath her eye, could be changing her from the inside out, changing her into a monster dedicated to Chaos. One of Nurgle's putrescent little pets.

She sobbed and concentrated on running. Thoughts like that would ensure one thing only – that she never left the island alive. The trees grew thicker as they ran, the occasional wink of the rush-knife in a patch of light the only leavening of the gloom. The sound of pursuit had broken up and Brida knew the twins were flanking them – or herding them.

The air felt lighter over to their left, but Cahn was there, his tall, muscled frame appearing in flashes through the trees. That was the direction they needed to move, she was sure of it. She pushed hard until she was level with Eron, then dodged ahead of him and then left. 'This way,' she gasped and was gone, Eron's protest lost in the air behind her. He had no choice but to follow and she prayed to the Lady of Leaves she wasn't leading him to his death.

Cahn let out a hungry, joyful bellow as they veered towards him. Filthy claws tipped the ends of his fingers and he swiped at them, too far away to cause any damage – yet. He too had a hanging flap of belly just waiting to be filled with their meat and bones, and it slapped against his legs with every stride, hampering his progress, slowing him just enough that they had a chance. She was sure they had a chance.

Sati screeched from their right, far closer than Brida had expected.

'Eron!' Brida yelled.

'Go,' he shouted, 'go, *go!*'

Brida put on a final burst of speed, leaping tree roots and bursting through and over shrubs, hurdling vines that would tangle her feet and hold her fast for the untender mercies of her friends. She could see a splash of grey ahead – the River Quamus. She ducked under a hanging branch, sped over a patch of bindweed, and emerged onto the shore, the long, mud-and-sand spit between the forest and the water. It was empty – no boat, no driftwood large enough to float on.

'Keep going,' Eron panted behind her and together they pounded along the mud. 'Rushes.' He pointed with the knife for a second and Brida saw them, tall and brown and upright. A huge, thick stand of them right at the edge of the water.

She angled for them, head down and knees pumping, putting all her terror and confusion into the single, simple act of running. The twins' shouts were fading with distance, but she knew – somehow just knew – that they wouldn't give up.

They might have to walk, or crawl, or even drag themselves along by their claws, but they were coming. They wouldn't stop; they couldn't. Hunger, madness, Chaos, drove them.

Eron stopped her at the edge of the rushes and stuffed a flint and steel into her hands. 'Use the rush heads and stems and build a fire,' he said. 'Signal fire, something to drive them back. I'm going to make a raft.'

She hesitated. 'Rushes won't support our weight, Eron. We'll sink in seconds.'

'Just make a fire,' he snarled at her, his eyes wild and the knife raised. Brida lurched away, panic drawing an icy finger down her spine. 'I'll cut wood,' he added.

'You shouldn't – the Everqueen,' she began.

'Then I'll pray for forgiveness, but without it we die. Now help me,' Eron insisted. He didn't wait for her answer, instead running back to the treeline and hacking wildly at the lowest branches.

Brida used up precious seconds watching him and offering a prayer to the Lady for forgiveness and aid, then began ripping the thick fluffy heads from the bulrushes and stuffing them inside her shirt for safekeeping.

She hadn't gathered many before she spotted a thick shape bobbing in the water – the reed bed was the perfect collection point for driftwood. Brida splashed towards it and began hauling it back towards land. It could form the spine of the raft. Eron dragged over what he'd managed to hack from the trees and they piled it all together. Even with the driftwood it wasn't much, a pitiful collection of branches that didn't look as if it would support the weight of a child, let alone two adults.

Still, it was all they had and they were running out of time. 'I saw strangler vine just up there,' Brida said, gesturing back the way they'd come. 'Not far. Give me the knife – I'll cut as much as I–'

'I'll get it,' Eron interrupted and ran off before she could stop him.

Brida pulled the branches together into a narrow platform ready for tying and then set about making the fire, pausing every few seconds to scan the trees for Eron or their pursuers. One of Demesnus' swift trading ships might see it, or even a slow, flat-bottomed rush punt – someone, anyone to rescue them, to tell them it was all right, that they were safe.

The fire was tiny but bright in the early sun when Eron came staggering back, swathes of vines trailing from his arms. 'Hurry,' he gasped. 'I could hear them.'

Brida snatched the vines from him. Movements automatic after so many years weaving, and with a speed born of renewed terror, she lashed the branches together with the vines and pulled them tight. Narrow, so narrow. If they so much as breathed wrong, they'd capsize. And what if there was more mutated river life? Still, the choice was between angry fish and an actual Rotbringer and his… disciples. *My friends.*

Tears pricked Brida's eyes but she blinked them back savagely, then blinked again at the shapes scudding through the trees close by. 'They're here,' she hissed and shoved Eron in the back. 'Lift.'

They dragged the raft into the shallows and it dipped alarmingly beneath the surface before bobbing back up. 'I should stay,' Eron said. 'Make sure they don't catch up to us.'

'Shut up and get on,' she snapped, clambering aboard. He followed as shouts of triumph and then fury erupted behind them. Sitting cross-legged on the almost submerged raft, they used their hands to paddle out of the reeds. 'Angle across the current. Doesn't matter how far downriver it takes us as long as we reach shore.'

Behind them, that hacking laughter broke out again. 'Chase them down, my pretties. One bite and Grandfather's joy will have them and hold them tight. Let them carry it home within them, nestled deep in their meat and bones to grow and consume them until they too must feed or die. Feed and spread his rot. Faster, pretties, faster! Don't let them get away.'

Sati and Cahn – or what was left of them – splashed into the shallows and began wading out. As soon as their tainted limbs touched the water, it began to boil with frenzied life – fish and frogs sped away from the approaching pair, some leaping onto the raft in their desperation to escape.

'Alarielle, Lady of Leaves, please, please help us,' Brida prayed as they paddled, but the words stuck in her throat when Eron slipped off the raft. 'What are you doing?'

'Swap places,' he ordered, treading water and clinging to the side.

There wasn't time to argue, not with him in the river and vulnerable to whatever might be down there. Brida slid forward, wincing as splinters ripped into her palms and through her trousers. Eron hauled himself back on, facing the way they'd come, the rush-knife clenched in his fist. A second later Cahn was clinging to the raft, nearly upsetting it.

Eron roared and swung, the blunt edge of the knife chopping into the bloated fingers, mashing them flat. Cahn squealed and vomited blood and half-digested meat across the raft, but Eron hit him again, in the face this time, and he lost his grip.

Sati reared up in front of the raft and Brida lashed out with one foot, kicking her squarely in her keening mouth; her friend hung on and chewed through the thick troggoth-hide heel of her boot as if it were rice paper. She could hear Eron grunting as he lashed out with the knife at Cahn. Sati fell back with a splash as the heel sheared away and then bobbed back up, a rotten apple in a barrel. Brida kicked her again and this time her lower jaw ripped free, flesh tearing. Maggots oozed from the hole and plopped into the water to feed fish and infect them. Brida screamed; Sati sank and didn't come back up.

'Ahoy, the raft. Trouble?'

A low-sided fishing boat was tacking towards them. *'Help!'* Brida screamed with everything she had. *'Help us!'* Oars slid out to aid the sail and she could see nets and long, wickedly barbed harpoons being passed among the rest of the crew. The distress flag was raised and, in the far distance, Brida saw the yellow sails of Demesnus' fishing fleet begin to drift in their direction.

The water boiled apart ahead of her and Sati rose again, jaw rehung and slavering with famine and the need to infect. The water around them was alive with diseased fish. Eron slammed into Brida's shoulder almost hard enough to pitch her into the water, but the knife point came down into Sati's head and through her skull. She thrashed and flopped, blood gouting into the air and spraying from her screeching mouth before, still writhing, she sank again.

Brida stared after her for a long, disbelieving second before Eron yelled. She turned to see Cahn holding onto the rear of the raft, his massive hands crushing the branches and tearing at the vines, snapping them like cotton. The raft shuddered and the branches began to move apart. Eron threw himself flat on the raft, both arms outstretched to cling to the narrow platform and push it back together, using brute strength to prevent them from sinking.

Brida lunged over him and punched Cahn in the face,

bursting his other eye. He disappeared in a swirl of bubbles. She hesitated for a second, then scrambled to the front and began to paddle again, faster and harder than ever before. The fishing boat was near now, but it was slowing – harpoons were jabbing down into the water on all sides as eels and pike – and Cahn – hurled themselves upwards to attack the fishers. One woman was dragged screaming into the Quamus and the water around the boat quickly turned pink.

'Alarielle Everqueen, I'll serve you all my days if you lend us your aid,' Brida gasped. It was a poor prayer, but it was all she had time and breath for as she paddled madly. Shouts and screams erupted from the boat – not just that boat, but all the boats that had come to help – ringing in her ears and drowning out her prayer. 'Lady of Leaves, hear me. Save us, I beg you.'

Eron was grunting and cursing, the water lapping at his nose and mouth as he lay on the raft and held it together. Sobbing, shoulders burning, Brida paddled on, leaving the battle between the fishers and their prey turned predators behind. The sounds of fighting slowly faded, though whether with distance or because everyone was dead, she didn't know. Didn't want to know.

They were trapped in the fastest part of the current, too fast for a broken raft and an exhausted woman to combat when Demesnus slid past, far away across the river. With the last of her strength, Brida tried to reach it, but as the sun slid across the sky and Eron fell silent, it disappeared in their wake, oblivious to their fate.

The sun was low in the sky when the great river began to curve and Brida spotted the telltale sign of a sandbank stretching far out into the river and angled for it. Eventually they ran aground. It didn't matter that they were on the wrong shore. What did matter was that they were on land and they'd left the monsters behind them. They were safe.

Brida sat and let her head hang to her chest for a while, just breathing as the agony in her arms began to fade. Then she licked the sweat from her lip and crawled off the raft onto the sand. 'Eron? Come on, we're safe.'

He whimpered and rolled over onto his back, cradling his arms against his chest. Brida's heart stopped. Great chunks of flesh were missing from his forearms, a finger gone from his left hand. His flesh was decorated with human bite marks. He'd held on – he'd saved her – while Cahn *ate him*.

Brida dragged him off the raft onto the sandy bank. 'Rest, love. Just rest.' Working quickly, she used the rush-knife to cut off her sleeves and wrapped them around the worst of his wounds. Crude bandages, but all she had.

She made a fire and pulled Eron close to the flames, holding him tight. 'Sleep now, my love,' she murmured in a cracked voice as he lay in her arms, shaking and muttering. For what felt like the hundredth time since their ordeal had begun, tears pricked at her eyes. This time she let them come, watching through their veil as the sun set and the world shrank down to orange flames and black night.

By dawn he was raving, and by its first light she saw how the wounds were pus-filled and rotting, how his skin had taken on the pallor of a drowned corpse. Eron's eyes were milky-green and his lips pulled back from snapping teeth.

Brida was empty. She stood and stepped away, evading the hand that reached to snag her ankle. Hollow, she walked around the dead fire and picked up the rush-knife, returned and knelt before him like a supplicant. 'Eron? Can you hear me?'

Claws burst from the ends of his fingers and swiped at her; she swatted them away. 'Eron?' she tried again. 'Come back to me.'

He laughed, mad and malevolent. There was no sign of the man she knew and loved, the man she was to marry. Eron was gone.

She was raw, no more emotions left inside her, and she was glad of it. If she could feel, she wouldn't be able to act. Brida rose up onto her knees and placed the inner curve of the rush-knife against Eron's neck. She didn't look into the face she'd once thought to wake beside every morning for the rest of her life. Instead she drew the blade across his throat hard and swift, leaning back from the spray of blood so it didn't touch her skin.

She counted the beats left to his heart, shuffled back from the final grasping of his hand, not sure whether it was offered in love or hunger. Not willing to risk finding out. What did that make her? As much a monster as the Rotbringer, to deny a dying man final comfort.

But a monster with a purpose.

When Eron was dead, Brida stood and stared back through the mist in the direction of the island. She wasn't sure she'd ever feel anything again, but she knew what she wanted. Vengeance. If any of the fishers had made it back to Demesnus, the city was already dead, and she wasn't strong enough yet to fight the shambling, diseased remnants of the rest of her kin.

Brida needed to be stronger. Strong enough to fight the evil that had taken everything she loved. And she knew who could make her so. Who would raise her up and make her vengeance holy. She had sworn to serve the Lady of Leaves if she was saved, and she had been, though Eron had not.

And while his loss was a knife in her heart, Brida lived free of disease and free to take her vengeance in his memory.

She lifted her hands in supplication. 'Alarielle, Everqueen, I am yours to command. My life for you, my service in the destruction of your enemies. Forever.' She felt something, a brush across her senses, as of sunlight dappling through leaves. Acceptance. A binding.

Brida looked one last time at the corpse of her lover, all that remained of her life before, and then she began to walk. There was a Freeguild company camped a few days' west. She'd make a new future with them. One written in blood.

RESPITE'S END

Marc Collins

Scotland-based Marc Collins – whose writing talents brought success in our Open Submissions – begins his Black Library journey with this gripping and thoughtful thriller from the 41st Millennium.

Respite is a model Imperial world. Its inhabitants are docile, obedient and disease-free, and quotas of invaluable medical supplies are consistently met, even exceeded, by the planet's industrious workforce. This is largely due to the efforts of Medicae Primus Arlen Cedano, whose ingenuity and unconventional experiments ensure the health and productivity of the population. However, the peace is shattered when a mysterious, highly virulent plague erupts, forcing Cedano to use all of his curative abilities to restore order. What's more, strange and disturbing transmissions are coming through the vox-network – it seems someone wishes to test their poxes against Respite's superior defences…

Respite was a world without night.

There was only eternal industry, the flare from spire-chimneys as they rendered the sky a greasy near-neon smear. Poison light bled into Arlen Cedano's chambers, as the shutters rose with their telltale clatter, and the first chimes sounded at the shift change.

Arlen glanced up from his writing desk, vaguely amused to notice the time. He had sat down to amend his notes at the end of the manufactorum cycle and now the dawn sirens were droning out across the complex. 'Foolish of me,' he muttered and stood, stretching. He was no longer a young man, and yet he often found himself working through the night – poring over shipping schedules, alchemical formulations and research proposals. He reached into a drawer and drew out an auto-narcotic phial, looking at it with weary familiarity. 'Foolish of us, old friend.' He braced his hand against his throat, and let the needle bite.

He felt the concoction hit his bloodstream in a rush of liquid fire. His pupils contracted madly in chemical sync, and his vision blurred. He blinked away tears, and ran one hand over his bare, suddenly sweating, scalp. *Prime*, he called it, an inoculation against idleness. The great macro-medicae forges of Respite had borne many fruits down the peaceful years of service, and Prime possessed the greatest utility – for workers in their multitudes, or singular minds such as his. He let his hands clench, flex, clench again.

The fog lifted, and he paced to the ablutionary chamber. He splashed his face with cold water, ignoring the chemical tang of it on his lips, shaking himself. He could feel the sensation of every droplet on his skin with almost terrifying clarity. Arlen looked at his haggard reflection in the mirror: grey eyes, the lines in his pallid skin. He sighed softly and wondered how long rejuvenat and determination would keep him going.

The insistent pulse of a message alarm startled him as he dabbed at his damp skin, and he grabbed a tunic before heading to the door. When it opened, a dark-haired aide was looking at him expectantly. Her arms bristled with data-slates and report wafers. She smiled apologetically. 'Forgive me, medicae primus. I didn't wish to disturb you so early, but matters require your attention.' She held them out, and Arlen nodded distractedly. There was something at the edge of awareness, a whispered summons scratching at his mind. He looked at her, and she smiled, unaffected. Unaware.

'Thank you, you are to be commended.' The girl beamed. 'Have them brought to my office. I have business to attend to first, then I shall be with you. Time and tithe wait for no one.'

'As you will, medicae primus.' She bowed, turning away

from the door, and Arlen looked back with a sigh. *It never ends, but then would I want it to?*

Arlen walked the corridors of Valderos Macro-Alchemical #1, crowds of menials parting around him as they trudged towards shift work. Cleansers idled as they scrubbed at the floors, jaws slack while brushes scratched against the cold stone and steel. Only the occasional worker nodded to him, acknowledging him by rank or name, their minds sharper.

The facility sprawled across Respite, a body carved of metal and willpower, fuelled by the ceaseless movement of labour. Crowds passed by winding filtration systems that glowed with strange inner lights, pipes weaving upwards with capillary grace. They moved under heaving coolant plants, with their mists and vapours, nestled like organs. The chill never crept into his bones; he felt nourished as he passed through it, tasting a semblance of the void's comforting embrace.

While the herd continued on, Arlen turned down a narrow side corridor, through the workings of the factorum itself. Lume-globes burned low and red as he passed below their stunted light, beneath the great vanes of stills and macro-alembics. He stood before a door, ornate and gilt-edged, letting his fingers drift down the heraldic device set into its centre. A familiar sight across these stars, across the manifold worlds of men. He traced its twinned heads and sharp edges, the reassuring depiction of a healer's helix, then to the wings behind it. It was a powerful symbol, one to endure even the most bestial of wars that threatened them. Before it he stood taller, a strength filling him that no chemical stimulant could ever replicate. Arlen held up his wrist and a scanner recognised the coiled electoo with a chirrup. The door opened, and he stepped forward into the sanctum.

The chamber before him was older than the rest of the manufactory that had risen around it – a gnarled bone bracing the flesh of the future. These had been the early laboratoriums, where the Creed had flourished, and they had grown in the intervening years. Rationality vied for space with religious trappings, islands of science amidst the air of temple superstition. Great containment tubes rose like columns, studded with wires. Things moved in the murk, or hung limp and unresponsive. Attendants and physicians bustled from one bench to another, considering results, or hunched over blood-slicked vivisection tables. Arlen smiled to see it, the labours of his kind. He shrugged off his tunic, extended his arms, and medic-serfs moved wordlessly to dress him.

The first sensation was the needle's sting along his spine, the cold metal of the armature against his skin – pain and numbness joined in the joy of re-communion. One serf held it as it bonded, while the other fitted the collar about his neck. There was another *click-hiss* of connection, nestling over the morning's injection site. Arlen rolled his neck slightly, adjusting to the weight of the device. He looked down as he heard the clatter of glass, and the last components locked across his shoulders. The chem-globes and bio-dispensers adorned him like the baubles of some ancient king, or a beast's warning colours. The final attendant handed him a fresh tunic and coat, and he accepted them both. 'Thank you, my children,' he whispered, and they responded with a zealot's awe.

'It is our honour, biophagus majoris.'

Arlen passed beneath arches of black iron and bone, the interred remains of the first martyrs to the new Vejovian science that had reinvigorated their world. Some were stunted things questing for perfection, while others bore smooth, flowing crests. They were an inspiration. Every time he passed, he understood their sacrifice, the progress of the Creed writ in death. He moved beneath the eyes of evolution until he came to the chamber's core, and the fragment of genetic purity around which their efforts orbited.

Vector Phi, their magus, was awe-inspiring. She floated in the amniotic tank, suspended somewhere between angelic rapture and burgeoning chrysalis. Her flesh was pale, hairless, coloured only by the violet fluid that surrounded her. Glassy eyes stared *through him*, un-seeing and all-seeing. Her awareness dwarfed him, forced him to his knees. He heard the whispered voice again as she graced him with the communion of the broodmind rather than base flesh-speech, his mind expanding in unity with hers.

+Arlen, my child, my father.+ He smiled; so many of the later generations, the ruling aspects of the cult, had been forged of his genetic experiments, given life in nutrient tanks and splice dishes. They were as much his children of the needle, as they were scions of the Helix. +How do our civilian concerns fare?+

'Well. Yes, quite well.' His head remained bowed, unwilling to look up at her avataric perfection. 'Exports remain steady. There have been no external inquiries.' He paused, weighing his words. 'We have overcome the setbacks from last month's meteorite impact. Queveron Production Hub has repaired the damage and restored itself to full operation. Void anti-emetics and pain-relief supplies have been dispatched to the Fifteenth Hydran Rifles at Rathla. All saturated. Within the year, we will have them.'

+Admirable. Within and without, our strength grows. The Deucalion Expanse knows the enlightenment of the Credo Vejovian, and the blessing of the Twisted Helix. He is pleased.+

Arlen looked up at her words, as something stirred in the darkness behind the great tank. The bloated shadow moved with a power and intelligence unmatched upon Respite, so graceful that he had not even noticed its approach. A primal shard of divinity, the pinnacle of their ambitions. The core of their faith nosed the air, tongue lolling from its mouth as though it could taste him. The progenitor watched him for a moment and he felt its scrutiny. Before it he was laid bare. He felt its psychic touch recede, and then it retreated through another arch of brick and bone. He finally allowed himself to breathe at the passing of a god.

'If it pleases you, I have arranged for the next rounds of inculcations. Support staff, mostly. Those who show promise despite the soporific intake. Hard workers all, minds yearning for purpose.'

The voice burbled with mirth inside his skull. +So even-handed with your blessings, Arlen. Your dedication shames many others. Though you must remember the credo – there are kin, and kine. Not all deserve our gifts, we must–+ She paused, hesitating as the first bells rang. Arlen had never heard them before, the muted, ancient alarm, dredged up as though from nightmare.

'What is that? Those bells never ring.' He looked around, as other biophaguses and their attendants started, confused. Guards straightened, while others clutched at helical symbols or muttered prayers.

+It has not sounded since our earliest days here. It is the Bell of Sorrows. It heralds disease within our blessed protectorate.+

'That's impossible. We have sheltered them from harm, we have kept the people hale.'

Arlen blinked, shook his head.

'There is no sickness here.'

Respite had known no ailment since the Twisted Helix caught it within its coils; a healthy populace was compliant and well prepared for the inevitable days of Biological Sublimation. Biophaguses maintained the drug regimens and clinics that kept them healthy, but there was always a divide.

It was as Vector Phi had said; there were kin and there were kine – exalted luminous beings and the base and bestial flesh. They were weak, fundamentally mortal, but a threat in their flailing multitudes. The Helix-touched could not afford to see them sicken, panic and die. Arlen gathered a small squad of sanctum guards, leading them towards the lower wards and the alarm. Whatever else he was, he was still a healer.

The tunnels beneath the mega-manufactories were inconstant, littered with dead ends and alcoves. Dust and cobwebs hooded the lights, pipes gurgled with runoff, and strange fogs coiled up from vents and drains.

Arlen and his escort pushed on towards the source of the disturbance, sanctified men all. Vox-links clicked as they moved, the guards talking amongst themselves. Worrying. The sound of the bells carried eerily, drawn out and made stranger by the acoustics of the underway. They wound their way down, spiralling into the darkness and the rot.

As they moved, the sounds of the alarms faded, beneath a low atonal moaning. The sounds of human agony, the dull bleating he had learned to live with. 'This way,' he breathed, and the guards followed without hesitation. The front two raised their lasrifles, while others dragged crates of medical supplies. They passed nests where acolytes had gathered, the blessed misshapen, to watch their intrusion. The acolytes nosed the air and keened, aware of the wrongness in their world.

We have ensured that this world is a paradise for those who toil for us! We have kept them quiescent. Tended their every need. How could this happen? Arlen could not put aside the doubts. Had they erred?

The door ahead lay half-open, and Arlen saw the bodies as he entered. Most were writhing, ever in motion. They coughed, spluttered and moaned, thick mucus streaking their chins or pooling on their chests. Bleary, bloodshot eyes looked up at him, full of pain and the yearning for comfort.

'Pater!' one of them crooned as he noticed Arlen, and the cry was taken up by the others. The air rang with the chorus of it, abating the sounds of agony. The rhythm of the word was like the pounding of a heart. *Pater. Pater. Pater!*

'Hold still.' Arlen muttered, his hand on the weeping man's shoulder, while fussing with the injector. He forced it to the victim's neck, depositing a mild anaesthetic while another needle dipped, and drew blood. He had to keep them calm, but he needed to understand. Was it contagion from the works? Chemical taint? Or from off-world? A darker cause?

There was a strange buzzing, like the wings of insects, though he hadn't noticed any on his initial inspection. The sound danced around the chamber; growing, changing, clarifying. He heard... laughing? He rounded on his aides. 'There is nothing amusing here!' They looked at him like he was mad, but he heard it. Again. The thick, mocking laughter flowed, and he became sickly aware that it was coming through his vox-bead. The man he was tending to spasmed, convulsing in seizure. Arlen struggled to hold him down, battered by bucking limbs. He jerked back as a fist collided with his skull. 'Hold him!'

Still there was the laughter. Hateful, tormenting, resolving slowly into a voice.

'Oh, Arlen.' It whispered, curdled like old milk and ancient spite. Arlen looked around at the patients. They had fallen deathly still; faces locked in rictuses, hideous strychnine grins. The guards shook and prodded at them, before retreating. Shaken. Terrified of the shadow of death.

'Do you like my opening move, in our little game?'

He sat alone in his private laboratorium, feverishly working over schemata and diagrams. He had torn the sacred, many-limbed depiction of Vejovian Man from the wall, replacing it with the documents that categorised the disease they faced. It was a coiled, terribly effective thing: morphogenic, hyper-infective. The only thing with similar adaptability was the holy germ-seed itself. He looked at the sprawl of data, spread across the walls like crawling mould. His stomach clenched; for a moment he feared the sickness was already within. Outside he could sense the psychic wailing of the broodmind, the frenzied communion between Vector Phi and the progenitor. If this continued, he would likely have to decant her.

'Arlen?' The voice hissed from the vox-emitter bolted into his desk, and he jumped back as though burned. *'I know you can hear me, Arlen. You alone are worthy of my attention here, such as it is. Do me the favour of at least engaging.'*

Arlen hesitated. He scribbled a single word on a scrap of paper and slammed it against the window to the outer sanctum. An assistant started at the sudden noise, blinked as he read the note, and then scurried off. Arlen waited till he was gone before picking up the broadcast horn. 'Who are you? What do you want?'

'Who am I? Well that is the question, isn't it? Who are any of us

truly? Are you Arlen Cedano, medicae primus of the salve-world of Respite? Biophagus majoris of the oh-so-holy touched of the Helix? Or just a man, flailing at the dark, convinced he is the light?' The toxic laughter burbled up again, filling the chamber in a heavy fug of bleak joy.

'You seem to know a lot about my world and my work. I should at least know the name of my admirer. This virus, it's your doing?' He gestured idly at the paper-colonised wall, more for his own benefit than his tormentor.

'Jast.' The word oozed out like an exhalation. *'You may call me Jast. It has served me long enough, it will suffice a trifle more.'*

'And what is it you want, Jast?'

The laughter returned, cruel and barbed. *'Isn't it obvious, Arlen? I want the world.'*

'The world?' Arlen blinked. 'A little artful biochemistry won't pry it from us. We are of the blood Vejovian – we have wrought divinity. You kill mind-dulled cattle – a loss certainly, but you cannot think to shake our order from the earth.'

It laughed again, and Arlen found himself despising the sound. Its crawling curdled sweetness. Wet and cloying like new rot. *'There is a broken beauty in you, Arlen. I have watched your world blossom from the bosom of malady, seen you pump poison and panacea into the Imperium's veins. Against such potential must the future be tested.*

'You have skill, Arlen. Let us cast it to the crucible. In suffering is advantage born.'

Death no longer scared Mortuary Clerk Dorval. It was an old friend, one he had looked in the eye a hundred times. The bodies before him, though, represented something else. A defilement beyond death.

The symptoms were odious. Widespread necrosis, threaded

through the organs to the point where it seemed the result of a long wasting sickness rather than a sudden total systemic collapse. Strange tumours flowered throughout the chest cavity of his current subject, and he lifted them cautiously with the blade of his scalpel.

'I've never seen a disease state quite like this before,' he muttered. His breath was close and tight in the confines of his respirator hood, the glass visor fogging. The anti-contamination gear made his movements clumsy, laboured, like walking underwater. It irked him. When the danger had passed he would petition Medicae Primus Cedano for a transfer; the older man had mentioned advancement before, induction into the mysteries of his special projects. He had put in his time, and he would be rewarded. He–

Dorval froze. There was a noise drifting through the mortuarium, a low rustling just out of sight. He turned, looking around, but he was alone. Alone with the dead. The drawers were silent, the cadaver-bags still on their slabs. There was only the cold tile, and the background reek of preservatives. He was safe; the dead could not hurt him.

He was turning back when it came again – louder, more insistent. The sound resolved, became familiar. He watched as the bags suddenly juddered and jerked, contents hideously in motion. There was a muted banging from within the drawers as limbs flailed at their confines, feet beating against the steel. He stumbled backwards, knocking over a tray of implements. Scalpels and bone-saws skittered across the tile. He felt something wet fill the suit with the stink of his own shame, barely able to stop sobbing.

He only began to scream when the body rose up before him and took hold of him.

* * *

'Yes. Of course. I understand.' Arlen had stopped truly engaging twenty minutes before. He gave token responses, and instead took notes as Jast rambled, threatened and cajoled. He was a determined orator, that much was clear, veering from pathological doctrine and religious fervour to intimate details of how he would vivisect the entire cult. Arlen only looked up when the door opened, and Heinrich sat opposite him.

The cult's clamavus, born of the Word Helical, was an odd sight in repose. His armour thrummed and clicked as it processed massed inloads of data. He toyed with the keypad chained at his wrist, fingers in constant motion. His eyes struggled to focus, and when they did they were black, pupils dilated as the information sieved through him. 'Your note found me. What do you require, biophagus majoris?'

'I've told you before to call me Arlen.'

'And I have told you before that hierarchy must be respected. How we order data is important – it shapes society, and so shapes victory.' He huffed, leaning back. The wan light of the chamber caught on the angular cast of his skull, making clear the gene-gifts of his generation. 'I ask again, you wished to see me? Why?'

'This.' Arlen waved his hand at the ongoing broadcast. 'There is an intruder. He's the source of the virus plaguing the underworks, the canker that threatens everything.'

'Are you there, Arlen?' The voice intruded again, and Arlen gestured for Heinrich to listen. *'Am I boring you? I would hate to think that you were not invested in this experiment of ours. You will be soon. The seeds are already planted, and when they blossom it shall be into a garden, worthy of his name. Stronger, and better. You should be proud, as you co-father the future.'*

His hand hovered over the horn. Heinrich nodded, and

Arlen took it up again, hearing the click as it engaged. 'I am here, Jast. I simply had to take down your… sermon. A most interesting faith that you practise. You must put great stock in it, to think that it can deliver you all that we possess.' He looked up; Heinrich was fussing with vox-baffles and signal splicers, brow furrowed as he carefully turned a dial. 'We will have the measure of your sickness. There is nothing that science cannot overcome. In the embrace of our most sacred gift, there can be no true infirmity of the flesh. There is only the Helix.'

'Shall we put that to the test? The next phase beckons. I have learned so much already.' Somewhere another klaxon began to ring. Automated voices joined it in a grating chorus, and Jast's laughter slithered behind the machine-parroted words.

Contagion. Contagion. Alert. Contagion in Core Mortuarium.

'Here is the game, Arlen. I will move, and you will oppose. Equals, opposites, as simple as a regicide board. Revelation is always painful, I know this myself, but in time you will all thank me, as I thank you.'

The line went dead. He looked up at Heinrich, who broke from his work to return Arlen's gaze. 'He's savvy, I'll give him that.' Heinrich breathed deeply. 'Hiding himself in our own systems, like a parasite. I can find him, but it will take time. Some creative systems analysis.'

Arlen swallowed hard, reached into the desk drawer, and drew out an autopistol. 'Find him.' The words left his lips in a snarl. 'Find him, while I undo what he has done.'

The mortuarium passages were cold and silent, lined with drawers, littered with abandoned trolleys. Arlen's makeshift fire-team pushed through the clutter, ten men of the Helix with flamers primed. Their leader, a hulking brute named Johan, grinned as he jostled the weapon, thrusting it at every shadow.

'Careful,' Arlen hissed. His gun was in his hand, its weight reassuring. There was a solidity to it that he clung to, beset as they were by the microscopic and the ephemeral. If Jast or his agents showed their faces, then he would end them. He would burn them from his world, cast the ashes before the progenitor and call it what it was. Justice.

Sometimes, one fought with needle, knife and vaccine; other times, the steady sword hand was required. Either way, the infection was driven out.

As they rounded the corner towards the Core Mortuarium, the group paused. A laboured shuffling greeted them, coming from the doors to the main chamber. The doors rattled open and a figure stumbled through, blood coating his containment suit, a ragged hole at the throat where something had torn through the material and the flesh beneath. Every weapon was raised as the figure sluggishly regarded them, dead eyes staring, already grey and unblinking. Arlen found himself thinking of Vector Phi's penetrating gaze. Bile rose in his throat at the blasphemy of it. His blood chilled. He knew this man, he was certain.

'Dorval?' he whispered. The dead thing turned, hearing without understanding, without knowing itself. It gave a snarl, shambling with greater urgency, arms outstretched, hands clasping. He could sense its feral hunger, the complete absence of any human sapience.

His hand was up before he was aware of it, already firing. He unloaded the pistol into the thing that had once been a colleague, someone he might one day have called brother. Arlen watched it falter, tumble, hitting the ground with a bloody thud.

'Burn it!' he snapped, surprising himself with his own vitriol. Johan grunted his assent and lumbered forward, tanks sloshing as he hefted the weapon. There was a splutter, like a consumptive's cough, and the flamer belched cleansing fire. The body crisped in the inferno as Johan directed the stream of burning flame onto it. The tiles blackened beneath it, cracking in the sudden furnace-rush of heat. He was so focused on the task that he never saw the other corpse as it barrelled through the doors towards him.

The pox-thing hurled itself through the flames, slamming against Johan as its arms wrapped around him. The man struggled, lost control of his weapon. There was the squeal of buckling metal as the cabinets were doused in fire, mixing with Johan's screaming. The corpse was one of the plague victims – its limbs emaciated, stomach distended with gaseous rot, gums drawn back over cracked teeth. It bit at him, blood spraying as it caught the artery, locked onto him like an animal. Arlen had no time to reload, his limbs were seized with shock. He could only watch as Johan grabbed for the fuel tank, and tugged the stop free.

The sharp smell of promethium drove back the stench of decay. The corpse looked up from the ruin of Johan's neck, from the flesh already beginning to putrefy, suddenly aware of the danger. They all ignited as the vapours caught, a sudden burst of light and sound that drove Arlen back onto the tiled floor. He flailed in panic, beating at the flames that had caught on his coat. More of them stalked through the tumult, passing through the fire that had consumed their fellows. It was almost as though they were learning, adapting. An immune response crafted from disease and ruin.

They laughed as they advanced – a brittle chuckle that was not their own bubbled up from ruined throats, behind the chorus of impossible wings. Arlen could see things writhing in their violated flesh, scuttling beetles and fat maggots boiling from their loose skin. He staggered to his feet, turning and running from the lurching horror. The others fell back behind him, flamers roaring as they sought to hold some semblance of a line, to create a buffer zone between themselves and the monstrous dead. Arlen made it through the airlock to the medicae wing, hitting the biological contamination override. The door slid shut with a heavy thud, locking mechanisms whirring. His hand was locked on the panel, fingers finding the right combination of buttons to enact the purgation protocols.

Something wet and heavy hit the glass, smearing it with fluids. Vasily, another of the soldiery, tried to wipe the blood from the viewport, mouth contorted in a scream as he pounded at the glass. It was soundproof, Arlen could not hear his desperate begging. His fear. His sense of betrayal. Arlen shook himself, took one gulping breath, and held the switch down.

Silence reigned. Arlen looked at the viewport, where Vasily was no longer standing. The dead, old and new, advanced like puppets. They watched him with cataracted eyes, babbled and laughed unheard. The victims mocked him, their skin already sloughing from the flesh below. They were becoming monstrous, not exalted by the Helix and the progenitor's gift. They were not worthy of the final sublimation, and that weakness shamed him. It was an insult to all their work. Arlen pushed the final button.

Sirens sounded, high and shrill, as superheated chemicals rushed from the sprinklers. There was a flash of irradiated light and heat, the fail-safes engaging one by one, before the final gurgle of fire-suppressant foam. He held the button, eyes closed, until he heard the scream of evacuating air, venting the toxicity of the chamber beyond. He slumped against the wall, beating his fists against the iron and tile of the door frame.

'You bastard,' he spat, 'look what you have driven me to.'

He was not sure how he had returned to his sanctum, who had carried him up from the toxic depths and then left him in silent contemplation. Sometimes he imagined he had dragged himself up through the hell below, as the rolling decontamination worked its way through the mortuarium. A cleansing flood, a necessary exsanguination. Draining the wound of its potency, and Jast of his vigour.

The laughter haunted him. He heard it everywhere: in the squeak of the door, in the rattle of a trolley's wheels, in the static of the vox. A dormant infection, waiting to surface. His hand trembled against his desk, fingers drumming erratically as he struggled to maintain his composure. Every time he closed his eyes, he heard Jast's voice and saw his monstrosities. Arlen raised both hands, pressed them over his eyes and tried not to scream.

A knock startled him, and his eyes snapped open to see Heinrich watching from the doorway. It did not last long, the man's eyes slipping away as if it hurt to look at Arlen. As though he were tainted by his experience.

'You recover? Good. We have work to do.' His armour burred as he walked, pacing the room with feral insistence. Heinrich's hands were always in motion, a focused echo of Arlen's nervous tremor.

'I'm not sure what I have to contribute. You weren't there, Heinrich. You cannot imagine.' He shook himself again, before the ghosts of the past day could lunge from the shadows, trailing ash and fire. 'It was like nothing I've ever seen before. It seemed…' He paused, struggling to find the words. 'Something out of a children's fable. A thing so inimical to life that it pushed beyond the known.' He shuddered to speak the words.

'I am close, Arlen.' He looked up at Heinrich's use of his name. The other man saw his look and his lips tightened as he tried to suppress a smile. 'You have been in shock, I understand familiarity is important in those circumstances.' Before Arlen could reply he pressed on. 'We are close. His encoding is a fiercely ancient breed, but I know we are gaining upon him. I have narrowed it to three outlying manufactory facilities. Soon we will–'

'And what of his works, Heinrich?' Arlen winced as he pushed himself up and out of his chair. Every muscle ached, his skin gleamed with an addict's sheen of sweat. He had been idle far too long, nothing to brace his system, nothing to fight his injuries. 'Have there been other incidents?'

Heinrich had the decency to look away, hesitant. 'There have been reports of the sickness spreading. Your decontamination was thorough, exacting. This is something else, another exterior vector. The sooner we pin him down, the quicker we can expunge his taint.'

'Leave me.' Heinrich looked at him as he said the words, but did not move. Arlen let his eyes drift down, like an ashamed child. 'I am so very tired, clamavus. This pursuit wearies me. I am not made for it, no wrath-shaped primus. I simply wish to rest.'

Heinrich sighed, shaking his head as he turned for the door.

'Perhaps when you are better recovered, biophagus majoris, we can discuss how best to proceed.'

Heinrich left and Arlen sat alone, idly toying with a quill; scribbling vague notions onto parchment, as though his musings could fight the infection before it consumed his world. He knew he had been evasive, but Heinrich could not understand. None of them could. He was locked in a battle for their bodies and their very souls. Without him there would be no sublimation, only the slow decay. Only the long, cold death that stalked below.

He reached out for the broadcast horn. 'Jast?' He spoke the word in a whisper, afraid that it would bring an answer. 'Do you hear me, Jast? I saw it. I looked your faith in the face. A hideous thing. Your words, they could not convey–'

'It means so very much to me that you have borne witness, Arlen.' The voice dissolved into giggling, a childish sound at odds with his guttural voice. *'Illumination brings agony, as it did for your comrades. Whether wrought from mortal flesh, or infused with notions of divinity.'*

'Don't talk to me of divinity, you know nothing of it. Your worship is abomination–'

'Abomination? A haughty claim from one such as you. You have shaped monsters of your own. Some wear their faces plainly, others hide behind smile and syringe.' Jast's voice oozed from the vox like smoke, coiling with a suffocating weight. *'I have seen so many talents come and go. Luminaries of every creed of mortal science – you could almost say that I have nurtured them, tested them for the days of wrath and horror to come. Cause and cure, growing together, all the stronger for it. Do you feel tested, Arlen? Do you think that you have offered enough?'*

'In all honesty? I think you enjoy this casual cruelty. You would kill a world if it entertained you, and pick nothing of worth from the ashes.'

'I have done so, many times. But the galaxy is a place of

wonderfully diverse ways to die. They flow like poison from Vejovium, Respite, a dozen other worlds, and they corrupt multitudes. You see blessing, and I see opportunity.' He sighed, wistful for a moment.

'All fathers will inevitably fail you, Arlen. Be they primarch, patriarch or progenitor.' Arlen stiffened. His fingers stopped drumming, clenching into a fist. To threaten the progenitor, the wellspring of their faith and power, the gift of Vejovium…

'You've been failed before, have likely failed in turn.' He smiled as he spoke the words, surprised at his own conviction. 'You think we're the same, that we can learn from each other. You're wrong.' Arlen began to write, his thoughts coalescing. He felt lightning in his veins, his mind and hands finally acting in unison. Formulae bubbled forth, etched onto the parchment alongside the scribbles of his doubt. It might work. An answer. An inoculation.

'We are from the same cloth. I have studied with theologians of the biological, true masters of disease and counter-immunity. They would put your bloodline to shame, no matter your innovation. You could have a place amongst them, if you are stalwart in your participation.' Gloating silence descended again, drawing out. Jast seemed almost hesitant as his voice came again. *'Arlen?'*

Arlen was not listening. His fingers were locked around the quill, so tight he felt they might bleed. He worked feverishly, the voice becoming a pleading background note. He rose and threw open the door, passing notes to questioning subordinates. Their eyes grew wide behind goggles, and they scurried off to oblige. The flow of work revolved around his office, a hive of frantic activity punctuated by his proclamations.

When he emerged days later, the world was changed. His own functionaries moved in their unceasing toil, automata crafted from flesh and set to motion by his hand; the frantic grinding of mortar and pestle, the turgid flow of chemicals through glass and steel. Bio-alembics hissed as they decanted into chem-crucibles, staining the air red in gasps of vapour, and the biophaguses chittered their enthusiasm. They looked up at his passing, nodding eagerly. All was proceeding well.

Around them moved other forces. More and more of the cult's power had mobilised in martial force, through hidden passageways and augmented work schedules. They siphoned their way to the heart of the world's true industry, their time at hand. Sea-green and purple armour glimmered in the light of the lume-globes and braziers. The Helix was worked into the plate, or styled as jagged tattoos upon their flesh. They checked and rechecked their weapons, anticipating that the world might end around them at any moment.

Arlen moved through them, like a predator through shoals, until he stood again before the central tank. He went to his knees, waiting for her voice. There was no light. No sound. He was about to look up when the hand trailed along the base of his neck, comforting and chastising at once.

'Arlen.' Vector Phi breathed, and her voice was a balm on his raging soul. He felt shame well within him; he had not been there. So consumed with vendetta that lesser hands had decanted the magus. 'Your war is coming to an end, Arlen. The war of needle and knife. Now, we rise up in our own defence. We spare the herd, and we exalt the Helix.'

'Exalt the Helix!' The words came unbidden all around him, and he felt them leave his own lips. There was a clanking, grinding sound and he looked up to see the progenitor leering from the top of the tank like a gargoyle. Beneath its gaze, he felt transformed. Illuminated.

All fathers fail...

Jast dogged his every thought, infecting them with doubt. Arlen rose, fixing his gaze upon the progenitor. 'I have served, I continue to serve. Everything is in place, my solution to our problem is synthesising. Simply a matter of contrasting his design methodology against our own, tweaking a number of ongoing lines of enquiry.' He smiled in what he hoped would be a reassuring manner. 'When we march to war, mortals and exalted together, we shall be armed to face down the future. We shall bear torches to dispel the darkness with the raw fire of faith.'

'Beautifully said.' Heinrich spoke as he moved to stand at Arlen's shoulder. His scrambler arrays clicked and whirred, his hailer whined with the yearning to amplify his words, yet it was his aura that had grown stronger and stranger. It was the whispered clicking of the broodmind, reaching into reality, to guide and nurture. It embraced them, and even when he did not speak, Heinrich's lips moved in constant rhythm. Where Vector Phi was a spear of psychic might, Heinrich cast forth a net of hushed prayer. No, not prayer. *Communion.*

'We have him, biophagus. Queveron Hub. It is there he likely made planetfall, and there we will purge him. All his works will crumble.' Heinrich nodded, and it seemed to Arlen as though it was more to convince himself than anyone else. 'This world has but one master, one creed!'

'One master.' The dull repetition thrummed behind them. 'One creed.'

'There will come a moment in proceedings where you will receive my signal, Heinrich.' Arlen kept his voice level, his eyes fixed upon the clamavus.

It cannot be this easy, he thought. *He would not allow himself to be found like this.*

'In that instant, the chemicals shall be released and the

infection will be purged from our midst, as though it had never been.'

When the symptoms confirm a disease state, then you know how it will be treated... But what if it is not as obvious as it appears?

'The progenitor blesses all who conquer madness with holy reason, who anoint the worthy, abhorring the base. You please us, Arlen.' Vector Phi's voice was saccharine, slick devotion where Arlen's was bitter, curdled with obsession. 'You will release the many-blessed and the gene-wrought to fight at our side. You are their father, they will heed you.'

'They will heed me.' He nodded, his hands balled tightly into fists. 'They will do the work of the divine, magus. Of that you may rest assured.'

The chambers below the sanctum were damp, echoing and badly maintained. Standing before the iron door, Arlen could hear the low ebb of breathing, the quiet cooing as something moved in the shadows beyond. He reached up, pulled a key from his pocket, and began to unlock the door.

The door had always felt unnecessary, there more for the comfort of others than because of any real fear of escape. He had never had cause to fear them. The unblessed would think them mistakes or malignancies. He did not. In them, Arlen saw the richness of their genetic legacy. Mutation and overexpression had occurred, yes, but that was not a failure. It was simply another aspect of their glorious cycle.

The children of flux slunk from the shadows. First came a twisted metamorph, feeder tendrils spilling from its lower face, with limbs like great scythe blades. Another spat a gobbet of bio-acid and flailed at the air with a whiplike appendage. The gaggle crowded in about him, clicking and snarling as they sniffed the air. They scattered as their larger kin unfolded from the darkness, dominance enforced with graceless ease. The aberrants stared down at Arlen and then pushed forward to nuzzle affectionately at him. He smiled, stroking one chitinous cranium. 'I have missed you, my children. Forgive me, it has been too long. Tell me, where is Alpha?'

They crooned and gestured with their lumpen heads to the figure sitting prone beneath a low arch. Its massive bulk was contorted as it rested, body curled with its knees up. It was watching him, four eyes aglow with a feral intelligence set in its bifurcated face. He could hear something hissing relentlessly in the dark and his eye was drawn up to the familiar that squatted, coiled like smoke, upon the abominant's shoulder. The awareness of the progenitor spilled from its psychic form. Once, long ago, Arlen had guided the parasitical thing to Alpha and watched it bestow its blessings. Now Alpha was beloved of the progenitor, exalted of the Helix. With its eyes upon him, Arlen felt surer in his course. 'We are being lied to,' he whispered, and Alpha looked up at him in confusion. The familiar stroked the abominant's head gently, bobbing with the motion. It almost seemed to be nodding at Arlen, as though in approval.

'Come, my children,' Arlen soothed, and Alpha growled as he rose to his full and towering height. 'It is time for war.'

The line of modified Goliaths seemed to stretch to the horizon, gleaming amidst the industrial sprawl that linked the great manufactories. They had been pressed into service, more to transport the men and Arlen's chemicals than to truly form a defensive cordon. The great thresher blades of agri-harvester variants were tinted crimson by the light of the hulking chem-sprayer Goliaths they squatted beside. Tanks sloshed and bubbled with the promise of salvation, ready to disperse the solution and safeguard them against contagion.

Vector Phi stood on the back of one, her robes whipping in the wind, casting her mind forth to probe the complex ahead of them. Queveron sat silent, dead to every conventional sense and deaf to their signals. It worried her, so used to Respite as a fertile world; so attuned to the never-ending cycles of reproduction. To live was to spread, to assimilate, to subsume.

She looked down at the ranks of gathered troops, in the mortal livery of the Respitian Hospitallers, or in the revealed glory of the cult. She could hear the human minds, their deluded thoughts of 'exotic foreign regiments'. It almost made her smile.

Heinrich climbed up to stand beside her, grunting with the effort, though she had barely noticed his ascent. She turned, nodded distractedly. 'Is there word from Arlen?'

'Nothing.' Heinrich shook his head and she could taste his anger. He considered it a personal betrayal. Almost a blasphemy. 'If he has set out with the gene-wrought, then he has not announced it or coordinated with us.'

'Strange, is it–'

The hub vanished, violently ceased to be. It erupted in an explosion of filthy green un-light, mushrooming into the sky like the clawing of vast talons. For a moment the seething sky was dispelled, peeled back in a rush of superheated air. Vector Phi beheld the wan light beyond her world, filtered through a lens of utter destruction. She tasted metal, harsh and cold, so strong that it made her gag. Heinrich braced her, horror-struck as the facility died before them. It made no sense – to sacrifice so much for so little gain; they were still outside the walls! Had the enemy sprung their trap too early?

And then he saw the extent of the enemy's spite.

The dead poured from Queveron's corpse like lice. A verminous tide seeped and ran like liquid, oozing from every sluiceway, door and gap. They tumbled over burning obstacles, traipsing through vistas of hell that any thinking being would run screaming from. The dead did not scream. They did not grunt or shout as weapons found their range. They did not speak, but nor were they silent.

As the dead storm-surged towards their lines, they were laughing.

The furthest under-levels of Valderos were moist with run-off and condensation, streaking the walls with strange patterns and lambent glows. Arlen pushed on alone, ignoring them even as they glistened in the corner of his eye. He had descended most of the way in an elevator, but the true depths were only accessible by stair, and so he had slogged on into the stolid darkness. It embraced him. It knew him. He leant heavily upon the goad-stave he carried, drew himself up. This was the right thing, and as he advanced he became more certain of the fact. *We have been deceived.*

Around him the passageways grew stranger. The sides of great mixing vats were whorled and gnarled like leprous coral, where elsewhere writhing ferro-cancers and vibrant rustmoulds furred decaying pipes. The very fabric of their efforts was eroding, and none had noticed. Not even Arlen. He sighed. The doors ahead of him were unnaturally aged, their metal brittle, but they shuddered to life at his approach, parting with an asthmatic sputter. Arlen stumbled as the sight beyond broke his stride.

It was a landscape of incomparable horror, far worse than the unsettling excesses outside. The ground seemed transmuted into an undulating carpet of living flesh. It crawled, it climbed up the mechanisms of the underworks – sinuous, grasping. Erratically pulsing organs had melded themselves to the machinery, violating the purity of their undertaking with something–

'Unclean.' The word slipped from Arlen's mouth as he stared in disbelief. 'Progenitor guard us.' Before him, kneeling amidst the despoliation, were three figures. They stood unsteadily, turning to look at the source of the voice. Where the room had seemed ungodly, these three were ruin incarnate.

His gaze darted from figure to figure, each singular in their corruption. The first was a giant in seeping plate, its face hidden behind the exaggerated features of a gas mask. It clattered as it moved, hung with phials and alembics, dusting some tincture from its hands. It regarded him with cold impassive lenses, and turned to vox inaudibly to its comrades. It was answered by a muffled guffaw from a hideously bloated warrior-thing hefting a gnarled bronze chem-sprayer. Something gurgled and Arlen realised that many of the pipes feeding the weapon wound their way back into the thing's twisted anatomy.

But worse was their leader. He had the air of a high priest of biological atrocity, draped in the profaned trappings of a healer. A faded pus-streaked helix was barely visible on one immense shoulder pad, and one gauntleted hand was surmounted by a mockery of a medical rig. It flexed its immense digits as it watched him with rheumy eyes, mouth twisted into a rotten-toothed sneer. A squat creature Arlen could only describe as a phantasmagorical imp clung to the figure's neck, cooing from a maw lined with needle teeth. 'Ah, Arlen. I knew you would not be as misled as your scrabbling brood.

You have tracked our metastasis as a true master of your art.' He knew the voice instantly – the voice which had haunted him, and driven him to this desperate confrontation.

'Jast.'

'Hektor Jast. Of the hallowed Fourteenth, and these are my brothers in arms – Aicard,' he gestured to the gas-masked fiend, 'and Carax.' The stinking chortling thing bent in a crude bow. Jast stalked forward, and reality seemed to warp palpably as he advanced. The air turned stale and lifeless, with only the entropic whisper of background radiation to fill the vacuum. 'Count yourself lucky, for if the Death Guard still cared about the common herd of man then your ilk would have been first upon the pyre. Suffice to say, we have better uses for you.'

'Perverting our work?' Arlen barked. 'Reducing this world to anarchy and monstrosity?'

'Do not talk to me of monstrosity!' Jast's eyes flared, genuine anger eradicating the jovial demeanour. 'You have embraced the xenos to your very core. We annihilated entire civilisations for less. You and your self-deluding creed disgust me, but *you* fascinate me. You are contagion given flesh – not in the ephemeral, but in practice. That is what brought you to me. You are an infection, Arlen, and so you belong to the Grandfather.'

'Your god?'

'The God of All.' Jast threw wide his arms, sword rattling in its scabbard. 'Before him you stand, alone and unshriven.'

'No,' Arlen whispered. 'Not alone.'

There was a tortured creak of metal. Jast looked up, surprised, as vent covers and rusted walls gave way. Arlen's baleful children flooded into the chamber, metamorphs in the vanguard. They spat as they hurled themselves at Aicard, acid hissing as it pitted his already ruined armour. The Death Guard reached up and grasped a phial, hurling it into the midst of them. The volatile mixture exploded forth in a shower of shrapnel and vapour, driving them coughing to their knees. Two of them screamed as the chemicals ravaged them, faces sloughing away even as their kin leapt over them. Blades scraped at his plate, scrabbling for purchase. He thrust his gauntleted hand up, crushing the skull of another squealing creature. A lash closed about his throat, dragging him down and out of sight as the bodies overwhelmed him.

There was a gurgling rattle as Carax turned his weapon upon the pile of writhing bodies that were drowning his brother. Great gouts of steaming green liquid doused the metamorphs, their cries shifting in agony. Flesh melted and bones shattered like glass, leaving only a stinking pool coating the half-devoured corpse of Aicard. Carax was turning to aid Jast when the first aberrants barrelled into him, almost knocking him over.

Jast did not seem to care as he lazily moved towards Arlen. His sword was drawn, turning in his hand, debating where to cut first. 'You are a crafty one, Arlen. Full of surprises. It won't save you though.' He laughed bitterly. 'I had hoped you might abase yourself before the Grandfather and be blessed. You would run with holy putrescence, be remade. You would speak your wisdom to me, eternally.'

Arlen fumbled for a button at his wrist and felt chemical relief flood through him. The censers on his shoulders bubbled as they dispensed their cocktail, and he felt the leaden weight in his limbs abate.

'I would rather die than be like you,' he spat. The crook of the goad came up and round, brandished like a club. His fingers found his autopistol and he jerked it up, pulling the trigger. A scatter of shots pinged uselessly against Jast's armour. One bullet buried in the distended plate, and foulness suppurated from the armour as though it were alive. Jast tilted his head wryly, unbothered, weighing options. 'Not an ideal outcome, but it can be arranged.'

Despite his terrible bulk, Jast was a thing of dark awe when he moved with killing purpose. He lunged forward, blade skittering across the floor as Arlen hurled himself to the side. Jast was laughing again, taunting him as he raked the sword against the grating beneath them. Sparks and debris danced before his plague-maddened eyes, and Arlen could tell the Death Guard was making sport of him.

He pulled the trigger again and the pistol gave a dull click. *Empty*. There was not time to reload before Jast batted it aside, as casually as disarming a child. His other hand, with its blades and drills, came round in a savage backhand, sending Arlen sprawling into the mucoid dust. The reek of blood filled his nostrils; he could feel the wetness where his ear had been. Jast looked at him with disdain.

'You don't even smell human any more. You are unworthy even of kneeling – I should have taken your wretched industry from the start.' He raised the blade, poised to impale. Arlen closed his eyes. It had been folly to think he could win.

The blow never came. His body tensed, expectant, but he did not die. There was a vast crash, and a bellow of inhuman rage. Arlen opened his eyes, and beheld his miracle.

Alpha hurled himself against Jast, a wall of vengeful muscle. He had torn free a length of piping and swung it down in great sweeping blows. Jast brought his sword up, the edge hissing as it clattered against the hardened steel and brute force. Alpha clawed at him, raking his twisted face and drawing turgid droplets of clotting blood. The Plague Marine bellowed into the abominant's faces, hissing acid spittle making the hulking figure rear back.

Behind them Carax had pinned an aberrant to the wall with his weapon, gurgling as its payload devoured the aberrant from the inside out. Steaming loops of intestine unfurled in a visceral rain. Carax turned as the other aberrant launched itself at him, emboldened by its loss or by Alpha's guiding might. It took hold of one of the creature's arms and pulled, wrenching the limb off with a rush of toxic waste. Carax twitched, grasped at the aberrant with his remaining faltering hand, and slumped forward. His already swollen armour bulged, steam whistling from between the plates as the pressure finally discharged. Carax exploded, showering the area in blood, bone and armoured shrapnel. The aberrant threw up its arms, but vanished in the miasma, consumed utterly.

Alpha rained blows upon Jast, the pipe buckling and snapping under the strain. The abominant cast it aside; his huge paws tore at Jast's chest even as the sword hacked at his malformed torso. The cuts flowed freely, soaking them both in the alien stench of his blood. The familiar hissed and snapped as the horrors clashed beneath it, and the daemonic reflection squatting on Jast's shoulders hurled its own shrill insults. The rival figments threw themselves at each other, tumbling away from the fray – snapping and clawing, an echo of the conflict in microcosm.

Arlen caught his breath. He had a chance, all that remained was to take it. He watched Jast drive his sword up through Alpha's chest, drenching himself in a torrent of gore before kicking the mewling war-form over. He looked at Arlen with undisguised loathing. Arlen merely smiled, and let his finger find the switch.

* * *

Heinrich battered back another drooling undead horror, baring his teeth in hate. He was slick with black blood, his augur stave battered and constantly whining with ultrasonic transmissions. A clutch of hybrids boiled up from a pipe in answer to his summons, lashing out against the creatures with fang and claw. One took hold of a zombie with its third arm, crushing its rotten skull, before leaping towards fresh prey. He spat, looking for Vector Phi. She shone with pale radiance, her helix-topped staff burning as she reduced any approaching foe to ashes. He had never felt more pride, standing with her. A low buzzing drew his attention to a signal rune on his augur as it flashed dully. *Arlen?* It surprised him; he had thought the biophagus dead. He bit back a growl as his hands moved automatically, splicing the signal into the local feed.

There was a low rumble as the chem-trucks churned and bucked, their hoses swelling. Crimson mist discharged into the air, enveloping the clashing forces in its warm embrace. Heinrich felt the flow of the broodmind shift, becoming urgent. His fellows fought with greater zeal, hurling themselves into the fray with a passionate intensity. The mortal soldiers suffered worse. They clawed at helmets and threw aside their rifles, launching into the undead ranks with no thought of their own safety. They bludgeoned and tore at the dead, ignoring bites and scratches. Their blood ran in boiling rivers from their wounds, yet they kept fighting.

This perversion is your cure? The thought stopped Heinrich dead, dumbstruck by the unfolding madness. *This is our salvation?*

Jast staggered. His necrotic features twisted in something resembling pain. It came again, like palsy. 'My children falter. What have you done?' The psychic weight had once been shared between three, and now it crashed down upon the wounded Jast like hammer blows. Every death was a cut. All unnatural power had its price.

Arlen threw up his goad, but the warrior bisected it with a sweep of his sword. The jagged spur of metal slipped from Arlen's hand as he stumbled backwards. He scrabbled on the ground, trying to get away even as a boot pinned him in place. 'I gave you a chance. No more, no mercy. Perhaps I will anoint your head and have it speak your secrets to me.' Jast raised his blade, poised to kill.

Another tremor wracked him. Arlen felt his own fingers close around the goad's haft, felt the last of his stimms ebb into his system, and pushed up. He pivoted the broken implement forward and felt it impact. He heard Jast's wheezing breath and the clatter of his sword as it hit the floor. The shaft protruded from the Plague Marine's throat, slick with blood and pus. Jast stared at him, his eyes wide with shocked spite as he sank to his knees. He gurgled, shook, and was silent.

Arlen felt fire spreading through his chest. His head was pounding, blood leaking slowly from his wounds in time with the dull throb of pain. He closed his eyes, and let the darkness take him.

Respite was a world without sickness.

He woke to that thought, to the absence of pain, as he pushed himself up from the sickbed. Heinrich stood before him, his clothing still stained with blood and smoke. He looked incongruous against the gleaming white of the room, and fixed Arlen with cold disappointment. Arlen looked down, sheepishly, and brushed his hand against his bandaged head.

'You found me, then?'

'We did, Arlen.' Heinrich grunted the words, but there was no camaraderie in his use of his name. 'Try as you might, you survived. For the moment, at least.' The clamavus' cold fury drained the room of warmth. He leant forward. 'You are aboard the medical relief ship *Fourfold Mercy*, and will soon be bound for Vejovium itself.

'There you alone will answer for your actions, Arlen. Not least to explain their impact upon the harvest to come. Whole hosts of mortals contaminated and lost, our own bloodline tainted. We sacrificed much in the tumult, and many more of the kine fled. The consequences will take years to assess – productivity already wounded by Queveron's fall will worsen with lack of viable bodies.' His lips drew back from his teeth. He had never seemed more like the progenitor than in that moment. 'So it is you who shall return to the sourceworld, and it is there that you will explain our enemy, having endured the most… moral contamination.'

Heinrich looked at Arlen sternly before he turned to leave. 'The magus sent me in her stead, Arlen. Do not reach for her, this is the progenitor's will. That you go, alone, and stand before the judgement of the Prime Specimen.'

'By the progenitor's will,' Arlen whispered, closing his eyes and listening as the door closed. He was truly alone now. The silence of the void closed in about him. He did not feel despair; he was not sure he felt anything, other than the pain. He winced as he sat up, his head spinning with sudden nausea. His gut roiled, his fingers dug into the mattress and he bit back a scream.

It's just the stress, the injury. Withdrawal? Arlen thought. Somewhere he was convinced he could hear laughter, low and mad. He squeezed his eyes shut.

He could feel it, bearing down on him. The inevitable. The impossible.

Alone, disgraced and broken, Arlen coughed.

NO MATTER THE COST

Michael R Fletcher

Canadian aficionado of all things grimdark Michael R Fletcher visits Shyish with this gritty, character-driven story. Bringing a unique twist to the forces of Death in the Age of Sigmar, this Faustian narrative features Fell, a mysterious and twisted figure who lives alone, shunning the other inhabitants of his village. We learn of Fell's bleak present and sinister past, his dabbling in the dark arts of necromancy, and the curse that afflicts him to this day. For one does not enter the domain of Nagash lightly, and without pledging one's soul to the Great Necromancer for all eternity…

Fell threw off the blanket and pushed into a sitting position with a wheezing groan. Thin legs stretched out before him. His left ankle hurt, its foot bent out at an odd angle, the instep crushed flat where a horse had once trodden on him. He eyed the offending limb. Such frail bones, so easy to snap.

He didn't have to suffer such wounds. It was a choice.

Fumbling at the side of the bed, he found his cane. For a score of weak and sluggish heartbeats he glared hate at his hand, the skin wrinkled and sunken. The last two fingers, fixed in their bent position, taunted him: how much is your oath worth, old man? Heal thyself!

Swinging his legs off the bed, he stood, groaning at the stabbing twinge in his lower back. Leaning heavily on the cane, he shuffled into the kitchen. The sad, timid steps of a man terrified of falling. His right knee clicked as he walked. He banged it years ago while digging in the garden and it had never been the same.

A tin cup of water sat on the table. Clutching it in the other hand, he drank. Stale. Brackish. The hard taste of rusting metal. He spat out a fly that had drowned in the cup as he'd slept. His eyes weren't great, especially in the early-morning gloom.

The front door slammed open with a bang, and little Rita stomped into the kitchen, a basket of bread and what looked to be a baked potato clutched in her arms. Red hair like an evening sunset, fringe cut short, two dishevelled plaits hanging down her back, she was all gangly limbs and bright green eyes.

'The hells!' Fell barked. 'Get out, you little rat! I'm not dressed yet!'

The ten-year-old frowned, head tilted to one side as she studied him. 'You need to wash your nightshirt. It's filthy.'

'Out, before I give you a bloody good thrashing!' He threatened murder with the cane, careful to lean on the table as he did so.

Rita ignored him as she slid past and set the basket on the seat of his rickety chair.

'I was going to sit there,' he muttered.

'Ashton gave me this bread for you,' she said, laying the loaf on the table. 'He says it's only a few days old and still good.'

'Great. Wormy bread. Now get out!'

'Terese sent the potato.'

'I hate potatoes.'

Rita placed the potato beside the bread.

'Galley said you can have his old horse blanket as soon as Ryder finishes the new one.'

'Fantastic. I love smelling like a gods-be-damned incontinent donkey.'

'It'll keep you warm in the winter,' she prattled on, clearing his dinner plate and fork from the table and taking them to the bucket where he kept his dirty dishes.

'I don't need their stinking pity.'

Glancing over her shoulder, she said, 'Wouldn't pity suggest that they like you, at least a little?'

'That's unlikely.'

'At the very least it means they care.'

'They like having someone to look down on.'

Grabbing the foetid cloth he used for cleaning, she dipped it in his water cup and set to scrubbing his dishes.

'Oi, you little wretch,' he barked. 'I was drinking that!'

She ignored him as she worked. 'Gallowglas said he'll give you a mug of ale if you come by the Dripping Bucket tonight.'

Fell had been once, back when he first came to Hollow's Dell. Many times he considered returning, just to hear Terese sing again.

'I hate the tavern. Too many people.'

'Terese is going to sing,' Rita said, as if she'd read his mind.

That stopped him. Terese sang like the very gods spoke through her. 'I do love the sound of someone skinning a rutting tomcat.'

'See?' she said. 'A reason to go!'

Rita babbled on as she cleaned, telling him about how Maz killed a deer on her first time out with Lawrence, the huntmaster. She talked of how beautiful Sarah looked in her new dress, how old lady Kalindy died the night before in her sleep, and was to be buried this afternoon in the town plot. She told him about how distant wars were going to affect the price of grain, and how the vile forces of Chaos were being driven from the Realm of Shyish. A thousand conversations between ignorant farmers overheard and filtered through the understanding of a ten-year-old girl. Half the time he hadn't a clue what she was on about.

'How old are you?' she asked over a shoulder.

'Why?' he demanded, suspicious.

'Terese asked me how old I thought you were.'

He swallowed a sigh of relief. 'And?' he asked, curious in spite of himself.

'I said sixty.'

Not too bad, considering the truth.

'Terese said she thought you were closer to fifty-five.'

Fell smothered a grin of pleasure. Not only had Terese asked after him, but she was also wondering if he was of a suitable age; whether they might spend time together without it being unseemly. Even though his back and knees were hell, he looked nothing like his true age.

Finishing, Rita wiped her hands on her trousers. 'Will I see you at the Bucket?'

'No.'

'All right. I'll swing by tomorrow.'

'You set foot in my house uninvited one more time,' he hefted the cane, threatening, 'and I'll crack your skull!'

'I'll probably be late,' she explained. 'I agreed to help Hellen collect eggs. I'll bring you a few.'

'I hate eggs.'

'I can make scrambled eggs, you know. Momma showed me. Maybe I'll try and find some cheese.'

'Get out.'

'I'll make you scrambled eggs and cheese,' she decided, collecting her basket and wandering out the front door, red braids swinging behind her.

'You're not right in the head!' he called after her.

By all the gods dark and bright she reminded him of Leona, his daughter.

Collapsing into the now vacated chair, he sat in silence.

His knees hurt. His back ached. One of the fingers on his left hand felt like it was going to lock up.

An eternity of slow decay.

Time devours us all.

Someday, he'd be a broken ruin, utterly helpless. His joints would seize, and his ancient bones crack. It might be a decade, or maybe another century, if he was careful, but that was his inevitable fate.

Rot and decay. Eternal life trapped in an undying body.

It doesn't have to be this way.

Break the oath he swore over the dust of his daughter, and he could repair himself.

Never.

He'd lie where he fell, mind as sharp as ever, awaiting an end that would never come. Carrion creatures would feed on what little meat he had. Insects would worm into his eyes, feast on his brain. Even that could not end him. Tied to these bones, his soul would remain forever trapped. He couldn't die, not ever. No escape.

'Grief,' said the woman who did this to Fell. 'I curse you with an eternity of grief.'

Fell and Ruhinn knelt over their daughter's bed. They'd cried themselves hoarse and now had nothing left.

Wrung out.

Emptied of all emotion except soul-staining misery. The one bright spark in the world, snuffed.

Leona lay still and pale, red hair brushed out and tied in plaits neater than she'd ever achieved when alive.

My girl. My beautiful girl.

Why go on? What was the point? How could anything ever matter again?

Ruhinn placed a hand on Leona's forehead. 'She's cold,' his wife said. 'So cold.'

He watched her glance about, as if in search of a blanket to warm their daughter.

She's not cold. She's gone.

But he couldn't say it, couldn't speak the word.

Gone.

Teeth clenched tight, his skull ached from the pressure.

'Daddy, am I going to die?' Leona asked on her last day.

And he lied. 'No, my love. Daddy will protect you. Daddy would never let anything hurt you.'

He was, he discovered, wrong. He *could* still feel. Something deep inside cracked then, never to heal. The kind of soul-deep wound that either breaks a man or twists him into something different.

This can't be real. This can't be.

Having a child changes you. You don't know who you are until you're a father. For the first time in his life, Fell had liked who he was. The selfishness of youth fell away, and he became a man. Tasks once daunting were nothing. Work hard to support your family, to give your beloved little girl everything she could need? Yes! Happily! Having a reason made all the difference in the world. His thankless job as a scribe for the Collegiate Arcane became bearable. That they couldn't have another, that Rue had barely survived giving birth to Leona, made their daughter all the more precious.

The Collegiate. Gods, he'd spent countless thousands of hours copying tome after tome for the masters. Much of the time he understood little of what he wrote. His eidetic memory and knack for penmanship and precise copying, even when he didn't know the language, earned him a place among the most prized scribes. Funny, as the work bored him to tears.

What a waste! Every hour there he could have been with Leona!

The Collegiate.

Something poked at his memory, demanded attention.

Copying books. Forbidden books, sometimes.

'Rue,' he said.

She looked lost, red-rimmed eyes unseeing.

'I copied a book once.'

Ruhinn stared at him with dull emptiness.

'It was a language book. A dictionary… for translating from the ancient tongue.'

She blinked. 'So?'

'I also copied another book. A book written in that old tongue.'

She waited. Not with patience, but with dejected disinterest. Nothing meant anything any more.

Fell pictured the worn leather cover, soft in spite of its age. Each sheet, warm to the touch. He remembered leaning close to inspect a page and seeing the whorls of flesh, the ink a strange, rusty brown with the scent of old salt. Blood. A thick tome; many hundreds must have died to make that one book.

One of nine.

Maybe.

'A forbidden book,' he said. 'A private commission, though I do not know for whom.' The idea built as he spoke. 'I didn't understand it at the time.' He'd always had a perfect memory, could clearly see the pages of every book he'd ever copied. 'I can apply one to the other. With some work, I can read that other book.'

Rue shook her head, lost. 'So?'

'I think I know what the book was.'

Closing his eyes, he remembered the text on the cover, flipping through the pages of his mind to find the translation. His breath caught.

'If I'm right,' he said, 'it was a book of spells. Necromancy spells.'

'Death,' said Ruhinn, perhaps beginning to understand.

Eyes still closed, Fell skimmed through several more pages of the ancient tome. 'A spell book.' He turned to Rue. 'Necromancy, my love. *Powerful* necromancy.'

'Necromancy,' she repeated, looking to where Leona lay.

'Maybe…' He hesitated, afraid to give voice to his thoughts.

Rue turned on him, curled her fingers in the collar of his shirt. She glared into his eyes, alive again, bright with desperate hunger. 'Bring her back to me. Whatever it takes. No matter the cost. Bring her back.'

Fell swallowed. Whatever it takes. No matter the cost.

He knew little of necromancy, but something of history. These were fiercely guarded secrets, and necromancy devoured its practitioners, twisted them, body and soul.

'Whatever it takes,' he said. 'No matter the cost.' He held his wife. 'I swear it.'

Purpose. Without it, we are nothing.

He had purpose now.

The next day Fell left his job at the Collegiate Arcane. He and Ruhinn sold their family estate in Glymmsforge and used the funds to pay a Scáthborn aelf to cease their daughter's rot. Fell would learn necromancy, but could not do so overnight. It would take years. They rented a single room over a cockroach-infested tavern, and Rue took a job cleaning dishes and scrubbing floors to support them while he studied.

Day by day the horror grew in him as he came to understand the task he had undertaken. But there could be no turning back. He would not fail Ruhinn. He would not fail Leona.

No matter the cost.

It became his mantra, repeated when he woke screaming from the nightmares, tangled in the sheets, face flushed and soaked in sweat.

He felt himself crumble beneath the onslaught of this terrible knowledge. The man he was died, hour by hour, day by day.

Year by year.

No matter the cost.

Fell crushed the potato with a fork, making sure there was nothing hard hidden within. In the past, he'd broken teeth on unexpected foods. Once, an incisor cracked in half when he tried to eat an apple Rita brought him, a treat from Terese. Pulling out the remains was unpleasant. When confident the potato was safe, he spooned it into the stale bread, making a hefty, if somewhat bland, sandwich. He ate slowly, chewing with care. It was, he was loath to admit, the most delicious thing he'd eaten in months. Maybe longer. After, he released a long belch and sat happy and sated.

He spent the day rooting about in his vegetable patch, pulling weeds, ever cautious not to injure himself, before returning inside to collapse onto his one chair with a groan. His back hurt. His knees hurt. His arms–

It all bloody well hurts!

He eyed the dirty plate still sitting where he'd left it on the table. Reaching out, he collected a few crumbs with a dirty finger and ate them.

He considered the Dripping Bucket. There'd be people. Few if any would talk to him, but they'd note his attendance. The town was small, everyone knew everyone and everyone knew everyone's business. Except for Fell. Though he'd lived here for years, no one knew him. To the people of Hollow's Dell, he was a grumpy old man probably named for his tendency to trip on things. Little Rita aside, people rarely talked to him. And that was fine. What could he possibly say to those with such brief mayfly lives? They'd age and die, and he'd still be here, rotting, falling apart one bone – one joint – at a time. In another decade he'd move on, find another town. It didn't do to stay anywhere too long. Better not to catch the attention of the townsfolk.

Still, it had been a long time since he'd immersed himself in the hubbub of humanity. It would be nice to see people, even if he didn't talk to them. There might even be news from beyond the Dell. Rumours of war had been trickling in for years. The forces of Order and Chaos would never rest until they'd subjugated or freed – the difference seemed non-existent to Fell – all the known world.

Gallowglas' offer of a mug sweetened the deal even further. It had been years since Fell had allowed himself alcohol. A man who doesn't heal can't afford the careless clumsiness of drink. But just one? It'd be nice to feel a little distance.

Admit it, you'd go just to hear Terese sing.

In a town like Hollow's Dell, there wasn't much for entertainment. Not like in Glymmsforge. He recalled how, years before Leona was born, he and Ruhinn used to attend concerts, visit galleries and see plays. They once saw a lavish production of *The End of Despair, Fall of a Mortarch*. The magisters shut the play down the next week, hanging the actors in the city square, displaying their tortured corpses in iron cages. But out here, out on the ragged edge of civilisation, a voice like Terese's was a wonder.

She's not hard on the eyes, either.

Fell laughed, a flat, humourless chuckle.

Nearing fifty, Terese was less than a tenth his age.

Funny how, as a youth, he'd never noticed older women. These days, anyone under forty looked like a child. There was something about women in the later half of life, a confidence, an understanding of what *actually* mattered, that was attractive beyond pert body parts.

Also, twenty-year-old girls don't know you exist.

Terese, on the other hand… Sometimes she watched him when she thought he wouldn't notice. And she often sent food along with Rita. He licked his lips at the memory of the potato.

It didn't matter. There could be nothing between them. She'd age and die, and he'd have to watch.

We all fall apart, just at different rates.

Having already lost one family, he was unwilling to lose anyone else.

Excuses, excuses, old man.

It wasn't like Terese was going to bear him children. Why could they not spend a little time together, make the passing years a little less brutally lonely?

No!

Rue might be centuries gone, but he would never betray the memory of her. And Terese deserved better.

How old do you have to be before you stop thinking about women?

He didn't know. Certainly, he had yet to reach that age. Would he ever? Would he miss it if he did?

'One drink,' he said. 'One quick drink, and then I'll return home.'

Home, a stinking hovel. Two rooms, one where he slept, another where he ate. A bucket to crap and piss in. Gods he missed the estate back in Glymmsforge. They hadn't been wealthy, not compared to some, but sometimes he dreamed of sitting rooms, soft divans, leather reading chairs and a small library of much-loved books.

Late that evening, cane in hand, Fell made the short walk to the Bucket. He moved at a careful limp he once jokingly told Rita was 'stately'. She'd pretended to understand, bouncing off the walls with the careless and enviable energy of youth.

Each time a foot slipped in the mud, darts of hot pain shot through his knees. The slight decline made the trip into town easier, but treacherous after a rainfall. The journey home would hurt, though he wouldn't truly appreciate how much until he woke the next morning.

He laughed, a mirthless cough. *Nothing ever gets better*. The axiom of the elderly.

Movement caught his attention, and he shuffled to a stop. There, to the west, up on what the locals called Hollow's Hill, stood a massive black beast of a destrier. Cloaked in white, the rider sat watching Fell. The wind gusted, whipped at pale wisps of cloth, teasing Fell with hints of a shapely body hidden beneath. The horse stood motionless, its eyes two shards of obsidian.

She found me.

A terrible sadness – a soul-crushing grief – overcame Fell, and he stumbled to his knees. Tears came, and he sobbed into his hands for a lifetime of loss. The pain of the fall was nothing. Flesh and bone and muscle mattered not when everything worth living for had been torn from your life, turned to dust before your very eyes, crushed in a skeletal fist.

When the misery had passed and his eyes were once again dry, Fell found his cane in the dirt and pushed himself back to his feet with a groan. He stood, staring at the blood on his hands where he'd scraped them on a rock catching his fall.

'I have to leave.'

He'd stayed in Hollow's Dell too long.

He felt it deep in his bones.

Turning, he saw the rider was gone.

She wanted to be seen.

It was a message: I found you.

Fell turned, looked back up the hill towards the wretched hovel of his home.

You can't leave tonight, not in the dark.

The only easily travelled path out of town was the single road cutting through Hollow's Dell, and that was the one place someone would definitely think to intercept his escape. On the other hand, creeping through the forest in the dead of night was a sure recipe for broken bones.

Doubt and fear.

They won't come tonight. She would want him to suffer. *I'll sneak out in the morning.*

He tried to shake off the lingering grief, but it clung like spiderwebs.

One last night. One more taste of Gallowglas' ale.

One last chance to see Terese, to listen to her sing.

Would Rita be at the Bucket? Sometimes her mother let her stay up late to hear a few of Terese's songs before bed.

I'll miss the brat.

The thought hurt more than expected. The precocious child was a constant annoyance, always letting herself into his home and prattling on with that incessant babble. A thousand small gifts littered his hovel, crude drawings sketched in charcoal on thin slabs of wood. She often brought sweets, treats saved from her own meals. Her constant thoughtless kindness was a pain.

So like Leona.

Fell sighed, and turned back towards the Dripping Bucket. One last night. He'd say goodbye to these people who had, if not welcomed him, still been kind. He'd say goodbye to Rita too, if she was there. And he'd thank her. She'd more than earned that.

Decision made, Fell set off down the hill.

On the outskirts he passed the town graveyard, and recalled Rita mentioning that old lady Kalindy had died and was to be buried there. Did she already rest in the earth?

As if death is a respite.

Though a small town, Hollow's Dell was old. Hundreds of stones marked graves. The eldest, further back, were stained black with moss, and smooth, wind-worn. Many had toppled over and lay half-sunken in the soil.

Perhaps, for people like Kalindy, death was an escape. Undying, Fell would never know.

Constructed of field-stones, the Dripping Bucket used to be a homestead. The wood shutters on the windows, warped and painted and repainted a thousand times, had been nailed shut. Probably to keep them from falling off. Judging by the colour of the stones and the crumbling mortar, the Bucket was one of the oldest buildings in the Dell.

A sodden and swollen wooden bucket, banded in rusted iron, hung over the door. It looked more like someone had hung it there, never bothering to retrieve it, than a tavern sign. Sometimes, after a heavy rain, it dripped for days.

From outside, he heard the raised voices of good cheer

and shared drink. Taking a deep breath, he pushed through the front door.

Grief followed with him.

For years Fell studied the dread tome. Time lost meaning. He and Rue aged, him bent from his endless hours hunched over the book, her from her time washing dishes and scrubbing floors.

Studying books was one thing, but he had to *know*. He had to practise what he learned to be sure it worked. He might get only one chance to save Leona.

At first, he practised on small animals, bringing the stiffened corpses of birds and rodents back to some twitching semblance of life. It was easy. Too easy. It was, however, difficult to judge success. Did they thrash and scream because their bodies were still broken, or had he got the spell subtly wrong? He had to know before he chanced anything with Leona.

He needed human subjects, and knew where to get them. There are always fresh dead in Shyish.

Each night he sneaked from the house as Rue slept, and visited a nearby graveyard. Sometimes he lay on fresh graves, talking to the dead, hearing of their sorrows. They all said the same thing: their greatest regrets were the things they hadn't done.

Leona never changed. She didn't age or rot. Every night they stood over their perfect little girl, read her stories, told her they loved her and would see her again soon.

Fell cracked the dark mysteries contained in the foul book, and they cracked him.

The nightmares stopped, an oddly terrifying occurrence. Such horrors should never become commonplace. The need to learn, to grow in power, consumed him. For it was not possible to learn a single spell and save his daughter. One mastery led to the next. Each terrible secret opened the gates to another. The man he'd been sank inwards like rotting fruit, became a dried husk of a being. Most nights he barely noticed Ruhinn, the love of his life, when she brought him meals, or tidied around him as he studied.

He made progress, fast at first, and then more slowly as the spells became more difficult. Finally, after years, he had but one last spell to learn – the only one that mattered.

And it defeated him.

Something held him back, hesitated like it knew that to learn the last spell was to surrender what remained of his humanity.

One last spell, and he couldn't do it. Week after week he smashed himself against the book, hammering his mind with repetition, struggling to learn what eluded him. Week after week he failed. He went days without sleep, weeks without bathing. He often forgot to eat, neglected every aspect of self-care, becoming a hollowed shell of the already thin man he was.

'Maybe you should stop,' Ruhinn said one day, standing over him as he sat at his desk. 'Maybe we should let her go.'

'No.' *I can do it. I* will *master that spell.*

'It's killing you. It's killing *us*.' She groaned, rubbed at the small of her back with gnarled fingers. 'It's not going to work. It's been years.'

'No matter the cost,' he said.

Some part of him struggled to the surface, a memory of who he'd been.

'Anyway,' said Fell, 'I'm almost there.' A lie. That spell defeated him.

Her breath caught. 'Truly?'

'This year or the next.'

She made a dry noise that might have been a laugh.

Fell turned to face his wife. 'We'll have her back, I promise you. I'm almost there. And then everything will be like it was.'

'Like it was,' she said.

He saw in her eyes that she wanted to believe. Desperate hope. Doubt.

'I promise,' he repeated.

How could things ever be like they were? Even if he returned Leona to life, and she was exactly as she had been, what of him? Was it possible to set aside a decade of necromantic study and become a loving father? Could he turn his back on all he learned? Gods, the secrets he knew, the powers he could access should he so choose.

Why settle for something so pedestrian as fatherhood? He could carve out a name for himself, raise armies of the dead! Someone, somewhere, must have use for such power! He and Rue could be wealthy, live in comfort! He glanced around their sad home, taking in the sparse and threadbare furniture, the stained curtains. Why live in such squalor?

As if sensing his thoughts, Rue took his hand, led him to the room where Leona lay.

He stood motionless, studying his daughter.

That's why.

No matter the cost. He understood now. To keep his promise, he must set aside all he learned once his task was complete.

If I can complete it at all.

Fell turned to his wife, took her in his arms. 'Give me one more year.'

She nodded, then lay her head against his chest. He held her, breathing the scent of her hair.

The next day, while Ruhinn was out shopping, a woman came to visit. Young and voluptuous, she had pale skin that glowed in the dim light of the apartment. She wore the rich clothing of the nobility, and walked with an assured grace beyond her years.

Unsure what to do, Fell invited her in. If the filth and poverty bothered her, she hid it masterfully.

She studied him without doubt or fear. 'You've done it. You've mastered the book.'

He twitched. 'What book? I think you've mistaken me–'

'I see it in your eyes. It should have broken you.' She reached up a fine-fingered hand to caress his cheek. 'But it didn't.'

He was less than sure. Something at the very core of him was dead, murdered by what he'd learned. He shook his head in silent denial and she ignored him.

'Rare is the mind that can hold such knowledge,' she said. 'Rare indeed.'

Surrendering the pretence, he said, 'One last spell to learn.'

The only one that mattered. The one he failed, over and over, to master.

'For your daughter,' she said.

He didn't ask how she knew.

'For Leona,' he agreed.

'Raising the dead is easy,' she said, studying him with dark eyes.

There was something deeply wrong with this beautiful woman; he found himself too aware of the skull beneath her skin.

That's the necromancy. It infected his every thought.

'If you want mindless minions,' he said.

'Ah. Yes. You seek to truly cheat death.'

'I can't do it. The spell is beyond me,' he admitted.

She flashed the slightest smile, unstained by humour or warmth. 'Nonsense. You are your problem.'

'How so?'

'You care too much.'

Was that true?

'But if I don't care, why bother?'

'Power for power's sake,' she said. 'Power because you can. Power because you want it. Power for what it is, for what it does.'

'I don't care about power.'

That twitch of a smile again, like she heard the lie. 'I can teach you the spell.'

His heart skipped, but caution held him. 'At what price?'

'I will give you another book.'

'What book?'

'The *next* book.'

The next.

'The second,' he said.

'Of nine,' she agreed. 'You will learn it as you have this one. I will guide you.'

'Why?' he demanded.

'You are skilled, but you could be great.'

'That's not an answer.'

An eyebrow quirked. Gorgeous as this woman was, skin flawless, body curved in all the most desirable ways, she sparked no lust in Fell. She terrified him. Her utter confidence spoke of a mastery he was decades – maybe centuries – from achieving.

'Lady Oh wills it.'

'Don't play with me. Who is she? What does she want?'

'She does not deign to share with me the reasons for her commands.'

'And the price?'

In Shyish, there was always a price.

'Once your daughter is returned to life, you will serve me as I serve her.'

'For how long?'

Unmoving, still like a statue, she stared at him for a score of heartbeats. 'Does it matter?'

No matter the cost.

'No,' lied Fell, 'it does not matter. And you are?'

'Nothing and no one, but you may call me Misère.' She glanced about his drab and ill-lit home before returning her attention to him. 'I will make you powerful beyond your dreams.'

Deny it as he might, a hunger burned in him. He'd lost Leona because he was powerless. He'd failed his wife. He'd failed his daughter. And now here he was, about to fail them again because he could not learn the one spell that mattered.

No matter the cost.

'Teach me the spell.'

The Dripping Bucket was warm and smelled of the boiled mutton Gallowglas had cooked up for the evening's meal. A fire crackled and snapped in the fireplace, occasionally shooting sparks out onto the stone floor before it. The scent of dry birch added a subtle spice beneath the mutton. A dozen men and women sat with their chairs turned towards the corner where Terese stood. She hadn't started singing yet, and was chatting with Rita, who sat on the table with her feet up on a chair.

Spotting Fell, Rita waved and beamed a huge, toothy grin. Terese flashed a more shy but no less welcoming smile that stuttered his heart.

He felt his face flush hot as he found an unoccupied table.

Scampering through the room, dodging around knots of people, Rita collapsed into the chair across from him.

'Go away, you wretched little monster,' he growled, but his heart wasn't in it.

She ignored him anyway, saying, 'I'm glad you came!'

Gallowglas brought Fell a brimming mug of strong ale, placed it on the table without a word, and disappeared back behind the bar.

Fell sipped the beverage and sighed.

'Are you all right?' Rita asked, examining him with bright eyes.

'No. My back and knees hurt.'

'Did you fall again?' she asked.

He remembered kneeling in the mud, sobbing into his hands. The woman on the horse.

They've come for me.

'Yes,' he admitted.

Tomorrow he would leave Hollow's Dell forever.

'Rita?'

'Yes?'

'Thank you. Thank you for bringing me food. Thank you for the blankets. Thank you for the potato and bread.'

She shrugged, embarrassed. 'You really should thank Terese for that.'

'I will. After.'

Somehow, knowing he was leaving, knowing he'd never see these people again, freed him. He didn't have to be grumpy. It was, at least in part, an act meant to keep people away.

He needed that distance, didn't dare get close. Everyone he ever cared about, everyone he ever loved, was dead because of him.

Never again.

'Why do you always pretend to be grumpy?' asked Rita, with the prescient understanding of youth.

'All old people are grumpy.'

'That's not true. Ashton the baker is older than you and he's much happier.'

I was alive two hundred years before Ashton's great grand-parents were born.

'Fine,' he said. 'All old people are grumpier than young people.'

She thought about that, head tilted to one side, as she played with the tangled mess of one of her plaits. 'I suppose,' she admitted grudgingly.

'If you can avoid ageing, do so.'

She gave him a perplexed look as she considered his words. 'Isn't dying the only way to avoid ageing?'

It wasn't, of course.

Not waiting for an answer, she stood, said something about helping Gallowglas in the kitchen, and jogged away.

The girl never walks anywhere.

So like Leona. Boundless energy. Such a pure heart, untroubled by the horrors of the world.

Someday that would change. Someday she'd be old and wrinkled, bent by the years, innocence scoured to nothing. Fell would be long gone. Not dead, but not here to witness it. Sadness crept up on him, a thief, stealing the warmth from the fire and the joy from the room. An ancient grief, centuries gone, but still sharp enough to wound.

The door to the Bucket swung open, and a large man

wrapped in heavy muscle entered. He wore a hauberk of double chain, the coif thrown back and hanging loose to show the shaved dome, pocked by countless scars, of his skull. Matt-black, his armour absorbed light. He wore an unadorned livery of black. A sword hung at his side, one hand resting on the pommel. The room stilled, everyone freezing in fear. The warrior surveyed those gathered with icy eyes, dead gaze lingering on each table, before finding Fell.

Grinning white teeth, he strode through the room to join Fell. 'Misère sends a message,' he said, waving at Gallowglas for a pint.

'The answer is still no,' said Fell.

The man shrugged broad shoulders. 'She said as much.'

Slowly, the conversations in the room stuttered back to life, the inn's patrons careful not to stare. They might not know who or what this man was, but everyone understood that, in Shyish, such men were dangerous and served even more dangerous masters.

'I'll leave in the morning,' said Fell. 'There's nothing for me here.'

'Really?' The man cocked an eyebrow, rubbing at dark stubble with a huge and scarred hand. 'Almost twenty years you've been here and you haven't made a single friend?'

'No.'

'Hmm.' The man turned in his chair, made a show of studying Terese. 'A bit old for my taste, but a good-looking woman.'

Fell stifled his reaction, shrugged.

Returning his attention to Fell, the big man grinned. 'You care nothing for what happens to these fine people?'

'Nothing,' agreed Fell.

'So you won't care when we ride in tomorrow and butcher the lot?'

Fell studied the warrior. 'No. Anyway, I'll be long gone.'

Carrying a pint of ale, Rita exited from behind the bar. Fell's heart dropped when she headed straight to his table.

'Who's this?' she demanded, when she arrived, delivering the ale. Turning on the warrior, she asked, 'Do you know Fell? From before?' She showed no hint of fear.

'Only by reputation,' said the big man, grinning at Fell.

'Begone, child!' snapped Fell.

As always, she ignored him. 'Is he your father?'

'Ha! No, child. My mistress has some… interest in him.'

'Interest? Why?'

'Your friend Fell possesses a rather singular mind.'

'Your mistress wants him because he's grumpy?'

Again the big warrior laughed. 'Quite. Now, if you'll excuse us, I have some things to discuss with your friend.'

With a careless shrug, Rita disappeared back into the kitchen.

'We're going to kill them all,' said the warrior.

'Go ahead.'

'I'm going to nail that girl to the wall of this shite-hole tavern and skin her alive.'

Fell leaned forward on his elbows and grinned death. 'I don't care.'

'I almost believe you.' The warrior stood, ignoring his pint. 'But we've been watching you. The singer,' he nodded in Terese's direction, 'sends you food almost every day. I'll gut her, let her die slow. It'll take days.' He adjusted the sword at his side. 'We'll be back in two hours.' He left without waiting for a reply.

Fell watched him depart, his chest tight.

If I leave now…

It didn't matter. Misère would make sure the people of Hollow's Dell suffered terribly. 'Grief,' she had told him as she stood over the ruin of his life, 'is a weapon.'

She thinks she can change me, make me like herself.

A servant to this mysterious Lady Oh.

He remembered the swirling dust, ash dancing in the wind, whipping about his legs, staining his hands. Everything gone. Life and purpose. Ash and corpses.

Rita exited the kitchen, bringing a tall mug of water to Terese. The woman accepted it with thanks, and tousled the girl's hair. Glancing at Fell, she flashed that shy smile. He had to look away for the shame.

'You all right?' asked Rita.

She stood at his side, face crumpled with concern. He hadn't heard her approach.

Walk away.

Maybe she wouldn't follow through with the threat if he left.

She would. He knew it.

There's nothing you can do to stop it.

Except there was.

Fell's fingers curled into a tight fist. A smouldering ember of rage sparked to life.

Misère, you push me too far.

Fell studied at Misère's side every day and long into each night. She guided him through the workings of the spell that had defeated him, but also insisted on teaching him spells from the second book. No longer did he sneak away to skulk in public graveyards. Her servants delivered fresh dead for him to practise his necromancy upon. Sometimes it was old men and women, or those who'd died in accidents, their bodies bent and broken. Sometimes it was children, seemingly unharmed, but quite dead.

He never asked where they came from; he dared not.

Leona. She was all that mattered.

No matter the cost.

'If you don't learn these spells in time,' she said one evening, 'you'll die of old age long before you're useful.'

Useful. She might have plans for him, but Fell had plans of his own. Being useful to this woman was not one of them. Dying of old age, he decided, wasn't part of his plan either. He and Rue had lost years trying to get their daughter back. He'd learn these spells, let Misère think he would honour his end of the bargain, and give him and his wife that lost time back. From the moment Fell agreed to study with the necromancer, he began scrimping and saving what funds he could. When the day came and his daughter was returned to them, he wanted to be ready.

Very quickly it became clear that Misère's understanding of necromancy – the raw power at her disposal – far outstripped his own meagre abilities.

'I could never have your skills,' he admitted after one particularly difficult evening.

Misère sat across the table from him, dressed in silks of pristine white that flowed loose and yet managed to cling seductively to the curves hidden beneath. Porcelain-perfect skin. Flashing dark eyes. If he were forty years younger, his wife might actually have some reason for the jealousy she harboured.

Misère studied him. 'When I was your age, I had a fraction of your abilities.'

She looked like she couldn't be out of her twenties, though Fell knew appearances could be deceiving.

'How old are you?' he asked.

That humourless smile graced full lips and died a fast death. 'This is not my age.'

For a moment he thought she meant that her body did not

accurately display her age, but that was more than obvious. Then he saw it. Did she date from the Age of Chaos? Could she be even older, and hail from the Age of Myth?

No! Impossible!

Whatever the truth, it didn't matter.

Once Fell had his daughter, he would abandon this dangerous woman. He'd flee with Rue and Leona. Maybe to another realm. Anywhere but here. Shyish was madness, in love with death, infected with soul-deep rot.

'You shall serve me as I serve Lady Oh,' Misère said. 'In time, you shall fight at our side, help turn the tide of war. Your potential...' She sighed with longing.

War? He dared not think about who this woman served.

Six months later, Fell had learned half of the second book – for learning with a skilled teacher was much easier than trying to translate and teach oneself – and knew he could cast the spell to save Leona.

That evening, after Misère left for wherever she retired to each night, Fell bolted the door and turned himself to the effort of raising his beloved daughter from the dead.

The spell worked, as he knew it would. He and Rue held Leona, this time crying tears of joy, as she looked around the room, trying to understand where she was, and how her parents had suddenly become so old.

Hurrying his wife and daughter, they rushed to pack what little they owned and fled into the night. Hailing a carriage, they rode to the docks. Fell purchased passage on the first ship heading south, not caring where it went, as long as it left Shyish.

Freedom. Time to finally start living again.

The next morning he stood alone at the rail, watching the sea flash past. Fish jumped and dived as they followed the vessel. A flock of seabirds, their twisting chaos staining the sky, followed too. They squawked a constant cacophony, fighting over scraps and defecating on everything. The sea air felt good on his skin. A strong breeze ruffled what hair he still possessed, and hurried the ship on its way.

He'd done it.

He'd mastered the spells and rescued his daughter from death. She was alive and beautiful, full of energy, and already exhausting Rue with her constant questions. Last night the three of them had shared a bed, all cuddled and clinging to each other, Rue and Fell unwilling to let go of their little girl.

And if she gets sick again?

No! He had power now, he could protect her, protect them all.

But is it enough?

He could learn more. There was always more. What if his talents extended beyond necromancy? Could he find a teacher? Maybe he should continue his studies. Having planned to escape Misère from the very beginning, Fell read through the second book in its entirety. It didn't matter that he hadn't understood much of it, for it was locked in his mind. He saw every page with perfect clarity.

I can teach myself.

Why stop? Better safe than sorry, surely!

I'll talk it over with Rue.

They were a family again. This would be a family decision. Whatever she decided, he would abide by it. And if circumstances changed, that book was forever in reach.

'She's a beautiful girl,' said Misère, standing at Fell's side.

His heart dropped into his stomach, a deep, writhing nausea. Worms in his gut.

'We had a deal,' she said.

A monster of a man, clad in angular plate armour stained a deep and arterial crimson, stood with her. A hand rested casually on the pommel of the great sword hanging at his hip. Eyes, blood-red diamonds, glowed from deep within the helm.

'I just want time with my family.' Fell hated the desperate pleading in his voice.

She laughed, a harsh bark of scorn. 'This was always your plan, and so it was always mine. You brought this on yourself.'

'I'll serve, I swear. Just let my family–'

'They were dead from the moment you agreed to learn from me.'

It's my fault. Guilt crushed him.

He turned on her, anger building. 'You don't *touch* them!'

Misère raised an eyebrow as if shocked by his outburst. 'Just as your fear of failure stopped you from learning the spell you needed, your family – your love for them – will stop you from learning everything she requires of you.'

'You don't need to–'

'Life is nothing. Love is nothing. To become one of us, you must shed such weakness. Someday you'll understand.'

One of us? Fell stared at her in horror. 'You're insane!'

'You thought that first book broke you. You still cling to hope.' Misère studied him, beautiful eyes in juxtaposition with the horror of what she was. 'We need you shattered.'

'You can never break me,' Fell swore. 'No matter what you do, I shall never serve.'

'Grief,' she said, 'grief will break you.'

Turning her back to him, she raised her arms as if to accept the adulation of a crowd. Several sailors stopped to admire the interesting things this did to her already interesting physique. White silk whipped about her as the wind picked up.

'There is only one escape from grief,' she said. 'Death.'

And the sailors collapsed. Those working the rigging plummeted, landing boneless and broken, leaking blood into the wood. Fell felt the impacts of them through his feet.

A heartbeat later, scores of seabirds crashed to the deck or splashed down in the sea.

Thousands of fish bobbed to the surface, floated belly-up, pale and dead.

No one screamed. Silence of the grave.

'There is but one universal constant,' she said. 'Decay.' And the stench of putrefaction filled the air as scores of bodies began to rot. Flesh sank. Faces became leering skulls, maggots feasted on festering eyes. Bellies swelled and burst.

The door to the cabins below-decks where Fell and his family stayed swung open, and Ruhinn and Leona exited, blinking in surprise at the littered corpses.

'No,' said Fell. 'Please.'

Misère beckoned Rue and Leona forward. 'Use your power,' she told Fell. 'Stop me from taking them, and they shall live.'

What could he possibly do? She was a powerful necromancer, maybe even a deathlord, though he couldn't bring himself to believe he'd captured the attention of one so terrible. For a mad instant he considered trying to leap past her guard to tackle her. But the thing in armour watched with glowing eyes. Fell had no doubt it would cut him down.

Dead. Everywhere. They littered the deck, fouling the air with the stench of their rot.

Raise them! Turn them against her!

There were enough that her guard couldn't possibly bring them all down. At the least, they'd keep him busy, leaving Fell free to put a knife in her back.

Misère grinned at Fell and her disguise fell away. While her body remained curved and beautiful, flawless in every way, her face shed its flesh. Empty sockets, deep holes of endless black, studied him. Her perfect, full lips shrivelled like strips of meat left in the sun, exposing the mad rictus of cracked teeth. Turning to face Ruhinn and Leona, she lifted her arms as she had when killing the sailors.

He had to act now!

With none of her finesse and mastery, Fell screamed out the spell. Eyes clenched shut, he pictured the book, flashed through the pages.

Don't fail! Don't fail!

Everything had to be perfect.

Fell poured himself into the spell, sacrificed the tenuous threads of his psyche to save his wife and daughter.

And failed.

Eyes open, he stared, stunned, as Misère undid the spell maintaining Leona's life. The necromancer was a master, a seamstress of unparalleled skill.

Fell watched, helpless, frozen by terror and grief, as his daughter unravelled. She came apart like ash in the wind, crumbling and falling in on herself, mouth open in an *oh* of terror. In an instant she was a dispersing cloud of dust, dancing on the sea breeze.

Kneeling, Fell screamed. He screamed threats. He screamed pleas for mercy. He begged forgiveness and swore vengeance.

Misère turned on Rue, her fingers hooked into claws. The necromancer shed the last of her false humanity, allowed the illusion of life to fall away. She was death. Clean white bone. That reaching hand squeezed into a crushing fist, and Ruhinn screamed as she suddenly aged at an increasing rate.

Rue's hair, already shot with grey, turned white and then fell out in fist-sized clumps. Her skin wrinkled and sank, her eyes dulling like turning milk. Flesh and muscle withered. Knees shaking, she collapsed. Her hip, brittle with age, snapped when she hit the deck, and she pitched to one side. Sprawled and helpless, she mumbled incoherent nonsense, her mind gone.

A score of heartbeats later, she was shreds of rotting flesh on bone.

Numb with horror, Fell sat back, staring up at Misère, broken by grief.

She turned to face him, once again whole and beautiful, and all the more terrible for the lie. 'Do you understand why you failed?' she asked.

He didn't answer. He couldn't. Words were gone from him, life and meaning stolen, his purpose murdered. Dead inside.

'Love,' she said. 'You loved them so much the fear of losing them made you panic.' Stepping closer, she patted his head like he was a favoured pet. 'I've saved you from that.'

Tears fell as he struggled to understand what had happened.

Rue's bones are still here.

It was enough. He might be able to raise her.

But nothing remained of Leona, the dust of her scattered to the wind.

If he raised his wife, he'd have to explain his failure, how he cost them their daughter. He couldn't face that, couldn't put Rue through that pain.

'I know this hurts,' said Misère, 'but in time you'll come to understand. You'll thank me for freeing you.'

He stared up at her in mute incomprehension, blinking tears as she continued.

'When you are immortal, godlike in power, this will seem a small price to pay. In time you will forget them.'

Forget them? Part of him desperately wanted that.

'You will serve, and in return I shall teach you,' she said. 'Someday, many centuries from now, when you are ready, you shall meet my mistress.' That hint of a mad grin.

Looking down at his hands, Fell saw them stained with dark dust. Leona. His little girl. His beautiful little girl.

'I will never serve,' swore Fell. 'Kill me if you want.'

'Kill you? No! Lady Oh has decided, and you shall be hers. You might be stubborn, but she is forever.' Misère stared down at him with what might have been pity, had she been capable of such emotion. 'All too human. Let me help you with that.'

Hooked fingers moved and twisted as she tore away some core part of his humanity.

'There,' she said, sounding pleased with herself. 'Now you will live forever. Know, however, that this is a curse, not a gift. You shall never heal. Every wound will haunt you for all eternity.'

'I don't care.'

'Give it a few hundred years. You cannot die. No wound can end you. Someday you will lie broken and unable to move.'

'I will never use necromancy again. I deserve this.'

'Deserve.' She snorted in derision. 'You already know the spell that will reverse my curse.' Misère knelt before him so she might look him in the eye. The dust of his daughter stained one knee. 'You will break your silly oath.'

He grinned madness at her. 'You've taken everything. You have no power over me.'

'Nonsense,' she said, standing and brushing the dust from her white silks. 'Grief is a weapon. Grief is *her* weapon. You think yourself beyond that now, but you are wrong. Some day you'll feel again. You'll love again. When that times comes, so shall I.'

* * *

Fell gazed about the Dripping Bucket – at Terese singing, Rita behind the bar wiping mugs because she had too much energy to sit still and couldn't stand the thought of not helping – and knew that time had come.

I tried to remain apart. I tried to be distant.

Their kindness undid him.

Their kindness was going to be their death.

Only if I do nothing.

But what could he do?

A limping cripple, he had no chance of escape.

His gut soured. Misère would force him to watch these people die.

Old lady Kalindy only beat them by a day. Unlike her, the rest of the townsfolk would never be buried.

Fell's breath caught.

Hundreds of graves, centuries of Hollow's Dell dead.

He wasn't helpless. All he had to do to save these people was break the promise he made to the dust of his daughter.

No! Never!

He watched Rita, red hair spilling from her braids, deliver a full mug to Ashton and return to the bar. Gods, she was so like Leona.

Will you let her die just so you can say you kept your word? Will you let them all die?

He knew the spell. He could raise the dead of Hollow's Dell. They wouldn't be like his daughter, not truly alive, but they could fight.

Fell stood so abruptly his chair toppled over backwards.

Startled, Terese stopped singing. All attention was on Fell, the spell of her voice broken.

Rita paused in wiping a mug. 'Fell?' she asked.

'All of you stay here,' he said. 'Bar the door behind me.

That man who was here, he came to kill me. To kill you all.'

They blinked at him in disbelief.

'Don't come out until it's over,' he commanded.

He left then, not waiting to see if they'd listened. He didn't have time, less than two hours if the warrior in black was to be believed.

Could he do it?

Fell's heart pounded in his chest and he remembered his failure on the ship. Misère's cutting critique: you loved them so much the fear of losing them made you panic.

She was right, he'd panicked.

But she was also wrong. Love wasn't why he'd failed.

Slamming the door to the Bucket behind him, Fell tossed aside his cane and sprinted as best he could for the graveyard. Gone was the careful shuffle of an old man afraid to hurt himself. Clouds blotted the night sky, choking the stars. Only tenuous hints of the moon punched through to light his path. He leapt puddles and potholes, taking risks he would have called insane an hour ago. Nothing else mattered. He would not fail this time.

An unseen crack in the path tripped him, sent him spilling to the ground. He felt the bone in his left forearm snap as he landed. Screaming from the pain and frustration, he rolled back to his feet and ran on.

The arm swung loose, grinding bone on bone, sending sparks of hot agony through him.

Nearing the graveyard, he tripped again, this time on a root hidden in the dark. When he tried to stand, he discovered he'd re-broken his left ankle and it no longer supported his weight.

Fell crawled the rest of the way, tearing his hands and knees.

You're ruining yourself.

These wounds would never heal. He'd be crippled, helpless.

He didn't care.

Reaching the graveyard, he found a branch to use as a crutch, and regained his feet.

Calm, he reminded himself. *You will not let your love for these people kill them.*

Closing his eyes, he imagined the book, flipped through the pages until he found the spell he needed.

Breathe. Calm.

Misère was wrong. Love wasn't a weakness, it was strength. Caring about the people of Hollow's Dell gave him reason and purpose. He would sacrifice himself to save these people. He would wipe out whatever she threw at him, and if she dared to show herself, he'd throw his strength against her too. She was always impressed by his potential. With nothing to lose and a willingness to sacrifice everything, he prayed he might at least wound her. More was too much to hope for.

Focus.

Fell lost himself to the spell. The sounds of the night and the damp smell of impending rain faded to nothing.

Misère had taken everything from him. All he had left was his word, his oath to the dust of his dead daughter, and she was taking that too.

She'd pay.

Oh, she'd pay.

I'll have my bloody vengeance.

Fell heard a whooping war cry from the hills surrounding Hollow's Dell. They were here, and he wasn't ready.

He'd failed again.

'No!'

Surrendering himself to the spell, Fell poured all he was into the dark necromancy.

The war cry grew closer, the rumbling thunder of hooves.

There were many ways to raise the dead. With skill and finesse, one could summon the spirit of whoever originally possessed the body. When time was of the essence, it was possible to call whatever souls happened to be nearest. In moments of desperation, there were infinite hells of suffering spirits one might contact.

Fell tore the fabric of worlds and threw it wide, a gaping wound. Wrenching open the gate he called upon the lost souls and savaged spirits trapped there.

'Come to me!'

They came.

They *all* came.

The soft earth of the graveyard heaved and buckled as generations of dead clawed free. Skeletons, held together by gristle and ill will. The more recent dead, still clothed in their decaying finery, meat rotten and frayed. Old lady Kalindy, dressed in her best dress, her normally peaceful face twisted in a feral snarl, milky eyes seething with madness.

It wasn't enough.

Fell screamed the spell, opened his soul to the darkest forces, unleashed countless hells. His voice echoed through the town and surrounding forest, and all the dead within hearing rose. Thousands of insects and animals. Wolves. Mountain lions. Deer and horses. Cats and dogs. Snakes. Slaughtered cows and pigs writhed and fought free of the hooks on which they hung and staggered from the butchery.

The dead heard, and they answered his call.

'Destroy them!' Fell commanded, and his army of decay hurled itself against the attackers.

He stood, transfixed, horrified at what he'd done. A score of armoured riders thundered into town, only to be met by a crashing wave of death. They fought, stabbing and hacking, but the dead care not for wounds.

Fell watched as old lady Kalindy, ignoring the sword stabbed into her belly, dragged a woman off her horse. The two struggled for a moment, Kalindy worrying at the warrior's armour. Finally, pulling the coif aside, she tore the woman's throat open with her teeth.

Everywhere such scenes of horror played out. A horse, mobbed by the corpses of vipers, their poison made worse for rot. Half a dozen dead wolves, still working as a pack, pulled another horse down and savaged its rider. The dead were unstoppable.

The woman Kalindy had killed rose, her throat a raw and gaping wound. Fetching her sword, she turned on her companion, attacking and killing him.

Fell laughed, a cracked cackling edged with madness. He succeeded. He raised the dead, and they obeyed his commands. But he also got the spell subtly wrong. Everything that died rose to continue fighting under his control. One of the raiders' horses, belly hanging in shreds, entrails dragging behind it, reared up to trample a man, crushing him to the earth.

It went on and on, death making more death, until the dead surrounded the last warrior, the big man in black plate armour who had threatened Fell in the Bucket.

'Don't kill him,' Fell commanded.

The warrior cut down scores of dead before they wrestled his weapons away and stripped him of his armour. They held him helpless, arms pinned behind his back.

Leaning heavily on his makeshift crutch, Fell approached. His left leg dragged, the ankle twisted to an impossible angle. His left arm hung limp and useless.

'This didn't quite turn out as you'd planned, I suspect,' he said.

'My plans matter not,' grunted the big man. He showed no fear. 'End me and be done.'

'Not yet.'

In truth, Fell wasn't sure why he spared the man. Perhaps he could, through torture, learn something of his opponent, Misère. He doubted it. This man would die before betraying his mistress.

Turning, Fell saw an army of the dead silently awaiting their next command.

Dull pain pulsed through his body. Everything ached. He'd done decades of damage in the last hour.

It doesn't have to be like this.

He could undo Misère's curse.

My promise to Leona.

What was that worth now? He'd broken his oath when he'd raised the dead. Why go on suffering?

Because I deserve this.

But someone else deserved it more.

Misère.

He knew now what she saw in him. She might have more skill, more talent. She might know more spells, but he was hardly helpless.

I've hidden for too long.

Flipping through the pages in his mind, he found the curse she'd worked against him, a slow path to undeath. He'd never given it much thought, but now realised there was a good reason he ate less every year, slowly becoming increasingly brittle. In another century his heart would stop and he'd be a walking corpse. There were other spells in that second book, too. Spells locked in his perfect memory but never studied.

Spells for repairing the dead. Spells for reversing the damage of time by stealing life force.

Misère's curse, he decided, was handy. No need to age. But this slow decay was unacceptable.

Skimming through the pages of his mind, Fell found a spell that tore life from the living to repair the dead.

He glanced at the helpless raider.

This spell is evil.

There was no way it couldn't be.

But this man serves an evil master. Fell laughed. *Two wrongs making a right?*

Taking his time to get it right, Fell worked the foul magic. The raider's screams, sharp and piercing agony at first, faded to dull moans and then silence.

In moments Fell stood whole, a man in his early twenties. After centuries of falling apart, he gloried in the feeling. A sunken husk, the raider stood staring at Fell with dead eyes, awaiting his new master's command.

'Come,' said Fell, and his army of corpses followed after him.

There were, he suspected, one or more of the nine books hidden somewhere in Glymmsforge. He'd find them. He'd learn the spells even if they shattered what sanity he had left. Nothing would stop him.

It was time to take the war to Misère.

He would bring her down. Her mistress too, if she got in the way.

No matter the cost.

Misère watched from the trees, Pharizair, her undead guard, at her side. Red eyes glowing from within his helm, he stood motionless and emotionless, untouched by the horror.

'I told you he had potential,' she said.

Pharizair remained unmoved.

'Grief is a subtle weapon,' she mused. 'Mere fear of it will move men to terrible action. Anything to avoid the guilt and loss.' She smiled fondly down at where Fell stood with his little undead horde. 'He just needed a push.'

'He'll come for you,' grunted Pharizair.

'They all do,' she agreed. 'But that was always the plan.'

CURSE OF THE LUCKY

Gary Kloster

American fantasy author Gary Kloster brings his talent for writing downtrodden underdog heroes to Necromunda, where life is cheap, brutal and short.

Cutty is one of many juves scraping a meagre existence in the rusted corridors of Hive Primus – yet he's one of the lucky ones. Having escaped the clutches of the gangers, he works as a back-alley chirurgeon's assistant, stitching up wounded Goliaths. But when a gang leader's hand has to be amputated, the Goliaths take Cutty as compensation. The juve is lucky in other ways, however, and priceless to a ganger who knows how to exploit his unique abilities. As Cutty is dragged into the depths of the hive and drawn into a turf war with House Van Saar, he begins to curse his luck – though it may yet prove to be his salvation.

When I was a little maggot, helpless and soft, Kicker told me that the lumens hanging around our locker were meant to last a thousand years. If he was right – and Kicker was right about most things, except when he was lying to you for fun – nobody'd wanted to see anything in this part of the underhive for a long time. The lumen strips running through these filthy halls were dark as a Delaque's sense of humour, except for the faded few that dribbled light the colour of old piss, an ugly glow that made it almost harder to see than just clean dark.

'Dust and nothin'. Nothin' and dust.' A heavy hand fell on the back of my neck, and thick fingers twisted my shirt into a knot. My collar tightened, almost choking, as Rast yanked me back.

The House Goliath ganger stood twice my height, and outweighed three of me. Four if you counted all the spiked metal plates and thick chains that he'd wrapped around his scarred body. 'Not what was bargained, Cutty boy. Not what you owe.' Rast tightened his grip, and the crude skulls tattooed on the ganger's shaved head blurred as my collar cut deeper.

'Soon,' I wheezed, but Rast wasn't listening. He was frowning at the bloody stump where his right hand had been.

'I'm owed,' he snarled, and the thick muscles in his maimed arm rippled. His elbow rose over my face and my hands scrabbled against his wrist, trying to escape his grip, but I might as well have been trying to tear a sheet of plasteel. Damn my dice and the Lady who spun them, and damn me, I thought, waiting for Rast to bring his elbow down to shatter my nose, break my teeth, smear my eyes across my cheeks–

'Rast!'

Rast's armour clanked as he turned towards the ganger who'd called to him. 'What?'

'Somethin' ahead.' The Goliath nodded down the corridor. 'Light, and noise.'

'What noise?' Rast asked, but the other ganger just shrugged. For a long moment Rast stood still, his thoughts clinking through his thick head like the rusty chains he'd wrapped around his biceps. Then he let me go.

'You owe.' Rast cuffed me with his stump, knocking me to my knees. 'Find me my gun.'

My hands were fists, grinding into the dirty rockcrete, wanting to hit him back, but a scrawny juve like me didn't stand a chance against a monster from House Goliath. So I scrambled up and moved ahead. Not laughter or screaming, I thought as the light got brighter and the sound louder. No, this noise wasn't human, but I didn't stop.

Whatever made that howl, I'd prayed for it, and all I could

do was hope that whatever sadistic joke Lady Luck was about to play on me would take Rast too.

This is what happened to heretics.

Kicker'd taught me about the Lady, the way he'd taught me to stitch up cuts with scraps of wire. He'd been a medic in the Imperial Guard, before some alien monster had bitten his legs off. The Imperial cult had been pounded in him deep, and he still said his prayers to the God-Emperor every day before his morning piss.

But the old man still believed in Lady Luck.

'She's just something people say,' I remember telling him, not long after my parents traded me to him for a bottle of black dreamers. 'She ain't real.'

'Oh?' he'd said. 'Then who's moving your dice?'

My dice. Everyone in our section tossed dice. Gambling, mostly, but sometimes they spun stories out of the pips and symbols that turned up on those crude cubes. Some even charged to tell fortunes, but they were fakes, Kicker said. He'd seen real wyrds when he'd served. Psykers, the Guard called them, and they used them to hex the monsters they fought. Dangerous people, psykers.

I wasn't dangerous. Sure, the dice told me things sometimes, like whose wounds would heal or rot, or when a slop riot was brewing, and sometimes, sometimes I could look at my dice and *know* where to go to find the supplies Kicker needed. But I wasn't a psyker. It was just the Lady having fun, like Kicker said, and maybe believing in the Lady was heresy, but heresy… was safer than being a wyrd.

So I hid what I could do with the dice from everybody but Kicker. Until Rast.

The ganger had shown up at our locker, bleeding and

bellowing. He'd been shot in some scrap with Van Saar gangers, but he seemed more mad about losing his bolt pistol than the hole in his palm. Kicker couldn't fix the ganger's hand, had to cut it off to save him, but try explaining that to a raging Goliath. Rast was going to kill us both, until I told him I'd find him a better gun.

That's how I'd ended up kneeling in a puddle of blood while Kicker watched me with sad eyes and Rast stomped around, telling me which bones he'd break if I didn't get him what he wanted. I'd prayed to the Lady and threw my dice, and now here I was, leading Rast to a weapon that would get him away from me. That's what I'd begged the Lady for, and when my dice had landed… I knew where I needed to go.

I just had no idea what'd happen when I got there.

The corridor ended in emptiness.

It was a ventilation shaft, at least fifteen yards across. I'd never seen one this wide, and it fell down, down into darkness and stretched up until the walls drew together into a blurry point of light. I wondered… was that light coming from what Kicker called the sky?

I shuddered. No wonder the underhive was deserted around here. When the storms swept in from the wastes, these corridors would run with poison rain. Even without a storm, the wind flowed from far above, dusting me with toxic ash as it played the hive's exposed corridors like a hideous flute. That was where that screaming, laughing sound came from, and it was loud enough to cover up Rast and his gangers catching up.

'Where, boy?' Rast grabbed me and hung me out over the yawning shaft. 'You said you'd find me a gun. Where's the gun, boy? Where?'

'It's here!' I shouted, even though I had no idea if there was any gun, what dark joke the Lady was playing on me, but I wanted him to set me down. My shirt stretched, and my pocket ripped, sending my dice bag tumbling, falling – then it stopped.

I hadn't noticed the crude bridge thrown across the shaft a few feet below me. My bag hit it and split, the dice inside spilling across rust-pitted plates, spinning then stopping, and the dots and symbols suddenly shifted into meaning. Opportunity. Revenge. Danger. Death. Weapon. Weapon.

Weapon.

'There!' I pointed at the dice. 'It's down there!'

'Better be,' Rast growled, and let me go.

I hit the catwalk before I could scream, and almost tumbled off. Rast laughed, then waved one of his gangers after me. The Goliath pulled a climbing rig from his pack and pressed it against the wall, where it drilled itself into the rockcrete. He grabbed the cable and swung himself down. I gathered up my dice, shoving them into the medkit strapped to my belt, and looked over the plate they'd landed on.

It was flat iron, fastened to the girders that supported the catwalk. Useless, but there had to be something here. Had to. I tried shifting the plate, but couldn't budge it. The ganger Rast had sent down grunted in disgust and shoved me away. He grabbed the plate and his huge muscles rippled, and with a snap a hidden catch broke and the plate scraped to the side. A coffin-sized compartment was hidden beneath it, packed full of… Of guns.

'Huh.' Rast grunted, and for once his face wasn't twisted in rage. He looked… bemused, and I felt the same. This was what I'd prayed for, right? A weapon to get rid of Rast?

But why did this feel unfinished?

'Maybe you gonna live, boy.' Rast pointed at the largest weapon, and the ganger beside me tossed it up.

Rast caught it, looked it over. 'Bolter,' he said, his deep voice solemn. 'Not a bolt pistol. Real bolter.' By the Lady, I swear he was about to weep.

'Rest are lasguns,' said the ganger, but Rast shook his head.

'Rest are scav.' He looked down at me, and his eyes *were* shining with tears. 'You live, and you work for us now. You and your dice.' He held up the gun and roared with laughter. 'You live, but so many gonna die!'

'Gonna break his other hand,' the ganger beside me growled, but quiet. Then he poked me in the back. 'Hand me up that scav, wyrd.'

'I ain't no wyrd,' I said, dropping into the compartment. 'Just lucky.'

Lucky. I'd prayed to the Lady for a weapon to get rid of Rast. Now Rast was going to keep me for a pet. What use was heresy, when–

There was a flash and a sizzle, followed by a sharp crack. Something hot and wet hit my back and I spun to look up at the ganger standing over me. One of his eyes was missing, the empty socket steaming, and his head behind it was gone, splattered across me and the catwalk. Pretty headshot, I thought in that endless dazed moment, then the Goliath toppled and I threw myself under the iron plate. Hiding from the sizzling rain of lasgun bolts slashing down, I jammed myself into the tight space, waiting for my flesh to burn and burst… but it never happened. Whoever was out there didn't want to risk shooting any of the guns I was half-buried in.

Who the hell was out there?

'Van Saar!' Rast bellowed. 'You owe me a hand!'

Of course. Somebody had hidden these guns here, and if

anyone had access to good guns it was the gangers of House Van Saar.

In my tiny hiding space, I started to laugh. Maybe the Lady had smiled on me. I'd found Rast's weapon, but it belonged to the gangers who'd just shattered his hand.

But now I was caught between them. I needed to *go*.

Outside, in the middle of the firefight, the thin line of the dead ganger's climbing rig swayed in the wind. I tapped my dice and whispered, 'Give me luck.' Then I moved.

I shot out of my hiding space, lasgun bolts sizzling around me, but my hand closed on the cable. The spool above spun, and I dropped. Not fast enough, and the only thing that saved me from having my head popped like that ganger's was the Lady's blessing and my swinging. But I picked up speed, and the catwalk vanished, Rast and the Goliaths and the Van Saars gone. I was free, I was safe, and then with a wrenching jerk I was at the end of the line and the cable ripped itself out of my hand. I had time to scream now as I fell, and I did until I crashed into a pool of black water and my breath was smashed out of me.

It fitted the Lady's sense of humour to save me with water. She knew I couldn't swim.

I thrashed, trying to keep from sinking, until my hand hit something and I grabbed hold. The thing bobbed but held me up, and I gulped air.

Water surrounded me, stinging and caustic. Remnants of the last poison rain, mixed with factorum waste and sewage, it made my eyes burn and my skin itch. If I'd stayed under, if I'd inhaled any of this stuff, it would have eaten holes in my lungs, but thank the Lady I'd grabbed hold of this... corpse.

The body of the Goliath, bloated with stimm, floated in the

water, adding its blood to the other contaminants. 'Thanks,' I muttered, and kicked my legs until I reached the edge of the pool, using the dead ganger as a raft. I heaved myself out and tried to look around, but the light spilling down the ventilation shaft far above was too weak. Reaching into my medkit, I dug past my dice and found the sparker I used to sterilise my blades all good and proper. Pulling it out I gave it a squeeze, and with a shower of sparks it sent out its jet of flame. But I didn't get a chance to look around. A spark landed on my sleeve, and the contaminated water soaking the cloth flashed into flame.

I yelped and slapped the fire out, dropping the sparker. Still burning, it hit a puddle of the toxic water, and with a pop it lit. I danced back from the sudden heat, but the firelight gave me a flickering glimpse of the massive room surrounding me. It was huge and empty, except for the rows of thick rockcrete pillars that held up the distant ceiling. The floor was slicked with puddles, but otherwise bare. Some kind of reservoir, probably part of the hive's drainage system. Perfect. The flames died, the shadows swept back in, and I picked up my sparker, hot but unbroken, and shoved it back in my medkit. How deep was I? Too deep. No one went this deep, if they could help it. There was nothing good down here.

Crouching down, I checked the corpse. A knife rode its hip, huge for me but that was OK. My eyes were on the water as I reached for it, searching for what had made those ripples. Nothing, nothing… until the body shifted its head.

I jerked the knife free and shoved back, watching the corpse's head bob. Something crawled out of the water, clinging to the ganger's hair. A rat. Not a fat meat rat like they had on the farms though. No, this was a mutie thing, its hairless skin split all over with oozing eye sockets. Those eyes stared at me as the rat crawled up the ganger's ruined head, dipped its muzzle into the shattered skull, and began to feed.

I'd helped Kicker with a thousand rough surgeries, but the sound of the rat's teeth made me sick. I backed away, trying not to retch, and I saw another rat scamper across the floor, its many eyes flashing as it dived into the pool. Then another, another. A flood of dripping-eyed rats rushed out of the shadows and into the pool, trying to reach the body to tear out their chunk of meat.

Cursing, I backed away. The rats ignored me, busy feasting, but that wouldn't last. The swarm would finish that ganger, and I needed to be gone by then. But how? I was deeper than I'd ever been, surrounded by darkness and mutant rats, and had no idea how to get back. And even if I did get back, I had no idea if Rast was still alive. I groaned, and dug out my dice.

They sat in my hand, symbols meaningless. What was I thinking? What good had the Lady done me? She'd got me into this hole. 'Damn you,' I whispered, wanting to throw the dice, wanting to throw them away.

'Damn who?'

The words cut over the sound of the rat's hideous feast, a high, sweet voice, like a juve's. I spun, the ganger's knife raised before me.

'Who's there?' I asked, my voice cracking as I tried to make it deeper and failed.

'I am.'

I could see them slipping around the columns, silent despite the shallow pools of water. They were shaped like people, but there was something wrong. They shimmered, and as they came close I shuddered, seeing why. They were twisted with mutation, like the rats.

Their skin was thin and crinkled like an old person's, but

split all over with damp, tearing sockets that held eyes that blinked and shifted. A hideous mob of mutants, clutching crude clubs and shivs that could split my head or spill my guts. They crept towards me on silent, blinking feet, pinning me against one of the rockcrete columns. Around them slithered more of the mutant rats, huge ones, almost waist-high. When I was surrounded, they stopped, staring, twitching, silent.

'Stay back,' I said, fighting to keep the knife from trembling.

'Why?' A shadow moved through the mutants, a dark little thing in a black robe, and that sweet high voice came from the shadows beneath its hood.

'Because I'll kill you if you come close.'

'You will?' Small hands reached up and pushed back the hood. It was a girl, younger than me, and though her skin was pale like the mutants', it flowed smooth over a face free of any extra eyes. She only had two, and like the rest of her features they weren't just normal, they were beautiful. Wide and blue, they glowed like a plasma torch. Her scalp was smooth, hairless, but I'd seen plenty of people like that. Not everyone was dark and shaggy as me. Nobody would call her a mutie, so what was she doing down here?

'Who are you?' I asked.

'I'm me,' she said, walking forward. She reached out and touched the knife I still held in front of me. 'Put this down.'

'No,' I said, now almost as confused as I was scared. Almost.

She frowned, then her beautiful eyes went hard. 'Put it down.'

I felt it, deep in my head, like a wire shoved into my brain, fishing to find something, to hook it out of me. It didn't hurt but it felt wrong, like having someone reach through your skin and touch your heart.

'What are you doing?' Whatever it was, I hated it, and I gritted my teeth and somehow *flexed* my thoughts as I spoke. 'Get out of my head!'

Her eyes went wider, and I felt that probing wire try to shove deeper into my brain, and my fear turned to rage. This *was my* head. 'Get out!' I shouted, and flexed my thoughts again, harder, and shoved the wire of her will away. I shoved it out and almost collapsed, nauseous and panting. The girl could have pulled the knife from my hand then and cut my throat, but she didn't. When I looked at her again, she'd cocked her head to one side, watching me, beautiful eyes curious. Not a mutant, I thought. No.

A wyrd.

'You stopped me,' she said. 'You're like me.'

'No.' Not a wyrd, just a heretic, like Kicker said. But the girl was shaking her head.

'You stopped me,' she said again. 'So you must be blessed too.'

'I never had a name. Teacher just called me student.'

The girl sat cross-legged on the floor, staring at me with her dangerous eyes. Behind her, her mutants worked, the only noise they made the slice of flesh, the crack of bone. While I'd sat here telling the girl about Rast, about gangers and guns and how I'd ended up here, they'd caught and killed as many of the small rats as they could, then dragged the corpse of the ganger out of the water. They'd stripped him of clothes, equipment, and now were stripping him of flesh.

I kept my attention on the girl and tried to ignore their 'cooking'.

'These don't speak.' The girl nodded at the ones who'd stayed near us, watching me, fingering their weapons with staring hands. 'No names. But you have one. How did you get it?'

'Kicker gave it to me,' I said. I met her eyes, and that wire feeling skittered through my skull, but I kept her out. I had no idea how, but I did. It was getting easier. 'I… didn't used to like to operate.' That was a way to say it. When I was little, I'd been terrified of slicing people, squeamish and sick when I saw blood. 'I didn't like cutting them, so they called me Cutty.'

She frowned at me. 'But then that's a wrong name.'

'That's the thing,' I said. 'It's a joke, right? To call me Cutty, because I didn't like to cut people.' She was frowning at me. 'It's funny. Like calling Kicker Kicker, cause his legs don't work so well, and the one time he tried to kick someone he fell on his ass.'

'Fell on his ass.' She held a hand out, and a mutant silently handed her a flask. She took a drink. 'Tried to kick, and fell on his ass. Kicker.' Then she laughed. Laughed, high and sweet and terrifying, and I had to fight not to scream. As suddenly as it started, she cut her laughter off and stared at me. 'I want a funny name too. Give me one.'

'I'll think about it,' I said. Her frown came back, and I tried to distract her. 'That man you call Teacher. Who was he?'

'He was the man who taught me.' The girl shrugged. 'That's what he was. He kept me in a room, alone except for machines that fed me and watched me and showed me things. Sometimes he came and taught me things. About being blessed.'

'Blessed?'

'I can do things that most people can't. Like you. We're blessed.' She smiled and patted my hand, and I tried not to twitch. 'He said that's why I had to be kept by myself. To learn and train, to count my blessings, until I was ready.'

'Ready for what?'

'I don't know.' The girl frowned, annoyed. 'He never told me. And then… then he stopped coming. I don't know why, and the machines were stupid and useless. They tried to keep me there, waiting for him, but they ran out of food and I got bored so I broke them and left. Went exploring, all by myself, until I met these.' She waved her hand at the mutants. 'They wanted to eat me, but I told them not to. They're… not blessed.' She looked at me, her eyes innocent and strange. 'Is Kicker like you? Are there more blessed where you come from?'

'I'm not–' I shut my mouth on the denial. This girl… raised alone, by machines and this nameless man… She was wyrd, and she was weird, and maybe I didn't want to argue with her. 'No. Kicker, everybody else, none of them are blessed.'

'Oh,' she said, disappointed. 'Teacher said there were more blessed. He said most of them were dangerous. You don't seem dangerous, Cutty.'

I felt her touch my mind again, poking at me, and I shoved her away and she smiled. My ability to reject her seemed to please her.

'Have you thought of a name yet?'

'Uh, no,' I said. 'Teacher. He never mentioned any names?'

'No. But I pulled some from his mind once, when he was asleep.'

'You–' I shut up again. What would happen if I couldn't keep that sharp wire of her power out of my head and she figured out I wasn't really a psyker, wasn't blessed? Would she lose interest in me, and let her mutants take me apart like they'd done with the Goliath? I didn't want to find out.

'Helmawr,' she said. 'That's the one name in his head that I remember. That name scared him.'

Helmawr. The Imperial Governor, the man who sat atop the

highest spire. Even I'd heard of *him.* Had this girl's Teacher served Helmawr, or had he been hiding from him? Which was worse? My gut twisted, and I wanted to run. Run from this wyrd girl with her mysteries, her talk of the blessed, and her gang of cannibalistic horrors.

I wanted to run, but I had nowhere to go.

'Helmawr's not a funny name,' the girl said. 'Not like yours.' Her eyes narrowed. 'What can you do, Cutty?'

'What?'

'What can you do?' She looked over her shoulder, and the mutant who'd given her the flask took it back and offered it to me. I flinched from its hand, from the little eyes that stared at me from between its finger joints, and despite my thirst I shook my head.

'I ask for things,' the girl said. 'And I get them. That's my main blessing. What's yours?'

My fingers tapped nervously on my medkit, right over my dice. What should I say? *Your blessing's a curse, you're a monster, and I'm not like you? Thank the Emperor.* No. 'I'm just lucky.'

'Lucky?'

'I can read fortunes in my dice. Sometimes.'

'Show me.'

I pulled the pouch out of my medkit and poured my dice into my hand. She examined the little cubes with their crude symbols.

'Teacher tested me, to see if I could read the future. He had these funny cards. But they never meant anything to me. What do you see now?'

'Now?' I shrugged. 'Nothing. I...' My eyes caught on the dice spread in my palm. The symbols danced and twisted, and spilled their message into my head. Malice. Death. Revenge. The Weapon. Opportunity.

Death.

'Something's coming.' I jammed the dice back into my medkit, and spun to face the pool. Dark lines were falling through the dim light coming from above, surrounding the water. Climbing cables, at least a dozen, and Rast had only brought eight gangers with him.

'Van Saars,' I said to the girl. 'Gangers. We have to run!'

She looked at me, and I felt the wire of her power pressing for a moment against the walls I'd built against it. Then she opened her hands like someone mimicking an explosion, and around us the mutants moved, scattering and hiding. She grabbed my hand and ran too, surefooted and certain in the dark, leading me behind one of the columns. She stopped, and we peered back around the rockcrete at the pool.

The cables jerked as the gangers slid down, a dozen, then more, definitely Van Saars. They wore tight bodygloves in black and grey, carried lasguns polished and decorated, and were the size of normal humans, not Goliaths. Except one.

He was one of the last, moving awkwardly. Lowered on one of the cables, because his arms were bound behind him. Rast.

'Where is he, you pink-skinned ork?' One of the Van Saars glared up at Rast. 'Where's your boy who can find such carefully hidden things?'

'Dead. Hope so.' Rast's voice vibrated with anger. 'Led us into trap.'

'If it'd been a trap, you wouldn't have killed three of mine.' The Van Saar shook his head. 'Today's been bad luck for both of us, thief, and I don't like it. I want the boy who brought that luck. I want to know how he knew about my guns.' The man looked at the others. 'Take him alive. Go.'

The Van Saars split into squads of four and began to move carefully away from the pool, leaving one squad with the talking man and Rast. I ducked behind the pillar, ready to run, but the girl was staring at one of the mutants close to her. Her blue eyes shone in the darkness, and the mutant stepped away, every eye blinking. Then it disappeared around the pillar, heading towards the pool.

'What–' I whispered, but she shook her head.

I heard a shout, the sound of a lasgun, and the leader shouting, 'Alive!'

'Not him!' another voice shouted back. 'Some kind of mut–' The voice suddenly ended with a hideous gurgle, and beside me the girl smiled.

'Watch,' she whispered.

The battle was short, choppy, vicious. The mutants were silent, knew the territory, and outnumbered the Van Saars four to one. But the gangers had lasguns and armour. I caught flashes of light as lasguns spat their bolts, saw clubs and shivs flash. Watched many-eyed giant rats scamper like roaches across the great columns and fall on unsuspecting men. I saw mutant after mutant fall, their flesh boiling, eyes bursting. I saw all this as the girl moved, dragging me with her as she scampered through the dark. Ordering her mutants to fight, sending them to their deaths with silent looks. *I ask for things, and I get them.* I shuddered and understood what Kicker meant when he said that wyrds were dangerous.

Then it was done. All the gangers that had moved away from the pool were dead, heads split, throats torn, guts spilled in tangles around them, each group surrounded by heaps of glazed-eyed mutant corpses. The only Van Saars left were the ones standing next to the pool – four terrified gangers pointing lasguns at the shadows, their leader, grim-faced and angry, and Rast, looking pleased.

'Bad luck,' the Goliath growled. 'Maybe you're right.'

'Shut up,' the man snarled.

We crouched behind another column, staring at the remaining knot of Van Saars. 'What now?' I whispered, and the girl smiled, raised her hood and took my hand, pulling me as she tried to move into the open. 'What? Are you trying to get me killed now?' I hissed, resisting.

'Of course not.' She shook her head, looking annoyed. 'You're blessed like me. C'mon.' She pulled again, and this time I let her lead me out.

'Help!' she shouted, sounding terrified, a little girl lost and afraid, and the Van Saars aimed their guns at us but didn't fire. 'They were going to eat us!' She led me forward, and the gangers watched us, wary but curious. All except Rast. He was focused on me, and the huge muscles in his shoulders shifted as he fought to break his arms free. So he could snap my neck, probably.

'Stop,' the Van Saar leader ordered.

'Please,' the girl said again, her voice quivering with desperation.

'What is this?' The ganger leader sounded furious, fearful, confused. 'What were those things? Who are you?' His eyes left the robed figure of the girl and landed on me. 'Thief,' he snapped. 'Is this the boy?' Rast's only answer was a growl, but that satisfied the Van Saar. 'Damn me, that's one thing at least. Come here.' His voice was cold, dangerous, and I didn't want to move, but his laspistol, lacquered pink with crimson veins, like a heart torn fresh from a body, was aimed at me. I started forward, the girl beside me. In her dark robe she was hard to see, though she kept her hands carefully visible.

'What's the matter? Are you shy, girl?' the ganger leader snapped. 'Show me your face.'

'Shy?' The girl pulled back her hood, revealing her small, pretty face, her lips curled into a smile that bared her neat, white teeth. They looked… sharp. 'No, I'm not shy,' she said and laughed, and then her eyes flashed. 'Kill the others. Now.'

The Van Saars all blinked at her, except their leader. With practised efficiency he spun and shot, each bolt making the deep-red veins on his laspistol glow and pulse as it burned a hole through the chest of each surviving member of his gang. They went down without a cry, faces confused, and then he turned on Rast. The Goliath ganger roared, his shoulders flexing, and with a crack his arms broke free, hand and stump raised as he started to dive forward – too late. The Van Saar fired again, hitting Rast in the chest, and the huge ganger stumbled back and crashed into the pool behind him.

Drops of stinging water hit my face and rolled down. I wiped them away, staring at the Van Saar. His face was blank, eyes empty, his head cocked, waiting for the girl to tell him what to do next. Behind him, the ripples in the pool slowly died. A weapon. I'd spun the dice, and asked the Lady for a weapon, so that Rast would leave me alone. A weapon.

'Do we need him any more?' she asked.

'Do we…' I trailed off, looking at her. Trying not to be terrified. 'What are you planning on doing?'

'Going with you, of course. Back to your Kicker.' She stared around at the shadows of the vault. 'I'm tired of this place, and I'm out of mutants. Blessed or no blessed, I want to see where you live.'

Go with me. This wyrd girl. Go with me? How long would it be before someone came looking for her, either her lost Teacher, or Helmawr's enforcers?

'Cutty?' she said.

There was something in her voice, and I risked a look at her. There was something I hadn't seen before in the set of her features. Uncertainty. Worry. Loneliness. For the first time she looked her age, looked like a juve alone in the dark.

Then the surface of the pool shattered.

A huge hand surged out, grabbed the leg of the Van Saar and ripped the man back. He flew across the pool and his head hit the edge on the other side with a wet crunch. His whole body spasmed, then sank beneath the water, leaving nothing but a smear of blood and tissue on the edge of the pool.

'Run!' I shouted at the girl, but it was too late. Rast, still alive somehow, lunged out of the water, his good hand pushing him up while his stump smashed into the girl's belly. The air came out of her in a single, sharp scream, then she curled around herself, trying to draw a breath. Rast pulled himself up behind her, his stump bleeding, the crude steel armour wrapped around his broad chest half-melted in a circle over his heart from the Van Saar's blast. He had to be in agony, but there was no pain in his eyes as he glared at me. Only rage.

'You owe, Cutty,' he snarled, picking up the girl. He held her with his maimed arm, his one hand wrapped around her head, covering her eyes. I could see her moving, thrashing in the Goliath's embrace, but she was like a rat-pup caught between the treads of a loader. Just a bit of meat, about to be crushed.

'Put her down,' I said. Why? What did I care about this strange, deadly girl? She was wyrd. Dangerous. So dangerous.

But that didn't mean I wanted to see her head crushed by Rast.

'You want?' Rast growled. 'Come get.' The muscles in his

hand flexed a little, and I could see the girl's small hands claw at the ganger's wrists. Dangerous, but helpless now, helpless as I was when Rast held me. Anger rolled through me, hot and searing, but right behind came fear. What could I do against Rast? Why risk myself to save this wyrd? Run. The words echoed through my head, as I argued with myself. Just run.

Run like a coward.

No. Run and find a lasgun. Kill Rast.

He'd kill the girl and run after me.

Who cares? She's wyrd.

I can't.

What's she to you? Run!

She's… she's blessed. She's wyrd. She's like me.

Speaking the truth to myself shut up the fearful voice in my head. Left me staring at Rast and the girl he held. I felt nauseous, and yet clear. Free.

'I owe you nothing, Rast. I got you your gun. It's not my fault you were too weak to hold on to it.' I watched his eyes narrow. I could see them so clear, clear as the blood dripping down from his stump, the iridescent, rainbow sheen of the contaminated water on his face, his armour. I stuffed one hand into my medkit. There were my dice, but I ignored them. The Lady…

The Lady was just something people say. I had to make my own luck. I found the smooth lump of metal I was looking for and pulled it free, while I held up the knife with my other hand.

'But if you think I have a debt… Come and collect.'

Rast bared his teeth and threw the girl away, sent her tumbling over the blood-and-water-stained floor. Then he started towards me, not caring about the knife.

'Going to tear you apart, boy,' he said. 'Bit by bit.'

'Try it.' My other hand came around, my sparker flashing to life as I ignited it and threw it at the ganger. It hit him, straight in his broad chest, then bounced off and landed, burning uselessly on the ground.

'Damn my luck,' I said, and Rast laughed, brutal and short, stomped down on the sparker.

That's when the toxic water caught.

Fire rolled up Rast's leg to his chest, down his arms, over his face, and he roared, blazing bright. I stepped forward and drove the knife into his belly, sinking it deep, so deep the blade twisted from my hand when the ganger stumbled back. But didn't fall.

His skin was cracked and red, his clothes still burned, but Rast jerked the knife out of his belly with a gout of blood. He raised it, snarling, but before he could bring it down a shape appeared between us. The girl, looking up at him with angry blue eyes in a bruised face.

'Step back.'

The Goliath blinked, but then took one step back. Enough to tumble backwards into the pool. The flames that still danced on him touched the contaminated water, and it exploded. Fire leapt up, roaring and bright, then slowly shrank down until all that was left was smoke and stench and ripples moving across the black water. Then they were gone.

'What was his name?' the girl asked, staring at the still water.

'Rast.'

'Not a funny name. He deserved to burn.' She turned to me, massaging her bruised neck. 'That man asked if I was shy. Am I shy?'

'No,' I said. 'You're definitely not. Is that what you think your name should be? Shy?'

'Do you think it's funny?' she asked.

'Hilarious,' I said, and collapsed.

Of course I brought her back.

What else was I going to do? Leave her in the dark, alone, after she had saved my life? She was just a juve. A wyrd juve, but… but so was I.

'Calling us blessed… that was another joke.' Shy crouched in the narrow service duct, surrounded by conduits, pipes and garbage. She peered through a vent in the floor, down into a corridor packed with gangers and workers, beggars and stimm-peddlers, all jostling past each other, a never-ending flood of stinky humanity. Shift change at one of the factorums, probably, and I was glad that I had ducked into these tiny tunnels when we'd left the abandoned area around the huge ventilation shaft. I didn't want anyone to see Shy yet. Or hear me talking to her about the realities of the world.

'I guess.' I shifted the pack I'd dragged back with me, stuffed full of weapons and all the other loot I could strip from the dead Van Saars. 'Kicker can't kick, I can't cut, you're not shy, and the blessed are cursed.'

'We're wyrd.' Shy made a face when she said the word, as if it tasted bad. 'And the people that aren't, they hunt us, catch us, pack us into the Black Ships and send us to your Emperor, to be killed or enslaved.'

'He's your Emperor too.'

Shy snorted. More heresy, and no wonder the Imperium rounded us up. 'Come on,' I said. 'We're almost there. We'll see Kicker, and he'll tell us what to do.'

'Hide and seek,' Shy said, shouldering her own pack and scampering away, moving more easily than me in the tight space. I'd told her that no one used these small spaces, especially in an area inhabited mostly by Goliaths, except kids playing hide and seek. Then I'd had to explain the game to her, but I guess she got the idea.

We slithered through the narrow tunnels, dodging searing hot pipes and swarms of rot beetles, until I finally found the grate that opened into the grungy corridor outside the locker I shared with Kicker. It was strangely quiet, but I was just happy to see it empty. I started to undo the catches holding the grate on, but Shy touched my hand, stopping me.

Four men appeared in the corridor, dressed in armour, carrying guns. I bit back a curse. Enforcers. The steel fist of the spires, sent down to keep order in the underhive. What were they doing here?

The men reached the door to my locker and pounded on it. It slid open, and inside I could see four more enforcers, the rest of the squad and their commander. He was tall, not Goliath tall but still head and shoulders bigger than me, with a livid, raw-looking scar that covered the right side of his face. His hair and ear were missing there, distorting his good looks, and that side of his mouth was twisted into a permanent frown. He was holding Kicker against a wall, and I could see blood and bruises on the old man's face.

'Well?' the commander snapped.

'Captain Har,' one of the enforcers said, snapping to attention. 'Everyone else in the corridor says the same thing. The boy was strange, could have been wyrd, and he left six shifts ago with a group of gangers. Gone scavenging.'

'Your story checks out then.' The man let go of Kicker, and the old man slid down the wall, his faulty legs not holding him up. 'The Imperial Governor thanks you for your cooperation.' He turned his back on Kicker and pointed at his men. 'You two wait here, in case he comes back.' He frowned at the men. 'Capture, not kill. Everyone else, with me.'

Captain Har stalked out, and I noticed the badges on his armour. When he was gone with the rest, and the two left had shut the door to my locker, I let my curses out.

'They came for you.' Shy crouched beside me, and I felt her mind brush mine. Not trying to dig in this time. More like a touch, like her hand touching mine.

'They did, damn me.' I shuddered. All my talk of the Lady, trying to fool myself… I hadn't fooled anyone. 'That captain bore Helmawr's marks. He's part of the governor's private guard.'

'Really? He never mentioned.' I blinked at Shy, and she shrugged. 'That was Teacher.'

'Teacher?'

'Yes. The scar's new. Maybe that's why he stopped visiting.' Shy raised her hands to the catches on the grate. 'You want things from there? Clothes, supplies?'

'I…' I shook my head. 'We can't. Those men–'

'Aren't blessed,' she said, and before I could stop her she'd popped the grate open and dropped into the corridor. I slithered after, but she was pounding on the locker hatch before I could catch her. It slid open, and the two enforcers stood there, weapons covering her.

'Hi,' she said. 'Shoot each other.'

They spun, and their lasguns pulsed. At point-blank range, they spread boiling blood across the walls behind them, and tumbled to the ground. Ignoring them, Shy stepped into the locker and went to Kicker, who was staring up at her with terrified eyes. 'Hi Kicker! I like your name,' she said. 'It's funny. Much better than my Teacher's. I'm sorry he hit you.'

'What the...?' Kicker rasped, then his eyes found me, standing in the door. 'Cutty. I hoped you were never coming back. You have to run, boy.'

'I know.' I looked at the old man, my only family for so long. 'I know.'

He sighed. 'I'm sorry, boy. I wanted to pretend. First that you weren't what you were. Then that we could hide it. But that was an old man's stupid dream.'

'And a juve's,' I said, moving to my cubby in the back of the locker, grabbing a pack and filling it with my few things. 'I'm going, Kicker. Going to run.'

'Escape is just another stupid dream, Cutty.'

'Maybe,' I said. 'But I'm still going.'

He looked at me, standing over him, Shy standing beside me in her dark robe, and sighed again. 'May the Lady bless you and your... friend.'

I reached down and clenched his hand. 'You too, Kicker. You too.'

Shy nodded, and met Kicker's eyes. 'I'm glad I met you, but I was never here. Neither was Cutty. Somebody broke in, shot the guards, and knocked you out, but you never saw who. Got it?'

'Got it,' Kicker breathed.

'Good,' she said. 'Now pass out.'

Kicker slumped back, unconscious, and Shy headed back out. 'I would have liked to talk to him longer,' she said, clambering back up into the service duct. 'But that's OK. Your locker kind of smelled.'

I hauled myself in behind her and snapped the grate back on. Lady bless us. I pulled my dice from my pocket and tossed them down. Danger and death clustered on one side. Danger and opportunity clustered on the other. I scooped them up and shoved them back in my medkit. 'Let's go,' I said, turning away from death.

'Hide and seek?' Shy said.

'Hide and seek,' I agreed, and she laughed softly as she followed me down the narrow passage, the lucky and the blessed, heading out into the world.

BEST DEATH WINS

Sean Grigsby

Sean Grigsby, an Arizona-based science fiction author with a flair for visceral action and gallows humour, offers up this original and characterful portmanteau story.

Malum is lost. The tyranids have overwhelmed the Imperial defences and three Guardsmen of the Astra Militarum await the inevitable in a fortified bunker. When a disagreement emerges about the most noble course of action – attack the tyranids in a final blaze of glory or detonate blasting charges to destroy as many of the beasts as possible – a contest is proposed: tell the story of the best death you've ever seen. The winner gets to choose the trio's demise.

Death surrounded them.

Then again, death had always surrounded Regula Morrison in her duty as an Imperial Guardsman in the Ferlian Seventh. She'd seen groups of men and women disintegrated in an instant, witnessed hordes of greenskins cut into a dozen ragged pieces under the fury of a chainsword. But one thing Morrison had never seen, not until that dark day on Malum, was a tyranid bite off a man's leg.

'I'll never walk again!' Consus screamed through gritted teeth and spittle. He slammed his head against the barracks wall. Once, twice, three times.

It would have given anyone a headache, if not a concussion. The one-legged man battered his skull against the wall as forcefully as the tyranids trying to claw their way inside.

'Will you stop that?' said Amulius, rubbing the back of his head. He ran his hand through short, grey hair, scattering sweat onto the floor like a misty rain.

Something heavy slammed against the wall where Consus leaned. Grunting, he dragged himself to the centre of the room, waving off Regula's offer of help. On the roof, multiple thuds sounded. Claws tore into plasteel just above their heads, growing closer. A chorus of screeching accompanied it all.

'Consus,' Regula whispered, kneeling in front of him, 'You might not have a leg, but you have both trigger fingers, don't you?'

With bloodshot eyes, he studied her face, trying to decipher her meaning. 'Yes?'

'Then you can shoot. We'll hold them off until help arrives.'

Amulius snorted a laugh and walked over to a rack of shelves filled with matt-black containers.

'Is something funny?' Regula asked.

Amulius tapped his fingers against one of the dark boxes. 'Help isn't coming.'

Colour drained from Consus' face, but Regula knew blood loss wasn't to blame. Amulius' words had taken what little hope the man might have clung to.

Regula stomped over to Amulius, pulling the old man to the side. Her words came quiet but sharp. 'That may be so, but he doesn't need to know that. The tourniquet I put on him has only slowed the bleeding. He's going to die, but I'd rather him go out fighting.'

'Were you promoted as you crossed into these barracks?' Amulius lifted an eyebrow. 'No? All three of us are still troopers equally then? Good. It's not your decision to make.'

Regula lifted her chin. 'It's our duty.'

'Let me tell you something about duty.' Amulius broke out of the whisper, filling the barracks with his weathered voice. 'Malum is lost to these monsters. This planet is an insignificant, minuscule piece of the Imperium. It is nothing. What do you think that makes you? Me? That blubbering wretch over there, trying his best not to release the rest of his bodily fluids onto the floor?'

'You get your leg bitten off and see how you like it!' Consus snarled.

Amulius pressed on. 'We're going to die today. Let's not pretend otherwise. So, if we're going to talk about duty, I say it's our obligation to take out as many of these creatures as we can.'

Regula gripped her lasgun. 'That's the first decent thing you've said in the last five minutes.'

'We've only known him for five minutes,' Consus said.

Regula shrugged.

'Do you know what these carry?' Amulius nodded towards the containers on the shelves.

'Power packs, I hope,' Regula said. 'Mine's nearly spent.'

The old man shook his head. He unlatched the container on which he'd been drumming his fingers and splayed it open, revealing a row of demolition charges. 'This is a breacher's barracks.'

Regula looked the old man up and down. 'You don't look like a breacher.'

'I'm not,' Amulius said with a smirk. 'I was the lone member of my squad to survive, and I found salvation in here just before you came knocking on the door.'

'Do you even know how to use one of those things?' Regula asked. 'What's your plan? To toss as many charges out there before they overtake us? It would be better to storm into the Emperor's glory, guns blazing. There's more honour in that.'

Amulius pointed to Consus. 'He won't be storming anywhere, unless he's suddenly learned to fly. But you're right.

I don't know how to detonate the charges, but I'm sure the three of us can work it out. And you're also correct that it would be ridiculous to throw the charges one at a time. We only have to set off a single explosive near the others. Right here. Right now. The rest will follow.'

Regula lowered her weapon to the side of her leg. 'You want to blow us all to bits?'

'It would be quick,' Amulius said. 'Honourable.'

Regula hissed through her teeth. 'That's not honour. That's suicide disguised as a noble deed. I won't be a part of it.'

Amulius frowned. Turning to Consus he said, 'And what do you say, One-Leg? A quick end? Or do you want us to feed what's left of you to the monsters?'

Consus coughed and winced as pain shot through his body. 'I don't care one way or the other, as long as it's quick. Death is death.'

Crossing his arms, Amulius groaned and stepped over the trail of blood Consus had painted across the floor. The old Guardsman stared quietly at the wall.

Regula had known plenty of men like him before. They turned even sourer when they didn't get their way. She touched one of the charges inside the box. *Press, twist, throw.* It had been a long time, but the words were forever lodged inside her mind like sticky sap.

'I have it,' Amulius said as he turned round. 'We'll play a game.'

Consus laughed, but it caused him to wince. 'What a sight that'd be. The monsters finally slithering in here to find the two of you locked in a staring contest. No? What's it to be then? Dice? If you need game pieces, you can use those demolition charges. And to mark the board on the floor, you can use my blood. I won't be needing it.'

'You're playing the game as well,' Amulius said. 'Regula is convinced she knows what a good death means. Well, I want to hear about it. The game is this – we will each recount the best death we have ever witnessed. It must be factual. No fictitious imaginings. You must have seen it with your own eyes. No stories overheard round the lunch table. We will vote in the end to see who wins.'

'A good death, you say.' Regula huffed, pinching the top of her nose. Of all the words she'd used to describe death throughout her career in the Seventh, 'good' had never been one of them. 'And what exactly would that look like? Some noble charge into oblivion?'

'That's up to you,' said Amulius, 'and the particular spectacles this cruel life has shown you. All three of us will decide which death is the best.'

'What'll we win?' Consus asked.

Amulius sputtered his lips as if it should have been obvious. 'The winner chooses our fate. If Regula wins, we'll drag you along outside until we're all squashed or digested. If my story takes the prize, we detonate the charges. Since you don't care either way, Consus, you'll be the tie breaker. If you win, the decision is once again in your hands.'

Consus blinked. 'And what if we each vote for our own story?'

Amulius' face boiled red.

Before the old man could begin yelling, Regula sat on the floor in front of Consus, legs crossed. 'We won't be allowed to vote for ourselves. Fair enough?'

Both men nodded.

'If nothing else,' said Consus, squeezing his eyes shut, 'it will take my mind off the pain for a bit. Care to sit with us, Amulius? I'll try not to bleed in your direction.'

The old Guardsman nodded solemnly and lowered himself to sit.

'We were talking about glory,' Regula said, 'honour. Amulius, you don't strike me as someone who cares much about those things. Please don't take offence. I don't mean it as such, but the truth is that you want to detonate those charges because it's easier than following our orders and fighting to our last breath. For you, honour can be tossed away when it doesn't suit you. You don't seek glory. But that's why you've survived for so long in the Astra Militarum. The best death I've ever seen belongs to a man who craved glory a little too much...'

REGULA'S STORY

'His name was Bernard Wellsmith. He was my sergeant, but how he ever came to that position was always a topic of debate between me and the rest of our squad. Some leaders think of themselves before their subordinates. With others, it's the other way around. Bernard, however, *only* thought of himself. The rest of us were just stones to step on as he crossed towards whatever goal he'd fixed in his mind. Thinking back on it now, I don't believe he ever called me by the correct name.

'I was in two battles with him, and in both cases he recklessly chased the opportunity to make himself look good. The first time had us guarding a small pass, while the majority of our forces held off an army of heretics less than a mile away.

'"If they retreat this way," we were told, "you'll be the ones to stop them. Blow the pass and crush them as they run through."

'That wasn't good enough for Bernard.

'We hadn't been at our post more than half an hour when he turned and said to us, "Friends," (he was always calling us that) "the fight calls to us. Follow me to victory."

'"Sergeant," I said. "Our orders are to stay here."

'"I give you your orders. Now, I've got a chill in my bones only the heat of battle can warm. Come. For the Emperor!" With that, he charged towards the clashing forces, raising his gun in the air and softly practising his war cry.

'Now, this left our squad in a conundrum. We all knew Bernard Wellsmith was a fool, and most of them thought he should be allowed to follow a fool's fatal endeavour. If he survived the battle, he'd be brought before a commissar and would eat a bolt-round for disobeying specific instructions. The squad would guard the pass as ordered and we'd have a new superior officer before morning.

'But I suggested that we follow Wellsmith. While I thought it inevitable our sergeant would fall under a commissar's final scrutiny, I considered that we also would be brought to the firing line if we didn't operate within the chain of command. More importantly, a dolt like our sergeant, unchecked, would likely get others killed on his march to fame and glory.

'That didn't sit well with any of us. With most of the squad grumbling, we pursued Sergeant Wellsmith.

'By the time we caught up to him, he stood in the thick of it, shooting his gun this way and that. The man was such a terrible shot, and he refused to aim his weapon properly. Instead, he roared and squeezed his trigger, allowing his shots to fly where they would.

'In the confusion of war, it was difficult to say for sure, but I'm almost certain his misguided shots killed several of our brothers and sisters that day, and I doubt he ever realised.

They were unlucky. Sergeant Wellsmith, however, seemed to have fate's grace upon him.

'You've heard that fools, because they can't be made wise, are made lucky? Bernard Wellsmith was the embodiment of that phrase. Bullets passed him by, flames diverted direction as if a whirlwind surrounded him. I saw a heretic launch a rocket at the man from less than forty feet away. Bernard turned at just the right moment, and all that touched him was the rocket's dark smoke across his shoulder. The Guardsmen behind were not so fortunate. Their parts scattered into the air, coating the battleground, and those standing or lying on it, in dark-red gore.

'Three in our squad were cut down as we made our way further in. Bernard wouldn't stay in one place, and this frustrated us more than having to fight our way to him. A fellow Guardsman, Bromidge was her name, made it to the sergeant before the rest of us. She must have been angry. We all were. She leapt at Bernard and shoved him to the ground. What she didn't realise was that a rather large heretic had been standing over Bernard, swinging down a spiked hammer. The blow, intended for our sergeant, broke Bromidge's back in two, folding her like wet cloth. You may not believe me, but I tell you, I heard her spine snap as if someone had cracked a twig beside my ear. I can hear it now.

'The rest of us grabbed Bernard and ran.

'You might think the tale ends here, that Bernard was executed and the rest of us moved on. But his luck, it seems, carried over from the battlefield to bureaucracy. The sergeant and his commissar had some family connection, and we remained stuck under the shadow of Sergeant Bernard Wellsmith. More unlucky Guardsmen were harvested and added to our squad to replace those we'd lost. From then on, Wellsmith had us perform pointless training drills and endless nights of study. We were made to read about tactics, known weaknesses of different xenos, the history of previous battles. The heretics hadn't yet been purged from the planet and, until we faced them again, we were to spend our time productively. Our hatred for him grew more and more, as we hoped he'd be placed in charge of a different squad. I, however, wouldn't be satisfied until he'd been transferred to a different world.

'Our hopes were dashed the day our squad faced the heretics' leader.

'This time we weren't given some lonely pass to guard. We were sent right into the battle, and our sole mission was to demolish a bridge before the heretics had a chance to cross. Things… did not go as planned.

'While we were setting the charges, the enemy had begun their advancement on the bridge, and several other squads had no choice but to meet them head-on. Bernard once again felt the call to pursue direct combat. I was to stay behind while the rest of the squad followed him onto the bridge.

'"You have the detonator," I told him.

'"Oh!" He stopped in his tracks and handed it over. "Now *you* have it."

'Nothing I could have said would have stopped him from running onto that bridge, and to say it plainly, I had no desire whatsoever to stop him. I'd learned my lesson from the previous battle. Guardsmen were going to die that day, but I wouldn't allow our squad to be among them, not because of Bernard Wellsmith.

'Wellsmith didn't hear me call the others back, nor did he see me lead them away from the bridge, shouting at any Guardsman I passed, imploring them to retreat unless they wanted to be vaporised. Word spread quickly and soon the Imperial forces ran from the bridge, but not Bernard. He charged ahead, a strange sort of joy in his steps. Luck would again be on his side.

'The warlord was a huge man, armour red as blood, two enormous prongs jutting from his helmet. He carried a pistol in one hand and a fearsome axe in the other. Chains jangled from his left hand as he turned towards two Guardsmen who hadn't been able to flee. As he sliced them in half, it gave Bernard the perfect opening for a kill shot, and our sergeant knew it. This was the glory he'd sought. Killing this leader of bloodthirsty heretics would write his name upon the scroll of eternity.

'As loud as his lungs would allow him, Bernard screamed, "For the Emperor!"

'My sergeant raised his weapon. And that's when I detonated the charges we'd placed on the bridge.

'I'd grown accustomed to the sound of explosions, but that had to have been the loudest sound in the entire galaxy. The blast, the fire, the tons of steel and rock that rained from the sky, they erased the warlord, his soldiers, and Bernard Wellsmith from this life.

'Luck, it seems, can be killed just as easily as any man. I did as I was ordered, and I am not ashamed to say it.'

Amulius scrambled to his feet. 'You *should* be ashamed! Your sergeant. How could you?'

Regula remained seated, looking at the old man with eyes too filled with exhaustion to have room for fear. At the door, something scraped at the metal. Screeching followed and several heavy bodies pummelled each side of the barracks. 'Are you going to use that gun or just stand there stroking it?'

'And you're a breacher?' Amulius' left cheek twitched. 'You

could detonate the charges. You can end this hell we've found ourselves in. Why didn't you tell me?'

'Excuse me,' Consus said. His face had grown paler. His words were airy, almost a whisper. 'But I believe... we still have a game to play. That was the agreement.'

'Game?' Amulius flicked sweat from his face and pointed at Regula with a wet finger. 'That story was a confession of treason. She's forfeited.'

'If you think her story wasn't worthy... that would be one thing,' said Consus. 'But you said the story had to be true and witnessed first-hand. Is it because you didn't like... the content? Or are you afraid she'll win?'

'I'm not afraid,' Amulius snapped.

'Then the game goes on,' Consus said. 'Besides, I haven't had... my turn yet. You want to die in a fireball like Regula's sergeant? You've got... to tell the best tale. Right?'

Regula popped her knuckles. 'It wasn't treason. I was ordered to destroy the bridge and I obeyed. But I'm dead anyway, so what does it matter?'

Amulius lowered his gun and, after a few seconds glaring at Regula, nodded and sat on the ground, although a bit further from the other two this time.

Consus coughed wet against his fist, but it came away clean when he lowered it. 'I... suppose I should... go next. Not sure how much time I have.'

'The floor is yours,' said Regula. Muffled by the roof, a tyranid roared just above their heads.

'Then I'll take up as much of it as I can, if you don't mind.' Consus lay on his back, taking a deep but staggered breath. 'I don't have the will to sit up any longer.'

Amulius and Regula shifted away to avoid the man's bloody stump.

'Well,' said Consus, 'my story is not a tale of one death… but many, all suffered by the same unfortunate man. I'd like to say he helped me… to never fear death, not ever again, and for several years I didn't. But that's the thing about living. You… get used to it. You grow covetous of time you're not sure you have.'

CONSUS' STORY

'His name was Veritus.

'My squadmates and I were as close as could be, and Veritus was the heart and soul of our group, though we didn't know it until after he'd gone. He was a quiet man, scrawny and almost sickly. But when he had a job to do, he never quit. Never. Not even when things got unbearable for the rest of us. We called him names like Veri-Tinius, and laughed at how wobbly he held his gun, but we respected his perseverance. Veritus had something in him that neither I nor the rest of the squad could ever hope to replicate.

'We were on a recon mission when we got caught by some greenskins. They had us surrounded and outnumbered. I was sure they'd kill us right then and there. Well, they didn't. Except our sergeant, who tried shooting out a path for us to escape. They squished his head like a pustule and laughed and laughed, re-enacting the murder in pantomime. A lot of grunts and snorts were exchanged as they spoke in their nasty language. I think they were trying to decide what to do with us.

'I knew they had come to an agreement when they all started saying the same word: *Kutrag*.

'At least, that's what my ears heard.

'They shoved us along. When I tried speaking to one of my mates, I was struck in the back of the head and berated with snarls and a spray of greenskin spit.

'It was a long way, wherever they were taking us, but my only thought was of Veritus. I worried I might stumble over his fallen body, the small man dead from exhaustion or lack of water. But it didn't happen that way. We finally got to where we were going, all of us accounted for, minus the sergeant, of course.

'I smelled the greenskin camp before I ever saw it. Think of the worst stench your nose has ever had the misfortune to breathe in, multiply that by a hundred and pour a can of fuel on top. That might come close to what we experienced. As bad as the smell was, the sound was even worse.

'When we crossed through their spiked and painted gate, we were assaulted by the sound of what seemed to be several dozen hammers pounding against metal. That ceased when they gathered to watch us, snarling and hurling whatever they had in hand.

'The whole camp came out to see us marching in, pushing and shoving at each other to get a better look. A short greenskin tried to squeeze past one of its larger brethren. The bigger one kicked it, sending it flying into a pile of rusty scrap metal.

'The ones guarding us laughed, but hurried the squad through a pair of doors. The heat of day no longer touched me, and the lack of light left me stumbling blindly. The sounds of dripping water and our boots descending down endless metal stairs told me we were heading underground. They shoved me against a wall, where they bound me with cold metal against my forehead, chest, arms and legs.

'Lights turned on with a *thud* and a shower of sparks. I had to blink away the blur from my eyes, but when they'd cleared... oh, what a sight.

'The other boys in the squad had been shackled to the wall just as I had. It was as if we were being forced to witness some gruesome greenskin performance. If that's what it was, then the platform before us was a stage framed by giant metal coils, one at each side. These coils suddenly sparked with electricity that danced around the poles and lit the stage, revealing a green-skinned devil who hobbled towards us, breath wheezing in its chest.

'Kutrag, I assumed.

'This slimy green beast was different from the others. A strange device covered Kutrag's right eye and glowed red as it examined each of us thoroughly, one at a time. On its right arm, a gauntlet, each finger adorned with knives, buzz saws, and instruments of different sizes and ill intent.

'When it got to me, the greenskin poked at my flesh with one of its instruments, babbling something as if I understood their slobbering language. I had no idea what I was being considered for, but I knew I wouldn't like it, whatever it was. Clanking as it turned, Kutrag shouted something to the other greenskins, and with its bare left arm, pointed at Veritus.

'They grabbed our scrawny brother and pulled him from the wall. All of us shouted and pleaded, cursed the greenies, threatened to kill them if they didn't leave him alone. We were each struck with fists or boots until we'd quieted again.

Veritus never said a word. He jerked his chin at Kutrag and called it something I don't even have the heart to repeat here.

'On the stage, two greenskins lifted a tarnished rack, where they chained Veritus and removed his shirt. He hung there like a worm on a hook, looking at us all with a sad acceptance, as if he'd been expecting this to happen sooner or later.

'Kutrag's wart-ridden hand grabbed two cables that had been lying on the floor, the ends of which were long and sharp, like spears. I then saw these were connected to the large, sparking coils. The greenskin plunged one of the cable ends into Veritus, piercing that fleshy spot where the shoulder and chest meet. We gasped, but dared not retort any louder. Our mate grunted, face twisted in pain, but he was doing his best not to give the greenies the satisfaction of hearing him scream. When Kutrag shoved the other cord into Veritus' belly, though, he roared like a mad berserker.

'A greenskin doctor. That's what I believe this Kutrag was. Don't believe me, do you? Of course you don't. I wouldn't have believed it either. Well, I'm not saying it was anywhere close to the skill level of our medics – Kutrag probably fell more in line with a common butcher – but hear what happened next and decide for yourselves.

'What sounded to me like lungs coughing up pus was apparently Kutrag ordering one of the greenskins to raise its pistol and fire a bullet into Veritus' head. One minute, our mate was breathing heavy. The next, he was still as stone, with a hole in his skull. The squad and I lost our restraint then. We shouted and cried and begged the Emperor's mercy. The greenie scum at our sides didn't even strike us that time. They laughed, delighting in our misery.

'I wonder. Do they even grieve for their dead the way we do? Well, I doubt either of you will grieve for me. But...

could I close my eyes? Just for a bit? You have my thanks. I… I feel so tired.

'While we lamented, Kutrag hurried to work. It cut into Veritus' head, removed the bullet with a pair of dirty tongs attached to its gauntlet and then filled in the wound with a syringe of thick, pink slime. Veritus was still. Dead. The man didn't breathe, and Kutrag used a hearing device to listen to a heart that held no beat. Nodding, the greenskin shuffled over to a lever near the electrified coil on the right of the stage. It flicked the lever once – forward, then back, as quick as a snap of the fingers.

'Electricity flooded Veritus' corpse, shaking him like a dead worm. I didn't understand it. Why torture a man after you've already killed him? But show me someone who says they understand greenskin logic and I'll show you a filthy liar.

'The shock from the coils was sudden, and vanished as quickly as it had come. The squad grew silent, myself included, all of us watching Kutrag as the mad butcher watched Veritus' body with anticipation. What were we waiting for? We didn't know. The only question that came to me then was who among us would be next?

'Veritus gasped, as if he'd been under water for a long time and had finally broken the surface. None of us men spoke, we couldn't believe what we'd just seen and heard. We weren't sure if we'd imagined it. The greenskins, though, either laughed or grumbled, one handing another a fistful of hard, white objects. Currency? It wasn't until the ones closest made their exchange that I saw they were teeth.

'On the platform, Kutrag shined a light in Veritus' eyes, used the hearing device to listen to the man's heart. When the greenskin pulled away, our resurrected mate shouted into its face, "I'm back, you ugly pile of rat droppings!"

'We men cheered then, rattling our bindings since we couldn't pump our fists or stamp our feet. Veritus smiled proudly, drinking in the praise.

'I... I am numb. I'll have to hurry if I'm to reach this story's end. Where was I? Oh, yes.

'Kutrag couldn't have understood what Veritus had said, but our reaction made it obvious that it'd been the butt of a joke, and for all the crudeness I'd seen in greenskin humour, this upset the doctor a considerable amount. It jumped up and down, swinging its oversized gauntlet of terror through the air. A vein throbbed at the side of Kutrag's temple as it screamed a short sentence of babble.

'Its rage reaching a climax, the greenskin raised its arms, as if daring us to challenge it further. Kutrag took a step but missed the top stair and tumbled forward, knocking over a cart of supplies. Bits and bobs bounced down the stairs after Kutrag, who landed in a heap under its heavy metal arm.

'I've never laughed so hard in all my life, but it was due to exhaustion, and I was also trying my best to annoy the beast. Everyone in the squad was in tears from a fit of giggles of course, but so were the greenskins who'd captured us. And Veritus, he was up there, dangling from the rack and making each of his laughs cut through the air towards Kutrag like a thrown dagger.

'The greenskin doctor groaned as it struggled to its feet, several smaller green creatures rushing in to help lift it. We continued laughing as Kutrag climbed its way back to Veritus. We didn't stop when it raised the gauntlet's middle finger, the one capped with a knife so sharp it could bisect a whisper. With this, Kutrag cut off our mate's left arm.

'Well, that shut us up. The greenskins that'd been laughing with us suddenly remembered themselves and cuffed us across the jaw or socked us in the gut. For whatever reason, I received both.

'Veritus was surely in pain, but I reckon dying had somehow taken the sting out of life, and our mate refused to yowl. Instead, he shouted angry defiance at his torturer. "Kill me again, you walking bogie! I got more lives than an alley cat. And I'd give them all for my brothers!"

'Now, as someone who's recently lost an appendage, I can tell you the only thing you want to do when it happens is scream or die to escape the physical agony and the pain of losing a part of yourself forever. So, it was really something when Veritus gave Kutrag what for.

'The whole of the squad shouted together thrice, almost in chant, a deep "Ve-ri-tus! Ve-ri-tus! Ve-rit-us!"

'The greenies at our sides stepped away. I'd like to say it was fear that made them do it, but what's more likely is they didn't know what to make of us. Veritus' stump steadily poured blood onto the platform. Scrawny lad couldn't have had much to spare. But as I said, he had more than enough mettle.

'Kutrag snarled and shot flames from a gauntleted finger, cauterising Veritus' gory shoulder. Sound didn't escape Veritus' throat, but his face begged for an end to the suffering. Unfortunately, our brother had a long way yet to go.

'They brought in a metal tub full of dirty liquid. I'd say it was water, but I've never seen water that black. The greenies turned the rack over and plunged Veritus' head in, all the way up to his neck. Bubbles thrashed the surface and our brother battered against the contraption as hard as any man could.

'None of us said a thing. This life we've been thrown into, the life of a Guardsman, it promises a likely end by blade or bullet. You accept the possibility – welcome it, in a way. But no one, not one soul birthed out of the deepest pit in the Imperium, would ever welcome a death by drowning.

'When Veritus was dead – again – they dried him off and Kutrag barked something at one of the bigger orks. This oaf grunted and began pounding a fist against Veritus' chest, as if sounding a war drum. It looked as though the big greenskin was pounding out the water trapped in our mate's lungs. Kutrag hobbled over to the lever by the electrified coil, and once again gave it a sharp flick.

'The one who'd been pounding Veritus' chest flew from the spot, landing hard against the floor in front of me. Tendrils of smoke rose from its neck and armpits, smelling of burned grox-meat. Its fellows surrounded the body, and after a snap of Kutrag's jaws, dragged the dead greenie away.

'Veritus hacked up black liquid, spitting towards the mad butcher. I was convinced this was not some defiant insult, but a means to evacuate as much of the dark water from his body as possible. He gasped at air like a starving man tearing into a loaf of bread.

'Weakly, he winked at us and smiled. "One more life for the Emperor."

'We cheered. Tears filled my eyes. I have never, not before that day or since, been so... proud or inspired. Veritus represented everything virtuous and decent. He gave us all a... reason to live, to keep fighting.

'The greenskins became hurried in their movements, as if they were searching... for a form of death our brother could not return from. They brought a hammer and crushed his chest. Kutrag operated and shocked him back into being. Next came the... next came...'

* * *

'Consus?' Regula crawled over to him, knees smearing his blood across the floor. She shook him. 'Consus!'

He'd closed his eyes, and would not open them. Regula checked Consus' throat for a pulse but found none.

'Has he gone?' Amulius asked.

Regula nodded.

Something heavy pounded against the door, causing them both to turn and look. Unlike the times before, when the tyranids would heft their weight or claws against the barracks and move on, this came repetitively, like a battering ram that wouldn't stop until the door had ripped open. Similar sounds attacked the walls and roof.

'The game is over.' Amulius stood and opened one of the boxes filled with bombs. 'Come now. You're a breacher. Set one of these to go off. If there's time, and you'd prefer a shot to the head, I'd be more than happy to oblige.'

Getting to her feet, Regula brushed at her knees, but stopped when she realised they were covered in Consus' blood. 'I will not.'

'We have no time for your misguided sense of honour!' Amulius threw the box to the floor, watching the explosives bounce and roll away.

Regula wondered if the old man had been hoping the impact would cause the quick death he wouldn't be able to get from her. A layer of sadness covered his face now. 'If you want me to detonate one of the charges, you have to win the game. Tell me the best story. Best death wins, right?'

Amulius kicked at the empty container. 'Consus is dead, and we're at a stalemate. You hear that sound at the door? Our time has run out.'

'If you didn't have a worthy death to recount,' Regula said, 'then you shouldn't have suggested the game.'

Amulius' jaw twitched. 'You want a story? I'll tell you a story!'

AMULIUS' STORY

'It started like any other day. Another planet, another day trudging through blood and muck as you hold the line against endless waves of enemy troops. We were entrenched and barely holding back a group of xenos-worshipping cultists. But I soon noticed what made this day different – I could look at the sky without shielding my eyes.

'Countless dark objects swarmed above, nearly blotting out the day. A woman in my squad wondered if these were our reinforcements, perhaps Astartes drop pods. But I knew different, not because I was sure of what was to come, but because I could feel it in my gut. When the objects in the sky began plummeting into the ground, showing themselves to be large fleshy pods, destroying whatever and whoever crossed their path, it confirmed my intuition. We would never leave.

'I'd thought I'd known fear. Sergeants had told me that bravery is not the lack of fear, but the strength to push through it and do what needs to be done. I held onto that belief my entire career as a Guardsman. But what I saw in the sky that day, it wasn't something you could push through. It pushed back. Where before I'd felt a heat that motivated me into battle, this day I felt only cold streams flooding my veins.

'I ran, ran as fast as my feet would take me.

'"Follow Amulius!" someone in the squad shouted.

'I hadn't wanted them to follow. I was propelled by a deep sense of fear and self-preservation, but I was also too focused on the ground ahead to look back and tell them to find their own path of retreat.

'The war sirens sounded, calling everyone to arms. Guardsmen stormed from their barracks, hefting their weapons, a horde of sacrificial meat driven by *duty.* What a word. What a lie. I'd given most of my life to duty, to the Imperium. And after all that, I was to die in this swarm of monsters? No. I was going to survive. That was my duty.

'Avoiding the pods became harder the further I ran. One landed right on top of the commissary as I was heading for it. I could have lasted a long time in there. Food for ages. But I didn't slow, didn't grieve the wreckage of a lost refuge. Those who do that have very short lives.

'My squad, still running after me, kept shouting that I stop. I refused. It was about this time the pods opened and things inside them ripped their way out. I fired my gun, saw how useless it was against them, how fast they were, how much damage their armoured bodies could endure.

'What slowed me, forced me to look back into the maw of certain death, was a scream. Lucia was her name. She'd been trying like mad to reach me, but she'd fallen to the ground and the creatures, not so mindless to turn down an easy meal, leapt upon her. The sounds of tearing flesh and twisted bone, the sight of blood and innards scattered across the sand, that's what got me to running again.

'The others in my squad diverted course to stay away from the feeding horde, but continued to follow me. When I saw a barracks ahead, a building more fortified than your standard issue, I locked myself inside. You think the monsters out there are slamming these walls? It's nothing compared to how hard my old squadmates pounded their fists to be let in.

'I never told them to follow me. Why did I have to let them in? If I let them in, then those things would be right behind and I couldn't allow that. My fellow Guardsmen screamed, calling me every name under the stars. But, as is the nature of humans, their rage quickly turned to supplication when the beasts were near.

'They begged to be let in. "Amulius, please!"

'They did that for a long time. Well, it *felt* like a long time. Their cries were cut short soon enough, but replaced with the shrieks of monsters. As the massacre raged out there, I was in here, looking through what I had at my disposal. Imagine my disgust at the unfairness of it. Bombs. Explosives. I took it as a sign, though. I'd tried to hide from death, and this was my punishment. That's when I dared a peek outside and saw a young woman dragging a legless man across the sand.'

Regula wished more than anything to raise her gun and end the miserable life of Amulius Vespan. But she didn't. 'You dare threaten me for what I did to my sergeant? You? After what you did? I saved lives that day on the bridge. You are nothing but a coward.'

Amulius threw down his lasgun. 'Then allow me to enact my own sentence. Please, Regula. Tell me how to detonate the charges. You can escape and die however you want. I realised too late that none of us will survive this. I was wrong. If you won't allow me the death I want, then shoot me.'

Regula shook her head. 'Shoot yourself, Amulius.' She walked towards the door, now barely hanging on its hinges. A claw slid through the crack and scratched at the wall.

'I can't!' The terror in his voice caused Regula to look back. The old man was on his knees, tears in his eyes. 'You're right. After all my years, I've become a coward. I can't even take my own life. I've got by this long on the courage and sacrifices of others. But don't let these monsters have me. Please, Regula.'

'That's why you let us in,' Regula said, nodding with realisation. 'You needed someone else to give you the best death you could hope for. You reckoned one of us could detonate the charge. Save you the trouble. And now you'd settle for a shot to the head. Amulius, I'm sorry to say, but yours wasn't the better story. Your squadmates' deaths–'

'The story wasn't about them.' Amulius shook his head, slobbering over himself as he shouted. 'It's about us. Our deaths. Our story.'

'In that case,' Regula said, 'I'm going to choose the ending.'

A thunderous groaning filled the barracks as the roof was peeled away. A large claw dropped down and impaled Amulius through his centre. The tyranid lifted its claw, dangling Amulius there like a limp piece of meat at the end of a stick. A dumb, surprised expression across the old man's face was the last Regula saw of him before his body was pulled into the sky.

She levelled her sights on the door. As the monsters tore into the barracks, dropping from the ceiling, slithering through the walls, charging her from all sides, Regula Morrison ran towards her death, lasgun blazing, and the Emperor's name on her lips.

TRAIL OF ASH

Graeme Lyon

With this intense story of redemption Graeme Lyon returns to the pages of Inferno!, *leaving behind the Blood Bowl gridiron for the wilds of Ghur.*

Jaqlyn Kouslo is in pursuit. Through a catastrophic magical mishap, she has unwittingly unleashed something horrible upon the Realm of Beasts, and now it is her responsibility to banish it. As she tracks the dire entity across the realm with a regiment of Freeguild in tow, we learn of Jaqlyn's guilt and her burning desire to atone for her failure. This thrilling tale explores the wildness and unpredictability of magic in the post-Necroquake Age of Sigmar.

The village was gone.

Jaqlyn Kouslo stood in what had once been the main square and looked around at the devastation that had been wrought upon it. Buildings of stone and stout timber and more esoteric materials unique to this region of Ghur had been reduced to ruins and ash by the bestial fury of the thing she hunted. And the people...

Many had fled, scattered groups of crying children and confused elders shepherded by those men and women clear-headed enough to see that they couldn't stand against the threat that had been unleashed upon them. Warriors who had fought to defend their homes for decades took one look at the enemy that now came for them and abandoned all they had known with barely a second look, making for the far plains and distant mountains, preferring to brave the monstrous predators of Ghur than to stand against this horror. Jaqlyn knew that few would make it. The beasts of this land were swift to fall upon the unwary and the defenceless, and most of those who had fled would end up as meals for the denizens of the region.

They were the lucky ones.

Those that had remained – the brave, the hopeful, the foolhardy – had died in agony as fire consumed them, body and soul. Jaqlyn had arrived too late to save them, but in time to hear many of them screaming. The sound, she knew, would haunt her to her dying days. It wouldn't be the first thing to do so. It was unlikely to be the last.

The worst thing about this, though, was the randomness of it. Farhold hadn't been targeted. No mad wizard or vengeful necromancer had unleashed this magical monster on the innocents. It was sheer, random chance that it had come this way. Some unfathomable instinct had driven it, and the citizens of Farhold had just been in its path. It had killed without mercy, but also without desire to inflict pain. It was as a force of nature, and just as impossible to understand. And it was her fault it existed.

'Shall we make camp, magister?'

Jaqlyn looked up from her reverie to see Sergeant Archus standing a respectful distance from her. His men – her men, she reminded herself, though she would likely never get used to being nominally in command of them – were still searching the village for survivors; it was a vain task, but she knew they wouldn't be satisfied until they had completed it.

She considered resting for the night amid the smouldering ruins, but the smell of burning meat, hair and bone remained too strong to bear, and too strong a reminder. Besides, she didn't want to sleep yet. The sooner she slept, the sooner she would dream.

'No, sergeant. We have a few hours of daylight left. Let's

use them. We're closer than we've been since we started this. With luck, we might actually finish it.'

Archus nodded sharply and turned away, calling to the rest of his Freeguild unit. He was exhausted, Jaqlyn knew. They all were. Their pursuit of this enemy had taken long months. They were far from home – not that there was a home to go back to now – and alone, save for each other.

All they could do was continue onwards. And so they did.

Half a day's walk brought the group to the edge of a forest. It was like nothing Jaqlyn had seen before. The magic that formed the core of each of the Mortal Realms shaped its character. Here in Ghur, it seemed like the flora, as much as the fauna, was monstrous. Towering… trees, she supposed they had to be called, of a substance that shone like amber, stood taller than the highest tower Jaqlyn had ever seen in settlements of man or aelf. They branched into shapes that were reminiscent of beasts of ancient legend.

As she took her first steps into the gloomy depths, the constructions around her made it feel as though she were surrounded by immense monsters – hippogryphs and drakes with wings outstretched, talons ready to strike, or stout gargants leering down, clubs the size of houses gripped in meaty fists. Even the patches of light that fought their way through the canopy to strike the ground resembled capering creatures.

Had these been immense beasts once? she wondered. Had they roamed these lands in the Age of Myth, fighting amongst themselves until some magical catastrophe had frozen them into amber like this?

The thought of a magical disaster brought with it a wave of memories and grief, which Jaqlyn pushed down. This was not the time. As she gazed at the forest canopy above, she noticed that the light was fading. Night would come soon.

'Let's make camp,' she called, and a chorus of relieved utterances followed. As Archus and his Freeguild soldiers busied themselves setting a fire and pulling bedrolls from packs, Jaqlyn made her way over to one of the trees and reached out a hand, hesitating for a moment before touching it. She opened herself up to the flows of magic that ran through the realms. An ancient power, raw and brutish, filled the crystalline structure of the tree, passing down through roots that spread deep beneath the earth and intertwined with others, creating an immense system that felt almost like a living thing.

She probed deeper, exploring the mystical energy and primal instinct that infused the root network, and realised that it *was* a living thing. It spread as far as she could sense, and insofar as it had emotions that could be compared to those of mortal races, it seemed angry… and in pain. She followed the sense of pain, tracing her way through a labyrinth of roots. The ecosystem of the forest fought against the intrusion. Already hurt, it lashed out in its unthinking way, and shocked her back into her physical body.

She removed her hand from the smooth surface of the tree. She was breathing deeply, heart beating quickly, blood pumping around her body. She was terrified, but also elated. This was it. She could use the forest's life force to track her prey. But not tonight. Not without rest.

The fire crackled and spat into the night. Jaqlyn lay facing away from it, watching the shadows cast by its light playing across the amber trees, oddly illuminating their depths. Behind her, the soldiers huddled around the fire, talking in low voices. She opened her magical senses and listened, though she felt a pang of guilt for it.

'Aye, we're close,' said one. She thought it was Amaro, who had been new to Archus' unit when Tantalum fell and their quest began. He blamed her, she knew. He was right to, though she would never tell him that. 'But what happens when we face it? Can we really trust her to stop it?'

'She's a magister, Amaro.' That was Cragen, the oldest of the unit. Solid and dependable, always calm. He had lost his family when Tantalum burned, but he had turned his grief into a steely determination to stop the thing they hunted.

'When did you last see her use magic?' Amaro pushed. 'I think she lost her nerve after the city fell.'

'No surprise,' said another – Baris, she thought. 'It was her fault as much as anyone's. She can't control it.'

'There was nothing she could have done,' said Cragen. 'And I've served beside her longer than either of you. When she needs to, she'll come through. She'll stop the thing.'

'I wish I had your confidence,' said Amaro.

'Enough,' barked Archus. 'She's a magister of Tantalum, maybe the last one left. We follow her, and we serve her. And we agreed long ago that we would see this thing undone.'

Jaqlyn silently thanked the sergeant for his support, but in her heart, she knew she couldn't argue with Amaro. She had failed Tantalum. And he was right about her use of magic. Since that night, she hadn't harnessed the threads of power that pulsated through the realms for anything other than the most mundane tasks. She couldn't risk it.

She put the thought from her mind and let sleep take her.

Around Jaqlyn, Tantalum burned. Everywhere she looked, corpses walked, shambled and crawled. Some were aflame, pulling themselves forward with arms that were blackening, the skin falling away as the fire consumed them. Others marched in serried ranks, ancient armour hanging from skeletal bodies, notched and pitted blades held in literal death grips.

That was bad enough, but they weren't the only enemy in Tantalum.

For years, the city had fought hard to keep the beasts of the local forests at bay. The brayherds lived in the deepest parts of the Ironwoods, and the various tribes fought one another more than anyone else. When they united though, Tantalum was too tempting a target to ignore. Jaqlyn was used to fighting their kind, but normally from the walls, with ranks of archers raining arrows down on the beasts, duardin war engines peppering them with hot metal and her fellow magisters devastating them with spells.

Tonight, on this worst of nights, everything was different.

She didn't know what it was that had swept across the realm, but in its wake, the dead had risen, ancient skeletons in corroded armour climbing from churned earth to stand alongside the recently dead, flesh still rotting from their bones. Worse, whatever it was had changed the magic as well, infusing it with the dark stuff of Death in quantities Jaqlyn had never imagined possible. With that, Tantalum lost its best defence. The change in the thread around them made it harder for the magisters to cast spells. It was taking them all longer, requiring more focus, and with the walking dead all around, it was time they didn't have.

Then the beasts had arrived, driven towards the city by even larger hosts of the dead that had risen in the depths of the forest. Skeletons with horned skulls, the dead of decades of internecine conflict between the herds, pushed their living brethren towards Tantalum. With no one free to defend the walls, everyone too busy fighting the risen within the city, the beasts broke inside, and all was anarchy as the two enemies fell upon each other as much as the rapidly falling numbers of defenders.

'Jaqlyn, the city is lost.'

She turned at the voice, her reverie broken, to see Nicol striding towards her. His robes were caked in mud, blood and worse, and he had gashes on his face. He carried his long staff of office, a closed eye at its apex, and a short sword with glowing runes on the blade.

'No,' she said, determination in her voice. 'We can save it. We can save these people.'

'The students are getting as many as possible to safety,' he replied. 'Taking them through the tunnels beneath the west tower. You should follow them.'

'And you?'

His bloodied face was grim. He didn't need to answer. Jaqlyn knew that he would stay, sacrifice himself to hold off the armies of the dead and the children of Chaos, giving his people time to get away. He'd always had an idiotic heroic streak. It was him she'd learned it from.

'I'm staying too,' she said. 'I'll fight with you until the end.' Not waiting for a response, she drew her own sword, a long and slender stabbing blade, and held it in a two-handed grip, turning to face the nearest skeletal warrior. 'Come, spawn of Nagash!' she screamed at it. 'You won't take Tantalum without a fight!' It stared at her blankly even as she lashed out, lifting its shield at the last moment and blocking the blow. It struck back, an ancient and pitted blade slicing through Jaqlyn's robes as she stepped back. It pressed on, blade swinging in tight arcs which she parried with her own. It paused, and seeing an opening, Jaqlyn went for its neck, separating its skull from the body in one swift blow. It fell into a pile of bones in the dirt.

'Jaqlyn,' Nicol said again. She turned back to look at him. 'Fight if you must, though it pains me that you embrace death so readily. But fight for a cause, not for vengeance. There are still people here. Find them, send them to the west tower. Do some good. That's what we were always for.'

She nodded, as much a goodbye as an acknowledgement, and closed her eyes for a moment. She could sense the dead, the Death magic animating them. She wished she could pull the threads of magic and end their abominable existence, but the dark power was everywhere. The magic of Shyish suffused everything. It came from all around, and unbinding it would be the work of more time than she had. Instead she sought its antithesis, the motes of Life magic, the very essence of Ghyran that clung to all living things. Some of them were muddied by the corruption that afflicted all who worshipped the Dark Gods. Those would be the beasts. But there were others. She grieved to see how few, for Tantalum had been a populous city just a few hours before.

She found a cluster two streets away and moved towards it... but hadn't she done this before? She remembered... no. No. Not again. She couldn't do this again. There was something else. Somewhere else she needed to be. A clearing in a forest of amber.

She woke.

The mood of the soldiers was dark. Jaqlyn suspected they'd been afflicted by dark dreams as well. She knew many of them had recurring nightmares, as did she. Drawing closer to the end of their journey and the thing that had been unleashed that night could only be making it worse.

They broke their fast in near silence, and repacked their bedrolls and gear. As they did, Jaqlyn turned her attention back to the trees, remembering her attempt the previous evening to tap into the life of the forest. She had to try again.

She wandered away from the group, and after a moment she heard footsteps behind her. She reached out her senses and recognised the life-pattern of Sergeant Archus.

'What is it, Archus?' she asked, and turned to face him.

He frowned. 'How do you always know it's me?'

'Magic,' she said, raising her eyebrows theatrically. Archus laughed.

'Of course,' he said. Then he fell silent, his gaze dropping to the mossy ground.

'What do you want to say, sergeant?' she asked softly. 'I know some of the men have doubts…'

He looked back up at her, surprise etched in the lines of his face. 'You heard that?'

'My hearing is more acute than you might think,' Jaqlyn replied sardonically. She felt that pang of guilt again. Archus didn't deserve to be lied to.

'It was nothing, magister. Just tired men venting frustration. They respect you and would follow you into the Realm of Chaos itself.'

'They weren't wrong though,' she said. 'Amaro said nothing I haven't thought about myself.'

'Still. You are our magister and we serve you. We trust you. We will finish this. It's just…'

Silence fell between them again.

'Go on,' Jaqlyn urged. 'What do you want to ask?'

'What do we do when this is over?' he sighed. 'Where do we go?'

They were good questions. Tantalum was no more. She didn't know what to tell him.

'I… I don't know, Archus. I haven't thought that far ahead. I just want to stop this thing. Make it right. And let tomorrow take care of itself.'

He nodded curtly and turned away.

It didn't take Jaqlyn long to find the path to her prey. Her second communion with the life force of the forest was as difficult as the first, but through the anger and pain that suffused it, she found a trail of devastation that her quarry had left behind it. Her spectral form glided between twisted and bestial trees that looked mostly unharmed, their surfaces perhaps a little smoother, a touch discoloured, but the crimson grass that grew to waist height in the spaces between them had been burned to ash, and the way was scattered with the shrivelled corpses of unidentifiable creatures that called the forest home. In all likelihood they were a vital part of its ecosystem, evolved over millennia into one larger entity. And now parts of that were dead and dying. No wonder it was in pain. Had she the time, she would have grieved for it.

As she continued, the magic around her shifted. She could feel a familiar malign energy nearby, and she was sure the wind carried the echoes of crackling flames. She glided on, coming soon to the edge of an immense clearing. At its centre was her quarry. It was larger than she remembered and utterly terrifying – a creature of shadow and fire, in the shape of a massive, monstrous bull, pawing at the ground as it faced its latest prey, a lone duardin. Jaqlyn tried to cry out, but her spectral form was as ephemeral as mist, and unable to make any impact on reality. With a thought, she unravelled it and awoke in her physical body, one hand pressed against the cold amber of a huge tree. She turned to the semicircle of soldiers standing around her.

'I know where it is. And we have to hurry.'

It wasn't far to the clearing.

The crackling of flames and stench of sulphur assailed the group as they approached.

'Definitely the right place then,' muttered Archus. He raised his voice. 'Soldiers of Tantalum, shields up, weapons at the ready. Do your duty for your magister, and for the memory of our great city!'

The soldiers unhooked their shields from their packs and pulled shining swords from scabbards at their waists. Jaqlyn looked at them, their grey and dark purple uniforms torn and muddy, worn from the months of travel that had brought them to this point.

'I am proud of you all,' she said to them. 'You have never let me down. And today, I promise, I will return that favour. We will defeat this rogue spell. For our fallen friends. For Tantalum.'

'For Tantalum,' they echoed as one, striking the flats of their swords against the Sigmarite icons adorning their shields.

'We'll buy you time, magister,' said Archus. 'You can do this.' He nodded, and Jaqlyn returned it, then he ordered his small unit forward.

Against any normal foe, they would be effective soldiers. But this was no ordinary enemy. The great shadowy bull turned to face them as they approached. Jaqlyn saw the duardin it had been threatening grab a pack from the ground and stumble back towards the treeline. If he was fleeing, that was for the best. This monster had claimed enough innocent souls. It stood ten times the height of a man, and its body seemed to have as much substance as smoke. Fire burned from its eyes, and consumed its rear half, the flames splashing around the shadow of its form. It opened its mouth and bellowed, a tongue of flame licking out. It lowered its head and pawed at the ground with one man-sized hoof, then charged.

As the monstrous spell approached them, the paint on the soldiers' shields blistered and melted, running like it was coming straight from the brush and pooling on the ground as they pivoted around the magical construct, avoiding its headlong charge. The metal of the shields heated quickly, and the men were forced to drop them as they burned through uniforms and charred the flesh beneath.

They should have been running, but they held firm, the bravest of them slashing ineffectually at the thing. Even blades blessed by a priest of the God-King could do little to the ephemeral form of the endless spell. The swords passed through its shadowy hide as though parting mist.

One of the soldiers had the misfortune to swing in such a way that his blade hit the flames that billowed from the dark form. His blade caught fire, and he screamed in agony, dropping it as the metal melted and the grip burned. He fell to his knees, his hand blackened and charred. The bull turned more quickly than something of its size seemed capable of and gored him, its great horns solid enough to run the soldier through. It pulled its head back and the corpse dropped to the ground.

The other troopers closed ranks and presented their half-ruined shields. They knew this was a hopeless fight, but they would do their duty.

The bull turned again, facing the small group, and prepared

once more to charge. Archus pulled a pistol from a holster at his waist, cocked it and fired into the great bull's horned head. The bullet parted the shadowy substance, which closed again behind it. He started reloading the pistol, and looked to the side. Jaqlyn could see him shouting something, though there was no way of hearing it over the unearthly braying of the spell.

She closed her eyes, took a deep breath and focused on it. Opening up her aetheric senses, she reached out. It was a complex, multi-layered spell, as any that could achieve a form of life and exist of its own accord would have to be. She took it in, part of her marvelling at the artistry of its very existence. To her magical senses, it was a web of energy, thousands of filaments in the eight colours of the magical spectrum, woven together to form something that should have been impossible, and would have been were it not for the flood of power that had saturated the realms – and the dark corruption of Chaos that infused many of the threads.

She sought an opening, a chink in its defences through which she could find a way in and unbind its essence. The densely woven magical threads resisted her, defying her attempts to penetrate them. She pulled back and looked again.

To another wizard, the spell would have appeared different. Each person attuned to the mystical filtered what they visualised through their own experiences and perceptions of the world around them. To one, it might have been a vast pattern of complex geometric shapes forming a puzzle, or cogwheels turning and shifting and linking with one another in a never-ending clockwork mechanism. Another might have seen countless serpents devouring one another, growing and shrinking. For Jaqlyn, it had always been trailing threads, intertwining and weaving together. When she cast a spell, she did so by visualising its elements and weaving them into the pattern of the casting.

When she undid another wizard's spell, it was the reverse. But she needed a loose thread to pull on. There was always at least one. Here, that was at its heart, beneath the outer layers that had accreted as it travelled, pulling in the raw magic that suffused the land and creatures around it. It had always been powerful – more so than it should have been – but it had grown ever more potent in recent months.

'There's no way in,' she muttered. 'Maybe if I–'

Her attention was captured by a shift in the magical energy around her. Something flashed from the direction of the soldiers. She turned, and saw them, the faint traces of magic clinging like lightly woven rags to each of the few that had survived the spell's malign intentions. She was struck by grief that several of the men who had followed her these long months were gone.

Behind them was something else. A beam of energy, bright and strong, was radiating from another figure, around whom the threads of magic were densely packed. It hit the great bull, which reeled back. To Jaqlyn's astonishment, what she saw as the outer layers on the weave of the spell began to fray and flake away. In moments, the surface layer was gone, and the beam continued, shredding another layer of threads to magical ash that drifted away on the aetheric winds.

Jaqlyn tried to take advantage of the situation, sending her magical form towards the endless spell and trying to find a thread on which to pull. The bull bellowed and surged forward. The spell broke the beam, overpowering it by sheer force of magical will, and, it seemed, absorbing its energies in an immense implosion. Jaqlyn's aether-self reeled in pain, and she drew back to her own body, which had been tossed against a tree. She looked at the bull. It grew before her eyes, the licking flames of its rear half becoming a mighty torrent of fire that crashed outwards against amber trees and incinerated unfortunate soldiers.

'Stand firm, men. Stand firm!' shouted Archus, but it was to no avail. Overcome by terror of the unimaginable monstrosity they faced, and undone by the death of their fellows, men threw down their useless weapons and fled. One by one, they were caught by the spell, tossed into the air by great shadow-horns, devoured in flame-wreathed jaws or trampled under monstrous hooves.

Jaqlyn pulled herself up, but her body was reacting slowly, the after-effects of the magical implosion disrupting the bonds between her aether-self and her physical body. She would recover soon, but not soon enough. Only Archus remained now, standing firm and shouting prayers to Sigmar as the spell's great jaws closed on him.

There was a thunderclap, and a bolt of lightning fell from the heavens and struck where Archus stood. For a moment, Jaqlyn thought she heard a booming voice and saw a stern, bearded visage in the flash of lightning. Then Archus was gone, and the spell bellowed again, angry at being deprived of its prize, as the God-King claimed a worthy soul for his own. What would happen to Archus now was beyond Jaqlyn's knowledge, but she hoped that his next life, whatever form it took, would be kinder to him than this one had been.

'This is not good,' she heard a thickly accented voice shout. 'This is not good at all. That shouldn't have happened, Steelfist. That big, burning beastie shouldn't have been able to take that energy. Why did it go wrong?'

Slowly, trying not draw the spell's attention, Jaqlyn edged

around the outside of the clearing until she saw the source of the voice. It was a duardin, his beard a shade of red not far from that of the bull-spell's flames. He wore a combination of leathers and scraps of plate armour inscribed with duardin runes. Somehow, they seemed to be holding back the spell, though judging by the way the runes glowed and spat, that wasn't going to last much longer.

The duardin was frantically rummaging in pouches on a wide bandolier that crossed over his barrel chest. 'No, not that one, you oaf, that's no good. Maybe the aetheric destabiliser?' He pulled a cylindrical device from one of the pouches, pressed a rune on the side and gripped it tightly, staring at the bull.

'Let's see how you like this!' he shouted and threw the device at it. When it made contact, it exploded and the spell reacted as if in pain, drawing its tendrils back into itself. Jaqlyn saw her chance and reached out once again. To her amazement, where the device had hit the spell, there was a great hole in its magical shell. She took her chance.

It was like diving head first into boiling water. The magic tore at her aether-self, but she ignored the pain, though it hurt her soul.

Frantically, she sought a thread on which she could pull. As she did, she could feel the spell's focus land on her. She only had seconds before it recognised her for what she was and incinerated her vulnerable body. She delved deeper, searching.

There. A thread.

She grabbed it, and pulled. In reality, what she was doing was infinitely more complicated. She was taking immense quantities of magical power and dissipating them, taking the complex creation that was the Burning Head and reducing it once more to its constituent elements of magic. But in the metaphor that her aetheric senses created to help her understand the impossible metaphysics of it, she simply pulled…

…and nothing happened.

The malevolent entity roared and turned towards Jaqlyn as she tried to pull her aetheric form back into her exhausted body. It lowered its head and gazed at her. As she looked into the fiery eyes, she realised her mistake. Human will warred against a magical desire to survive. This spell, the product of her folly, her error, could not be unbound. Not by her. Instead, it would be her undoing.

It was going to kill her, and that would be her penance.

She couldn't look away from its burning gaze. Instead, she felt as though she were falling as she remembered the last time she had stared into that monstrous visage, the night the spell had come to be.

Jaqlyn made her way down the street, screams echoing strangely around her. Death was everywhere. Corpses, broken and brutalised, littered the ground around her, both human and beast. She watched them as she passed, constantly aware that at any moment, one of them might be returned to a semblance of life by the deluge of amethyst magic that swirled around her. A grasping hand at her ankle, or a body suddenly rising, broken teeth snatching for her throat, could spell her end.

She followed the screams to a group of townsfolk clustered together, defended by a makeshift barricade constructed from doors, barrels, broken statuary and whatever else they had managed to drag over. At the front, a pair of old men and a burly duardin leant crossbows on the top of the barricade, firing shots at deadwalkers and beasts alike as they approached. Around them, grim-faced men and women held long makeshift weapons – brooms with kitchen knives or cleavers tied to them – with which they stabbed at any beastman or skeleton that came too close. Behind them, more old men comforted crying children.

Jaqlyn hurried towards the group, swinging her sword at foes who drew near, severing limbs and breaking bones. She fought towards the barrier, every step earned with another fallen enemy. But there were too many, and their numbers were growing. Swearing under her breath, Jaqlyn stepped back. With a deep breath, she focused and opened her magical senses.

The familiar swirl of threads surrounded her, but it was different than it had been just a few hours before. There had been balance in the weave of magic before, with just the warm golden threads of Metal magic outnumbering the others. Now, threads of amethyst were everywhere, their total greater, she thought, than that of the other seven colours of magic put together. Death truly was everywhere. And there was something else, a further corruption in the magic around her. It reached out from a locus of power, fraying threads and turning them from their natural colours to pulsing, sickly darkness. It was the raw stuff of Chaos, and it was being shaped into something hideous.

She quickly found the source – a monstrous bray-shaman standing in the midst of a group of hulking bestigors. Its tall staff, topped with the horned skull of another of its kind, was planted in the ground. It was chanting in its dark tongue, and to her magical senses, the syllables themselves took life and formed into threads, meshing with one another and pulling in other nearby threads. Whatever the bray-shaman was casting, it was powerful, and it was nearly done.

Jaqlyn had a choice. There was no way to reach the bestial wizard and stop it with a blade. She could wait until the spell was complete and hope to unbind it, or she could try and disrupt the magic that was forming it. She scanned the threads it was drawing in. Besides the stuff of Chaos that spewed from the beast's throat, the bulk of the magic it was using came from the winds of Fire and Shadow, the magic of Aqshy and dread Ulgu. Jaqlyn sought threads that would stand in opposition. Chamon would be no good – the fire could overpower it as flame melted metal. The soothing light of Hysh was a good bet, the antithesis to the shadows of Ulgu. To combat the fire, she drew on the pure magic of Azyr, the Celestial Realm. Known more as the magic of stars, it also encompassed all that came from the heavens – including the furious storms that could quench any flame.

Jaqlyn reached deep inside herself, plucking glowing white and blue threads, weaving them together into an inchoate form and pulling them out into the aether before her. What she was creating didn't follow the structure of any spell she knew. Instead she was just trying to create something, anything, that could disrupt the weave that was taking form before the bray-shaman.

The magic was resisting her. She persisted, pulling more threads towards her, knitting in some gold in an attempt to balance the magic. But even as she did, sinuous filaments of Shyishan purple drifted into her spell, turning its bright glow darker. The spell started to struggle in her grasp as more of the Death magic was attracted to it. The pale blue became purple, and the purple started to turn black. Jaqlyn was losing control. Panic rising, she tried to pull some calmly drifting Ghyranian green into the mix. The opposing force to Shyish, that magic of Life might bring the spell back into balance.

It was to no avail. For every piece of Life magic she added, more Death magic infiltrated the weave, until it was too late. The spell was no longer hers. With a prayer to Sigmar on her lips, she let the spell go in the direction of the bray-shaman's magical construct.

The results were catastrophic. What emerged into reality was no ball of blazing light. It was a dark mirror of what she had intended, alive with pure Death. It surged forward, bringing an end to all that it touched, undead and living alike. Skeletons and deadwalkers were silently incinerated, wood and even stone scorched with purple flame, and the screaming from behind the barricade intensified as the defenders and their charges were burned alive. The screaming continued even after they were no more, as the magic of Death consumed their souls, sending them to one of the underworlds of Shyish to be playthings for the King of Bones. Again, Jaqlyn heard that otherworldly laughter as the spell slammed into the pack of beastmen and met its target.

The world turned dark as spell met spell. She saw the bray-shaman's magic pull out of its control, and had the fleeting impression that the beastman was consumed and absorbed by it. There was a flash, impossibly both light and dark at the same time, and she shielded her eyes. When she dropped her arm, what she saw before her filled her with such terror as she had never felt before.

A monstrous flaming bull towered over her, and it stared down with eyes of roaring fire. It was looking at her, and she felt its magical gaze pierce her soul. It recognised her as someone who had tried to stop it from being birthed. And it hated her. Around it, the remaining beastmen who had not been consumed in its birth jabbed spears and clubs in the air, chanting in worship of this godly creature that had been unleashed.

'What did you do?' Nicol grabbed her by the shoulder and spun her around. 'What did you create?'

She had no answer for him.

'Go, Jaqlyn. Get out. The west tower. Sergeant Archus and his men will take you.'

Nicol turned away and raised his staff towards the great spell, chanting words of power. That was the last Jaqlyn saw of her mentor as Archus ordered his men to lift her and carry her with them, her struggles to no avail.

The journey to the west tower was quick. Archus' unit battered their way through the enemies in their path, losing many of their number as they did. Those that reached the tower and escaped into the catacombs below, and thence out of Tantalum, were few, but they were determined. There was no question of what they would do next, after they emerged into the daylight once more and saw the ruins of their once great city, and far on the horizon, a vast creature of shadow and flame bellowing into the sunlit sky. Jaqlyn watched it until it passed out of view, unable to forget the depths of hatred in those blazing eyes.

Jaqlyn came back to herself, standing before the unstoppable spell that was the result of her failure. It would be her end. But… if she died here, what could stop it? What could possibly stand against it as it rampaged across Ghur, drawn by some unfathomable instinct to settlement after settlement, extinguishing them of life. How many more deaths would Jaqlyn allow?

'No,' she said firmly. 'I will not be defeated. Not by you.'

She took a deep breath and reached deep inside herself to the core of her being where the physical and magical were one. It was here that her spells began. It was here that she hadn't dared touch since that night. It was here, at her very heart, that she needed to reach to end this.

Back in Tantalum, she had sought to disrupt the equilibrium of the spell, and had succeeded only in making it stronger. In the months since, she had discovered more about what happened that night. About the great power that had swept across the realms – the Necroquake, it was being called. It had originated in the underworlds of Shyish, which explained the way it infused the weave with the power of Death.

It was that power she called on now, in a way. The spell before her was too great to defeat by any normal magical means. So instead she would create something that could meet it on its own terms, something that used the greatest concentration of energies around her – the natural threads of Ghurian magic, what scholars called the power of Beasts, and the abundant Shyishan magic of Death.

She let instinct take over, not consciously guiding her casting. Instead, she let the magic take the shape it desired. It wanted to be cast, to become... *something*, and she would be the conduit by which it took form and was given life.

She had mere moments before the great bull charged her and she suffered the same fate as the Freeguild soldiers. Grief and pain welled up at the thought of their painful deaths, and she embraced it, pushing it into the spell that took form before her. She reached deeper, and unleashed all the emotion that she had pushed down since Tantalum's fall. As she did so, she knew the spell was ready.

Jaqlyn let go, and the magic flowed through her. She felt like she was being torn apart, every fibre of her being slipping away onto the aetheric winds. She held on to the core of who she was, gripping tightly to thought, feeling and memory as the magic passed through her.

Then it was over. She collapsed to her knees and looked up. Above her was a great sphere of living crystal, gnarled and trailing streamers of liquid amber. It was as if one of the monstrous trees around her had returned to life and birthed some grotesque child. It radiated power, and even the bull felt it, taking a step back.

'Here, lass.' She looked in the direction of the voice, seeing the strange duardin by her side. 'Come on, I think we should go,' he hissed, pulling at her. She didn't resist, and he dragged her away as she watched her conjuration fall on the prey she had sought for so long.

The two spells met. The gnashing maw of the amber creature was lined with immense teeth, each larger than a man and looking like it had been plucked from the jaws of a dragon. They closed around a horn of shadow and snapped shut. The amber beast pulled back and tore the horn from the magical bull, which bellowed in pain and rage… and perhaps terror. It charged, head lowered, its remaining horn piercing the side of the maw. The wound bled liquid amber that streamed onto the bull and, rather than passing through its immaterial hide, sizzled and burned it, pocking what passed for its flesh.

An idea came to Jaqlyn.

'Do you have a weapon?' she hissed to the dwarf as the two endless spells circled one another above them. 'Any kind of bow or pistol?

'I've got my arm,' the duardin said, rapping his knuckles

against what Jaqlyn had taken to be a metal gauntlet, but she now saw was some kind of mechanical limb. 'I've a wee one-shot gun built in there in case of emergencies.'

'I think this counts,' Jaqlyn said, gesturing to him to do what he needed to get it ready. The duardin nodded and twisted the metal arm at the wrist, pulling the hand to one side to reveal the snub barrel of a pistol.

'I've only got one shot, lass,' he said. 'What do you need me to hit?'

'You see where the blood has burned the bull's hide?' She pointed to the wounds. 'One of those.'

'Small targets,' the duardin said, shaking his head. 'I'll need to get closer.' He started forward and Jaqlyn followed. Together, they circled around the duelling spells, which were continuing to strike at one another. The gnashing maw had torn away half the bull's face with its massive teeth, revealing what looked like a skeletal structure made of flame beneath the shadow-hide. In return, the bull's fiery jaws and remaining horn had wrenched chunks from the amber creature, and the liquid that trickled from the wounds stained the ground of the clearing.

Jaqlyn prepared a conjuration, a mystic shield, should they need it. It felt good to use magic again. Months of fear and doubt had been exorcised by casting the gnashing maw. She felt, for the first time since Tantalum, like herself again.

The amber maw lunged at the bull once more, and it batted the thing away, roaring.

'Now,' Jaqlyn shouted, and the duardin opened fire. His accuracy was unerring, and the bullet pierced the shadowed hide in the very centre of one of the amber stains, creating an entryway for Jaqlyn. To her aetheric sight, it was a mess of threads. She grabbed them – not seeking any one, just following her instincts once more, and pulled with all her might.

There was an explosion, and a wave of powerful magical energy rushed towards her. When it hit her, Jaqlyn fell into blissful oblivion.

When Jaqlyn woke, she knew it was over. Even without dipping into her aetheric senses, she could tell that the magic around her was cleaner than it had been. She pulled herself to her feet and checked for injuries. She'd been lucky – her body had been far enough from the duelling spells that she'd escaped more or less unscathed. She had the duardin to thank for that.

She looked for him, steeling herself for the sight of a hideously burned corpse. But there was no sign of that. Further away, she saw him lying on the ground, smoke rising from many of the runes carved into his armour. She moved towards him, reaching out with her magical senses. He was alive.

'Are you well, master duardin?' she called cautiously.

The duardin's eyes opened. He rolled onto his side, looked over at her, and slowly pulled himself to his feet. He made a show of dusting himself down, and trudged towards her. When he reached her, he peered curiously at her for a moment, then rummaged in one of his pouches and pulled out a small oilcloth, from which he extracted what looked for all the realms like a monocle on a metal arm. He adjusted something on its side and fitted the arm into a slot on the side of his helmet, flicking the lens over his eye. He closed the other eye and squinted at her before stepping back.

'Well,' he said at length. 'I don't know if I'd say well. That was a mighty explosion back there. But I'm alive, and that's a start. The real question is, what are *you*?'

'What am I?' she repeated, dumbfounded.

'Aye, lass. What are you? You don't look like a wizard. No staff, no robes, no haughty superiority. But this,' he tapped the eyeglass, 'this suggests that you are. And so does what you did back there. That was… well, I'm not easily impressed by manlings, but that was quite something.'

'I… thank you,' she said. 'You can see magic with that lens?'

'Aye,' the duardin said. 'But that's not important. What did you do to stop that thing? What did you cast? Why did my aetheric destabiliser not work? And just what are you doing here at all?'

Jaqlyn laughed bitterly. 'There is a long story that will probably answer all of that.' She trailed off. 'Most of it anyway. I don't know about your… whatever you called it.'

'Didn't work how it should,' the duardin grumbled.

'Nothing works quite the way it should any more,' Jaqlyn replied.

The duardin nodded. 'Aye. I've noticed. And the rise in that purple magic lingering around these past months. I have a feeling you know more about that than I. Maybe you can help me out actually. I'm Thorri Steelfist,' he held out his non-mechanical arm, 'magical investigator for hire.'

She took his hand and shook it. 'Jaqlyn Kouslo. I'm not sure what I am any more.'

'You're here, and I thank you for that,' said Thorri.

'Why were you here?' she asked. 'How? I was following that spell for months. If you were too, we would have crossed paths before now.'

'Aye, well, I wasn't following it so much as waiting for it. My gadgets picked up something powerful and magical coming this way. I wanted to try and capture it. Study it. Or stop it if I had to.'

'I didn't think duardin had wizards,' said Jaqlyn.

'We don't, really. I'm not naturally attuned to magic like you seem to be. I use a mix of duardin engineering and runic secrets instead. It's... new. It doesn't always work. And I could use a real wizard to help me perfect it.' Thorri looked up at Jaqlyn, his broad brow furrowed.

'What do you say, Jaqlyn Kouslo? How about we partner up for a while? I reckon we could work quite well together. And who knows where the tides of magic will take us?'

Jaqlyn considered the offer. She had nothing to return to, and with the tragic deaths of Archus and his men, she had no one to be responsible for. She could seek out one of the other magical colleges that dotted the realms and continue her studies, as she had done at Tantalum. But that had been all she had known before the disaster. And with the wild magic unleashed by the Necroquake, there were all sorts of new things out there to discover... and perhaps more threats to be stopped. She considered Thorri.

'What did you have in mind?' she asked.

'Well, I heard tell of something strange in a town a few weeks' travel from here. A giant sinkhole and rumours of ratmen being sighted. It has the stink of Chaos magic to it, if ye ask me. Want to come with me and see what we can do about it?'

Jaqlyn smiled. 'Lead the way,' she said.

CASTLE OF THE EXILE

Gareth Hanrahan

Irish author and games designer Gareth Hanrahan takes his first steps into the world of Warhammer 40,000 with this unique look at life in the 41st Millennium.

On a distant, feudal world, the Emperor has been forgotten. The Exile, however, is remembered; a mysterious figure that visited many generations ago, bringing an end to the wars that raged between the human kingdoms. But the Exile's legacy is now passing into myth, and war threatens to return. Three treasure hunters attempt the impossible – a heist of the Exile's castle. There, amidst the crumbling stonework and ancient relics from beyond the stars, they will gradually uncover the truth behind his story.

The road was so overgrown that Elorn had to dismount and cut a way through for the three travellers. He chopped at the tangled vines and branches in the same detached, methodical way he fought, never wasting a blow. Like one of the ancient threshing machines in Wrmonoc's museum.

Wrmonoc remained on his horse while Elorn cleared the road, offering the occasional word of encouragement or warning. 'Beware the vines,' he called, 'they're poisonous!'

Elorn acknowledged the old scholar with a grunt. He knew the vines well; he'd once killed a man by driving him into a patch of those lethal plants. That was… six years ago? Seven? In some other forest, closer to the kingdoms.

'The ancients referred to such plants as *xenoflora*,' said Wrmonoc. 'You can tell them by the texture of the leaves, you see?' He babbled on about how rare such plants were on this continent, but how the lands across the seas were overrun with them.

The third member of their group, Lanig, remained mercifully quiet. His grey eyes scanned the forest and the road behind them. Looking for dangers, finding none.

As far as Elorn could tell, they were the only living souls in this whole forest.

He chopped at one heavy branch, letting the weight of the hanging vines finish the job and bring the whole limb crashing down. He jumped back as a cloud of purplish pollen rose into the air. 'Why the *gell*,' he muttered, 'did the Exile build his damn castle in the middle of nowhere?'

'Oh,' said Wrmonoc, 'well, it's said that the Exile's chariot came to rest here in the Border Forest three hundred years ago, and he built his castle in the very spot he descended from heaven. Why, this road was built to carry the wagon-loads of cut stone needed for his fortress. Records in the Kingdom of Lan Din say–'

Elorn shoved the branch off the road and trudged back to his horse. 'The question,' he said, 'was rhetorical.'

'Oh.'

'Onwards,' said Lanig, spurring his horse past both of them. 'No more delays.'

No one's come this way in years, thought Elorn, but Lanig was in charge. This whole expedition was Lanig's brainchild. Lanig had the purse of gold. And so, he followed Lanig.

The road took a sharp turn, running down a deep furrow in the earth. The trees around them were younger here, and more light penetrated through the canopy above. It was as though some great sword had swung down from heaven and cut a great wound in the land, now scabbed over with forest. Wrmonoc squeaked with joy when Lanig's horse kicked over a clod of earth, revealing something shiny and metallic.

'Look! Look!' Wrmonoc nearly fell off his horse in his eagerness to examine the tiny flake of metal. It looked like it might have been good steel, once, but too small to be turned into even an arrowhead. Quite useless.

Elorn grunted dismissively.

Lanig was equally disinterested, but indulged the old man by waiting. 'What are you going to spend your share on, Elorn? Buy land and title? Maybe you've got some aged parent who needs a place to live out their dotage? Or is it all going on wine and women?'

'Mercenary company. And a better sword.'

Lanig grinned. 'A man of vision,' he said approvingly.

Wrmonoc looked up at them from the mud, an expression of disgust plain upon his features. 'It is forbidden for man to make war on man.' He reminded Elorn of his father, reciting the Exile's credo like it still meant something.

Three hundred years ago, the Four Kingdoms were at war. Man made war on man, and then some. Huge armies marched across the land, cities were put to the torch. *Those must have been the days,* thought Elorn, *when a man like me could really prosper. Instead, I got stuck with the Exile's bloody peace.*

In his father's stories, the Exile arrived in a heavenly chariot of fire. There were three nights of omens before he came – lights flaring in the heaven, meteors streaking through the skies, the old towers of Lan Din waking for the first time in many centuries and screaming with the voices of ghosts.

Three months of silence, and then the Exile came out of the forest.

Single-handedly – or so the stories said – he brought down Calbech, the Lost Kingdom. The other three kingdoms applauded the defeat of their rival. And then, fearing he would destroy them too, they banded together against the Exile. They met him at the Battle of Esstesea Field, forty thousand men against one.

One man walked away victorious. A giant of a man, ten feet tall, girded in impenetrable armour and armed with fury and thunder.

At least, so the stories said. Elorn knew an exaggerated tavern boast when he heard one. The Exile, he was sure, was just another warlord, dead for more than two centuries now. He probably retired to this castle and died of gout.

Wrmonoc kept digging in the mud, looking for more fragments of metal – then he stopped.

'Oh.'

He held up the remains of a human thigh bone. From a fresh kill, Elorn guessed, and cracked open to expose the marrow.

'Back on your horse,' ordered Lanig. 'And be on your guard. Looks like there's a reason no one else has ever tried to burgle the Exile's castle.'

The Castle of the Exile was singularly ugly. The outer walls loomed over them like a landslide caught in stasis, uneven and unadorned, even unfinished in places. The forest had grown up, and now vines and creepers spilled over the parapets and onto the far side. There was only a single gate, and it was shut.

Beyond the walls rose the drum-shaped main keep. No flags or banners, just the worn sigil of the two-headed eagle on the outer wall. No lights burned in any window. No guards stood watch.

It looked empty.

Wrmonoc brushed his fingers against the wooden gate. 'It is said that the Cult of Man intended to make the Exile's castle a place of pilgrimage, but he forbade it. So they built the Great Cathedral in Lan Din instead.' He pushed at the gate, but it didn't move. 'That was before it was burned, of course.'

'And the Exile did nothing,' said Lanig. He joined Wrmonoc at the gate and shoved it, to no avail.

The Exile founded the Cult of Man, right here in this castle. He banned the surviving kingdoms from practising their old faith, the worship of the ancestral sky-lords, declaring that he would destroy any who defied his edicts. He sent out preachers, armed with his new creed, to bring his word to the people.

But the Cult never took hold, not really. The surviving kings worshipped in the old ways – in secret at first, and then more openly. They ignored the Cult's commands, and the Exile did not respond. They burnt down the Great Cathedral, and the Exile did not respond.

Finally, they came for the few who still believed in the Exile.

Elorn's father, Eldred, had been one of those last holdouts. And when the soldiers broke down the door, Eldred did not fight back or flee. He just prayed to the Exile, beseeching the warrior to return. Elorn watched the swordsmen cut his father down, and the Exile did not respond.

On that night, Elorn swore that he would be the man holding the sword, not the fool calling on a vanished god.

'Give us a hand, you big brute!' called Lanig. Elorn shook his head, abruptly jerked back to the present. His mind had wandered. Such inattention was foolish. He joined the other two, but their combined efforts did not move the heavy gate in the slightest. It must be barred from within, he guessed.

'We'll have to climb,' said Elorn, looking up at the steep walls. The uneven stone offered plenty of handholds, but was slick with moss and moisture. He could make it to the top, and he guessed Lanig could too. Wrmonoc, though…

'But not here,' he added. 'Let's circle the castle, see if there's an easier route.'

They left their horses near the gate, and set off with Lanig in the lead. Elorn took up the rear, so he could keep an eye on Wrmonoc. The scholar scrambled doggedly through the forest, eager to show he could keep up with the younger men, but he was tired now, and kept slipping in the mud. All that kept him going, Elorn suspected, was his desire to see what relics and secrets remained in that castle. The last act of a life obsessed with secrets and forbidden lore. Wrmonoc was not only a devotee of the life of the Exile; he also espoused nonsensical theories about the origins of the kingdoms, about the works of the ancestors. On the journey to the castle, he'd babbled about ships that sailed above the clouds, about other lands beyond the sky. He believed that the Exile came from the same place.

Lanig slipped through the forest like a shadow. Elorn did not know what to make of him – a spoiled rich brat who'd turned to tomb robbing and mercenary work when the family fortune ran dry? Maybe the bastard son of some sky-lord priest, here to finally discredit the myth of the Exile?

'Here,' said Lanig, pointing to a section where the forest had encroached upon the wall. Tree branches brushed against the battlements, and the stones were lost beneath ivy creepers. Elorn caught up with Lanig, tested the strength of one of the creepers. It held firm, strong enough to support the weight of a man.

Or something else. There, in the mud at the foot of the wall, was a footprint. Not a human print, but not an animal track either. Humanlike, though – and there were scratch marks on the wall nearby that suggested something used its claws to climb.

'I'll go first,' said Elorn, 'just in case.'

From the top of the wall, he could see the inner courtyard of the Exile's castle. It was bowl-shaped – the outer wall ran along the lip of a great hollow in the land, and the central keep stood on a pile of earth that reminded Elorn of a burial mound. The courtyard was partially overgrown, but the trees were small and stunted, their leaves discoloured, as if they'd leeched poison from the soil.

'Impact crater,' whispered Wrmonoc as he looked down. Another of the scholar's gnomic statements.

They crouched atop the wall, watching, waiting. Wrmonoc was out of breath after the climb, but Elorn could feel the man vibrate with excitement at the sight of the Exile's tower. It was just there, across the field! Nothing between them and the castle door…

…except the grey-furred creature that emerged from the shadow of the twisted trees. The creature ambled out towards a stone trough half-filled with rainwater. Another followed, and another. The things were man-sized, almost man-shaped, but their bodies were covered in rank grey hair, their long jaws were filled with fangs, and their four eyes were bulbous and red.

'Xenofauna,' muttered Wrmonoc. 'From across the ocean. There are tales – I thought them apocryphal – of the Exile wandering the world for seven years, after the defeat of the Kingdom of Calbech. Stories that he brought back monsters…'

A fourth grey-furred beast emerged, dragging a huge carcass behind it. 'Gell,' whispered Lanig, 'is that one of our horses?'

'Looks like.' Elorn shook his head. The gate was still closed – the beast must have scaled the wall with the horse carcass on its shoulder. That sort of fearful strength would make for an immensely dangerous foe. He watched for a moment longer.

'I can't tell how many there are,' he said, 'but there could be dozens of those things living here. I guess they're… guardians, of some sort.' A memory: his father telling him that the Exile would come back one day to bring the kingdoms into the light, and that until that day, he slept, watched over by Custodians. Could those ape-wolf things be the guardians out of legend?

One of the creatures twisted the hind leg off the horse with alarming ease, like you'd tear a drumstick off a roast fowl.

'Maybe we can sneak past,' said Lanig, 'while they're eating.'

'Maybe,' said Elorn, 'we can't.'

'We must not turn back now!' said Wrmonoc. 'Look! Stairs!'

There was, indeed, a narrow stone staircase running down from the battlements to ground level. The scholar wobbled towards it, stepping over vines and uneven stones. One slip to his left, and he'd fall to the courtyard below. One slip to the right, and he'd fall to his death on the other side, landing outside the castle.

Lanig glanced at Elorn and laughed. 'Come on!' He leapt up and followed Wrmonoc.

They nearly made it to the stairs without being detected.

Nearly.

Wrmonoc tripped, and dislodged a rock that fell from the battlements and shattered on the ground below. The crash echoed around the courtyard, resounding from the walls.

The hollow filled with roaring and whooping. Beasts

emerged from the shadow of the trees. The four feasting on the remains of the horse looked up, then joined the mob rushing towards the stairs.

'Back! Back!' urged Elorn. If they were fast enough, maybe they could climb down and escape into the forest. He drew his sword. He could kill one or two of the beasts, buy them some time to–

And then, answering roars from the forest. There were more of the beasts outside the castle walls. They were trapped.

Elorn lunged forward, pushing past Wrmonoc. The top of the stairs was a choke point. He'd make his stand there.

'Watch the bloody wall, Lanig!' he ordered. Lanig drew his own blade, a wickedly sharp rapier. A fancy weapon, but as much use as a knitting needle against brutes like these. This was butcher's work, not a duel.

'What-what do I do?' Wrmonoc asked, his face pale with terror.

'Throw rocks instead of dropping them.'

The first beast rushed up the stairs, bellowing a challenge, its four eyes bulging, some reddish liquid spurting from holes like tear ducts. Elorn kept his head, waited until the beast was nearly at the top, and then struck. The sword cut through fur and meat and bone.

The brute was tough, and strong, and monstrous – *xeno-fauna*, as Wrmonoc called it – but it still died when he cut off its head. Elorn kicked the body back down, knocking another two creatures off the stairs. *A good start,* he thought, *only thirty or so more to go. A last stand that wouldn't be out of place in the stories of the Exile.*

He killed another, hewing at it as the mob came up the stairs. Maimed a third as it climbed. Behind him, he heard Lanig shouting, heard the whistling of the rapier through the air, the gurgling of a monster as it choked on its own blood. Wrmonoc was screaming, but Elorn couldn't tell if the scholar was screaming in terror or pain, or if it was an attempt at a battle cry.

Another came over the top, and Elorn brought his sword down, cleaving the monster's skull. Purplish goo spurted out over grey fur – whatever the things had in their skulls, it wasn't like human brains. Stabbing still killed them, though.

A fifth, and that one nearly got him. It fell on top of him as it died, nearly taking him with it over the edge. Elorn pushed the hairy corpse off his legs, swung at a sixth brute, chopping its forearm as it reached for him. Wrmonoc bounced a stone off the creature's head.

'Elorn!' called Lanig. 'Hold them off on this side!'

What the gell does he think I'm doing here? thought Elorn. He fell back to the top of the wall. Lanig knelt there, frantically digging through his backpack. 'What are you–' Elorn started to ask, but there was no time to finish the question, no time to do anything except stab and thrust and cut and dodge, nothing in all the world except red eyes and grey fur and roaring.

The forest and the castle fell away around him, his existence circumscribed to the narrow space atop the wall. The edge of the universe was a field of grey fur, filled with clawed arms reaching for him. He fought like he'd never fought before, desperate yet dispassionate. Stripped down to nothing but the instinct to survive, the razor-edge calculation. It wasn't enough to strike each monster – he had to do it perfectly, efficiently, his sword moving from one to the next without time to recover. If his blade became lodged in bone, or if he was too slow killing one, he was a dead man.

Wrmonoc was still screaming, but it sounded different now, lower and drawn out, like time was slowing down.

His arms ached. His eyes burned. He couldn't remember the last time he'd blinked, the last time he'd taken a breath. The world contracted again and again, a circle of grey fur and red-tipped claws, and all that held back the end of everything was his blood-drenched blade.

'Ready,' said a voice from very far away. Lanig stood up. In one hand he held a black leather pouch; on his other hand he wore an elegant jewelled glove, long fingers wound around with silver filigree. The glove was black, of the same strange substance as the pouch.

He dipped his gloved hand into the pouch and took out a handful of crystal shards. He flung the shards into the air where they hung, impossibly, hovering above his head.

Lanig pointed his gloved finger at one of the beasts. Shards flew at the creature, slicing its eyeballs, bursting them, blinding it. The monster howled in agony, flailed its arms, and fell from the wall.

Laughing, Lanig pointed again and again. More shards shot through the air. More bulbous eyeballs exploded in fountains of gore. Elorn dragged Wrmonoc out of the way as half a dozen brutes, all suddenly panicked and blind, staggered around the narrow path atop the wall. Two more fell. Elorn pushed a third down, stabbed a fourth. The fifth bolted, running away along the battlements until it lost its footing and fell.

Lanig picked up his rapier and dispatched the sixth. He wiped the blade clean on the grey fur of one of his victims, and looked down at the courtyard below.

Another twenty or so of the creatures were down there. All stumbling, all pawing at their ruined faces, bellowing in confusion or whimpering in terror. Lanig peeled the glove from his hand and tucked it into his belt.

'What was that?' croaked Wrmonoc. He cradled his arm – one of the brutes had dislocated his shoulder.

'An heirloom,' said Lanig. 'An ancient treasure.' He turned the pouch upside down and sighed. 'All used up now. But the way is clear.'

He strode down the blood-slick steps into the courtyard below.

It was Wrmonoc who discovered the secret switch. The door to the inner castle was forged of steel and decorated with an image of the Exile seated on a throne.

'It's not the Exile,' muttered Wrmonoc. 'It's the Emperor.'

'Aren't they the same person?' asked Elorn. He vaguely recalled his father mentioning an 'emperor', but he'd forgotten the litanies of his childhood. The Exile and the Emperor, he vaguely recalled, weren't quite the same being, but the Exile was born of the Emperor's seed. Something like that. Elorn still felt shaken by what he'd seen on the wall. His armour of cynicism, built up over many years, had been cracked by the sight of that miraculous, ghastly weapon.

'No. The Exile served the Emperor in heaven,' said Wrmonoc. He pointed at a symbol on the door, a winged skull. 'But that symbol there is the Exile's sigil, not the Emperor's mark. I wonder…' He pressed the symbol, and it moved slightly. 'It's rusted shut. Push it!'

Elorn pressed on the sigil, and there came a distant click in response. The door shifted a fraction. He shoved it open and stepped inside, crossing the threshold of the Exile. The others followed, passing into the darkness of the empty keep. Lanig produced a lamp from his backpack. He fumbled in the gloom for a moment, then light flooded the room.

'Oh my,' breathed Wrmonoc.

Gold. Gold all around them. It was a chapel, its rows of pews facing a shimmering golden altar set with jewels. Paintings and banners hung on the walls, an illuminated book lay on the altar top. A suit of ornate golden armour stood behind it all, an angelic guardian of this holy sanctum.

Lanig tensed at the sight of the armour, as if worried it would spring to life.

'Is that… is that the Exile's armour?' whispered Elorn. His mouth was dry. He wanted to speak out loud, to spit on the mosaic floor and blaspheme, to stuff his pockets with loot, but he couldn't raise his voice. He imagined his father here in his stead.

Wrmonoc shook his head. 'No. It's said the Exile stood ten feet tall. I'd wager it's a replica, made by the faithful.' His voice was equally quiet, equally reverent.

Lanig strode forward to examine the armour. Lanig had no fear. 'So where is the original?' He wrenched the helm from the suit's bulky shoulders, held it up to show them it was empty, like a conjurer's trick, then flung it to the ground.

'There's a bloody king's ransom here,' said Elorn. He hadn't moved from the threshold. What was wrong with him? He'd come all this way to loot the castle, and here in this room there was more wealth than he'd ever seen before. Just one of the jewels in the altar was worth a fortune. Every surface glittered with gold. That armour, too, was ornamented with gems and precious metals.

'A king's ransom? Try three kings, and the entirety of one *kingdom*,' said Lanig. He sounded almost angry.

'True,' said Wrmonoc. 'After the defeat of the Kingdom of Calbech and the surrender of the other three kingdoms, the Exile demanded tribute from all the lands. He asked for gold and other metals, and the finest smiths and builders. The builders, clearly, raised this castle. The smiths made this armour at least. There'll be more wonders within…'

'There's enough wealth here for Elorn, I'm sure.' Lanig flipped through the illuminated book on the altar. Images of a war in heaven – armoured warriors fighting against monsters and devils. Images of worlds floating in the void, under siege by horrors. The only light in the darkness shining from within a golden throne…

Lanig slammed the book shut, then took out a knife and started to cut the pages from the jewelled cover. A manic energy drove him; the light from the lantern beside him made his face seem bestial, his features distorted by shadow.

'What are you doing?' shrieked Wrmonoc.

'It's just the litany of the Exile. The same nonsense his followers used to preach. You've read it before, Wrmonoc. We all know it. But this case is worth a fortune.'

Loose pages spilled across the floor of the chapel. Lanig finished dismembering the book, then held up the jewelled case, as empty as the Exile's helmet. He tossed it across the room to Elorn.

'There – a down payment on the fortune we've found. I want you to stay here and guard the door. There might be more of those monsters still out there. You watch our way out, while Wrmonoc and I search the rest of this place.' Sword in hand, he opened another door in the back wall of the chapel.

Wrmonoc lingered a moment, loath to leave the chapel, but even more unwilling to stay. His eyes darted about, trying to commit every inch of the place to memory. His hands shook as he lit a second lantern. 'So much to learn. So much – but what else might be here?' He glanced at Elorn. 'It's all true. All of it.'

He darted after Lanig.

The door shut behind the pair, leaving Elorn alone. The sounds of their footsteps quickly faded away, swallowed by the gloom of the Exile's castle.

The swordsman turned back to the outer door, scanned the courtyard. He could hear distant yowling and whimpering, but there was no sign yet of pursuit. Maybe Lanig's ghastly glove-weapon had blinded the entire pack.

He roamed the chapel. Elorn's father had taught him his letters, but he disliked reading. The paintings and icons on the walls were more his speed. Stories out of legend – there was the Exile's chariot of fire. There, he guessed, was a fanciful depiction of the battle between the Exile and the king of Calbech – but the king was shown as a horribly twisted, bloated monster, and there was a fallen angel on the ground nearby.

A third picture showed a whole army of men in the Exile's army fighting against devils. Elorn paused in front of that image. He'd seen it before – a copy of it at least, a drawing. A memory of it bubbled up from his childhood. His father told him it depicted the holy days to come, when the Exile would bring an army of heroes to cleanse the world and eradicate all evil. As a child, Elorn dreamed of being part of that army.

More nonsense. He cursed himself – he'd risked life and limb getting here, and now he was getting dewy-eyed over a painting.

That is the point of this place, he reminded himself. *To use pomp and glory to batter a man's soul into submission.* The Exile hadn't saved Eldred from the swordsmen. The Exile wasn't real.

The painting, while beautiful, wasn't portable. The jewels in the altar, though – a man could carry a fortune in his pocket with those. Elorn knelt by the altar and started to pry rubies and emeralds from their golden settings. He hacked at the icons, like Lanig had cut the holy litany, eager to prove to himself that this place had no power over him. The Exile was not a god or an angel – just a warlord with delusions. If he wasn't going to come back to stop Elorn defacing his altar, he certainly wasn't going to come back to stop the kingdoms going to war, or to lead a holy army against mythical *devils*.

He pushed one jewelled skull, and it went *click*.

Elorn flung himself back, fearing that he'd triggered some hidden trap. The front panel of the altar fell away, falling to the ground like thunder, revealing a concealed compartment.

Inside was a casket or coffer, a box like a child's coffin.

Elorn dragged it into the middle of the aisle. The casket was sealed with copper bands. Stamped on the lid was the sigil of the Lost Kingdom of Calbech, the kingdom brought down by the Exile.

Might it be full of gold and jewels, looted by the Exile from fallen Calbech? It didn't seem heavy enough. It was light enough that he feared it was empty – but then why hide it away in the altar? And why seal it? Elorn fetched a hammer and chisel from his bag, and the chapel rang with the sound of metal on metal.

One by one, the copper bands fell to the stone floor.

Holding his breath, Elorn wrenched the lid off the box – and recoiled in horror.

If Wrmonoc had still been present, maybe he'd have called the thing xenofauna, but it wasn't anything like the blind beasts outside, anything like any of the creatures Elorn had fought in the wild places of the world. The skeletal remains in the casket were almost human, but uncannily wrong. The bones were too thin, almost translucent, like the scales of fish. The skull was too long, the eye sockets too large.

Worst of all, though, was the cruelty that emanated from those bones. As he stared at the alien skull, Elorn could suddenly feel the grotesque excess of his own flesh, the glutinous layers of fat and skin and offal larded over his own crude, bulky skeleton.

He sensed the nerves threaded through that sludge of ugly meat.

Could feel glass-thin needles flensing those nerves, stripping them to the point of exquisite agony.

Could feel liquid fire dissolving his brain and holding it forever at that point of torment.

COMMORRAGH, whispered the bones.

Elorn slammed the casket shut and fell whimpering to the floor. He lay there for a long, long time, shivering, muttering a prayer to the Exile his father had taught him.

The thing in the casket was a *devil*. He knew that with a bone-deep certainty, a loathing written into every cell in his being. An actual *devil*, a supernatural horror out of myth.

And if those stories were true, then what else might be true? Elorn crawled across the floor, away from the hateful casket, and collapsed at the feet of the golden armour of the Exile. The golden armour stared down at him – in judgement, or forgiveness, he could not tell.

What if the tales of the Exile were all true, too?

Elorn wept like a child, feeling as though he'd been cracked open by the ordeal. The world he thought he knew washed away. It was all real, all terrible and wonderful. There were divine heroes out there amid the stars, and there were horrors there too.

And as he lay there, he saw something glittering on the ground next to him. It had fallen from the casket when he'd opened it.

A long spindle of purple crystal, just like the shards Lanig had flung at the guardian beasts.

An heirloom, Lanig said.

Still shivering, still feeling that phantom suffering in every sinew, Elorn slowly dragged himself upright, using the golden armour to support him as he rose. He shoved the crystal spindle into his pack, then staggered across the chapel.

The Exile will come back one day, whispered his father in Elorn's memory, *but until then he sleeps.*

He had to stop Lanig.

Elorn stumbled through stone corridors. Archways yawned on his left, on his right, leading to empty rooms whose purpose he could not guess. Had Lanig and Wrmonoc come this way, or taken another route?

He found a stairway, and nearly fell down it. Another archway, and this one led into a huge cylindrical chamber that must be right in the heart of the castle. It was open to the sky – far above, he could see clouds bloodied by the setting sun. And ahead…

Ahead was a great slumbering hulk of shattered metal, half-buried in the earth. The celestial chariot of the Exile – what else could it be, forged from the same unbreakable star-metal that Wrmonoc had found earlier? But the metal was torn in places, scorched in others. The chariot was a shattered wreck.

Above the chariot, blossoming from its ruined flank like a beautiful flower growing from the rot, was a wheel of filigreed gold. This bizarre ornament, at least, was the work of mortal hands. Elorn could imagine the craftsmen and goldsmiths hammering the plundered gold of Calbech, drawing it out into fine wires, and then weaving it all together into this heavenly mandala, this wheel of frozen fire. In the centre of the wheel was a golden spike, a spire aimed straight at heaven.

He crept closer. The wheel was vibrating, pulsing like a beating heart. Thick cords of some flexible material ran from the base of the wheel into the wreckage of the chariot. Fascinated, Elorn followed the cords back to where they vanished into the machine. He pressed his ear against the cold metal, and the Exile spoke to him in a voice of crackling thunder.

'Battle-Brother Cromadus of Fourth Company… only survivor of crash… eradicated xenos cult… stranded… now awaiting rescue… entering hibernation… in the name of the Emperor, if you are receiving this vox, harken… This is Battle-Brother Cromadus of Fourth Company…'

The Exile was calling him. The Exile needed his aid.

Another chamber. A hall of wonders.

Two rows of plinths, each one bearing a treasure or a trophy. Some Elorn recognised – crowns and swords out of legend. Others were things he could not comprehend, like the four glowing jars, each one holding a lump of flesh, that stood at the four corners of the hall in places of honour.

One plinth was empty.

At the far end, the armour of the Exile. It was like the golden replica in the chapel below, but half as large again, towering nine or ten feet tall. It was so battle-scarred that Elorn could not discern its original colour.

'Beautiful… is it not?'

Wrmonoc sat on the ground by the empty plinth, his hands clasped tightly over his belly. Blood welled up between his fingers, ran down his legs to pool around him. Elorn knelt beside the dying man.

'What happened?'

'Lanig…' Wrmonoc groaned. 'He took a weapon. Went away. But it's all right.' He smiled through red-stained teeth. 'I've seen this, at least, Elorn. I got here before the end. So much we'll never know. But…' He struggled to breathe.

'You were right,' whispered Elorn, 'the Exile is real. It's all true.'

'It is forbidden… for man to make war on man,' muttered Wrmonoc, 'but I don't think that Lanig…'

But whatever the scholar's last thought was, it was lost forever.

One hand slipped, limp and lifeless, to the floor.

If Elorn had Wrmonoc's wit, he might have searched the room of treasures for some weapon he could use.

If he had his father's faith, he might have remembered some tale of the Exile's deeds, and learned from that.

Instead, he rushed, sword in hand, towards a final archway. Lamplight streamed from within. It had to be Lanig.

Elorn charged in, screaming a battle cry – and was struck by a wall of agony.

Eldritch energies boiled through his body. He fell to the ground. He could feel every bone in his body, as if they'd all been heated red hot or turned to molten lead.

'Oh, good,' said Lanig.

Elorn couldn't stand, couldn't reach his sword. He couldn't even focus his eyes. He could see Lanig standing over him, holding a small device in his hand. It looked to be of similar wicked design to the black gloves tucked into his belt, made by the same cruel, monstrous mind.

Beyond Lanig was a long stone bier, and on that bier lay the body of a gigantic man. He was eight feet long at least, thickly muscled, inhumanly beautiful. So still that Elorn might have assumed he was dead, but that blood slowly trickled from a fresh wound on his cheek.

The Exile. The Exile existed. The Exile lived.

'I was about to go looking for you,' continued Lanig. 'I need to calibrate this–' He made a guttural noise, a word in a language that Elorn did not know. 'It wouldn't do to kill the Usurper *painlessly*, would it? But with you here I can work out exactly how to inflict the proper suffering.' He aimed the device at Elorn again, and again a searing wave of pain washed over him.

'My great-great-great-grandmother,' remarked Lanig as Elorn writhed, 'was queen in Calbech, until this brute fell from the sky and ruined everything. He murdered her – but worse, far worse, he killed the Pale Folk. They came from afar, from the dark place between the stars, and they brought us wonderful things like this.' He held up the device. 'I don't know if torturing their killer to death will be enough to bring them back, but I'll settle for revenge.'

He knelt down next to Elorn and gently pushed Elorn's sword out of reach. He was close enough that Elorn might have throttled him, if only he could move his hands. 'I just hope the Usurper wakes up from his enchanted sleep so he knows who killed him.'

Again, the wave of pain. This time, it was more focused, the energy swirling through Elorn's body to gather and pool at specific points – his right temple, his shoulder, his left hand, left thigh. The pain reached a crescendo, and his skin split, ghastly jagged wounds opening up as the underlying nerves burned.

'Nearly right,' said Lanig, straightening up.

In his torment, Elorn managed to speak a name. A prayer.

'Cromadus.'

Maybe it was a trick of the dancing lamplight.

Maybe it was a side effect of the eldritch torment.

Maybe it never happened.

But in that instant, Lanig saw it too. The slumbering Exile stirred, woken by the invocation of his name. Terrified, Lanig's finger lifted from the control of the agony device.

Elorn grabbed the black glove from Lanig's belt, pulled it onto his own blood-slick hand. Pointed at Lanig.

The purple crystal burst free of Elorn's pack and flew through the air for an instant, embedding itself in Lanig's throat. The last prince of the Lost Kingdom gurgled, his face turning as purple as the crystal. His lips moved, but produced only blood-flecked spittle. He took two slow steps towards the Exile, then fell to the ground, dead.

The agony device, the weapon forged by the Pale Folk, landed nearby. Wearily, Elorn lifted up his sword and struck the hateful thing over and over until it shattered.

The wound on the Exile's cheek continued to bleed sluggishly. Elorn stumbled over to the bier, staunched the flow with a cloth. The Exile did not respond.

'You're real,' said Elorn, 'it's all true. You commanded the kingdoms not to go to war, told them to follow the Creed. They've lost their way – but my father said you'd come back when we needed you. So wake up.'

The armies of the Kingdom of Inginerin laid siege to the walls of Lan Din for six days. Inginerin brought a great host, the greatest gathered in one place since the Battle of Esstesea Field. For six days, war returned to the kingdoms.

And on the seventh day, a single armoured knight arrived, and he alone challenged that host.

The knights and lords of Inginerin saw the golden armour of the Exile. They remembered the Exile's old edict, but more than that, they remembered how the Exile had single-handedly defeated their ancestors. No one dared raise a sword against the warrior of legend.

Their courage failed them, and they yielded the field to the Exile.

Inside the replica armour, Elorn breathed a sigh of relief, then rode off to accept the surrender of the three kings.

In the years that followed, scribes and preachers visited all the remaining kingdoms, and restored the Exile's Cult of Man to primacy of place among the faithful.

The sound of distant voices woke Elorn.

He lay there in bed for a long moment, wondering if he was dreaming. Then he threw back the furs and rose, his old body trembling with the effort. His leg had never wholly recovered from the torment Lanig had inflicted on it; he could ride, even in armour, but he could not walk quickly. He limped through the corridors of the castle that had been his home for fifty years.

He entered the vault where the Exile slumbered.

The bier was empty.

The voices came again, from the reliquary. 'Collect the stasis tubes, quickly. Return the progenoid glands to the ship.'

'Wait,' shouted Elorn, 'who are you? Where have you taken Cromadus?'

A figure stepped out of the door, and Elorn fell to his knees.

The figure was another armoured giant, like the Exile.

'Our battle-brother has been returned to the ship after his long exile,' said the warrior. 'The Apothecaries will rouse him from suspended animation and restore him to health.'

'And then he'll...' Elorn's voice cracked. He choked back tears. 'He'll come back to us?'

'No. Other worlds have need of the Adeptus Astartes. He has done enough for you. But now that we have found your world again, other ships shall follow mine. You shall be brought into the Imperium, and give tribute to Holy Terra,' said the Space Marine.

Elorn swayed, his wounded leg unable to bear his weight. His wounded mind, unable to comprehend the words. The Space Marine reached out to steady him. He clasped Elorn's shoulder, his armoured gauntlet heavy as destiny.

'Rejoice! Your long exile is at an end.'

AT THE SIGN OF THE BRAZEN CLAW: PART FIVE

Guy Haley

All good things must come to an end, and this volume of Inferno! *concludes with the last chapter of Guy Haley's episodic tale, which brings the serial to a dark and shocking finale.*

As the sorcerer Quasque reveals the truth behind his presence at the inn of the Brazen Claw, the travellers find themselves besieged. Nagash dispatches his hounds in a remorseless hunt for souls, and Prince Maesa leads a desperate defence. Meanwhile, the innkeeper, Horrin, furiously attempts to keep the fire lit lest the giant god beneath the inn awakens. Can the travellers prevent disaster, or is this the end of all of their journeys?

Trapped in a storm in an inn built atop the stone hand of a buried demigod, Prince Maesa and Shattercap have passed the night listening to the tales of their fellow travellers. The final story was that of Pludu Quasque, sorcerer of Hysh, and his tale ended on a disturbing note – that the Hounds of Nagash, the dreaded glaive-wraiths, were pursuing him to recover a treasure the Great Necromancer regarded as his own. As the eye of the storm passes over the inn of the Brazen Claw and the wind rises once more, fell screams are heard outside. Nagash's servants are at the door…

THE HOUNDS OF NAGASH

Manic light gleamed in Pludu Quasque's eyes, and he sat down hard.

'They are here!' Quasque whispered. His fingers fluttered nervously against each other.

Screaming blended with the wind's music, adding wordless lyrics of pain and misery to its gusting wail.

Maesa and Stonbrak got to their feet and drew their weapons, facing the door. Something heavy slammed into the other side, making it jump in its frame. Ninian shrieked. Barnabus gripped her waist and whimpered.

The door leapt again. There was a deafening shriek. Sharp nails scraped against the wood, scratching and scratching, the soft rasp of splinters being picked free and the creak of timbers tested by inhuman strength followed. Grave-cold seeped underneath the door, chilling the air to mist and spreading a web of frost up the walls. Iron nails and studs gathered small thickets of ice. Over the bar Horrin's warding charms danced with violent magic, then swung out from the wood and hung straining towards the door.

Maesa watched in silence. The wooden edge of the Song of Thorns gleamed with the magic of Ghyran.

'Curse you, mage, for what you have done!' growled Idenkor Stonbrak. He hefted his axe. The runemarks upon the head glowed with cold fires.

'It's not my fault – I was a boy, a foolish boy!' Quasque collapsed into tears.

Shattercap scampered onto Maesa's shoulder, craned his neck and sniffed deeply.

'The dead, master, it is the dead at the door!'

'What manner of undead are they?' growled Stonbrak at Quasque.

'The Hounds of Nagash! Can you not hear them bark?' blubbered Quasque.

'What?' spat Stonbrak.

'A breed of nighthaunt,' said Horrin softly. 'They are well known to we of Shyish. They chase down those that displease the Great Necromancer. It is said they were cruel hunters in life, now doomed in death to wear the skeletal heads of their hounds in place of their own. They are implacable, tracking down their quarry wherever it may be.'

'Then they are wisps, and wisps pass through solid matter,' said Stonbrak. He groped for his pint pot and drained the last of his ale. 'Let them come! I have a surprise of steel for them. My axe will see to their second deaths, as will that stick of the aelf's, I'll warrant. It has a gleam of magic almost as good as my own.'

'My sword is inimical to such ghasts,' said Maesa softly. 'But the glaivewraiths are deadly. We must be ready.'

'Oh, I'm ready,' said Stonbrak.

The thing picking at the door planks moved away to try the shuttered window along the wall. It rattled violently. Plaster dust shook out from the bouncing frame. Streaks of water ran from fresh cracks. Ice spread around the window and the glass broke. A plant on the sill withered and died.

Ninian shrieked again. Barnabus was crying, but he stood up, fists clenched.

'Go away!' he shouted bravely.

Horrin rested his hands on his foster son's shoulders. He smiled through his fear.

'They cannot get in,' he said quietly.

Maesa looked at the innkeeper.

'The charms over the bar,' Horrin explained. 'I have many, from all manner of wizards and sorcerers. They cannot get in.'

'They will not last,' said Maesa. 'This magic is strong, and yours is not.'

Horrin glanced to his left, at the bar. All the charms were shining red, and smoking with the dust burning from them.

The first shutter fell still. The thing outside moved on. There was a brief pause before the next shutter shook to a furious pounding.

'Master Horrin,' said Maesa. 'I suggest you arm yourself. Do you have any weapons bearing enchantment?'

'This is Shyish,' said Horrin gravely. 'What use is any other kind? Barnabus, come with me. Fetch the silver balls for my gun and bring the daggers out for you and your mother. Barnabus!'

Barnabus was panting, staring at the patches of ice spreading all along the inn wall. His breath steamed from his mouth, thin threads at first, then huge billows. They were all breathing steam. The temperature was dropping rapidly, carrying frost deeper into the room along the beams. Shattercap shivered.

Stonbrak narrowed his eyes. 'The aelf is right. Your charms will be insufficient, Master Horrin.'

The party looked upwards. Noises were coming from the upper floors.

'They're trying the shutters upstairs!' said Ninian.

'I said they can't get in,' said Horrin, but he no longer believed it.

The party jumped, except Maesa, as all the shutters and the door commenced banging at once with great ferocity. Several things outside shrieked and screamed.

'Your gun, innkeeper!' Maesa said. 'Now.'

Horrin nodded dumbly and hurried to the bar, dragging Barnabus with him.

The charms were floating parallel to the wall, straining on their chains, and now glowing brighter than a tree of candles. As Horrin took up his gun, the first charm exploded, showering the room with red-hot fragments that hissed on the spreading ice.

Barnabus leapt over the counter. He rummaged about and shoved a rattling box at his foster father. Horrin half-spilled the contents and swore as he fumbled powder and ball into the mouth of his gun. Shaking hands took three attempts to push the ramrod home. Barnabus scrambled over the countertop again, clutching a pair of identical sheathed daggers to his chest. He gave one to Ninian, and drew his own. As soon as it cleared the sheath, flames licked along the edges.

'Now that's more like it!' growled Stonbrak. He was shifting about, eager to fight. Maesa stood completely still, the Song of Thorns pointed at the door. Shattercap hissed.

Horrin finally succeeded in priming his gun. He pulled back the hammer with a click.

The banging stopped.

Soot sifted down the chimney. A cold wind blew out from the fireplace. The flames in the grate sank.

Horrin paled. 'The fire!' he said. 'The fire must not go out!' He banged himself on the counter as he rushed to the fireplace.

Another charm exploded, then another. The whole string of them went off like duardin firecrackers, banging in succession until only one remained. Stonbrak growled at a fleck of molten gold burning his cheek. The temperature dropped further. Frost raced over the bar, up the bottles. Glass broke as the contents froze solid.

Maesa kept a wary eye on the last charm. It floated, buzzing with failing magic, flickering like a firefly heading deep into the woods.

More soot fell down the chimney, damping the flames further.

'They're going to come in through the bloody fireplace!' Stonbrak shouted.

'The fire! The fire!' Horrin wailed. He tossed dried mosses onto the blaze. They sputtered, but would not take. Barnabus ran to his side with a flask.

'Try this, Master Horrin!' he said.

Horrin uncorked the flask and upended it over the fire. Thick oil glugged onto the embers. The fire roared up and Horrin cheered. His jubilation fled when a bone-chilling wail echoed down the chimney, and the fires died back again.

'Get away from the fireplace,' Maesa said.

'It cannot go out!' Horrin was in a panic, spilling matches and kindling as he tried to revive the dying blaze.

The last charm exploded. To Maesa's aelven vision, the chain fell slowly, each link clinking in turn on the wood.

As the last link stilled, the candles in the bar-room extinguished all at once. Lightning flashed somewhere far off in the depths of the storm, sending sharp slivers of light spearing through the gaps in the woodwork of the shutters and door. Maesa saw a shadow moving fast outside.

'The fire!' Horrin said. The last spark guttered out.

A moan fluted down the chimney.

'Get away from the fire!' the prince cried.

With a rush of soot and ash, a cloaked thing plunged into the room. Horrin threw himself aside. It sped over his head, wailing piteously. Green and ghastly light flooded the bar. A dog's skull jutted from under its filthy cowl. It had no legs, its body and robes blended into a long, glowing tail of magic. Clawed hands swept at Maesa as it flew overhead. It raced around the room, its passage leaving a trail of ice and soot upon the walls. The touch of its spectral form knocked pictures down and shattered glass ornaments. As it came at the group again, a glaive appeared in its hands, solidifying from shadows into full reality: a black wood haft hardened by centuries in a tomb, a sword-long blade eaten with rust but sharp as death's bite.

The ghast levelled its weapon and sped towards Quasque, who let out a low, animal moan. Balefires glowed in the thing's empty eye sockets. Its shriek carried notes of triumph as it stooped to kill. From far away, the party heard the baying of hounds and the shouts of wicked men intent on their quarry.

Maesa stepped in front of the ghast. The Song of Thorns sang through the air, intercepting the blade before it could claim its prey. Green sparks fountained along the point of contact. Maesa encountered a wiry strength he had not expected, and the ghast pushed him back, its fleshless muzzle snapping in his face.

Stonbrak gave a shout. His axe blurred through the air, cleaving through the phantom as if it were composed of nothing but mist. The blade dragged the stalker into shreds of vapour. The runes cut into the steel flared. The phantom discorporated into nothing, and Stonbrak's axe thunked into the wall.

'That's you done,' said the duardin matter-of-factly. He clumped across the room to where his axe was embedded, and grasped the haft.

'Master duardin!' Maesa called.

Stonbrak looked back. Maesa dropped the Song of Thorns, drawing his bow in the same movement. His lithe arms moving too fast to follow, he plucked an arrow from his quiver, drew and loosed. The shaft sped towards the outraged merchant, passing his nose by a finger's breadth, and buried itself in the skull of a second wraith emerging through the wall. It disappeared with a moan and a shower of grave dust.

'We need to remove ourselves from here,' Maesa said.

Stonbrak tugged out his axe and brushed the dust from his arm with distaste.

'Upwards, into the storm,' Stonbrak said. 'There's too much ground to cover here. We should hold at the sky-dock and await my cloud-dwelling cousins. If we fight back to back, we might be able to hold them off for long enough.'

'Boy, which way?' said Maesa.

'The stairs are here, good sirs!' Barnabus said. He hurried to the far corner of the room and opened up a door.

'But the fire!' Horrin said.

More shrieks passed close by the inn.

'It will have to wait,' said Maesa.

The party waited tensely. No more wraiths attempted entry.

'They've learned caution,' said Stonbrak. He hauled Quasque to his feet. 'Up you get, master mage.'

'They will attack soon. They do not fear us,' said Maesa.

Horrin spoke up from where he was stacking the fire anew. 'The dead know no fear at all.'

'That is not true,' said the prince. He fetched his helm from the table and put it on. 'They know fear of failure, for their lord will punish them in unimaginable ways if they do not bring their quarry down. Barnabus, lead us out.'

The eye of the storm was passing on. Rain was falling again, and its pattering on the shutters took on a fresh foreboding. The gusting of the wind increased in strength and frequency. The shrieks of the ghasts sounded from all around the pinnacle of rock.

'I cannot go,' said Horrin. 'I must tend the fire. I must tend the fire!'

'The fire is out,' said Maesa. 'It is likely it will not burn while the creatures assail us.'

'I am aware of that!' snapped Horrin. He took up steel and flint and sent sparks fountaining into fresh kindling. It did not take, and Horrin cursed.

'It will not burn,' said Maesa. 'Come.'

The ground stirred beneath their feet.

'It is beginning!' Horrin said. 'Oh no, oh no! I must relight the fire. The god awakens. Please. Leave me here. I will–'

The moan of shifting timbers and grinding stone drowned out Horrin's voice. The whole inn shifted like a storm-tossed ship. Only Maesa rode the motion with any dignity. Stonbrak stumbled. Ninian gripped at a table that almost pulled her over as it scraped across the floor. Quasque wept all the harder. Chairs toppled over with wooden clatters.

'We must leave now!' Maesa said.

Without warning, a ghast plunged through the door. Horrin snatched up his gun and fired. The bullet burst into pink fire as it punched through the phantom, sending it shrieking back to the netherworlds.

Horrin reloaded. The room was still moving. A persistent rumbling set up in competition with the storm; the low bass, tooth-jarring grind of stone on stone. The room shook. The few bottles behind the bar that were not frozen in place fell to the floor and shattered. Wood splintered. Windows burst in warping frames.

'Masters!' Barnabus said. He glanced into the dark stairwell. Tears glinted in his eyes. The boy was terrified.

'Don't need to tell me again, lad,' said Stonbrak. He shoved past Maesa, dragging the shivering Quasque with him. Ninian went to her son's side.

The inn swayed. The room tilted. Loose objects fell from the tables and bounced across the planks.

'Get out of here!' Horrin said. He primed his gun again. 'With luck, I can hold them back. They'll follow the sorcerer. They're not interested in me. Please watch my family. Help them live the night through. I have to stay here.'

Maesa nodded. 'Very well.'

'Your highness, this way!' said Ninian. 'If we get the mage away from here, they will leave my Horrin alone!'

Horrin smiled. 'Thank you for your story, good aelf. Maybe, tomorrow, you can tell me an–'

A howling wraith burst upwards from beneath the inn. Its phantom glaive point slid through Ninian's chest with no resistance. Horrin's eyes and mouth went round in shock.

When the tip emerged from beneath her sternum, it suddenly phased into solidity, parting Ninian's skin with a sudden rush of gore.

Barnabus screamed. Ninian opened her mouth to speak, but a sheet of black blood poured over her jaw in place of words.

The phantom passed through Ninian's dying body, stilling her heart and covering her in frost. It raced with a shriek at Maesa in order to get to Quasque. Maesa sidestepped at the last possible moment, brought down the Song of Thorns and decapitated it. The hound skull fell towards the ground, the body began to dissipate and fade, but then the Song of Thorns shone with ruddy thirst, and the shreds of the doomed hunter's soul were sucked screaming into his blade.

'Grungni's beard!' Stonbrak swore.

'Run,' said Maesa. 'I'll hold them back.' He looked at the stone finger where the fireplace was set. 'I do not think they can pass through the body of the god. Horrin, get out!'

'Ninian... My Ninian...' Horrin stood, hands shaking.

'Aelf...' grumbled Stonbrak.

'Go!' shouted Maesa. More of the phantoms were coming into the room, slipping though the walls as if they were not there, weapons transitioning from ghostly to solid forms. The ghasts clacked their canine teeth together, drifting into a line six wide. The inn shook again. 'The god is waking. The dead are here. Get aloft before it is too late! Get aloft and pray for morning.'

Stonbrak glanced from the line of ghasts and back to the prince.

'Go!' said Maesa. He spoke no louder than a whisper, yet his words flew with the force of arrows.

'Oh, very well!' Stonbrak snapped. He shoved the humans out of the room and slammed the door behind him.

The wraiths attacked.

They came at Maesa in a group, glaives pointed at his heart. The Song of Thorns flashed out and took the heads from two of the weapons, causing their bearers to wail furiously and discard the hafts, which boiled off into glowing smoke. One of the disarmed raced at the prince. Maesa leapt lightly onto the table, parrying a flurry of jabs from the others, his eyes ever on his principal opponent as it reached out with a heart-stilling touch. Its fingers never brushed his skin. A swift thrust from the Song of Thorns, and its soul was sucked away into the prison of his sword.

The others became wary.

'There are more terrible things in these realms than Nagash,' Maesa told them. 'This weapon I bear was the gift of the Goddess of Life. It is inimical to your kind. Come at me, and know a true end.'

They circled him, trying to surround him. Maesa followed their movements with an aelf's easy grace, switching his stance just enough to execute deflections and counter-attacks in a way all but the greatest human swordsman would have found impossible. The inn's movements increased in severity, not fits and starts this time, but a smooth, purposeful motion towards the ground, steady as a piston drop. The ceiling cracked as the great finger poking up through the roof twitched. Furniture upended and skidded to and fro. Maesa leapt from tumbling chair to sliding table, his feet light, as if the battle were a well-choreographed dance and not a struggle against death itself. The inn swung downwards faster. Objects lifted. He heard Horrin's muffled shouts from upstairs. The phantoms, not anchored to reality, were taken unawares, and passed screaming in fury through the walls and floor as the building moved rapidly from them. As Maesa waited warily for their return, the great stone digit the inn was built around flexed further. Timbers cracked with such force that splinters exploded across the room.

'Master!' wailed Shattercap.

The inn tipped sideways, until the hand that carried it stopped abruptly. Furniture crashed down. Aelven grace was no protection against such a landing, and Maesa was flung clear across the room, landing in a tangle of broken wood and glass. Shattercap gibbered terror into his ear.

'Master! Master! Master!'

'Silence,' said Maesa. The inn had come to rest at an extreme angle. One wall was now the floor, another the ceiling. All surfaces were broken and bent. 'My pack. Ellamar,' he said.

He pushed himself out of the pile of debris and searched frantically for the sack containing his beloved's grave sands and bones. Finding it, he tied it across his back, leaving his other baggage, and clambered for the door to the stairs, now above him and hanging open. He sheathed the Song of Thorns and leapt, grabbing the edge of the turned-about doorway and hauling himself lightly upwards. Once inside the stairwell, he ran along the walls, for the stairs hung broken over his head. Great tremors of the god's waking affected the inn, splintering the timbers further.

Maesa found Stonbrak in a heap of armour and beard in the coign of the new floor and wall.

'The others, where are they?' Maesa demanded.

'Ran ahead!' Stonbrak said. 'Quasque fled gibbering up there after them. He refuses to use his magic.' Stonbrak spat a huge gob of saliva and dust from his mouth. 'What's going on?'

Maesa peered out of a crazed window onto a vista of grey grasses and black-barked trees.

'The arm of the god has come down. We are on the plain. We do not have much time before it fully wakes, I think.'

In answer to his warning, the hand shook, and the inn tilted a little way back towards its proper position. Horrin shouted from somewhere ahead.

Stonbrak got himself up, and immediately put his heavy boot through the lath and plaster of the wall currently making the floor.

'I do not think this will end well,' said Maesa. He sprang ahead, barely troubling the fractured building, while Stonbrak swore and blundered his way through broken wood.

The upper floor of the inn was ruined. Maesa pushed his way through a rent in the wall to emerge onto a slippery mess of tiles caught in the angle of a gable. Water ran from the smashed inn in floods. Rain pounded at his eyes. The fingers of the god were half curled, the giant hand resting blade down on the ground, the mighty thumb blotting out a huge part of the sky, black stone on black clouds.

Atop a higher portion of the ruin, Quasque held Barnabus to ransom. He had the boy's flaming knife pressed up against Barnabus' throat. Horrin balanced on the tiles. He'd lost his gun, and stood helpless.

'Get back from me!' Quasque said.

'Leave the boy, Quasque,' said Maesa. 'Let him free to his father.'

'No!' shouted Quasque. He searched the sky frantically for the ghasts. 'When they come back, I'm going to give him to them. Then they'll leave me alone. I'm sorry. It's the only way.'

Maesa withdrew his bow from its case and nocked an arrow to the string. 'They want you, master sorcerer. Spilling that boy's blood will make no difference.' He drew his bow, taking sure aim on Quasque's head.

'He's just a stable boy! I am a mage of Hysh! I carry a dead god's tear! It is obvious who should die!'

'You are just a man, for all that,' said Maesa.

Quasque laughed wildly. 'I know the spell that will see me safe!' He stiffened. From the corner of his eye, Maesa glimpsed what Quasque saw; looping down through the sky on trails of ghostly vapour came a group of the glaive-wraiths. They flew at the terrified sorcerer.

'Drop the knife, Quasque. I will protect you.'

'No!' Quasque shrieked. 'You don't know what I've been through, what I've done! I won't let them take me. I'm sorry, boy,' he wheedled. 'I've avoided this until now. It can't be me, it has to be you.'

Rain washed over them all. The wind buffeted them, yet Maesa's aim did not waver.

'Then you leave me no choice,' said Maesa.

The ground lurched as he released the string. The giant fingers of the god curled in. Maesa's shot went wild. Horrin slipped and fell, bouncing from ruin to ruin, and fell tumbling through the torrents of water pouring from the god's hand into the mud of the plain.

Maesa swayed in time with the movement. He plucked another arrow from his quiver, and drew his bow, only to see Quasque vanishing over a pile of timbers, dragging the boy with him. The inn was high up on the god's palm, giving the aelf a good view out over the plain as it bulged upwards. The turf broke, soil ran in muddy torrents, then massive boulders beneath lifted up like jagged sets of teeth opening. A stone head as large as a hill burst through the earth. The land further out rippled, and a second hand punched its way from the soil and reached for the sky. Lightning flashed, stabbing into the giant's splayed fingers. The left hand fell and hit the ground. The elbow angled upwards. Palm flat, the giant pushed, heaving its shoulders free. The hand bearing the inn curled tighter, stopping before making a fist that would have crushed them all. Wood shattered. The god pushed hard on the earth. Slowly, water and mud running off its face and from its mouth, it forced itself out of the ground. Its shoulders emerged, then its chest and back.

Horrin slid towards the gargantuan hole left in the plain. Maesa watched, unable to help, then sighed in relief as Aelphis leapt down the crags of the grounded fist and hurtled towards the man. He tilted his noble head to the side as he charged at him. Horrin grabbed onto the points of his antlers, and Aelphis bore him away. He ran as fast as he could, bounding from crumbling sod to falling boulder, brown water surging up to his chest, his head bowed by the weight of the innkeeper.

'Take him to safety, Aelphis!' Maesa cried.

The stag tired near the lip of the growing crater as the giant lifted one leg free from the ground, placed its foot flat, and bent forward, then pushed, and dragged up the other leg from its subterranean prison. Water, soil and rock tumbled into the gaping void it left behind. Aelphis dwindled in Maesa's view as the giant rose higher and higher into the sky until finally it stood tall in the storm. Lightning flashed all around, thunder roared. The giant roared back, a cry of rage that chilled Prince Maesa's soul.

Aelphis raced from rock to rock as they plummeted into the hole. For all his speed, he was going nowhere, until finally the avalanche slowed, and he jumped free, galloping off to the side of the rising god and finding safety among the sparse trees.

Stonbrak shoved his way out of the building just as the inn

tilted again. The giant brought up its palm to its face to see the drama unfolding there. The motion led Stonbrak to slip, and he would have fallen to certain death had not Maesa loosed his arrow at the duardin, pinning his clothes to the wood of the inn. The whole ruin groaned, and Maesa was forced to run and leap as his stag had, until the palm was flat and the ruin of the Brazen Claw, still clinging to the finger of the giant, was brought up before a stone face as tall as a cliff. Eyes of fire peered from sockets deep as caves at the ruin and the tiny figures around it, much as a man might examine a beetle scurrying over his skin.

Stonbrak was left hanging by his cloak from a high beam, struggling and cursing against the arrow.

'It is ironwood, it will not break,' said Maesa, 'you must draw it out.'

'The god does not like us,' said Shattercap. 'I see it! It will devour us!'

'Its thoughts are slow,' said Maesa. 'We have time to save the boy yet.'

'He's there!' said Shattercap, pointing to the stairs running around the giant's finger to the platform high above. Stairs and dock were both in disarray, but being of duardin make they were not easily dislodged. Quasque was dragging the boy after him. In the sky, the ghasts circled about, floating up the side of the giant after their prey.

Still peering at its palm, the giant god took one ponderous, earth-shaking step. It moved slowly at first, but each stride took it hundreds of yards away from its grave and became quicker, like a rockfall building speed, until it was moving over the land like the wind.

The storm boomed around them, thunder mingling with the thump of the god's feet so that it seemed the ground exchanged blows with the heavens. Rain flew at Maesa in horizontal rods. The glaivewraiths shrieked in the turbulent air left by the god's passage. One bounced from the chest of stone and was torn away by the wind.

'Help me down!' growled Stonbrak, still slapping fruitlessly at Maesa's arrow.

Maesa's eyes squinted against the wind and rain. Quasque continued his clumsy ascent, hampered by Barnabus' struggling. A flash of lightning lit them as Quasque threw the boy against the stone and slapped him hard across the face with the back of his hand, stunning Barnabus into submission. Thereafter his ascent became easier.

'Release yourself,' Maesa told Stonbrak. 'I must save the boy from his fate.'

The prince ran to the broken stairway. His feet flashed over cracked timbers and bent iron pins, bearing him unerringly upwards.

Behind him Stonbrak growled and yanked the arrow hard. He fell loudly to the palm.

'Wait!' The duardin called. 'Wait!'

Maesa lost Stonbrak's voice in the storm. He rounded the finger quickly, then again, gaining on the fleeing sorcerer. In little time he had caught up to Quasque. Barnabus was unconscious, draped over Quasque's shoulder.

'Stop!' shouted Maesa.

Quasque glanced back. He grinned in triumph and hurried on.

'Master!' shrieked Shattercap. 'The wraiths!'

Maesa switched targets from Quasque to a trio of ghasts bearing down on him. His arrow pierced the first, tearing it to rags of ectoplasm. The second two met their end to swift blows from the Song of Thorns. They were pulled wailing into the sword, but valuable time was lost in their slaying. Maesa recommenced his pursuit. The god held its palm mercifully still in its fascination, but the plunge of every step rocked the aelf, and its great fingers twitched and moved, making the way perilous.

The god curled its fingers. The stairs shifted. Overhead, the damaged sky-dock swung from a fingertip by threads of iron and steel.

Around and around Maesa went, daring creaking, wet wood and slick iron staples where the steps had been torn away. Quasque evaded him, pushed on by terror, and perhaps a little magic of his own. By the time Maesa caught up, Quasque had reached the sky-dock and lodged himself firmly into an angle of wood, his feet braced against further movement. He had laid the insensible boy across his thighs, the dagger to his neck.

Quasque was muttering the words of a spell. Maesa whispered to Shattercap. The spite jumped from his back and vanished into the rain. The prince drew his bow.

'Let him go,' Maesa said.

Quasque opened one eye. 'I can't,' he said.

'I have killed many creatures, both fair and foul, during my cursed life,' the prince said. 'But I will not stand by to see this boy's soul carried off. It is your error that led to your predicament. He is innocent. Let him go and face your punishment.'

'No,' sobbed Quasque. He spoke the words of his spell quickly. The shrieks of the stalkers were coming nearer.

'Then I will do what must be done.'

Maesa loosed his arrow. It sped at Quasque's face, but flashed into nothing.

'I have a great deal of magic. Have you not learned your lesson?' sneered Quasque.

The prince put his bow away, and drew again the Song of Thorns.

Quasque finished his spell. A nimbus played around Barnabus. A phantom outline of the unconscious boy overlaid his physical being. Quasque grinned at the prince. 'You will strike me down with your blade then? I know a soul stealer when I see it. I would not if I were you. Already you provoke Nagash's wrath by stealing the essence of his servants. They are but scraps of being. If you take my soul, so plump and full of recent life, then his attention will be fixed on you.'

'It already is,' said Maesa, 'but it is not my time yet.'

'Aye,' said Quasque. 'I know what you hide in your satchels. The grave sands of Shyish are his as much as this jewel I carry. I wonder, how far behind my hunters are yours?'

'That, you will never know,' said Maesa.

'You've already lost,' said Quasque. 'My magic has loosened the boy's soul from his body. I must now strike the final blow, put the mark on him, and I will be free for a while.' He raised his dagger to strike. The wraiths howled.

A tiny figure darted out from behind a leaning post. Shattercap, his teeth bared, leapt upon the sorcerer's arm and bit hard. Quasque howled. Maesa lunged, his blade piercing the shield of magic around the sorcerer, and with its tip he knocked the dagger from Quasque's hand. Quasque jumped up. Barnabus fell down and slid towards the drop at the edge of the tilted platform where he lodged upon a broken post. Quasque shook his arm until Shattercap was flung free. The spite went crying over the edge of the dock, and was lost in the storm.

Maesa watched him go.

'You will pay for that.'

Ghostlight shone through the rain. The distant baying of hounds carried on the wind.

'They come. I could have saved you,' Maesa said.

'Then save me now!' Quasque pleaded.

'By your own actions, you have damned yourself,' said Maesa. He sheathed his sword. 'Prepare yourself for Nagash's judgement. I warn you, the God of Death knows no mercy.'

'Please!'

Five stalkers floated down towards the dock. They passed by Maesa, bony snouts twitching up and down as they sniffed at his soul. Maesa held up his hands.

'It is not I you want, your quarry stands there. The mage of Hysh.'

As one, the ghostly huntsmen turned, black eye sockets locked on Pludu Quasque. Their blades pointed at him. They surged forward, each voicing a soul-piercing shriek, and transfixed the screaming Quasque with their rusty weapons.

Quasque's death was not quick, and he screamed all the way through and beyond. He aged rapidly, his skin wrinkling and sagging, his teeth falling out, his hair growing long and fine until it blew away on the wind. Weakening bones and failing tendons drew him into a hunch. He was ancient now, but still alive, still screaming, even as his flesh turned to dust and yellowed ribs emerged through disintegrating skin. As his body vanished, his soul was left, howling in agony, pierced by five blades it could not escape no matter how hard he writhed.

The last of Quasque's body fell away. The wraiths rose, carrying his still-screaming spirit with them.

They floated into the storm. One of the ghasts pulled its glaive out and turned to face the prince. It uncurled its bony finger and pointed. Balefire glared in its eye sockets, the baying of hounds rose over the giant's footsteps and the thunder. Then the five wraiths and their spectral prey faded from being, and the barking receded.

Maesa wiped the rain from his eyes. He looked up into the face of the god, who stared back with unguessable intent at the aelf.

Seeing the drama done, the god set its face into a grinding frown.

The fingers twitched. The hand moved. Barnabus hung on the edge of death. Maesa leapt for him, scooping the boy up and slinging him across his back. Part of the sky-dock collapsed. Maesa grabbed a plank of wood and swung himself back onto the remains of the platform. He secured a safe position, and through the driving rain saw a mountain approaching, the first of many rocky fangs lining the horizon. A cliff of stone, black in the wet, loomed ahead, close by the god's right hand.

The giant reached out.

'Shattercap!' Maesa shouted. 'Shattercap!' But he could see his companion nowhere.

He raced away from the sky-dock as the finger extended. The palm bent back. The cliff drew closer. Stone rushed by. The god scraped its fingers against the rock, dislodging a tumble of boulders. The dock caught on the mountain and, with a screaming wrench of metal and broken timber, came free. The palm got closer and closer to the stone, tilting so that it too became a cliff parallel to the mountain's face.

Seeing the god's intention to scrape the inn off its hand, Maesa ran along the cracks of its palm, then through the chasm between its fingers. From behind came a squealing and shattering as the inn of the Brazen Claw snagged on stone and was crushed to matchwood. Maesa leapt for the cliff face, legs wheeling, one hand clamped about the boy's wrist. He slammed into the mountainside, sliding down, tearing the skin on his hand until, at last, his feet found purchase upon a grassy ledge. With great effort, he shifted his weight and fell into a crouch, coming to a rest a hundred feet above a slope of scree.

The giant strode on, the hand still trailing against the rocks, showering bits of shattered wood onto the land below. Like a man divesting himself of something distasteful, it wiped its fingers back and forth on the stone, then upon its leg. The inn removed, with quickening strides it headed off towards the mountain peaks and vanished into the rainy night.

The storm was easing. The rain caressed rather than pummelled.

Barnabus moaned on Maesa's back. Though slight, the aelf was strong, yet now the ache of his exertions threatened them both.

'Rest easy,' Maesa said, panting. 'Do not move suddenly.'

Barnabus opened his eyes and gasped.

'I said, be easy,' said Maesa.

With some difficulty, Maesa guided the frightened boy from his back and onto the ledge. The angle of the cliff there was not too steep, and the ledge was wide enough to keep them safe, but the climb down was nigh impossible, and Maesa doubted Barnabus would make it. He looked upwards, and saw a similar climb where the rock grew steep again.

'Ninian… Horrin…' the boy said. He kept his eyes screwed tightly shut.

'I am sorry for your loss, boy. Ninian was a good woman, as your people go. Your foster father escaped. I saw it myself. My stag took him away from the ghasts and the god, he will keep him safe until we return. Sit. Put your back against the rock. We are in no danger here.' Maesa's words were true, but the boy was beginning to shiver. He could die of the cold. How long that would take, the prince did not know. Humans lacked the fortitude of aelfkind.

Barnabus took one look at the drop then shut his eyes again. 'How will we get down?'

'I will find a way,' the aelf said. He checked over Ellamar's remains. Finding them to be undamaged, he started to look for a way down. The ledge went for a dozen yards in one direction, a little less than half that in the other. Everywhere he stopped to look down, the stone below the lip was smooth for many feet, without handholds.

The rain eased to nothing. The wind dropped its voice to a gentle whisper. Away to the east, Hysh was approaching the edge of the realm. Already the sky was turning silver, and the clouds were breaking.

'The weather turns,' said Maesa. 'That is a good start. The day will warm you.'

He tried a few times to lower himself down, but his feet rasped on featureless rock.

As he was about to make another attempt, a piping voice called from above.

'Master!'

'Shattercap?' Maesa said. 'You live!'

'Yes, yes, I live.' Shattercap landed with a soft thump upon the grass. There was the hiss of rope on stone, and coils of it piled on top of the spite. He groaned, and picked himself up, then shook his fist above.

'Stupid beardy!' he shrilled. 'Rope's too long!'

He untied the line at his waist, showing it to Maesa before nonchalantly tossing it over the edge.

'Shattercap didn't die on purpose. Stupid beardy didn't

save me, no, no, not at all. I make sure to stay alive all by myself to save nice master!' He poked his thumb into his chest. 'Shattercap good spite, yes?'

'Yes,' said Maesa. 'You are a good spite.'

The spite stuck out his chin in delight.

'Though I suspect the rope is not yours, but rather Master Stonbrak's,' Maesa said. 'Which means he must at least have found you, if he did not save you.'

Shattercap scowled. 'Stupid beardy,' he said again. 'Shattercap needs no rope for this little climb.'

'I am grateful,' said Maesa.

From above came the clash of hobnails on stone, accompanied by heavy breathing and rough curses. Stonbrak rappelled efficiently if gracelessly onto the ledge. His face was badly grazed, and one eye swollen shut, yet he grinned at Maesa, exposing a missing tooth.

'I'll wager you thought me a goner, eh?' said Stonbrak. 'Not so easy to kill off old Idenkor Stonbrak! Takes more than wraiths or gods to put an end to me.'

'Or, indeed, mountains,' said Maesa.

'Mountains! *Mountains* he says! Mountains won't kill me, aelfling. Ha! You might get duardin floating in the sky, living in manling cities or rolling about in the fire, but the only real duardin is a mountain duardin if you ask me, and what kind of real duardin goes anywhere without a good bit of rope?' Stonbrak winked.

Maesa looked him over. There did not appear to be anywhere the duardin could have stashed his rope. He bowed.

'Your kind are a marvel to me,' he said.

'And yours an irritation to me,' said Stonbrak, 'but I won't hold it against you, because that was a great deal of fun.' He peered over the edge. 'Now then, I've got about two hundred foot of good strong line here. Should be more than enough to get us down.'

Stonbrak attached the rope to the rock by means of a small iron spike hammered into a crack. He went first, then Barnabus, who was accompanied by Shattercap, hissing hard encouragement at him all the way down. When Maesa at last reached the bottom, Stonbrak gazed mournfully upwards.

'Be a shame to leave my rope behind,' he said.

Maesa drew his bow and shot off an arrow without looking. The rope went slack, and a few seconds later came racing down the cliff, tangling up the merchant.

'My thanks, master aelf!' Stonbrak said, his voice muffled by the line. 'Ow!' he shouted, as Maesa's arrow bounced off his head. Shattercap scampered up and snatched it with a glower.

'Come on!' Barnabus said. His teeth were chattering, and he was running about to keep warm. 'We've come a long way, I have to get back. I have to see if Master Hor–' He paused. 'If my father is all right,' he said firmly. He started off. Stonbrak struggled himself free of the rope and began to coil it.

'Don't run far, lad! The night might be over, but there are many perils in these parts!' Stonbrak called.

The striding god had covered many miles, and they had ascended high into the foothills in only a short space of time. On the grey plains hung a mist turning gold in the light of rising Hysh.

Maesa looked up towards the mountains. He saw, far off towards the snow line of the highest peak, a glint of bronze catch the sun. It flashed several times as it proceeded upwards, then was lost.

'Brazen claws indeed,' he said.

'Your highness!' Barnabus came running back. 'Your highness, look what I found!'

The boy held out an eager hand. He turned it up, and opened it.

In his palm was the lost tear of Adembi, the weeping god of Hysh.

'Oooh,' said Stonbrak and Shattercap simultaneously.

'You should take it, your highness,' said Barnabus. 'Please!'

'Perhaps you should, to pay your way,' said Maesa. 'You have lost much. It will be some recompense.'

'No!' said the boy in horror. 'It still bears a curse. Besides, it is worth a fortune. He'll want to keep it, but me and Horrin will be in danger if we do, not just from the dead,' he gabbled. 'Take it back to Hysh. Put it back where it came from. Then we'll be safe. Then…' He became downcast. 'Ninian…'

'She died protecting you, my boy,' said Stonbrak, gripping the youth's shoulder and shaking him. 'Remember her bravery, and honour her. Now, if you'll give me that pretty thing, then…'

Before Stonbrak's eager fingers could pluck the gem up, Maesa's hand closed over it.

'I will do as you say, Barnabus, and return the tear to Hysh, in memory of your foster mother. Maybe Adembi will give me his counsel. There are matters he could help me with.'

'Oh no you don't!' said Stonbrak. 'We won that bauble together!'

'Then you are more than welcome to accompany me, master duardin.'

Stonbrak stroked his beard, his eyes beady and fixed on Maesa's palm.

'Knowing humans, they will be grateful to have their treasure back, once adequately prompted. There will be a reward.' He cleared his throat. 'Then I might well come with you,' said the duardin. 'To see the world set to rights. Any money paid for tasks done and all that will be gratefully received. But even if there's not gold involved I'll come,' he added hurriedly, 'it's only right.'

'Come with me or not, I do not care,' said Maesa. 'First we must make our way back to the site of the inn, and deliver this boy to his father. I must recover my steed, and my belongings. We cannot make the Argent Gate by land. The Plain of Teeth is deadly. We must hope that the skylords are true to their schedule and return to the site of the Claw.'

Stonbrak looked up into the lightening sky. 'It's not natural, duardin living in the clouds. We need stone under our boots and stone over our heads as it was for thousands and thousands of years, not air! Even so, they are duardin nonetheless, and now the storm is done they will be on their way.' He looked out over the misty landscape. 'Ten miles, I'd say.' He sniffed. 'We'd better get on with it.' He'd wound his rope into fine coils, and he now secreted it beneath his armour. As he did he peered at his chest and moaned. 'It'll take ages to polish the scuffs out of this, it's damn near ruined.'

'Then ask your cousins on the boat,' Maesa said. Shattercap scampered up onto his perch on Maesa's shoulder. When the spite was comfortable, the prince strode off down the hill. Barnabus followed. 'The voyage will take three days or more, and there will not be much to do.'

'It's customary to swap tales on voyages,' said Stonbrak, trotting to keep up.

Maesa kept his eyes on their destination.

'Like it is at inns? I beg your leave, master duardin. I for one have had enough of tales for now,' he said.

ABOUT THE AUTHORS

Ben Counter has two Horus Heresy novels to his name – *Galaxy in Flames* and *Battle for the Abyss*. He is the author of the Soul Drinkers series and *The Grey Knights Omnibus*. For Space Marine Battles, he has written *The World Engine* and *Malodrax*, and has turned his attention to the Space Wolves with the novella *Arjac Rockfist: Anvil of Fenris* as well as a number of short stories. He is a fanatical painter of miniatures, a pursuit that has won him his most prized possession: a prestigious Golden Demon award. He lives in Portsmouth, England.

Award-winning author **Rob J Hayes** has been a student, a banker, a marine research assistant, a chef, and a keyboard monkey more times than he cares to count, but eventually his love of fantasy and reading drew him to the life of a writer. He is the author of the Warhammer 40,000 short story 'Anarchy's End'.

Ben Galley is an award-winning author of dark and epic fantasy books who currently hails from Victoria, Canada. 'Mournclaw' is the first story he has penned for Black Library and he couldn't be prouder to be writing in the Age of Sigmar.

Gavin G Smith is the Dundee-born author of, amongst others, the science fiction novels *Veteran* and *War in Heaven*, the survival horror novel *Special Purposes: First Strike*, the fantasy novella *Chivalry* and the short story collection *Crysis Escalation*. He also penned the Warhammer 40,000 short story 'Apex Predator'.

Anna Stephens is a UK-based writer of epic, gritty, grimdark fantasy. She is the author of the Godblind trilogy and the Age of Sigmar short story 'The Siege of Greenspire'.

Marc Collins is a speculative fiction author living and working in Glasgow, Scotland. He is the writer of the Warhammer 40,000 short story 'Ghosts of Iron' and when not dreaming of the far future he works in Pathology with the NHS.

Michael R Fletcher is an author and grilled cheese aficionado with several dark and grim science fiction and fantasy novels to his name, including his first story for Black Library, 'A Tithe of Bone'. He lives in the endless suburban sprawl somewhere north of Toronto.

Gary Kloster is a writer, a stay-at-home father, a librarian and a martial artist – sometimes all in the same day, seldom all at the same time. He lives among the corn in the American Midwest and his short fiction can be found in *Analog, Apex, Clarkesworld* and others. His short story 'Curse of the Lucky' is his first for Black Library.

A former firefighter in Arkansas, **Sean Grigsby** writes novels, comics and scripts about everything from dragons to robots, and has been featured in *Amazing Stories* magazine, Tor.com, and several other short story anthologies. 'Best Death Wins' is his first story for Black Library.

Graeme Lyon is the author of the Age of Sigmar novella *Code of the Skies* and the Space Marine Battles novella *Armour of Faith*. He has also written a host of Warhammer 40,000, Warhammer Age of Sigmar and Warhammer short stories including 'The Carnac Campaign: Sky Hunter', 'Kor'sarro Khan: Huntmaster', 'Black Iron', 'The Eighth Victory', 'The Sacrifice' and 'Bride of Khaine'. He hails from East Kilbride in Scotland.

Gareth Hanrahan's three-month break from computer programming to concentrate on writing has now lasted fifteen years and counting. He lives in Ireland and has written more gaming books than he can readily recall by virtue of the alchemical transmutation of guilt and tea into words. 'Castle of the Exile' marks his first foray into the worlds of Warhammer.

Guy Haley is the author of the Siege of Terra novel *The Lost and the Damned,* as well as the Horus Heresy novels *Titandeath, Wolfsbane* and *Pharos,* and the Primarchs novels *Konrad Curze: The Night Haunter, Corax: Lord of Shadows* and *Perturabo: The Hammer of Olympia.* He has also written many Warhammer 40,000 novels, including *Belisarius Cawl: The Great Work, Dark Imperium, Dark Imperium: Plague War, The Devastation of Baal, Dante, Darkness in the Blood, Baneblade* and *Shadowsword.* His enthusiasm for all things greenskin has also led him to pen the eponymous Warhammer novel *Skarsnik,* as well as the End Times novel *The Rise of the Horned Rat.* He has also written stories set in the Age of Sigmar, included in *War Storm, Ghal Maraz* and *Call of Archaon.* He lives in Yorkshire with his wife and son.

YOUR NEXT READ

KAL JERICO: SINNER'S BOUNTY
by Josh Reynolds

With a Guilder armoury looted, and the culprit racing downhive in a mining hauler bristling with stolen weaponry, Kal Jerico chases the bounty… but with a prize like this, every other Venator worth the name will be after it too.

YOUR NEXT READ

WATCHERS OF THE THRONE: THE REGENT'S SHADOW
by Chris Wraight

As Guilliman heads off to lead the Indomitus Crusade, Terra is a world still in turmoil. The Custodians and Sisters of Silence lead the recovery effort, and when the warship Phalanx returns it seems that stability will at last be assured. But not every enemy is corrupted by Chaos, and the prospect of civil war looms...

For these stories and more, go to blacklibrary.com, games-workshop.com, Games Workshop and Warhammer stores, all good book stores or visit one of the thousands of independent retailers worldwide, which can be found at games-workshop.com/storefinder

YOUR NEXT READ

BEASTGRAVE
by C L Werner

In the untamed wilds of Ghur, darkness is rising. Rival warbands battle over the dread Beastgrave. Will Beastlord Ghroth prevail or can Branchwraith Kyra and her dryads stop his foul plans?
